NEW YORK TIMES BESTSELLING AUTHOR EILEEN GOUDGE "IS BACK AND BETTER THAN EVER"*

"This exciting tale . . . . Vivid and engaging . . . . on-versation between . . . . ne chat you don't want to miss."

—aromancereview.com*

"[An] entertaining tale."

—thebestreviews.com

"Fun, romantic, and heartwarming. . . . Goudge explores the power of loving relationships."

—romantictimes.com

More Praise for Eileen Goudge

"A writer who knows how to entertain in a lively and credible way."

—*Kirkus Reviews*

"Goudge . . . reminds us of the delights to be had in explo-rations of the improbable."

—*New York Times Book Review*

"[Goudge] consistently explores intense family relationships and turns out bestsellers that feature women on the verge of major change."

—*Publishers Weekly*

Eileen Goudge

Otherwise Engaged

POCKET BOOKS
New York   London   Toronto   Sydney

This book is a work of fiction. Names, characters, places and incidents are products of the author's imagination or are used fictitiously. Any resemblance to actual events or locales or persons, living or dead, is entirely coincidental.

 POCKET BOOKS, a division of Simon & Schuster, Inc.
1230 Avenue of the Americas, New York, NY 10020

ISBN-13: 978-0-7434-8341-4
ISBN-10:   0-7434-8341-3

This Pocket Books paperback edition October 2005

10 9 8 7 6 5 4 3 2 1

POCKET and colophon are registered trademarks of Simon & Schuster, Inc.

Front cover photo © Pure/Nonstock

Manufactured in the United States of America

For information regarding special discounts for bulk purchases, please contact Simon & Schuster Special Sales at 1-800-456-6798 or business@simonandschuster.com.

To my darling husband, Sandy,
who reminds me daily of what it's all about.

Acknowledgments

A novel written without assistance from others, whether it be editorial guidance or the kindness of strangers, is, in my opinion, all the poorer for it. This one, I'm happy to report, had more than one cook seasoning the soup. As always, I'm grateful to my friend and agent (in that order), Susan Ginsburg. I owe thanks, too, to Louise Burke, another dear friend who most happily, and not so coincidentally, is also my publisher; my smart and hardworking editor, Amy Pierpont, who, if she minds having to read and edit multiple drafts, never lets on; and Maggie Crawford, whose insight and enthusiasm spurred me on.

For an invaluable peek behind the scenes of a bed-and-breakfast, I'd like to thank Charles and Valerie Bin-

Acknowledgments

ford, of The Place at Cayou Cove, on Orcas Island in Washington. In addition to providing useful information, they welcomed my husband and me as if we were family, even letting me use their kitchen to bake pies. Their inn overlooking a peaceful harbor, with its three separate cottages, each with a water view, is so magical that words fail me in describing it, so I'll let the photos on their website do it for me. You can see them by logging on to *www.cayoucove.com*.

I'd also like to thank Jim Langan of The Full Circle Ranch, in Cave Creek, Arizona. If Jim had been a character in this book, it wouldn't have been a stretch to make him larger than life. His unique desert retreat must be seen to be believed; suffice it to say, my husband and I didn't mind a bit not having a water view. Check out his website at: *www.fullcircleranch.com*.

A special thanks to the dogs and cats that made us feel as welcome at each of the inns we stayed at as did their owners: Hannibal, Coco, Bruno, and Max. What would a B&B be without its furry critters?

Last but not least, for his help in adding flavor (pardon the pun) to the scenes set at the fictional Cooking Channel, I am indebted to Reese Schonfeld, founder of the Food Network, who put me in touch with the right people, and who also arranged for me to attend a taping of *Emeril Live*, where I sat in the front row and was allowed to sample the scrumptious dish Emeril prepared.

"Men's courses will foreshadow certain ends, to which, if persevered in, they must lead," said Scrooge. "But if the courses be departed from, the ends will change. Say it is thus with what you show me!"

— FROM *A CHRISTMAS CAROL*,
BY CHARLES DICKENS

Otherwise Engaged

Chapter One

"I won't be long. My house is just down the road," Jonathon said as he pulled into the Great Neck station, its parking lot nearly deserted this early on Saturday. "You're sure you don't mind? It's just that it'd be sort of awkward, with Rebecca and all." He eyed Jessie anxiously.

"Really, Jon, it's okay." She flashed him her best we're-in-this-together smile.

They'd discussed it, and she'd told him she didn't mind waiting at the station while he picked up his kids at his ex-wife's, so as to avoid a possible scene. The truth was she *did* mind, but only a little, and why rain on the parade? He'd arranged this outing so she could meet Zach and Sara. She wasn't going to dwell on his calling it *my* house, which was only technically true. Nor would she think about the message it would send his kids, that Daddy's girlfriend wasn't quite kosher. She must avoid even using such words as kosher—his family didn't need any reminders that she wasn't Jewish. Like the other day, when she'd mispronounced his Uncle Chaim's name, to rhyme with shame, and Jonathon had corrected her, saying it was *Hiy-am*.

"Thanks, Jess." His eyes were soft with gratitude, and she felt an answering tingle, reminding her of why she'd fallen in love with him in the first place. Besides looking like he'd stepped from the pages of *GQ*, he was caring and sensitive, with just enough of an edge to make him interesting. Now all she had to do was pass muster with his kids. . . .

"No problem." Her mother had raised her to be a Good Sport, which meant that unless you were bleeding to death or having a heart attack, you sucked it up. Noting the flicker of uncertainty in his eyes, she placed a hand on his wrist, adding, "It's easier for everyone this way."

She was unbuckling her seat belt to get out when a wave of panic swept over her. "What if they don't like me?" She twisted around to face Jonathon, her stomach executing a slow cartwheel at the thought.

He frowned in consternation, absently brushing back the adorable Clark Kent comma of dark hair that was in the habit of falling over his brow. "It's bound to be a little awkward at first," he said in that slow, thoughtful way of his that let her know he was taking her concerns seriously.

"But once they get to know you, I'm sure they'll love you as much as I do."

She wasn't so sure. Her stomach did another lazy half turn. "Still . . . I wonder if this is such a good idea." They were driving up to his parents' house in Rhinebeck. Jonathon saw it as a chance to kill two birds with one stone—introduce her to his kids and his folks all at once—but she was afraid she was biting off more than she could chew. Her best friend, Erin, back in Willow Creek, had advised against it, but when Jonathon first suggested it, Jessie had been so excited to be taking this next step, to be a part of his life, not just the faceless Girlfriend tucked away in the wings, that she hadn't thought it through at the time.

"Relax, it'll be fine. Mother and Dad . . . they're not your run-of-the-mill parents, I'll admit, but they're great people. You'll like them."

Yes, but will they like me? She forced herself to smile, more afraid of appearing neurotic than of the possible ordeal ahead. Lately it seemed she'd been focusing less on being herself than on how *not* to be like Jonathon's ex-wife. "I'm sure you're right. I'm just a little nervous, is all." Who hadn't heard the joke about the Jewish mother with her head in the oven because her son was dating a *shiksa?*

She thought back to when she and Jonathon had first met, six months ago, at the salad bar in her neighborhood Korean deli. She was spooning garbanzo beans over her greens when some internal radar caused her to glance up.

A tall, dark-haired man stood in front of her. All she could see of him were his broad shoulders and the back of his head, but she felt a humming awareness, like when her cell phone was on vibrate mode. He must have sensed her presence as well because he turned around just then, as if looking for some salad fixing he might have missed while he surreptitiously checked her out. It was all she could do not to stare. This wasn't your average good-looking guy, just flawed enough to keep you from peering obsessively in the mirror, wondering what he saw in *you*. This was the kind that made you go limp all over, as if you'd been punched in the stomach.

He looked to be around her age, well over six feet — he towered over Jessie, who was tall herself. His wavy hair was the glossy black-brown of molasses, flecked with gray at the temples, his eyes the blue of Van Gogh's *Starry Night*. His face had the planed, architectural look of a Ralph Lauren model's — sharply defined jaw and cheekbones, full lips that curved enticingly, just begging to be kissed. Only there was nothing fey about him; he exuded testosterone.

She eyed the modest pile of greens in his plastic clamshell before her gaze dropped to his left hand, with its pale band on the ring finger where a wedding band must have been. *Divorced*, she thought. Recently, from the looks of it.

She realized she was staring when he flashed her a quizzical little smile, as if to say, *Do I know you from somewhere?* She became so flustered, the garbanzo beans went sliding off the spoon onto the floor, scattering every which way. *Great, just great,* she groaned inwardly. The cutest guy she'd seen in ages, and she'd blown it without even opening her mouth. But to her relief Mr. Tall-Dark-and-Handsome only made a joke of it, breaking into a soft shoe routine as he nudged beans out of his path with the toes of his loafers.

She cast a sheepish glance at the store owner, busy ringing up another customer's purchases. "I suppose I should offer to sweep up."

The man smiled, showing an adorably crooked front tooth. Another point in his favor—she had an unreasonable distrust of men with perfect teeth. "Are you always this considerate?" he asked.

She shrugged. "It must be in my DNA."

"Ah, just as suspected. You're not from around here." He regarded her with bemusement, his head cocked to one side. "Let me guess—Ohio? No, Minnesota."

Jessie mock-groaned. Though she'd lived in New York City the better part of fifteen years, her naturally blond hair, peaches-and-cream complexion, and body that looked equally suited to pitching hay or riding down Main Street on a parade float, screamed corn-fed. She was, as her darling landlord, Clive, had once wryly observed, "sooooo west of the Mississippi."

"Consider it a compliment," the man said. "You look like the kind of person who means it when she says, 'have a nice day.'"

She grimaced and made a shoveling motion to indicate that he was only digging himself in deeper. But the ice was broken, and maybe something else as well . . . the firewall she, like most single women in Manhattan who'd been dashed against the rocks of their romantic aspirations, had erected around herself. They chatted for a minute while they helped themselves to salad fixings. When he finally got around to introducing himself, "Jonathon. Jonathon Silver," holding her gaze a beat too long and giving her hand a little squeeze, as if to let her know that he didn't make a habit of hitting on strange women, she felt as if she'd known him all her life.

Now, seeing the love and concern in his face, she felt her reservations melt away. On impulse, she leaned over, taking his face in her hands, and kissed him full on the mouth. He responded greedily, putting his arms around her and pulling her in tight, reminding her of what a sacrifice it'd been dragging herself out of bed this morning just after dawn, instead of making slow, luxuriant love as they usually did on weekend mornings.

She thought of last Sunday, at her place, when he'd surprised her with breakfast in bed. The pancakes were a little soggy, but the raspberries on top more than made up for it. She'd pointed to them, asking, "Where did these come from?" She couldn't remember the last time she'd bought raspberries, they were so pricey out of season.

"From the corner market," he'd told her. He'd looked so adorable, with his hair as rumpled as the bed, it was all she could do not to drag him back under the covers with her, breakfast be damned. "Sorry they're a little squished.

It was the last box." She'd looked out the window and seen that it was sleeting outside. He'd gone out into *that* to buy her raspberries, knowing how much she loved them. There was something so sweetly old-fashioned about it, tears came to her eyes. *It'll work out,* she told herself. *It has to* . . .

Leaving the box of chocolates for his parents on the front seat, she climbed out of the car. "Be back before you know it," Jonathon called cheerily out the open window, his frozen breath trailing vapor as he pulled away from the curb.

She settled on a bench, wrapping her arms around her to ward off the cold. It was January, a month when even the English ivy along the embankments waved in tattered surrender. She shivered as a gust of wind sent crumpled wrappers and dried leaves scuttling along the tracks below. She wished she'd worn her down jacket instead of her more fashionable, but lightweight, suede one. Sensible boots, too, not the J. Tod loafers she'd splurged on with the check from *Atlantic Monthly.*

Jessie fished her notebook from her shoulder bag and began jotting down some thoughts on a plastic surgery piece she planned to pitch next week to Kate, the senior editor at *Savvy* magazine. By the time she glanced at her watch, twenty minutes had gone by. She frowned. There must have been some sort of last-minute holdup. Or maybe Rebecca had decided to throw a fit regardless. Wasn't Jonathon always saying she could make a Shakespearean tragedy out of a missed bus? Oddly enough,

Jessie felt she knew Jonathon's ex-wife, a woman she had yet to lay eyes on, better than people she'd known all her life. But of course she only knew what Jonathon had told her.

Twenty minutes stretched into half an hour. Jessie began to worry that something was *really* wrong. But wouldn't Jonathon have called? She checked her cell phone to make sure it was still on, her worry turning to irritation. What could be so earth-shattering that she had to be kept shivering in the cold without so much as a courtesy call?

After what seemed an eternity, she heard the toot of a car horn and looked up to see Jonathon's midnight blue Nissan glide up to the curb. She jumped to her feet and began walking toward it, only to come to an abrupt halt a few yards away. A teenage boy with Jonathon's blue eyes and wavy dark hair occupied the seat in front. But it was a girl peering out the window in back, her eyes red slits in her tear-swollen face, that set off a trill of alarm.

A train rumbled in the near distance, and for a wild moment it seemed the deus ex machina Jessie's creative writing teacher in college had labeled the province of cheap fiction. The screech of brakes as it slid into the station was a siren call, urging her to jump on board—she'd be at Grand Central in less than an hour, with the whole rest of the day to do as she pleased. Coffee and Danish at Le Bergamot with Clive, if he was around, followed by the new Muriel Spark novel she'd picked up yesterday. Or, if the rain that was threatening remained at bay, the El Greco exhibit at the Met she'd been wanting to see.

Only a sense of obligation, along with a spark of hope that the day might be salvaged yet, kept her from bolting. She paused just long enough to take a deep breath before climbing in the backseat next to the damp, crumpled heap that was Jonathon's daughter.

"Hi, I'm Jessie. You must be Sara." She put on her friendliest west-of-the-Mississippi face as she stuck out her hand, from which Sara recoiled as if from a dead fish before turning her back.

Jonathon twisted around to give Jessie a rueful little grimace. "Sorry we're late," he apologized. "Sara couldn't find her sneakers." As if the real reason for the delay wasn't painfully obvious. In a misguided effort to smooth things over, he announced brightly to no one in particular, "Jessie's a writer." When neither child remarked on the fact, he went on, "Sara's our budding author. Sweetie, maybe Jessie could give you some tips."

Sara shot her father a murderous look. From the photos Jessie had seen of Jonathon's ex-wife, Sara took after her mother. She had Rebecca's straight, honey-colored hair and wide-set brown eyes, her petite build. In low-rise jeans and a pink Hello Kitty sweatshirt she looked younger than her age, and at the same time old beyond her years.

"Zach's our resident athlete," Jonathon went on in that fake hearty tone as he edged the Nissan into traffic. "He holds the school record in the hundred-yard dash and took second place in the regionals."

"*Daaaad*," Zach groaned.

"You should hear how he talks about you behind your back," Jessie said.

Zach turned to give her a halfhearted smile that showed a mouthful of metal. Jessie's hopes were briefly buoyed, until Jonathon, after they'd gone several miles without a peep out of Sara, called over his shoulder, "You okay back there, sweetie?"

Sara went on staring mutely out the window. Jessie couldn't help thinking that if it'd been *her* at that age, she'd have felt the flat side of Beverly's hand. If there was one thing her mother refused to tolerate, it was rudeness, especially toward adults.

But could Jessie blame the girl? Divorce was hard enough on kids without their parents' love lives complicating the matter. And what could Jonathon have been *thinking*, forcing them to sit together back here? He should have insisted that Zach sit in back.

When the silence became too much, filling the car like some noxious emission, Jessie took another stab. "You must be anxious to see your grandparents," she said, addressing the wall of Sara's resolutely turned back. Jonathon's parents, both retired professors, traveled extensively, so according to Jonathon the kids didn't see much of them.

Sara swung around to face her. "I was when I thought it was just *us*."

"You knew she was coming. Dad told us," Zach reminded her.

"I know what he *told* us," Sara shot back. Clearly, she hadn't believed her father would actually go through with it.

She has a point, Jessie thought. *I was crazy to agree to this*.

"Guys, please. You're making me look bad here," Jonathon cajoled. "What happened to your manners? Jessie's our guest."

"But Mom said . . ."

"Your mother has no say in this," he cut her off, gently but firmly.

Sara lapsed back into mutinous silence.

The spark of hope went out like a guttering wick exposed to an icy blast. *Be careful what you wish for*, Jessie thought. She'd been fooled by her closeness with her fourteen-year-old goddaughter into thinking this would be, if not a piece of cake, then at least the first step toward a meaningful relationship. But Sara wasn't anything like Kayla. And in all fairness, in her shoes would Jessie have been any happier about the situation?

The drive to Rhinebeck seemed endless. Jessie and Jonathon's joint effort to lighten the atmosphere was about as effective as rubbing sticks together to make a fire. Sara remained mute, and Zach only grunted from time to time. After a while, Jessie subsided into silence as well. When Zach turned on the radio, tuning it to a rock station, the blare came almost as a relief.

Jessie's nerves were frayed, tiny muscles twitching under her skin, when they finally pulled up in front of the

Silvers' house, a starkly modern cube on a block of older Tudor-style homes. As she made her way up the front path, lined with stiff spears of juniper that cast zebra stripes of shadow across the winter brown lawn, Jessie thought there was a greater likelihood of her winning the Pulitzer Prize than of being welcomed into this family.

They were met at the door by a tall, distinguished-looking gentleman with wavy silver hair that dipped over his forehead exactly like Jonathon's. After greeting Jonathon and the children, he extended an elegant, long-fingered hand to Jessie. "You must be Jessie," he said. "I've heard so much about you." His eyes twinkled, as if he knew something she didn't.

"Same here. It's nice to meet you, Professor Silver," she said.

"Leonard, please. My days of terrorizing undergraduates are long past, I'm afraid," he said with a chuckle, taking her arm as he ushered them inside.

He took their coats and hung them in the hall closet. As they stepped through the arched foyer into the living room, an older woman, large and formidably handsome, wearing some sort of caftan and jangling with heavy ethnic jewelry, sailed over to greet them, hugging her son and grandchildren as if she hadn't seen them in years. She offered Jessie a cool, beringed hand, introducing herself as Ruth. "Pardon the mess," she apologized, gesturing about the room, which was tidy except for a few boxes stacked in one corner. "Len and I just got back last night. We haven't even unpacked."

"Did you have a nice trip?" Jessie inquired.

"Divine! Everyone should be *required* to go to Africa at least once in their lives. There are simply no words to describe it. Len must've taken at least two hundred pictures." Jessie found it a bit unsettling, Jonathon's blue eyes looking out at her from Ruth's lined face framed with crisp iron hair.

"Not everyone can afford to, dear," Len reminded her.

"Nonsense," Ruth scoffed. "It's not as if *we* stay in four-star hotels." Their sense of adventure bordered on the extreme, Jonathon had told Jessie, which had led to disaster on more than one occasion—like the tent-cabin in Costa Rica that was infested with scorpions and the "quaint" Parisian *pension* that was next door to a whorehouse.

"Ruth and I aren't your typical tourists," Len informed Jessie with a wink, as she settled into a chair by the fireplace, where a welcoming fire crackled. She could have guessed as much from the artifacts scattered throughout the room—an intricately tooled leather ottoman, carvings of various animals and religious deities, a large Japanese scroll on one wall. No tacky giant sombreros or painted conch shells for this pair.

"That reminds me, I have something for you two," Ruth said, beaming at Zach and Sara. She disappeared into the next room, returning moments later with a rumpled shopping bag. "Good thing I got these in extralarge. You've each grown a foot!" She produced a pair of bundles wrapped loosely in brown paper tied with string. "They're dashikis," she explained when the children had opened their gifts and stood staring in bewilderment at what no self-respecting adolescent would be caught dead in. Remembering the frilly dresses Grandmother Holland used to send her every birthday, which were always a size too small, Jessie felt a pang of sympathy.

"Thanks, Grandma," Zach said with forced enthusiasm. "It'll go good with the congo drums you got me last time." He nudged Sara with his elbow, and she thanked Ruth, too.

"I understand you're originally from Arizona," Ruth remarked to Jessie when they were sipping wine in front of the fire, the kids off in the den watching TV. Before Jessie could reply, she added, "Our friends, the Rosenblatts, have a house in Sedona. We were there over the holidays. You remember Al and Esther, don't you, darling?" She turned to Jonathon. "Their daughter was in Becca's class at Princeton." He nodded, looking vaguely uncomfortable, while a distant alarm went off in Jessie's head, like the sound of an approaching siren. Ruth brought her pleasant, smiling gaze back to Jessie. "Do you have family there?"

"My mother," Jessie told her.

"Well, in that case, you must visit often."

"Actually, it's been a few years."

"Ah." Ruth gave her a sharp look, and Jessie realized how it must sound.

She felt she should explain, but what was there to say? The plain fact was she and Beverly were all but estranged. Years ago, her mother had made it clear she'd never forgive Jessie for her role in the accident that had claimed Jessie's father's life. In one way or another, Jessie had been a disappointment to her ever since.

She was relieved when Ruth changed the subject. "I enjoyed your piece in *The New Yorker*," she said. "I found it rather remarkable, actually." She arched a brow, her expression making it clear she was more amazed that Jessie had managed to infiltrate Williamsburg's tight-knit Hasidic community than by her writing ability.

"Thanks." Jessie warmed at the compliment nonetheless. "I wasn't sure I could pull it off."

She'd spent months befriending several Hassidic women, who couldn't have had less in common with her—wives who wore the traditional marriage wig and who sat in a separate part of the synagogue from their husbands and sons. At the time, she couldn't have known her foray into Judaism would one day prove useful in more ways than one. That is, if Jonathon ever got around to popping the question.

"Did you study journalism in school?" Len asked, leaning back in his club chair and sipping his wine.

"Not really. I sort of picked it up along the way." Jessie scanned the collection of framed photos on the mantel. There were ones of Zach and Sara at different ages, and of Jonathon and his two brothers, including one of Jonathon in a cap and gown posed against an ivied brick wall—he'd graduated from Yale before getting his master's in journalism at Columbia. She thought better of mentioning that she'd gone to Arizona State.

"Well, you've obviously done well for yourself," Ruth said.

"I'm lucky. Most writers don't make a living at it."

"What counts most is that you're doing what you love. And how nice that you and Jon have that in common." Jessie detected a note of irony in Ruth's honeyed tone, or had she just imagined it?

"I'll toast to that." Jonathon raised his glass. One of the things she loved about him was that he didn't differentiate between his position as New York bureau chief of CTN and her considerably less-well-paid career as a freelance journalist. They were both equally worthy in his eyes.

"Of course, it was different in *our* day," Ruth went on. She and Leonard exchanged a coded glance. "We did what we thought was *right*, not just what struck our fancy. Take divorce, for instance. It was practically unheard of. Couples simply worked things out. You think it's luck that your father and I have been together all these years?" Her voice remained mild, but now the honey was laced with arsenic.

Jonathon was visibly pained.

The awful realization swept over Jessie that she'd been duped. The warmth with which his parents had welcomed her had been nothing more than a false front hiding their true feelings: They wanted no part of her.

She barely managed to get through lunch. The Silvers made small talk that excluded her, while Zach ignored her and Sara darted evil glances at her across the table. Jonathon's encouraging little squeezes did nothing to alleviate the dull ache in her belly that had little to do with the stringy corned beef and leaden potato knishes.

"All right, I admit it wasn't a roaring success," he acknowledged in the car on the way home, after he'd dropped off the kids.

"That's putting it mildly," she said coolly. "The town stocks would've been preferable."

"Come on. It wasn't *that* bad."

"I felt like a party crasher."

"You could've fooled me. It looked like you were enjoying yourself."

"What can I say? I was raised by a woman who, if there was a cockroach in her soup, would sooner eat it than risk offending her hostess."

"Well, you were spared that at least," he said with a chuckle.

Jessie hadn't meant it as a joke, but she was too drained to get into it right now. All she wanted was to be home, in her pj's, curled up in front of the TV with her cat purring on her lap.

"Give it time," he added, more gently. "They'll come around." But she thought she detected a note of uncertainty in his voice.

"Who, your parents or your kids?"

"My parents liked you," he said, a bit defensively.

Was he delusional? "Yeah, like pilgrims liked the Indians."

"There were Jewish pilgrims?" He cast her a wry, sidelong glance.

Jessie glared at him. If he thought he could jolly her out of this, he was sadly mistaken. "I wouldn't know. Not being Jewish myself."

The storm that'd been threatening all day had finally broken, and rain was pouring down in sheets, drumming on the roof and sizzling off the windshield. Jonathon slowed as they sloughed through a puddle the size of a small pond. "Look, okay, they weren't exactly rolling out the red carpet," he admitted, "but it didn't have anything to do with you. They're still upset about Rebecca and me splitting up—she's the daughter they never had."

"It would've been nice if you hadn't left me swinging in the wind. And I don't mean just with your folks."

He grimaced. "I'm sorry about the kids. They weren't on their best behavior."

"It didn't help that I was stuck in the backseat." Jessie had sat up front on the way back, but she was still smarting from this morning's ordeal.

He shrugged. "Zach climbed in before I could stop him. I didn't want to make a big deal of it."

"Well, it was a big deal to me. And to Sara," she was quick to add.

He looked chagrined, but she didn't know if it was because of her or Sara. Probably a little of both. "I never said it would be easy." He strained to see past the torrent that had made a waterfall of the windshield, his body angled forward against the steering wheel.

"I didn't expect it to be," she told him.

"It's nothing against you. They're just not used to the idea of their father having a girlfriend."

"Is Rebecca seeing anyone?"

Jonathon shot her a look that seemed to say, *Get real.* But was it so out of the question? His ex-wife was an attractive woman. Or was it that the idea made him uncomfortable? Was he, like his children, hanging on to the shell of his former life?

"I can see it from their point of view," she said, struggling to be fair. "On the other hand, they should know you have a life outside of them."

"Maybe if we hadn't met so soon after Becca and I separated . . ." His voice trailed off and his expression turned inward for a moment. Then he shook himself free of whatever memory he was caught up in and flashed her a contrite smile. "They don't call us the walking wounded for nothing."

She snorted. "I wasn't exactly twisting your arm, as I recall." A week after their serendipitous meeting in the Korean deli, they were sleeping together.

"All I'm saying is that you've never had to go through a divorce. You don't know what it's like."

"I have a pretty good idea," she said. She'd been engaged once and still carried a residue of guilt for all but leaving Mike at the altar. "I know what it's like to hurt someone you love. I know about waking up at 2:00 A.M. feeling like you've swallowed a handful of razor blades. If I don't know what it's like to get divorced, it's only because I've never been married. And at this rate, it's not likely I ever will be." Her voice rose on a trembling note. She was dismayed to realize she was on the verge of tears. Until now, the M-word had been only vaguely alluded to, something that might occur in the distant future. But she could no longer hide her true feelings.

"I'm not sure where you're going with this," Jonathon said cautiously.

"I'm not sure, either. Why don't you tell me." *He* might have all the time in the world, but she didn't have that luxury. She was thirty-five years old, with rapidly aging ovaries and a well-meaning gynecologist who frequently reminded her of that fact. She took a deep breath, all thoughts of snuggling with her cat on the sofa eclipsed by her rising emotion. "Okay then, let me put it another way: Where do you see us in six months?"

She waited for the answer that could change her life, a breath trapped high in her chest like a small, quivering bird. At last, in a flat voice that didn't exactly inspire confidence, and that even sent a small chill up her spine, he answered, "Still together, I hope."

"Can you think of a reason we wouldn't be?" She struggled to keep her tears in check, not wanting him to see how much she had invested in this.

They plunged into the shadow of an overpass, where he navigated his way through another pond-sized puddle. "Is this a trick question?" he asked, with the faintest edge in his voice.

"All I want is an honest answer."

He sighed. "I love you, Jess. You know that. And I don't want to lose you, but . . ." His face was a pale mask in the glare of oncoming headlights. As a newsman, Jonathon dealt only with facts. His biggest drawback was also his greatest asset: He'd never lie to her. "I can't make any promises. I don't know when, or if, I'll be ready for more than this."

"We hardly see each other as it is," she reminded him.

"I know," he said. "I wish it didn't have to be this way, but my children come first. For now, at least."

Jessie was doing her best to understand, but right now she was too upset. *What would Erin do?* she wondered. But Erin, with her adoring husband and perfect child, might as well be in a different universe. How could she possibly know what it was like to have the man she loved slip through her fingers?

Not that it was over. She knew Jonathon had been telling the truth when he'd said he loved her. But was it enough? She wasn't sure how much longer she could stand being in limbo.

They drove in silence the rest of the way. The rain had tapered off by the time Jonathon pulled to a stop in front of her building, a converted brownstone in Chelsea, on the corner of Twentieth and Ninth. Glancing up at the third floor to see her windows ablaze, she realized that she'd forgotten to turn out her lights as she was dashing out the door, hours ago that seemed more like a lifetime. Damn. As if her overdue Con Edison bill wasn't already enough to bankrupt a Third World nation, more than most people paid in rent in her hometown of Willow Creek. It served to remind her of her career slump, which at the moment seemed to mirror the state of her love life.

"See you tomorrow?" Jonathon said hopefully.

"I don't know. I'm going to be pretty busy," she hedged.

"You're not still mad at me, are you?" He shut off the engine, turning to regard her gravely.

"Mad? No." More like crushed.

"What about Tuesday then?"

"Don't you have therapy?"

"Right. I forgot." Tuesday evenings he and his ex-wife and children had family therapy. Until she'd started seeing Jonathon, Jessie hadn't even known there was such a thing, postdivorce.

"Just as well," she said airily. "I promised Drew I'd help him go over the photos for his show." Let Jonathon wonder if her upstairs neighbor was more than just a good friend.

He took hold of her arm as she was climbing out of the car. In the glare of a streetlamp, through the rain dribbling down the windshield, his face was cast in a queer, undersea glow. "I'm not saying it'll always be this way," he said softly. "I just . . . I want to be honest about where things stand."

"I think I have a pretty good picture," she said in a low, quivering voice.

"I'm not going to lie to you, Jess."

"All right then, since we're being so honest," she said,

"don't count on me sticking around until you make up your mind." Unlike Erin, who never had any trouble speaking her mind, Jessie usually found it hard to express her feelings. But this time the words came easily. The hard part, she knew, would be following through.

He arched a brow. "Is that an ultimatum?"

"No, just the way it is."

With a sigh, he let go of her arm. "Look, we're both tired. Can we talk about this tomorrow?"

"Fine. Whatever." She was getting out of the car when her foot bumped up against something on the floor—the box of Teuscher chocolates she'd meant to give to his parents. With the excruciating trip to Rhinebeck, she'd forgotten all about it. Now she snatched it up and tucked it under her arm. Just as well. They didn't deserve it anyway.

Dashing up the brownstone steps, rain mingling with the tears that trickled down her cheeks, she thought about Erin, the days when they'd console each other with chocolate chip cookies and ice cream in times of heartbreak. Jessie couldn't wait to call her. Just talking to her best friend would make her feel better. Erin's perfect marriage shimmered in her mind's eye, the touchstone that had been a constant throughout her string of failed relationships, reminding her that such happiness *did* exist, that it wasn't just in fairy tales. Though at the moment it seemed unlikely that she'd ever find it.

Jessie trudged up to the third floor to the lush strains of *La Bohème*—she wasn't alone in her misery, it seemed; Clive always listened to Puccini when nursing a broken heart. She unlocked the door to her apartment and before she was all the way inside Delilah began twining in and out between her legs, meowing piteously. Jessie picked her up, burying her face in Delilah's thick black fur, thinking, *At least someone's glad to see me.*

Glancing about, she took in the marble fireplace and parquet floors, the French windows that opened onto the street below, telling herself how lucky she was to have this place, that she could be living in a dump or one of those sterile high-rises where you'd get a nosebleed going up in the elevator. But tonight there was no consoling herself. Even the homey touches—the worn Oriental rug, the deep sofa with its scattering of bright throw cushions, the fifties atomic lamp, an oak bookcase displaying her collection of vintage Nancy Drew titles—served only to remind her that she had no one to share it with.

She sank down on the sofa, not even bothering to take off her coat, which was probably ruined from the rain. Delilah leapt off her lap at once; the only thing she hated more than being left alone all day was getting wet. Jessie remembered the box of chocolates and pried it open. She was starving after having choked down only a few bites at the Silvers'. But instead of truffles in neat rows, there was only a gluey chocolate sludge; the floor heater in the car must have melted them. With a low cry, she hurled the box at the wall, where it stuck for a moment, then slid halfway down before plopping unceremoniously on the floor, leaving a brown snail trail on the yellow paint. She

stared at the mess, then let out a burbling sound halfway
between a sob and a laugh. She couldn't even manage a
grand gesture without it looking ridiculous.

Erin will make it better. She always does. Slumped on
the sofa staring into space, Jessie found herself remembering the day they'd met, in the girls' bathroom at Yavapai Elementary. The day she climbed aboard the
supercharged V-8 engine that was Erin D'Amico, and
never looked back.

It was 1980, and Jessie had just moved with her
mother from Pasadena to the small town of Willow
Creek, Arizona, in the mountains north of Phoenix. And
if the worst thing that had happened to her thus far was
her father dying, entering the sixth grade at Yavapai Elementary was a close second. As the New Girl, she was an
easy target. It didn't help that she was an inch taller than
the tallest boy in the class, with strawberry blond hair so
pale it was almost pink and translucent skin that showed
every blush like a stain. Everything about her was
wrong—her clothes, even the lunches her mother
packed. Instead of regulation peanut butter and jelly or
bologna on Wonder Bread, Beverly, on some kind of
health kick then, made her sandwiches with wholesome
brown bread glopped with hummus or runny egg salad.
Her first day, in the cafeteria, Jessie had taken no more
than a bite of her sandwich when Amanda Coolidge wrinkled her nose and pronounced loudly, to the snickering
amusement of her friends, "Eeww. It looks like diarrhea."
Jessie thought she would die on the spot.

The torment continued, day after day, forcing her to spend lunch recesses holed up in a bathroom stall. She was perched on a toilet seat one day, absorbed in *Jane Eyre*, when a piece of the apple she was nibbling on went down the wrong way and she was seized by a coughing fit.

"You okay in there?" called a loud, raspy voice. Unmistakably that of Erin D'Amico, a wisecracking girl in her homeroom who was always getting in trouble with Mrs. Ahern for mouthing off in class.

Jessie gave a last explosive cough that sent her pitching forward, the half-eaten carton of yogurt on her lap tumbling to the floor with a splat. After a stricken moment, when it became clear that Erin wasn't leaving, she crept from the stall. Thankfully, they were alone. Erin's gaze dropped to the mess on the floor, then traveled slowly back up. *What kind of weirdo eats lunch in the bathroom?* her eyes seemed to say. Jessie's face was on fire.

But to her relief Erin merely shrugged and grabbed a handful of paper towels. Together they cleaned up the mess, Erin chatting away as if they were old friends. Before she knew it, Jessie found herself confiding about Amanda. She didn't know quite what to expect—sympathy seemed too much to hope for in her currently beaten-down state—but she was startled nonetheless when Erin let out a laugh.

What would have been truly amusing, had years later they come across a snapshot of that moment, was the odd pair they made—Jessie, a great pink-cheeked girl with legs to her armpits, and Erin, small but perfectly formed, a miniature replica of her adult self, minus breasts, with hair the color of root beer that fell in a glossy wedge over one eye. But back then, certain she was being made fun of, Jessie only ducked her head to hide her brimming eyes.

"Screw Amanda," Erin said. Jessie's head jerked up to meet her own astonished reflection in the mirror. "She's so dumb her brains would fall out if she sneezed." The bell rang, and Erin linked arms with Jessie on their way out. "Tomorrow you'll sit with me."

The following day Jessie's heart sank when she found Erin seated at Amanda's table in the cafeteria. Then she caught the twinkle of mischief in Erin's eye and knew she had something up her sleeve. When Amanda, frowning in puzzlement, pulled something lumpy wrapped in waxed paper from her lunch bag, the mists began to clear. Amanda's face reddened as she unwrapped a fat chunk of salami and wedge of runny cheese. Those around her fell silent, everyone staring. Amanda turned even redder as the stinky cheese smell rose around them, as if someone had farted. The stink hung in the air even after she'd stuffed the offending items back in the bag, muttering about some kind of mix-up. But Jessie knew that Erin had put it there, and she gave a silent cheer.

Amanda left her alone after that—perhaps not wanting to remind anyone of her own brief descent into social pariahdom—and things began to look up for Jessie. She stopped feeling so shy and began noticing things about other people rather than simply praying not to be noticed. More importantly, she had Erin. They had a lot in common, it turned out. They were both only children, though Erin lived in one of the poorer neighborhoods while Jessie's house was on a shady street lined with gracious homes. And if Erin didn't know what it was like to lose a parent, she knew how to fend for herself—her dad was a bus driver and her mom a waitress, and their shifts often overlapped.

It wasn't until their junior year of high school, when Jessie caught the notice of popular senior, Mike Delahanty, that she and Erin stopped spending almost every free moment together. Looking back years later, Jessie knew it must have been hard for Erin, though she never let on. She occupied her time running for student council and taking a cooking class at night—in self-defense, she claimed, since both her parents were hopeless in the kitchen.

After they graduated, Jessie went off to Arizona State and Erin to UC Davis. Jessie and Mike were still dating— he'd gotten a job on a local construction crew—so she often came home on weekends. Her senior year, when Mike presented her with a diamond engagement ring, it seemed the inevitable next step. In many ways, it was like they were married already. She was closer to Mike's family than to her mother, especially his younger brother Skip, who'd been in her class at Yavapai High and who'd palled around with her and Erin.

Jessie was so over the moon at first she scarcely noticed how out of sync she was, a diamond solitaire on her finger while other girls on campus sported nose and belly rings.

Between term papers and exams, she tried on bridal gowns and flipped through binders of sample invitations. It wasn't until she and Erin were both home on spring break that she became aware of just how out of step she was. Taking in Erin's newly pierced eyebrow and shredded jeans, her spiky hair dyed the color of rooster feathers, Jessie was suddenly and acutely aware of the gap between them. As Erin chattered on about various student groups she was involved in, and her plans to house-sit for her roommate's parents in New York City that summer, Jessie felt the gulf widen. *A year from now I'll be throwing Tupperware parties*, she thought, gripped by a strange, new panic.

Erin told her about the summer job she had lined up at a restaurant in Greenwich Village owned by friends of the Shapiros. If it worked out, she planned to stay on in New York and fulfill her dream of becoming a chef.

"You'll be so far away," Jessie moaned.

"I'm not the one getting married," Erin said, giving her a long, assessing look.

As the Big Day drew near, Jessie's uncertainty grew. Often she became short of breath for no reason, or found herself bolting awake from a sound sleep, drenched in sweat. The only other time she'd felt this way was in the weeks after her father's death.

One day, Jessie fainted while being fitted for her wedding gown. Mike's mother insisted on taking her to a doctor, who diagnosed it as an acute anxiety attack. He wrote out a prescription for a mild sedative, which Jessie didn't fill. *It'll pass*, she told herself. Besides, what would it mean if she had to medicate herself in order to march down the aisle?

The day before the wedding Jessie awoke while it was still dark to discover she'd been buried in her sleep by an avalanche. Each breath was like sucking in air through a straw, and when she tried to sit up she found she could barely move.

Somehow she managed to pull herself upright. In the darkness, her bridal gown, hooked over the closet door in its plastic shroud, seemed to hover ghostlike. She extended a trembling hand to pick up the phone on the nightstand and punched in Erin's number.

"I'll be right over," Erin told her.

Half an hour later, huddled over mugs of coffee at Denny's, it all came pouring out—the doubts Jessie had been having, the panic attacks. Erin listened, her forehead furrowed in consternation. It wasn't until Jessie slumped back in her seat that Erin said calmly, "You don't have to go through with it, you know."

"Of course, I do. It's all planned!" Jessie didn't see a way out. Besides, this was probably nothing more than a severe case of cold feet.

"I know. It's too bad it got this far before you realized . . ." Erin's frown deepened, and she took a sip of her coffee as if to keep from saying what was really on her mind. "Not that Mike isn't a great guy, but you haven't had a chance to be on your own, to live a little. How can you know this is what you want if you have nothing to compare it to?"

It was what Jessie had been thinking without being able to express it. Softly, she asked, "Even if you're right, what other choice do I have?"

"Come with me to New York. At least until you know for sure if this is what you want."

"New York," Jessie echoed in disbelief, as if Erin had suggested a canoe trip down the Amazon.

"You can stay with me," Erin went on in that maddeningly calm voice. "I'll ask the Shapiros, but I'm sure they won't mind."

Jessie's heart raced, and she felt slightly sick to her stomach. How could she do that to Mike? None of this was his fault. Besides, she knew in her heart that if she postponed the wedding, there'd be no turning back. She wouldn't just be burning her bridges, she'd be torching them.

She was opening her mouth to refuse Erin's offer when a clear, cool wave of sanity washed through her, banishing all but the shining reprieve Erin held out to her. Instead, she asked, "How soon can we leave?"

"Right now, if you like."

Jessie had only a vague recollection of what came next. She dimly recalled throwing clothes into a suitcase back at her house. She didn't even take the time to shower; she wanted to be gone by the time her mother woke up. Some instinct told her that if she were to linger any longer than it took to scribble a note to Mike, and one to Beverly, she'd lose her nerve. Later, when she and Erin were well on their way, the full impact of what she was doing, the hurt she was causing, would sink in. But at that moment, as she was flying out the door and across the dew-damp lawn to where Erin's orange VW bug, aptly nicknamed the Pumpkin, idled at the curb, the guilt that in the days and weeks to come would consume her was but a distant voice faintly heard amid the roar of blood in her head. She felt like a thief making a getaway. Not until years later did she realize she'd only stolen what was rightfully hers: the destiny she was meant to fulfill.

Whatever that was.

Now, fifteen years later, what did she have to show for it except a bunch of articles in magazines growing dog-eared in doctors' offices? That, and a string of failed relationships. The only thing that allowed her to keep the faith that she'd one day find her soul mate was knowing that Erin had found that kind of happiness with Skip. If he had yet to forgive Jessie for what she'd done to his brother, he was good to Erin. They had the kind of marriage other couples envied. Despite the odds against them—they'd been so young, with Kayla on the way and Erin still reeling from the deaths of her parents—they'd made it work.

Briefly, Jessie wondered what would've happened if she'd married Mike. Would it have been so terrible? True, he was nothing like his brother. Where Skip was the still-waters-run-deep type, Mike was white-water rapids. Yet she knew that Mike had truly loved her and that she'd wounded him deeply. Maybe this was her punishment, to be forever disappointed in love.

She stared at the chocolaty ooze on the floor, which

Delilah was tentatively sniffing at before she roused herself, as if from a deep sleep, and reached for the phone. She punched the speed dial button for Erin's number.

"Darby Inn," Erin answered after several rings.

After all these years Jessie still hadn't gotten used to the crisp, professional voice Erin used at the inn. "It's me," she said. Jessie waited for Erin to say something in her normal voice, low and smoky, with a little laugh waiting to break out, but there was only a choked sound at the other end.

Instantly, Jessie forgot her own troubles. "Erin, what is it? What's wrong?"

There was a long pause, then Erin answered in a low, trembling voice, "It's Skip. He's left me."

Chapter Two

Earlier that evening, Erin was locking up for the night when she paused to scan the guest book in the foyer. *Gorgeous setting and great food (the Grand Marnier pancakes are to die for!)*, read the most recent entry. *You and Skip are the perfect hosts. What a dynamic duo! See you again next year!* Her mouth stretched in a mirthless smile. What would Mr. and Mrs. Baumgarten say when they returned to find that the dynamic duo was now a solo act?

She closed the book, absently fingering its faded denim cover, fashioned from an old pair of Skip's jeans—one of her early craft projects, which now seemed to symbolize everything that was wrong with her life. Once, she'd dreamed of moving to New York and becoming a renowned chef. Instead, she was still here in Willow

Creek covering things in fabric and coming up with new and creative recipes for pancakes.

Could she blame Skip for wanting out? There were days when she herself felt it was too much to handle. But if she sometimes questioned her sanity in buying this place, she'd never wondered if it had been a mistake marrying Skip. Until now. All day, she'd seesawed between wanting to tear him a new one and missing him so bad it was like a hole in her gut.

"What are you doing?" she'd cried in panic when she walked into their bedroom that morning to find him stuffing clothes into a suitcase.

"What does it look like I'm doing?" he'd responded coldly.

"You can't leave because of a little argument. That's . . . that's . . ." *Crazy*, she wanted to say, but bit her tongue. "Skip, what's going on? Why are you doing this?" she demanded instead.

"I've had enough."

They'd disagreed earlier over whether or not to pave the driveway and it had escalated into an argument, but nothing that would account for this extreme of a reaction. "Look, if it's about the driveway, you can have it paved if you like. I just thought that crushed gravel would look—"

"It's not about the driveway," he said, cutting her off.

"What then?"

He shook his head slowly, incredulously, as if her obtuseness were only reinforcing his decision, before he went back to his packing.

This wasn't just about some stupid argument, she knew. She could no longer deny it: Their marriage was in trouble. Like a faulty appliance they'd put off fixing that was now blowing up in a shower of sparks.

Erin, in shock, struggled to wrap her brain around the fact that her husband was leaving her. Despite all the harsh words and cold silences, she'd never imagined it would come to this. Leaning into the doorframe to keep her knees from buckling, she forced herself to ask, "Is there someone else?"

He cast her an aggrieved look. "No." From the flatness of his tone she knew he wasn't lying.

It wasn't for lack of opportunity, God knew. There was no getting around the fact that her husband was a babe magnet. Skip was the guy women batted their eyelashes at when their car wouldn't start or when they needed a hand lifting something heavy. Waitresses who didn't normally flirt with customers would linger to chat with him, and female clerks rushed to wait on him in stores. Looking at him now, brown and stripped to muscle from working outdoors, his sandy hair brushed with silver, the color of a windswept beach, she felt her heart catch. How could she possibly let him go?

Realization sank in at last. "This is about Coburn, isn't it?" she said. Coburn Moss, Skip's old boss at Red Rock Landscaping, where he'd worked before they were married, was retiring and had offered him a honey of a deal on a buyout. Skip had come to her the week before brimming with excitement. It was what he'd always wanted—innkeeping was just something he'd fallen into, she knew, not what he'd have chosen on his own. But instead of giving him her blessing, Erin had reasoned that they couldn't afford to take out a second loan, much less hire someone to replace Skip.

Too late, she saw that in shooting down his dream she'd broken more than his spirit.

She remained motionless in the doorway, her gut twisting as she watched him toss things into his suitcase— shirts she'd ironed, boxers and undershirts she'd folded, socks rolled into balls like a litter of orphaned puppies. All her life, she'd believed there was no such thing as an insurmountable obstacle or crisis. Even the nightmare of her parents' deaths she'd coped with somehow. But for the first time ever, she felt utterly helpless.

"All I wanted was a little support from my wife," he said. "Is that too much to ask? It's not like I don't pull my weight around here. It's not like I don't *deserve* a fucking break. Instead, what do I get—a load of crap about how we can't afford it, how it'll ruin us." He whirled around, and she flinched at the raw fury in his face. "Thanks for the vote of confidence, Erin," he hurled at her. "It's nice to know you believe in me."

"I *do* believe in you," she said, but it came out sounding weak and unconvincing.

"Yeah, I can see that," he scoffed.

Where was this anger coming from? He must have been stewing about this for days. She'd noticed that he'd been quieter than usual, almost sullen at times, but she hadn't realized the extent of it. Her own anger stirred and broke free of the paralysis that gripped her. Wasn't that typical of Skip? Nursing a grudge instead of hashing it out then and there.

"It has nothing to do with you," she insisted. "I just didn't—don't—see how we could swing it, at least not until you were in the black." Coburn wasn't in the best of health and business had fallen off as a result, part of the reason he was offering Skip such a good price.

"You didn't see it because you didn't want to."

"So it's all *my* fault," she said.

He gave a tight shrug and went back to his packing. "Blame me, if it makes you feel any better."

Erin winced. It took every ounce of her self-control to say in a placating tone, "It's nobody's fault. We hit a bad patch, that's all. It happens. Maybe if we saw someone . . ." Skip cut her off with a look that would have sliced through case-hardened steel. He'd sooner go to a Navajo medicine man than see a marriage counselor.

"I don't need a shrink to tell me what's wrong with our marriage." He snatched a blazer from its hanger, the navy one he wore to church, which was missing a button. She felt a crazy urge to yank it from him and make him stay put until she'd sewn the button back on. How would he manage without her? How would she manage without *him*?

She took a step toward him, still hoping she could appeal to him, that she could reach the man she'd slept next to every night for the past fifteen years, the man who loved his family more than anything in the world. "Is it so terrible? We have a good life, Skip. You should be proud of what we've accomplished." She gestured about her, thinking of how they'd killed themselves just to turn this old wreck into something habitable. Why wasn't it enough?

"I only did it to make you happy." The quiet coldness with which he spoke robbed her of any comfort she might have taken from his words.

Erin found herself remembering when they'd been picking out a wall color for this room. Skip had wanted Williamsburg blue, and she'd had her heart set on Devonshire cream. She'd won. Now she wondered why she couldn't have given in. Such a little thing, would it have hurt? Jessie had once joked that she was a one-woman Panzer division. Erin had laughed at the time, but it didn't seem funny now.

But if she could be bossy and opinionated, she didn't hold grudges the way Skip did, like the one he'd carried all these years against Jessie. If he'd felt this strongly about going into business for himself, he should have done something about it years ago.

She knew why he hadn't, and that only made her feel worse: Skip had always bent over backward to please her. But you could only push a man so far.

"We didn't have a whole lot of options at the time," she reminded him. They'd been expecting Kayla and barely making ends meet on his salary. When she came into some money from a small life insurance policy her parents had taken out, buying this former dude ranch and turning it into an inn had seemed the perfect solution, a way to utilize both their talents.

Skip dropped his head, kneading the back of his neck. She knew the exact spot where it was kinked, and even now her fingers itched to ease the knot. "You're right," he acknowledged with a sigh. Erin felt a surge of hope, until he brought his head up, and she saw the unforgiving look on his face. "But did it have to be set in stone? Christ, I've put fifteen years into this place. If I want something more, don't you think I've earned it?"

She bristled at the unfairness of it. Hadn't she worked her tail off, too? "What about Kayla?" she snapped. "What were we supposed to tell her when she's ready for college? 'Sorry, we don't have the money.'"

He crumpled the jacket he'd been folding and hurled it at the wall. The buttons made a little pinging sound as they hit the metal base of the lamp on the dresser. His whole body was clenched so hard it was quivering, and his eyes blazed like a struck match. "Don't you dare drag Kayla into this!" he roared. "She's the only reason I stuck it out this long!"

Erin took a wobbly step back. Abruptly, the anger went out of her, and she sank down on the foot of the bed. "Where will you be? In case I need to reach you," she asked in a strange, dead voice she hardly recognized as her own. Thank God Kayla wasn't here to witness this— she was spending the night with her friend Devon.

"My brother's." He zipped his suitcase shut with a

sound that went through her like a serrated knife. "He's giving me a job, too, but don't worry, I'll keep up with my chores around here until you find someone to replace me." As if he were a broken lawn mower part she could replace.

"I wasn't . . ." She squeezed her eyes shut, realizing it was useless to argue. His mind was made up. She felt something wet nudge her hand, and opened her eyes to find Otis peering up at her with a worried look, his tail fanning slowly back and forth, as if to ask, *What's wrong?* She stroked his silky yellow head, answering silently, *Where do I begin?*

Skip brushed past her, suitcase in hand.

"I was only doing what I thought was best," she said in a last-ditch attempt to defend herself.

He paused, looking down at her. Some of the hardness went out of his face, and he lifted his arm as if to console her, only to let it fall heavily to his side. "Yeah, I know. What's best for *you*," he said wearily.

Somehow that hurt more than the harsh words. Hadn't she always put her family first? Often at the expense of her own wants and needs. And what about the dreams *she'd* sacrificed? If she'd denied him his, it wasn't because she was selfish.

Now, hours later, Erin looked about in disbelief at the walls that were still standing, the roof that hadn't caved in. The pendulum still swung in the burled grandfather clock in the foyer, relentlessly measuring out the minutes. And in the great room down the hall, she heard the faint crackle of a log collapsing in the fireplace. It seemed a cruel joke almost, that nothing had altered in the wake of something so earth-shattering.

To top it off, all day she'd had to act as if nothing were out of the ordinary. Every room and both casitas were booked, so she'd had her hands full with guests. She'd put together the wine and cheese plates, and carried a tea tray up to Mrs. Cooley, who wasn't feeling well. She'd spent twenty minutes on the phone with a woman in Philadelphia who'd wanted to know everything there was to see and do in Willow Creek. By the time she'd hung up, Erin had felt like screaming.

The only thing keeping her sane was the hope that Skip would return home any minute. *He'll come around*, she told herself. *It's just a squabble that got out of hand.*

But she knew it was more than that. Or why she hadn't phoned Jessie? When it was just some stupid argument, she'd turn it into a humorous tale that would have her friend chuckling. Like the time she and Skip had gotten into a fight over his lifting a curfew she'd given Kayla, without consulting her. They didn't speak to each other for a whole day, and she'd missed him so much that after a night of tossing and turning, she woke the following morning to find herself twined about him like a piece of barbed wire around a pole.

Not that Jessie wouldn't sympathize. Erin could talk to her about anything. Growing up, they'd been closer than most sisters. In the seventh grade when Jessie got her period, it was Erin she'd gone to, not her mom. And the time Erin, to her horror, spied her own mother going at it hot and heavy with her boss, Jessie was the only person she could bring herself to confide in. These days, they talked on the phone at least once a week and emailed each other every other day. Erin consoled Jessie after each of her breakups and Jessie listened patiently when Erin let off steam about everything from her despised in-laws to impossible guests and health inspectors from hell.

Erin often reflected on the irony of Jessie's having taken the path that would have been hers if fate hadn't intervened. If she hadn't urged Jessie to come with her to New York that long-ago summer, her friend might well have married Mike . . . while Erin would probably be living in New York if not for her parents' sudden deaths, perhaps with her own restaurant. But if she occasionally regretted that lost opportunity, she knew that given the chance to do it over again, she wouldn't change a thing. Otherwise, she wouldn't have Kayla. Or Skip.

Make that past tense, she thought bitterly of her husband.

As Erin made her way down the hall, her yellow retriever padding at her heels, she could hear the creak of floorboards overhead as guests settled in for the night. It wasn't all drudgery. There were people who sent thankyou notes, as they would after a visit to a friend's. And those who came year after year who'd come to seem like family.

In the great room, she pulled a notepad from her pocket on which was scribbled, in her nearly indecipherable shorthand, a punch list of all the things in need of attention or repair:

> *fix lky faucet in dwnstrs bthrm*
> *call Vince re: furnace*
> *dry-clean slipcovers in grt/rm*
> *replace bulb in chandelier*

She stared at it vacantly for a moment, then wrote, *talk to S. about frwood.*

Normally it was Skip's job to keep the wood box stocked and to light a fire in the morning before the guests came down. Now, as she warmed herself before its dying embers, she wondered how she would cope. Maria worked only four days a week, and the maids, Suzy and Petra, alternated days, which often left Erin shorthanded. She didn't doubt Skip would keep up with his morning chores until she found someone to replace him, but what about all the little things that cropped up during the day? Heavy suitcases to lug upstairs, trips into town to pick up items she'd run out of, the little fix-it jobs he'd always seen to.

Swamped with fear, she abruptly dropped onto the sofa. The great room was dark except for the firelight and sepia glow from the mica floor lamp, which she left on for any guests who happened to wander downstairs in the night. The sturdy Mission chairs and tables were pooled in shadow, their dark, polished oak glinting with reflected firelight. Her gaze fell on the Navajo rug by the fireplace, a souvenir from the last trip she and Skip had taken together, to Canyon de Chelle. How long ago was that? Six, seven years. How could they have let so much time pass without a vacation? Had they thought they could simply tuck away that part of their lives until they got around to it, like the good silver wrapped in felt?

She thought about helping herself to a glass of sherry from the cut-glass decanter on the sideboard, or curling up with one of the books that lined the built-in shelves on either side of the fireplace. Anything to put off having to face the emptiness of her bed. It didn't help knowing that Mike would do his best to reintroduce his brother to the joys of bachelorhood. It wasn't that Mike had anything against her; it was marriage in general he had a problem with. Erin was convinced, though Mike wouldn't have admitted it, that it was because he'd never gotten over Jessie, the only woman he'd ever really loved. It had soured him on longtime commitments of any kind.

With an effort, she hauled herself to her feet. Tomorrow she had to be up at the crack of dawn, same as always, breakfast started and coffee set out by the time the guests began stirring. She made her way down the hall to her cramped office in what had been a storage closet back in the Darby Inn's heyday as a dude ranch, when Arizona was the Mecca of quickie divorces. Sitting down at her computer, she quickly scanned her email. Most of it was inquiries about room availability and dates, along with the usual spam hawking everything from low interest rates on a home equity loan to promises of a bigger penis. She was responding to an email from a woman in Ohio who wanted to know if she and her husband should pack sweaters and warm jackets for their stay—out-of-towners seemed to think the entire state was nothing but desert and cacti, with blistering temperatures to match—when the phone rang.

Her heart leapt. Skip? He'd know to call her on the business line at this hour. Her hand was trembling as she snatched up the receiver. "Darby Inn," she answered crisply.

But it was only Jessie. The concern in her voice when Erin broke the bad news was what finally pushed her over the edge. She began to weep.

"My God, I can't believe it. Skip?" Jessie was incredulous. "I'm sure it'll all blow over by tomorrow. I mean, how bad could it be?"

Erin choked back a sob. "He moved in with Mike. I don't . . ." She forced herself to say it. "I don't think he's coming back."

Jessie sucked in a breath at the other end. "What happened?" she asked. "What's he so mad about?"

It all came pouring out then. About Skip, wanting to buy out Coburn and Erin, putting the kibosh on it. About other things, too. He thought she was too strict with Kayla; she thought he spoiled her. She wanted him to stick up for her more with his parents; he was always pushing for her to make more of an effort with them, like *they* had been anything but hateful toward her since day one. Lately, they couldn't even agree on rare over medium rare when it came to roast beef.

Jessie was silent for a moment. "Oh, Erin." She sounded more than just dismayed; all the wind seemed to have been knocked out of her. "Why didn't you tell me?"

"I didn't want to admit to myself how bad it'd gotten."

"So what now?"

"Your guess is as good as mine."

"Are you going to be able to manage on your own?"

Erin sighed, staring at the pile of paperwork in her in-box. "What choice do I have?"

"If you need me, I'll fly out tomorrow."

"Thanks, but I'll be okay." She appreciated the offer, but Jessie wasn't exactly the domestic type. She didn't know what a hospital corner was, and she could barely boil an egg.

"What about Skip?"

"Mike gave him a job on one of his crews." That was how Erin knew how bad this was: Skip was proud of his older brother, but it stuck in his craw that Mike was so successful—he'd built most of the newer subdivisions around town. To swallow his pride and accept Mike's offer, the alternative would have to have been intolerable.

"This is worse than I thought," Jessie said.

"Oh, Jess. What am I going do?" Erin's voice broke. Jessie was the only person who ever saw this side of her. To everyone else she was the Rock of Gibraltar, supplier of endless advice, a shoulder to cry on, cakes for bake sales, Kleenexes and Wet Ones.

"I know one thing," Jessie said. "You can't just sit back and do nothing."

"It takes two to tango." Erin's voice hardened. At this point Skip wouldn't come back if she begged him to. Not that she ever would. She had her pride.

"This is no time to be stubborn." The urgency in Jessie's voice bordered on desperation, as if her own future were at stake.

"Why should I be the one to apologize?"

"One of you has to go first."

"In that case, let him come to me."

"What if he doesn't?"

"Screw him then."

"You don't mean that."

"If he thinks he's punishing me," Erin growled, "I'll show him a thing or two."

"You're not thinking of divorce!" Jessie gasped.

Erin's stomach dipped as if she were plunging down in an elevator. "No," she said softly. "No one's said anything about divorce." *Yet.*

"I still can't believe it. You always seemed like the perfect couple." Jessie sounded on the verge of tears. Hesitantly, she asked, "He isn't, um . . . seeing someone, is he?"

"Not that I know of." Though Erin almost wished it were that simple. Another woman she'd know how to deal with; she'd pull every hair out of the bitch's head.

Silence fell. She could hear the inn settling, like an old person full of creaks and groans. Most of the guests would be in bed by now, blissfully unaware of the drama taking place below.

"You sure you don't want me to come out?" Jessie said.

"I'm sure. Thanks for offering, but right now it'd be about as much fun as a trip to Guantanamo Bay. I'd only drag you down with me."

"I wouldn't have far to go," Jessie muttered.

Erin remembered that today was the Big Day. "I'm guessing it didn't go all that well with Jonathon's family," she ventured.

Jessie groaned. "They acted like I was Typhoid Mary."

"That bad?"

"The kids didn't say more than two words to me." She sighed. "His folks weren't much better. All their small talk was just fattening me up for the oven."

Erin murmured in sympathy. "Believe me, I've been there." She'd endured the same treatment from her in-laws, who'd made it clear they thought she wasn't good enough for Skip.

"I probably should have expected it. I mean, after everything I've heard about stepchildren." Jessie gave a bitter laugh. "Pathetic, huh? I'm wondering what kind of family we'll make, and he hasn't even asked me to marry him. In fact, he's made it pretty clear that's not on the agenda."

Jonathon must be pretty special. Jessie hadn't talked this way about any of her other boyfriends, even the ones she'd professed to be in love with. If anything, that whole business with Mike, what Jessie referred to as her close call with "suburbicide," had left her skittish about commitment. "You're talking to the wrong person," Erin said. "At the moment I'm not exactly a walking advertisement for marriage. Not with mine in the shitter."

"Don't say that! There's still hope."

"As in 'hope springs eternal'?" Erin pulled her cardigan around her to keep from shivering. "Sorry, but I don't think I'll live that long."

"Have you thought about seeing a therapist?"

"Skip doesn't believe in shrinks."

"That's ridiculous! Practically everyone I know is in therapy."

"This isn't New York," Erin reminded her. Jessie had been away long enough to forget that in Willow Creek the clock had stopped sometime during the Nixon administration. Around here, such matters were still talked about in whispers.

"Even so, it's crazy not to at least try. You two love each other."

Erin recalled as if it were yesterday the exact moment she'd known she was in love with Skip. It was the week after her parents' funeral, and she was still reeling from the shock. It had all happened so suddenly. One minute she was in New York having the time of her life, and the next she was flying home in the wake of the accident that had claimed their lives—they'd been on their way home from a night of bowling when a drunk driver smashed into their car. Jessie had gone with her, but after the funeral she'd had to fly back to New York to start her new job as editorial assistant at *Mademoiselle*. It was Skip who volunteered to help Erin pack up her parents' things.

She was in their bedroom sorting through her mother's jewelry box when she came across the gaudy rhinestone brooch Erin had bought her for her birthday one year, when she was thirteen. She hadn't cried once throughout the funeral, but for some reason that ugly brooch only a kid would've thought was beautiful, and that her mother had worn as if it were diamonds from Tiffany's, affected her more deeply than the sight of her mother's coffin being lowered into the ground. She cracked, and the tears came pouring out in a torrent.

Skip sat down next to her on the bed and put his arms around her, holding her tightly as he rocked from side to side. In school, they'd hung out together, mostly because of Jessie and Mike; it wasn't until now that he'd shown what a good friend he was, scarcely leaving her side throughout the ordeal. When she was finally out of tears, he used the tail of his shirt to pat her cheeks dry—the sheets and towels, along with every box of Kleenex, had been packed up.

"Why don't you stay with us for a few days?" he offered. "I'm sure my folks wouldn't mind. I'll drive you back tomorrow, and we can pack up the rest then."

"I can't ask you to—" She started to protest, knowing that he and his brother had tickets to a ball game.

He brought a finger to her lips, silencing her. "You're not asking me. I want to."

"I can manage on my own," she said weakly.

Erin was used to handling things. Though it pained her to admit it, her parents had been hopeless when it came to household matters. Money had run like water through her dad's fingers, and her mom had always joked that she didn't want it on her tombstone that she had the cleanest oven in town—a joke that seemed grisly in light of the present circumstances. As soon as Erin was old enough to reach the counter, she'd done most of the cooking. The cleaning, too. Things other kids took for granted, like shampoo and toothpaste, she'd often had to buy with the money she earned from babysitting.

Putting a hand under her chin, Skip tilted her head up to meet her gaze. "I know you can manage," he said. "But that doesn't mean you *have* to."

She'd known then he would always be there for her. Her throat tightened at the memory.

"I used to think love conquered all," she told Jessie. "Now I'm not so sure."

Jessie fell silent, no doubt thinking about Jonathon. Then she sighed, and said, "Do you ever wonder what would've happened if you'd stayed in New York?"

"Sometimes." It was as if Jessie had read her mind. Hadn't Erin been thinking about that very thing just before Jessie called? She picked up a framed photo of her and Skip and Kayla taken the summer before last, at the county fair where Kayla had won a blue ribbon for the Plymouth Rock hen she'd entered in the 4-H competition. Had they really been as happy as they looked? "My life would be different, but I'm not sure it'd be better." She never made it back to New York. That summer, she and Skip were inseparable, and by fall she was pregnant with Kayla. They'd gotten married soon after that.

"I wonder about it, too. What would've happened if I'd married Mike." Jessie hastened to add, "Not that I have any regrets. Just in general, you know—I wonder what it'd be like to be a wife and mother. I never really noticed before, but now when I walk down the sidewalk, all I see is moms pushing strollers."

Erin gave a knowing laugh. "Your biological clock isn't just ticking—the alarm is going off."

"It's more than that," Jessie said. "It's like I woke up one day and realized that the little rock I'm on that I thought was the center of the universe is just a *place*. I used to look down at people living in Queens or Jersey. But am I a better person because I ride the subway? I buy my coffee at Starbucks like everyone else, and you don't have to live in a 212 area code for that."

"From where I sit, it looks pretty glamorous." The times Erin had visited her, she'd felt like a starving person at a banquet—she could never seem to get her fill.

"Maybe we should trade places," Jessie joked. "Find out if the grass is really greener on the other side."

"I'd be getting the best of the bargain." Erin knew Jessie wasn't serious, but at the moment she found the idea appealing.

Jessie snorted. "Fat chance. You'd be living off ramen noodles and saltines."

They shared a laugh, and Erin felt the heaviness that

clung to her like a wet cloak lift a little. By the time she hung up, she was feeling marginally better. It was times like these that she realized how much she missed her best friend. If Jessie lived just down the road, they'd be at the kitchen table right now with a tub of ice cream and two spoons.

Erin retraced her steps down the hallway and let herself and Otis out the back door, easing it shut behind her. The dog raced ahead of her as she made her way down the gravel path that led to the former bunkhouse they'd converted into family quarters. The only sound was the crunching of her footsteps and the faint rustle of the breeze in the trees overhead. Moonlight glinted off the corrugated toolshed and the wire enclosure beyond, which was meant to keep the rabbits out of her herb garden but hadn't done much to deter them. She whistled for Otis, and a moment later he came bounding back to snuffle furiously at the most recent hole under the fence, whining deep in his throat before throwing his head back in a howl of frustration. Erin knew just how he felt.

An hour later, she lay staring up at the shadows playing over the ceiling above her bed. *What if I could just pick up and go?* she thought. Anywhere but here, where the cold expanse on Skip's side of the bed was mute testament to her failure.

Chapter Three

"You don't look so hot." Kate set aside her menu to eye Jessie with concern. "Are you getting enough sleep?"

They were having lunch at Eleven Madison, which overlooked Madison Square Park and was within walking distance from the offices of *Savvy* magazine, where Kate was a senior editor. Sunlight slanted in through the soaring windows of the former Met Life building, setting the glass of white wine in Kate's hand aglow and casting its shimmery reflection on the tablecloth below. Who wouldn't look haggard next to Kate? With her gorgeous face and body by Equinox, she had to be the envy of every woman in the restaurant.

Jessie gave a rueful laugh. "I sleep alone. Need I say more."

"So you and Jonathon . . . ?" Kate arched a perfectly plucked brow.

"No, we're fine," Jessie hastened to assure her. "It's just that we've both been really busy lately." She wasn't being completely honest, but she didn't want to admit the truth: That between weekends with Zach and Sara, school events, and therapy sessions, Jonathon had very little time for her. And after that disastrous trip to his parents', another family outing wasn't an option. At least not until the dust settled.

"I'm glad to hear it," Kate said. "Because if you ever do break up with him, it would start a feeding frenzy. I know at least a dozen women who'd dump the guys they're with for so much as a *speed* date with Jonathon." She was referring to the latest trend among Jewish singles, the dating equivalent of musical chairs. Jessie shuddered inwardly at the thought, reminded anew of what she'd faced when she was unattached. On the other hand, she might as well be single for all the time she'd spent with Jonathon lately.

"How's *your* love life these days?" she asked, eager to change the subject. Kate made a face. "So the Bolivian polo player's out of the picture?"

Kate shrugged. "I found out he was cheating on me. Not that I hold it against him. He was more than one woman could handle. It's true what they say about Latin lovers—they give new meaning to south of the border," she added, with a sly smile.

Jonathon was no slouch either, Jessie thought. They

must have tried every position in the *Kama Sutra*. What she missed most, though, was just snuggling with him in bed. "Knowing you, I'll bet you haven't been sitting home alone." Kate could wallpaper her office with the business cards slipped to her by men interested in more than business.

Kate rolled her eyes. "Please. I barely have time for my morning coffee, much less a relationship."

Jessie didn't comment. Kate's would be another woman's dream job. She got to interview the likes of Tom Cruise and George Clooney. Glamorous parties and movie premieres were de rigueur. Perks included the latest designer fashions left over from photo shoots, trips to London and Paris, not to mention freebies sent by advertisers. While Jessie was lucky if she got paid for an article in a timely fashion.

She cleared her throat. "Um, speaking of work, I was wondering what you thought of my proposal." Jessie assumed that's why Kate had asked her to lunch.

Kate didn't beat around the bush. "No go, I'm afraid. Julia feels it's been done to death." Julia Hicks, the sixty-plus managing editor of *Savvy* and Kate's boss, prided herself on having her finger on the pulse of their readership—urban women in their thirties and forties. "I tried telling her yours would be a fresh take, not just the Wax Work set, women *our* age getting face-lifts, but I couldn't get her to bite. I'm sorry, Jess."

Jessie's heart sank, but she did her best to hide her disappointment. She was too proud to let Kate know how desperate she was—if her current slump didn't end soon, she'd be looking at homelessness. Her neighbor Drew had offered to put her up if it came to that, but his apartment upstairs was even smaller than hers, with only one bed.

"Too bad. I was hoping to get free liposuction out of it, at least," she joked.

Kate didn't even crack a smile. She eyed Jessie almost pityingly. *Oh God, this is worse than I thought,* Jessie thought. Her last two proposals had been turned down as well. Kate must think she'd lost her touch.

"We're always open to new ideas, though," Kate said.

"The thing is, I seem to be fresh out. Any suggestions?"

They were interrupted just then by their waiter arriving to take their orders. Jessie was so caught up in her thoughts she didn't mind that he looked at Kate the entire time he was rattling off the day's specials. As usual, Kate was oblivious. "Don't you hate that?" she leaned across the table to whisper when he'd left. "All I want is lunch, not the goddamn Magna Carta." When men stared at Kate, she assumed it was because she had something on her teeth. "Anyway, where were we? Ideas, yes." She frowned in concentration, tapping a French-manicured fingernail against the stem of her wineglass. "What about a piece on boomerangers? You know, women who move to the 'burbs and after a year or two run screaming back to their fourth-floor walk-ups and pooper-scoopers."

"What about the ones who think it's the best decision they ever made?"

"They're probably just saying that to make themselves feel better." For Kate, a dyed-in-the-wool New Yorker, there could be no worse fate than being stranded in the suburbs. She was more likely to wind up with an STD than an SUV.

"Some maybe, but not all," Jessie said. "My friend Cynthia was bitching the other day that she pays more to garage her car than she used to pay in rent."

"Where, in North Dakota?"

"The point is, she's thinking of moving out of the city. She's tired of being broke all the time. A dollar won't even buy you a decent cup of coffee these days." No one knew that better than Jessie. "Is it so hard to believe someone would happily exchange a fourth-floor walk-up and a MetroCard for a house and a Chevy Suburban?"

"Sounds like you're warming to the idea yourself." Kate sipped her wine, eyeing Jessie thoughtfully.

"It wouldn't be the worst thing in the world," Jessie said a bit defensively.

She loved New York. She loved that everything she could possibly want or need was within walking distance. She loved curling up with a Sunday paper as thick as her arm. She loved bagels so hot they steamed a hole through the bag. If she had a craving for sushi at two in the morning, there was sure to be a Japanese restaurant that was open. But in light of her present circumstances, she couldn't deny that the idea of moving to a place where the cost of living was considerably lower, where she wouldn't always feel the pressure of making ends meet, had a certain appeal. She realized she was *tired*—of scrambling to make ends meet, of being thirty-five and single with only a part-time boyfriend and no prospects in sight.

Kate eyed her curiously. "Just for the sake of argument, where would you go?"

"Home." The word was out before Jessie realized it.

"You mean, *home* home?" Kate said in the same tone she'd have used if it were Newfoundland.

"It's not so bad." Okay, there were only a few decent restaurants, and Saturday night was more likely to find you at the local Blockbuster than a swanky nightclub (not that she frequented nightclubs as a rule). But . . . "For one thing, people are friendlier. They actually *smile* at you when they pass you on the street." In New York when people smiled at you, it was because they were trying to sell you something.

"The last time you visited, you couldn't wait to get back," Kate reminded her.

"That was only because my mother was driving me crazy." Erin had offered to put her up at the inn, but Jessie had known it would be uncomfortable for them all, given the way Skip felt about her, so she'd stayed with Beverly instead. "As a matter of fact, I was joking with my friend Erin the other day that we ought to trade places. We could both use a break. She's having some problems with her marriage, and I'm, uh . . ." She faltered, before adding, "Between assignments."

Kate brightened. "Now *that*," she said, "would be a great story."

"It was a *joke*."

"You know what Freud said: There are no jokes."

"What exactly do you have in mind?" Jessie asked uneasily.

Kate lapsed once more into thought. When she brought her gaze back to Jessie, her eyes were glowing. "What if you gave it, say, six months? I'm not suggesting you swap partners or anything. But a lot of our readers are probably wondering the same thing you are. *Is* the grass greener on the other side? You'd be acting out the fantasy of every urban woman who's ever thought of chucking it all for the quiet joys of country living."

"It sounds like more than an article," Jessie replied dubiously.

"Good point. Hmmm, let's see . . . I know! We could run it in weekly installments." Kate was working up a real head of steam. "I'll talk to Julia about it when I get back to the office, see what she has to say."

Jessie shook her head. "Erin would never go for it." As if *she* would!

"How do you know until you ask? Didn't you just say she could use a break."

"I was thinking more along the lines of a spa weekend. Besides, she's not a writer. I'm assuming you'd want both our points of view."

Kate waved a hand as if it were a minor detail. "All she has to do is put her thoughts down on paper, and we'll do the rest. I'm telling you, our readers would eat it up!"

Their food arrived, but neither moved to pick up her

fork. "I'll give it some thought," Jessie said, more to appease Kate than anything. Who in their right mind would seriously consider such a thing?

A *woman with nothing to lose*, replied a voice in her head.

"You're not worried about Jonathon, are you?" Kate said, as Jessie picked listlessly at her salad.

"The thought crossed my mind." How could it not?

"Do you think he'd hesitate if the shoe was on the other foot? If, say, he were covering a story overseas?"

"He's a bureau chief, not a foreign correspondent."

"You know what I mean." Kate wasn't letting her off the hook that easy.

Jessie pondered what it would mean to Jonathon if she were to do this assignment. He was so preoccupied with his work and his kids, would he even notice she was gone? "I get your point," she said. "But there's another problem: my mother." Six months of close proximity to Beverly would be dangerous to her mental health.

"More grist for the mill," Kate said. "Who knows? It might even bring you closer."

Jessie snorted. "You haven't met my mother."

"Think about it, and talk to Erin. That's all I ask."

"I *will* think about it," Jessie promised.

"In the meantime, I'll run it by Julia."

"This is crazy. You know that, don't you?" Jessie stared at Kate, shaking her head slowly.

"The best things in life usually are." Kate speared a sliver of cucumber and brought it to her lips.

"What do I know about innkeeping?"

"You'd learn. How hard could it be?"

"I could learn to drive a forklift. That doesn't mean I have any interest in doing so."

"Maybe that's not the only thing you're afraid of." Kate shot her a challenging look.

"What are you saying?" Jessie's eyes narrowed.

"That you might like it enough to make it permanent."

Jessie felt a moment's panic at the thought. "I don't think there's any danger of that," she said with an airy laugh. "After six months, I'd be climbing the walls."

Kate broke into a grin, and Jessie realized she'd played right into her hands. "Well then, what do you have to lose?"

Chapter Four

"You should do it, Mom." Kayla pried the lid off a container of yogurt. When she was little, her favorite after-school snack had been peanut butter and honey on toast; now that was deemed too fattening. "Think of it as a vacation. When was the last time you went anywhere?"

Three years ago, her last trip to New York, Erin recalled. And even then, Jessie had had to twist her arm. She dried the last pot and placed it in the drainer. "You don't go on vacation from life," she said. Why had she even mentioned Jessie's crackpot scheme? It wasn't as if she were considering it. "Besides, this isn't a good time."

"Because of Dad you mean." Kayla's tone was elaborately nonchalant.

When they'd all sat down together, the day after Skip

moved out, Skip had explained to their daughter that he and Erin needed a break from each other. Kayla knew the real score, though, and she'd been furious at them both. For days afterward she'd skulked about, red-eyed and exuding near-radioactive levels of reproach. But in the last week or so she'd done an abrupt about-face and was now acting as if it were no big deal—half of her friends' parents were divorced, she'd said, why should she be any different? Erin wasn't fooled, however; she knew it was just Kayla's way of coping.

"It's not just about your dad," she said, which wasn't quite true. These days everything seemed to revolve around Skip, or rather, the gaping hole he'd left in her life. "I was thinking more of you." She folded the dishtowel over the drainer and turned to face her daughter, who sat perched on a stool at the counter, wearing baggy jeans and her Yavapai Scorpions sweatshirt that was at least two sizes too big, her sandy hair pulled back in a ponytail. Erin was about to add that this was a difficult time for them both, but thought better of it. Kayla didn't need reminding.

Erin watched her spoon up a quivering pink glob of yogurt. "No offense, Mom, but I can manage without you for a few months."

"You're only fourteen," Erin reminded her. "Besides, I think we've had enough changes around here as it is."

Kayla went on, undeterred, "Remember Rose Fahey, who used to be in my class? Well, she's at some boarding school back East now, and I don't see *her* mom freaking out about it. Anyway, I wouldn't be all alone. There's Dad. And I'd have Aunt Jess."

"Aunt Jess?" Erin snorted. "I'm still recovering from when you visited her at spring break—wild parties, men in drag, and God knows what else."

"It was *one* party. And Mom, I *know* about transvestites. In fact, I know more than you think."

Erin didn't doubt it. Kayla, at fourteen, was far more mature than she'd been at that age. But while Erin secretly approved of her daughter's broadening her horizons and knew that Jessie would never act irresponsibly where Kayla was concerned, having her best friend play surrogate mom for six whole months was out of the question.

"There's no point in discussing it," she said. "So I guess you're stuck with boring old me."

When did you become such a stick in the mud? whispered a voice in her head. She recalled the time she and Jessie had hitchhiked all the way to Phoenix on a lark, when they were only a little older than Kayla, spinning some wild tale to the trucker who gave them a lift, about being on their way to Las Vegas to become showgirls. Of course, if Kayla were ever to pull such a stunt, she'd be grounded for a year. Being a parent had changed Erin's outlook, not necessarily for the better in some respects.

She pulled open the fridge, packed as tight as a ship's hold with various Tupperware containers holding everything from butter pats to leftover pancake batter, a variety of cheeses, jams, and jellies. She took out a bag of grapes and washed its contents at the sink, then began snipping it into smaller bunches for the evening cheese plates.

How could she get away for a few weeks, much less months? Her days were so full she scarcely had a moment to herself. Mornings there was breakfast to prepare for anywhere from a dozen to two dozen people, and the rest of the day endless inquiries to field, confirmation letters to be sent out, and individual needs of guests to attend to. In addition to that, she had to oversee the housekeeping, make sure every room was spotless—woodwork gleaming, silver and brass polished, fresh flowers in all the vases.

And that wasn't even counting the events they hosted at the inn. Tomorrow morning she was meeting with the event planner for the Travers wedding, a former classmate who'd been the school spirit commissioner in high school and who still tackled every event as if it were the season playoff. If Erin didn't rein in Cricket, she'd have the poor Travers girl running for the hills instead of the altar.

"If you went away, Dad would be sorry, I'll bet," Kayla said. She darted Erin a sly look out of the corner of her eye as she picked at a hangnail.

Erin paused in the midst of her snipping, shears poised in midair. "I see. So this isn't just about my needing a vacation." Kayla probably saw this as a way to get her parents back together. If only it were that easy! "Too bad. You almost had me convinced," she added with mock regret.

"Seriously?" Kayla's head shot up.

"No." Erin went back to her task. *Snip, snip.* "And as

for your father, I shouldn't have to go to New York for him to remember he has a family." She spoke more bitterly than she'd intended.

Kayla regarded her sorrowfully. "You don't make it any easier, Mom."

Her words were a knife in Erin's gut. *Et tu, Brute?*

"I know, honey. I'm trying," she said softly. The truth was, she'd have taken him back in a heartbeat. But he had to bend a little, too.

"He still loves you."

Erin's heart leapt. "Did he tell you that?"

"No. I just know."

The shears slipped, the sharp tip stabbing Erin in the tender groove between her thumb and forefinger. She let out a little yelp and brought her hand to her mouth, sucking at the drop of blood that welled. "If your father decides to come home," she said when she could speak without her voice quavering, "it won't be because he was tricked into it."

"Yeah, whatever." Kayla slumped in defeat, staring morosely into space, elbows on the counter and chin propped on her hands.

Erin was struck, as she often was, by how much Kayla resembled her father. They were both tall and fair, with the same refined features and direct blue eyes, except that where Skip was lean, Kayla was what salesladies in dress shops referred to as big-boned—which her daughter was sure was just a polite way of saying she was fat. When Kayla looked in the mirror, she didn't see her fine features and clear skin, her shiny hair that was five different shades of blond, only that she wasn't a size 0. And yet, ironically, she idolized her Aunt Jess, whose build was similar to hers. Erin would sometimes catch a glimpse of Kayla out of the corner of her eye and think she was seeing Jessie at that age.

Erin shook her head, muttering, "Aunt Jess and her big ideas."

"At least she's not an old lady in a rocking chair."

"I'm not old!" Erin wondered when Kayla had gotten to be such a smart mouth. At the same time, she couldn't deny that there was some truth in her words. At the moment, she'd love nothing more than to rest her weary bones in one of the wicker chairs on the porch.

"Aunt Jess told me about some of the stuff you did when you were my age. Like the time you drove your dad's car without a license."

"I had my learner's permit!" Erin made a mental note to strangle Jessie. "Even so, it was stupid and reckless." *Not* the same as adventurous. "Besides, I have responsibilities now that I didn't have back then." Even as she spoke, a little chill went up her spine. Hadn't Skip, too, accused her of being inflexible? "You'll know what I'm talking about when you're married with kids of your own," she threw in for good measure.

"No way. I'm never getting married." Kayla's mouth was set in the stubborn line that was also like her father's when he was determined about something.

"You say that now, but—"

Kayla didn't let her finish. "What's the point," she said darkly, "if you're only going to split up in the end?"

Erin turned away to sponge down the already clean counter. She couldn't bear to see the look on her daughter's face. Had she and Skip done that to her? She realized how foolish she'd been, believing a closed door was enough to keep raised voices from being overheard.

But it hadn't always been like this. There'd been good times. Times the bedroom door had been closed because she and Skip were making love. Evenings when she couldn't wait to be alone with Skip after a hard day's work. Little offerings he'd brought her—a handful of the first spring cherries from the orchard; an abandoned bird's nest he'd found while clearing the pasture; a chunk of rose quartz he'd unearthed from the garden, which he'd teased was the same color as the strawberry mole on her left butt cheek. She'd had it made into a pendant, which hung on a chain around her neck, and which she now fingered absently.

She blinked back tears. She didn't want Kayla to see how close to the breaking point she was. Clearing her throat, she jerked her head toward the now-empty yogurt container, saying briskly, "If you're done with that, I could use a hand." She passed Kayla the bowl of grapes and a stack of small plates, the good china they used for the guests.

Kayla rose with a sigh and began setting out the plates in a row along the counter. She was distributing the bunches of grapes among them when she said, as if it had just occurred to her, "Uh, I forgot to tell you. Devon and I are going to the movies, if that's okay with you. Her mom's picking me up." In other words, it was all planned, and Erin would be the bad guy if she said no. At the prospect of being left alone, she felt a twinge of panic, and was about to suggest that Kayla invite Devon to watch a DVD here instead. But she thought better of it; it wasn't Kayla's job to keep her company.

"You all done with your homework?" she asked.

Kayla rolled her eyes. "Mom, it's *Friday*. I have the whole weekend."

Erin nodded distractedly. Whole chunks of her mind seemed to have disappeared along with chunks of her life. "It's all right with me, but you'll have to ask your—" She caught herself. Oh, God. Would she ever get used to thinking in terms of I instead of we?

Not that Skip wasn't still an active part of Kayla's life. They saw each other every day, when he stopped by in the morning to do his chores, and they spoke on the phone every night. Last weekend she'd stayed with him at her uncle's, and this Sunday he was taking her to church with him. All of which served to make Erin feel even more abandoned.

She was rescued from such morbid thoughts by the sudden appearance of her assistant. "Damn toilet is stopped up again," Maria growled, crouching to root around in the cupboard under the sink for the plunger. From where Erin stood, all she could see was a cloud of curly black hair and the back pockets of Maria's Levis' stretched across her generous rear.

"Which one?" Erin asked.

"Paloverde."

"Oh, Lord." As luck would have it, the woman staying in the Paloverde suite was a writer working on a piece for *Arizona Highways* on the best inns of Arizona.

Maria straightened, brandishing the plunger, her plump, freckled cheeks flushed with exertion—Diana the huntress meets Josephine the plumber. Erin silently blessed her, as she did at least a dozen times a week. Maria, a former loan officer, had seemed overqualified for the job when she'd applied six years ago. But after she'd thrown herself on Erin's mercy, saying she'd do anything to escape the stultifying atmosphere of the bank—scrub floors, trim trees, clip guests' toenails—Erin had decided to give her a chance. It was one of the best decisions she'd ever made.

"I don't know why we even bother to put up signs," Maria said. She was referring to the discreet one in every guest bathroom that read, *While we strive to meet your every need, our delicate plumbing thanks you in advance for not flushing your tampons.*

"One of these days somebody might actually read one," Erin said dryly.

Maria rolled her eyes. "Yeah, the same person on airplanes who listens to the flight attendant's spiel."

Maria dashed off, and a moment later Erin heard her pelting up the stairs.

When she was alone in the kitchen, the cheese plates assembled and Kayla off getting ready for her movie date,

Erin took a moment to rest, sinking with a weary sigh into a chair at the table. Looking around, she recalled when it had seemed an impossible undertaking to make this place inhabitable. What a wreck it'd been! Everything but the foundation and the structural beams had had to be torn out and replaced. The kitchen was nonexistent—in the days of the dude ranch, the cooking was done outdoors or in a lean-to out back. Now, as she took in the glass-fronted cabinets and gleaming copper pots over the butcher-block island, the walk-in pantry, and the walls on either side of the stove hung with vintage plates, what she and Skip had accomplished seemed nothing short of miraculous.

If we could salvage this old wreck, she thought, *couldn't we do the same with our marriage?*

The following morning, Erin and Maria were in the kitchen washing up after breakfast—cranberry-corn muffins, and scrambled eggs with chorizo and roasted tomatoes on the side—when a familiar voice called from the next room, "Yoo-hoo! Anyone home?" Erin groaned aloud. The event planner from hell had arrived.

Maria arched a brow, muttering, "Livingston, I presume?"

They were still recovering from the Arabian Nights—themed wedding Cricket had staged at the inn last spring, at which one of the elderly guests had fainted when the rubber cobra emerged from the snake charmer's basket, a cobra which, from a distance, had looked real.

Erin went off to deal with Cricket, leaving Maria to

finish washing up. She found her former classmate in the breakfast room chatting up the Morgensterns, who wore the pained smiles of passengers aboard a luxury liner being corralled by an overzealous cruise director.

"Why, hello there!" Cricket greeted Erin in that chipper voice that always made her feel as if she'd stumbled onto the set of a game show. "I was just telling these nice folks here that if they ever decide to renew their vows, I'm just a phone call away." At thirty-five, Cricket was even perkier than in high school, if that were possible. Blonder, too—every year she went a shade lighter. In her pink pantsuit and ruffle-necked cream silk blouse, she looked like a large strawberry sundae. Erin watched in dismay as Cricket dug into her Louis Vuitton shoulder bag and handed Mrs. Morgenstern her card. "I'm Cricket Shaughnessy, by the way," she introduced herself. "And you're—?"

"Don't you two have a plane to catch?" Erin swooped in to the rescue.

"Yes, of course. We must be going. So nice to meet you." Mr. Morgenstern flashed Erin a grateful look as he and his wife hurried off.

Earlier in the week, observing how sweet they were with each other, this gray-haired couple who'd been together longer than Erin had been on this earth, she'd asked what their secret was.

"Growing old disgracefully," Mrs. Morgenstern had replied with a chuckle, hooking an arm through her husband's.

"That, and a hearing aid," added her husband, casting his wife a fond look.

"When he's tired of listening to me, he turns it off," Mrs. Morgenstern explained.

Erin was stepping outside with Cricket, on their way to the garden where the ceremony would take place, when a midnight blue Lincoln Navigator caromed up the drive, lurching to a stop. She recognized it as the Nicholses, who were staying in the Blue Willow suite. Watching Mr. Nichols climb out, a burly man with hair everywhere but on his head, she noticed he was limping. Mrs. Nichols gestured frantically to Erin, who rushed over to assist them. "We'll need some ice," she ordered breathlessly. "And Tylenol."

"Do you want me to call a doctor?" Erin asked.

"A lawyer is more like it." The woman's lips looked like they'd been drawn on with a red Sharpie. Erin's mother used to say about such people that there'd been a drop of vinegar in the silver spoon in their mouth when they were born. Despite their obvious wealth, Mrs. Nichols was clearly unhappy. All she'd done since they'd arrived was complain—the room was too small, the mattress too soft, the food not to her liking. Now it appeared even the Lazy Q was at fault for the trail ride they'd gone on earlier this morning. "That horse isn't fit to be ridden. My God, it's a miracle nothing's broken!"

"I'll speak to Ted about it." Erin could only imagine what Mr. Nichols had done to cause the poor animal to throw him; all of Ted Kimble's horses were gentle as lambs. "In the meantime, let's get some ice on that leg," she told the grimacing Mr. Nichols as she helped him up the steps, casting Cricket an apologetic look on her way inside.

"Take your time. I know my way around!" Cricket called after her.

Together Erin and Mrs. Nichols half dragged and half pushed Mr. Nichols up the stairs to their suite, the couple barking orders at her the whole way. It was all Erin could do to remain civil. *If only Skip were here*, she thought. Words she repeated throughout each day like a mantra. Without him, every molehill was a mountain. She hadn't realized how much she'd depended on him until now. If he were here, he'd have Mrs. Nichols eating out of his hand, while all Erin could do was think of where else she'd like to put that ice pack.

As soon as the Nichols were settled, Mr. Nichols's hairy leg propped on a pile of cushions with an ice pack, Erin hurried back outside, where she found Cricket in the former paddock, which Skip had transformed into an oasis of flower beds and ornamental trees accessed by winding paths. Cricket had her tape measure out and was measuring the distance between the gazebo and the grassy clearing where the tent was to be pitched.

Erin followed the little trail of divots left in the turf by Cricket's high heels. The wedding before the one Erin and Skip had dubbed the Arabian Nightmare, Cricket had insisted the tent be pitched in a more shaded spot than the one Skip had recommended, despite his warning her that the runoff would collect there if it rained. She'd dismissed his concerns, as if perfect weather could be ordered up like champagne. When it *did* rain, a deluge that turned the tent floor into a pond, the wedding party had had to be moved indoors, where everyone had been crammed like so many soggy coats in a too-small closet.

Erin took in the raised flower beds covered in mulch that in spring would be lush with blooms, recalling when this whole section had looked less like a garden than an archaeological dig. With his own hands, Skip had hauled rocks up from the creek for the retaining walls; he'd built the gazebo, too, where countless couples had taken their vows, on a knoll overlooking the creek on one side and rolling pastures on the other.

Her mind drifted back to her own wedding day. The only ones in attendance were Skip's family and Jessie, who'd done her best to ignore the fact that Mike wasn't speaking to her. Skip's mother had argued that a big wedding would be in poor taste with Erin's parents' deaths so recent. But the real truth, Erin knew, was that Skip's parents were embarrassed by her; they thought she was beneath them. In their minds, she'd accidentally on purpose gotten pregnant, in order to trap Skip into marrying her.

At the time, Erin was so blinded by love she'd been able to shrug it off for the most part. But over the years, those hairline fractures had become rifts. It wasn't just her in-laws. She and Skip argued about how best to raise Kayla. On one occasion, after Erin had caught him feeding three-year-old Kayla cookies before supper, she'd slammed the cookie jar down so hard on the counter it broke.

Most of their fights were over money, though. Growing up, Skip had never known what it was like to go without, and while she wouldn't have described him as a spendthrift, he didn't stint and believed in buying only top of the line. Whereas Erin grew panicky at the thought of running short—if it wasn't on sale, she bought it used.

"The folding chairs will go here, of course." Cricket's voice broke into her thoughts, and Erin turned to see her gesturing toward the grassy area that skirted the gazebo. "And the string quartet"—Cricket's pink mouth pursed in concentration—"over there, I think." She pointed toward the mock cherry trees, their boughs twined into a bower. "I just hope the weather—" She broke off, her nose wrinkling. "What is that *smell?*"

Erin caught a whiff of something foul. Oh, God. The septic tank—it must have overflowed when Maria was working on the toilet. Of all the times for this to happen! "It's nothing. We're having a little problem with the plumbing," she explained, deftly steering Cricket to the other end of the lawn, where the smell was a little less noticeable, "but don't worry, we'll have it fixed in no time."

By the time Cricket left, Erin was ready to collapse. Her temples throbbed with the onset of a headache, and each step was like trudging knee deep through mud. Nothing a good night's rest wouldn't fix, but sleep was elusive these days. She'd drift off, only to wake with a jolt, her heart banging against her rib cage and her blindly groping hand meeting nothing but cool sheets on Skip's side of the bed.

"What you need is a night on the town," Maria pronounced later that afternoon.

Erin looked up from her desk, where she was busy sending out confirmation letters. "A long soak in a hot bath is more like it," she said.

"It's country western night at Murphy's," Maria went on, leaning into the doorframe. "Some of the bands are pretty good. My ex-boyfriend's in one, the Texas Rattlers. Seriously, you should go."

"Some other time." Erin folded the last of the letters and tucked it into an envelope.

"You don't want to end up like Callie." Callie Viner down at the post office, the industry standard for long-suffering exes. The way Callie carried on, you'd have thought her ex-husband had run off with Posy Drummond the week before. She still referred to Posy as "that tramp," never mind Posy and Ed had been married for ten years, longer than he and Callie had been.

"Is this your idea of tough love?" Erin asked.

"I'm just saying it wouldn't hurt to get out more."

"I get out."

"Yeah, to the store . . . and to pick up Kayla from school. That doesn't count. What good is it, moping around? It's not going to get Skip back, that's for sure."

"I don't know what would," Erin said.

"One thing that *won't* work is acting like you don't give a shit."

Maria's words stung. Was that how she came across? "Believe me," Erin said, "if people knew how I *really* felt, no one would come within a mile of this place."

Maria's expression softened. "I don't know how you do it. Honestly. I'd be a wreck. But if you don't lighten up a little and have some fun, you're going to crack. I can hold the fort down for one night."

No one would ever accuse Maria of being a stick in the mud. Recently she'd taken up line-dancing. And the summer before she'd gone rock climbing in Yosemite, making it all the way to the top of El Capitan. If a guy she was seeing didn't treat her right, she dumped him at once. She never had trouble finding a new boyfriend, no matter that she was a size sixteen and practically lived in her jeans, and that she spent more time fussing with toilets than with her hair. Maria was sexy in a way that had nothing to do with size or fashion or trips to the beauty parlor. What attracted people to her, men and women alike, was her can-do attitude and utter fearlessness. When you were with her, anything seemed possible.

"All right, you win." Erin gave in with a sigh. It wasn't as if she had anything better to do, and Kayla would probably be relieved to have her out of the house for a few hours.

That evening, on the way into town, she drove past the chapel on Cayuga, where dances were held when Erin was in high school—the only place where you could sin on Saturday night and pray for forgiveness on Sunday. As if they'd been so wild! Back then wild was getting drunk on Boone's Farm wine or letting a boy's hand graze your breast.

Funny, how everyone had thought it was Erin who would set the world on fire. She'd been voted Most Likely to Succeed, not because she'd been such a great student but because she'd been so hell bent on getting out of Willow Creek. She'd planned to support herself working in restaurants in New York until she had enough money and experience to attend the Culinary Institute of America, the Harvard of cooking schools. She'd seen herself rising through the ranks, working under top chefs, maybe even doing a stint in Europe, before one day achieving her dream of owning her own restaurant.

Instead it was Jessie who'd flown the coop while Erin was still in Willow Creek. Not that she didn't have her share of accomplishments. She was proud of the Darby Inn's reputation as one of the finest bed-and-breakfasts in the Southwest. She was proud, too, of the job she'd done in raising Kayla. But the plain fact was that it wasn't what she'd set out to do.

Suddenly Jessie's proposal didn't seem so outlandish. Why *couldn't* they trade places? What was stopping her? Her husband obviously didn't give a damn if she stayed or went, and her daughter was practically pushing her out the door. As for the inn, Maria was more than capable of managing it with or without Jessie's help.

Erin was picturing herself sipping a cappuccino at a sidewalk café in Greenwich Village when she arrived at

Murphy's to find the parking lot packed. She circled around for at least ten minutes before she finally found a space. Already this wasn't seeming like such a good idea.

Climbing out of the car, she could hear the throb of music from inside. It grew louder as she neared the entrance. Pushing her way in through the louvered doors, the sound was like smacking into a brick wall. As she checked her coat and handed over the four-dollar cover charge, Erin wondered again if this had been a mistake. She and Jessie used to love going to rock concerts and cranking up their stereos full blast. But in recent years she'd gone from preferring loud music to feeling assaulted by it.

As she weaved through the crowd, she spotted several people she knew. Jordy Kimble, Ted's son, from the Lazy Q. A tattooed young man named Chuck from the garage where she got her Toyota repaired. Jayce McDonough, one of the other mothers from school, sitting in a booth with a group of friends, beckoned to Erin, and she waved back, relieved that she wouldn't have to sit alone.

She was making her way toward them when she spied Skip and Mike, beers in hand, amid the crush at the bar. It had always amazed her how two brothers could look so much alike and yet be so different in every other way. Mike was the souped-up model, with a killer smile and eyes the blue of the artesian waters in the illuminated Coors sign over the bar, while Skip was the quieter, less flashy one. The two were chatting with a pair of women, a blonde and a redhead, who looked like they'd just come off the evening shift at Hooters. Mike had his arm around the redhead. The blonde was leaning in close to Skip, hanging on his every word. Erin watched him smile in response to something she'd said, and bend down to murmur in her ear, nearly brushing it with his lips. His hand rested lightly on her smooth-skinned back below the ties of her plunging halter top.

Erin felt as if the floor had dropped from underneath her. Dizzy, she grabbed hold of the person standing next to her, and a bleary-eyed, bearded face swung into view. "Hey, sweet thing, wanna dance?" the man slurred, pulling her in close enough to smell the beer on his breath.

Erin shook him off, growling, "Get lost."

She was turning to flee when she heard Skip call out, "Erin!"

She didn't stop. She pushed her way through the warm, beery sea of bodies, the beat of the music throbbing in the pit of her stomach. She paused only long enough to retrieve her coat before plunging into the frigid night air as she hurried off in search of her car.

When Skip caught up with her at last, she didn't even slow her stride. "Jesus, Erin, will you wait up?" He was panting, his cheeks stamped with cold and maybe something more: guilt that he'd been caught red-handed. "At least give me a chance to explain."

"I'm not interested in your explanation," she told him.

"It's not what you think. I don't even know her." Despite his long legs, he was having difficulty keeping up with her. "Mike offered to buy her and her friend drinks, and we ended up talking. That's all, I swear."

"Yeah? Well, from what I could see it looked like you two were pretty cozy."

He let out a low grunt of expelled breath, raising his arms heavenward in a gesture of supreme exasperation. "I don't know why I bother. You never listen."

Erin shot him a withering look. "Right. *I'm* the one who's being unreasonable. Just like always."

"I didn't say that. But why do you have to assume the worst?"

"Oh, let's see. Maybe it has something to do with the fact that you walked out on me. That I've spent the past few weeks trying to pick up the pieces while doing the work of two people. And the whole time I was thinking, at least, *at least*, he's hurting as much as I am. Instead, you and your brother have been out whooping it up in bars like a couple of frat boys.

"There's no need to be sarcastic."

"What do you want from me then?" She ground to a halt and whirled around to face him. In the harsh glare of the mercury vapor lamps overhead, the parking lot might have been another planet. She'd never felt so alienated from this man she'd once thought of as her soul mate. All that joined them now were the frosty plumes of their breath, doing a slow dance in midair. "Tell me, because I'd really like to know. I seem to be without a clue here."

When he didn't respond, she resumed walking. Finding her Toyota, she climbed in, slamming the door shut in his face. Skip rapped on the window, but she ignored him, turning the key so hard in the ignition the engine ground before finally sputtering to life. *Kiss my ass*, she swore silently as she peeled out of the lot with a squeal of tires.

She wasn't all that surprised when a minute later she glanced in the rearview mirror and saw Skip tailing her in his truck. Hurt and fury gave way to a kind of twisted triumph. If he cared enough to chase after her, there was still hope, wasn't there?

They arrived at the inn within moments of each other, Skip's truck grinding to a halt beside her car in a spray of gravel. Erin leapt from her Toyota, breathing as hard as if she'd run the whole way as she darted up the path to the family quarters, Skip at her heels.

"You think running away is going to help?" he shouted as he stomped in after her.

"*You're* one to talk!" she shouted back, slamming her purse down on the hall table so hard it scattered dried petals from a bowl of potpourri.

"If you'd just listen . . ."

"To more of your lame excuses? No thanks! God, I can't believe I was stupid enough to believe you when you told me you'd never cheated on me."

"I was telling the truth." Skip stepped around her, blocking her as she attempted to move past him. "But it's more convenient to think what you want, isn't it?" He seized her by the shoulders, gripping them hard. "That way you don't have to face that *you* brought this on yourself. You and your pigheaded—"

"So now you're giving me a taste of my own medicine? Is that what this is about?"

"Stop it, you two. *Just stop it!*"

Skip's arms dropped to his sides, and Erin spun around to see Kayla poised in the hallway, ashen and trembling. In her flannel pajamas, with her hair in pigtails, Erin was reminded of when her daughter was little, when she used to crawl into bed with them after she'd had a nightmare. The anger went out of her, and a tide of shame and mother love rushed in.

"Honey, I'm so sorry. I didn't realize—"

Kayla didn't let her finish. "What? That I might hear you screaming at each other? I *live* here, in case you've forgotten!" Gone was the mature young lady who'd pretended to be taking this in stride, in her place the child who felt caught in the middle.

"Pumpkin . . ." Skip took a step toward her, looking as stricken as Kayla.

She shrank away, shooting him a warning look that stopped him in his tracks. She cried, "You know what? I wish you'd *both* go away and leave me alone!"

Watching her retreat down the hall, Erin longed to go after her. Wasn't that what she'd always done when Kayla needed consoling? But for some reason she found she couldn't move. What held her rooted to the spot was the horrifying realization that for the first time ever, she might be doing her daughter more harm than good.

Chapter Five

It was the first thing that caught Erin's eye when she arrived at JFK: a large hand-lettered posterboard sign above the crush just beyond the security checkpoint that read WELCOME, ERIN!

Moments later she was enveloped in a fierce hug. Erin stepped back to take in the sight of her best friend in a black leather trench coat and designer jeans that bore little resemblance to the baggy Levis' she had on. Jessie, from her expertly styled hair to her black ankle boots, was pure *Cosmopolitan*, while Erin, in her wool socks and Dr. Scholl's, her shaggy hair pulled back with a butterfly clip, was straight out of *Mother Jones*.

"You look amazing," Erin told her.

"So do you," Jessie said, with all the sincerity of a dear friend lying through her teeth.

"You shouldn't have." Erin cast a wry glance at the sign.

"I wanted a brass band, but they were all booked."

"Darn. And here I am, all dressed up for nothing."

They laughed as they headed off toward baggage claim.

"The limo's waiting downstairs," Jessie informed her.

"Limo? I thought you said you were broke."

"I am. It's on Drew—a friend of his owed him a favor."

"Your neighbor Drew?" His name popped up frequently in Jessie's emails.

Jessie nodded. "You'll meet him tonight. I invited him for drinks." He'd moved in upstairs only in the past year, so he and Erin had yet to be introduced.

"I can't believe I'm actually here," Erin marveled aloud as they waited at the baggage carousel. Their conversations debating the pros and cons of this venture had seemed more like the what-if games they'd played as girls than something they were actually going to embark on. Now it was real. *This is going to be my home for the next six months,* she thought. "Tell me again why we're doing this," she said through gritted teeth as she hefted the heaviest of her suitcases off the carousel.

"Because," Jessie reminded her, "in a few years it might be too late."

"According to Kayla, I already have one foot in the nursing home."

"In that case, there's no time to lose. Anyway, what's the worst that could happen?"

"Do you want me to make a list?"

"Later. We have the whole weekend." Jessie wasn't leaving for Arizona until Monday. She grabbed hold of Erin's remaining suitcase and headed for the exit. "Tomorrow I'll show you around the neighborhood. You won't believe how much it's changed. There're tons of new shops and restaurants. I thought we'd do some shopping while we're at it. You're going to need some new clothes."

"How did you guess?" Erin replied, with an ironic lift of her brow. In addition to her country mouse wardrobe, she'd lost so much weight these past weeks a belt was the only thing holding up her jeans.

"There's this boutique in SoHo that sells the most amazing secondhand stuff. Designer labels mostly, and no one would ever guess it was used," Jessie prattled on, as they searched for their limo among the cars, taxis, and gypsy cabs idling triple deep along the curb. "I'm sure we'll find the perfect outfit for your interview."

"What interview?" Erin asked, lurching to a halt.

Jessie flashed her a grin. "I wanted to surprise you. There's an opening at the Cooking Channel for a production assistant. You're meeting with them first thing Monday morning."

"How did you manage that?"

"A friend of a friend works there."

Erin felt a giddy rush; then it occurred to her that she

didn't even know what, exactly, a production assistant did. "Are you sure I'm qualified?" Her résumé, if she'd had one, would consist of the part-time jobs she'd held in high school and her four years in the cafeteria at UC Davis.

"It's not that different from what you do at the inn— looking after guests, smoothing ruffled feathers, making sure the trains run on time," Jessie informed her.

"In that case, I'm *over*qualified."

Their limo wasn't the black stretch Erin had envisioned, but a somewhat decrepit town car driven by a Rastafarian man named Jerome. As Erin settled in the backseat next to Jessie, she found herself staring in fascination at what appeared to be a massive lime green growth sprouting from the back of Jerome's head—his dreadlocks bundled into a crocheted snood. Listening to him chatter in his indecipherable singsong, it was a moment or two before she realized he was speaking English. He seemed good-natured, though, and the little bit of island sunshine he brought to this cold February day was welcome.

On the drive into the city, her thoughts turned to Skip. "Have you lost your mind?" he'd roared, when she'd informed of her plans. "You call *me* irresponsible, and yet you want to traipse off to New York and leave *Jessie*, of all people, in charge!"

Erin had reminded him coolly that Jessie would have plenty of help from Maria, and, besides, it was only until July. She'd been afraid it would get ugly; they were equal partners after all, so he'd be within his rights to insist that any decision involving the inn be a joint one. But that would have meant his resuming full-time duty as innkeeper, and he wasn't prepared to do that. The only sticking point was Kayla: Skip wanted her to stay with him. In the end, it was Kayla who resolved it by saying they'd put her through enough as it was, she was *not* going to spend the next six months sleeping on her uncle's fold-out sofa and living off pizza and microwave popcorn.

Among Skip's objections, it didn't appear that he was sorry to see her go. Had he told her he was going to miss her, had he so much as shed a tear, she might have changed her mind about going. As it was, she'd become even more resolute. Damn him. If he thought he could tell her what to do, after the way he'd treated her, he had another thing coming.

Forty minutes later, Jerome was dropping them off in front of Jessie's building, an ivy-covered brownstone on a quiet block, across the street from an Episcopal church. As she and Jessie lugged the suitcases up three flights, Erin was glad she'd shipped the bulkier stuff, like her books and laptop, on which she was to keep a daily journal, one that Jessie would draw from for their weekly column in *Savvy*.

Home sweet home, she thought, collapsing on the sofa in Jessie's sun-drenched living room. A wave of anxiety washed over her. This wouldn't be like the times she'd visited; she'd be on her own, with only her wits to rely on.

"It's all yours." Jessie threw out her arms in an expansive gesture. "Cat hairs and all." As if on cue, Delilah leapt up onto the sofa, purring loudly as she settled on Erin's lap.

Erin stroked the cat. Already she missed Otis. "It's a little overwhelming," she confessed.

"Don't worry. Between Clive and Drew you'll be in good hands."

Erin remembered Jessie's landlord from her last visit. To call him eccentric was putting it mildly, though he'd seemed like a sweet guy. "I'm just wondering how I'm going to be able to afford this." While Jessie's rent wasn't sky-high by Manhattan standards, it would have paid for a small mansion in Willow Creek. Even if Erin was careful, the money from the government bond she'd cashed in wouldn't last long if she didn't find a job right away.

Jessie didn't seem too concerned, probably because she was used to Erin's fretting over money. She wandered off, calling from the kitchen, "Is white okay? It's all I have." Erin told her white wine would be fine, and Jessie returned with two glasses and a bottle of Chablis. "I'm the one who should be worrying," she said, pouring them each a glass before curling up in the Eames chair opposite the sofa. "I can barely cook for myself, and now I'm supposed to feed a cast of thousands? Whenever I think about it, I break into a cold sweat."

"I left instructions," Erin reassured her. On Post-its, stuck to every shelf and appliance. "Also, a file of my simplest recipes. And Maria's coming in early the first couple of weeks to help with breakfast. It's not brain surgery— you'll get the hang of it in no time."

Jessie looked less than convinced, but she put on a brave face and lifted her glass. "To country roads and city lights," she toasted.

Erin leaned forward, clinking her glass to Jessie's. "And to shaking the small-town dust off my shoes."

She tried not to think about what else she was leaving behind.

Jessie gave her a rundown on the other tenants. Besides Drew, there were the newlyweds next door who fought night and day. And Doug Fitch, on the floor below, a quiet middle-aged man who Jessie had assumed was married until she got a close look at his wife one day and saw that it was Doug in drag.

Then there was Mr. Ghupta, who owned the Pakistani deli on the corner, and who was currently under attack from the block association president, a loud-mouthed woman on the warpath over the cabs double-parked in front at all hours. And the elderly French sculptress next door, who'd declared war on Clive by dashing a pitcher of water over his beloved pug, MacArthur, after Mac had peed on her front steps. Clive had retaliated by blasting Wagner out the window, which he knew Madame loathed, every day for a week. They'd been happily making each other's lives miserable ever since.

Jessie was launching into another tale when she was interrupted by a knock at the door. She got up to answer it, and a man about their age, dressed incongruously in a tuxedo and Converse sneakers, strolled in to plant a kiss on her cheek. "Hi, honey, I'm home."

"You're just in time. I was warning Erin about the other tenants."

He winked at Erin as she rose to greet him. "Don't listen to a word she says. I'm really quite normal when I'm on my meds."

"Drew, Erin. Erin, Drew," Jessie introduced them.

He was several inches shorter than Skip (Erin had a bad habit of measuring every man against her husband), and stocky where Skip was lean, with rumpled brown hair that curled over the starched collar of his tuxedo shirt and eyes the color of strong ale. Eyes that held her gaze as he clasped Erin's hand. "It's great to finally meet you. The way Jessie talks about you, I wasn't sure whether to shake your hand or genuflect."

Erin laughed, feeling instantly at ease. "Just don't ask me to walk on water."

Jessie fetched a glass for Drew and poured him some wine. "How was the wedding?" she asked.

He dropped into the easy chair by the fireplace with an expelled breath, tugging off his bow tie.

"The usual highlights," he said. "Old farts making fools of themselves on the dance floor, the best man giving a drunken toast, the bridesmaids knocking each other down to catch the bouquet." He looked so rakish sprawled in the chair with his wineglass, like the leading men in the old movies Erin had watched as a child all those nights her parents had been working late—Cary Grant and Fred Astaire, William Powell in *The Thin Man*, who were always in tuxedos and who tossed off witty lines while downing martinis—that she found her-self smiling.

"Drew's a photographer," Jessie explained.

"Mostly weddings and bar mitzvahs," he said.

"He's being modest." Jessie said. "You should see his stuff—it's amazing. In fact, his new show's opening a week from tonight."

"You doing anything next Friday?" he asked Erin.

"I'll have to check my calendar," she said facetiously.

"She'd love to go," Jessie accepted for her.

"It's only a few blocks from here," he told her. "We could walk over together."

"I'd like that," Erin said, blushing a little. She won-dered if it qualified as a date.

Don't flatter yourself, said a voice in her head, the voice that noted every flaw when she looked in the mirror. He was just being neighborly. Anyway, she was married, if in name only.

A short while later, when Drew suggested they go out on the stoop to watch the sunset, Erin wondered if he *was* a little crazy—it had to be thirty degrees outside! Nonetheless, she bundled up in her coat and gloves and followed him and Jessie downstairs. Even with the blan-ket Jessie spread over the steps, it was freezing. But as Erin sat there sipping her wine and watching the fiery ball of the sun, framed between two buildings, descend slowly, like a grand dame taking a bow, into the Hudson River, she scarcely noticed the cold, she was so entranced.

The shadows of the buildings folded in around them.

She took in the unfamiliar sights and sounds: the blare of traffic, the steady stream of pedestrians hurrying past, the lighted windows in the apartment complex across the way, like living shadow boxes—in one, a woman was setting the table, in another a bare-chested man was working out with weights. People she might never meet but who seemed a part of this strange new adventure, a part of its warp and weave, not unlike the strangers who moved in and out of her life at the inn. All at once Erin didn't feel so homesick.

The following morning she was given a tour of the neighborhood. A lot *had* changed since she'd last visited. Chelsea was bustling, with new shops and eateries everywhere she looked. The Chelsea Market, a vast indoor mall devoted entirely to food had opened up on Ninth Avenue, in the old Nabisco building. Taking in its dazzling array of baked goods and imported foods, as well as cheeses, meats, and fruits and vegetables so fresh they might have been harvested that day, Erin thought she must have died and gone to heaven.

They ate lunch at a Venetian restaurant on Eighth Avenue, Le Zie, where they gorged on grilled pizza and steaming plates of pasta, with the best zabaglione Erin had ever tasted for dessert. Afterward, it was on to Shakra, the trendy salon where Jessie got her hair styled. Erin, glancing about at the plush sofa and antique gilt mirrors, the large canvases of nudes on the exposed brick walls, murmured, "It looks more like a bordello."

Jessie patted her arm. "Relax, and leave the driving to us."

An hour later, emerging from the expert hands of a swan-necked stylist named Giorgio, Erin hardly recognized herself. When she swung her head from side to side, her hair swung with it in thick glossy sheaves instead of sticking together in frizzled clumps.

"I feel like a whole new person," she said with awe, staring at her reflection in the mirror.

"You *look* like a whole new person." Jessie beamed like a big sister.

The next stop was Sephora on lower Fifth, where Erin tried on makeup while Jessie supervised. Then it was on to Redux, in SoHo, the high-end used-clothing store that Jessie had raved about, at which they found a gently worn Donna Karan suit that fit Erin like a glove. If she was nervous about her interview on Monday, at least she'd look the part.

They rode the subway up to Bloomingdale's, and Jessie helped her pick out separates she could mix and match that wouldn't break her budget. By late afternoon they were both exhausted and numb from tramping around in the cold. When Jessie treated Erin to tea at the Pierre, easily the fanciest hotel she'd ever been inside of, where she found herself speaking in whispers as if in church, it seemed the perfect end to an almost perfect day: The only fly in the ointment was knowing that Jessie would be leaving the day after tomorrow.

On Sunday, Jessie slipped away for a few hours to be

with Jonathon. When she arrived home, her eyes were red from crying. Erin knew that Jessie felt torn about leaving him. Later, as they were getting ready for bed, Jessie confided that she'd secretly hoped this would be the nudge he'd needed to pop the question. That hadn't happened, though he *had* reassured her that he loved her as much as ever and promised to visit as soon as he could get away.

Monday morning arrived all too soon, and before long it was time for Erin and Jessie to say good-bye. Erin helped Jessie carry her luggage downstairs to where Jerome's town car was idling at the curb.

They clung to each other. There were tears in Jessie's eyes when she drew back.

"I wish we'd had more time," Jessie said.

"Me too." Erin swallowed hard.

"Are you going to be all right?"

"I'll be fine," Erin said, with more bravado than she felt.

Jessie gave a shaky laugh. "I don't know about you, but I'm scared shitless."

"You'll be fine, too," Erin assured her.

"Promise?"

"You'll have Maria and Kayla. And Skip." She felt a sharp pang at the thought of him. "And if you need me, I'm only a phone call away."

"Don't worry about Kayla. I'll take good care of her." A corner of Jessie's mouth hooked up in a crooked smile. "And I'll do my best not to drive away any guests."

"If the pilot light goes out on the stove, don't forget to turn off the gas before you relight it."

"Delilah's picky about what she eats," Jessie reminded her. "I left extra cans of her food in the cupboard."

"Oh, and—"

Erin was interrupted by Jerome tapping on the car horn.

"Good luck with the interview!" Jessie called out the window, as they were pulling away from the curb.

"Good luck with your mom!" Erin called back, shivering in the coat she'd thrown on over her nightgown.

Two hours later Erin was walking into the building that housed the Cooking Channel, a glass-and-steel complex situated on a pier along the West Side Highway between Chelsea and Hell's Kitchen. She informed the security guard at the entrance that she had an appointment with Ms. Powers, and after consulting his clipboard he buzzed her in. Latrice Powers's assistant, a pretty young woman wearing designer jeans and a trendy plum blazer, appeared a few minutes later to escort Erin through the cavernous, concrete-floored space that housed the studios. They passed a brightly lit, glass-enclosed set inside which a petite brunette in chef's whites was tossing ingredients into a pan, her lips moving soundlessly as cameras zoomed in for tight shots. Just beyond it was an edit bay, in which consoles and monitors glowed beyond sliding glass doors, manned by a small army of technicians.

The assistant led the way up a steel catwalk to the floor above, which wrapped around the soaring central

space, and at last Erin was ushered into the executive producer's office. Walking in through the door, she was so
dazzled by the panoramic view afforded by floor-to-ceiling
windows that looked out over the Hudson River, glinting
like polished steel below, that it was a moment before she
noticed the attractive, light-skinned black woman stepping out from behind the desk.

"Latrice Powers." She shook Erin's hand with a firm,
executive's grip.

Latrice was dressed in a chic pearl gray pantsuit that
left Erin feeling almost dowdy in her Donna Karan of two
seasons ago. But she quickly recovered her wits and
smiled, introducing herself.

Latrice settled back in behind her desk, a slab of glass
the size of an ice floe set on brushed nickel legs, motion-
ing for Erin to have a seat. She sank into the chair opposite the desk, hoping the run in her panty hose that she'd
gotten on the way over wasn't too noticeable.

"So you're interested in working for us," Latrice
prompted when Erin didn't immediately launch into the
spiel she'd rehearsed on the way over. "What kind of experience have you had?" She must have done this a thousand times, and it showed. She sounded as if she were
merely going through the motions.

Erin felt suddenly tongue-tied, which was unusual for
her. Then she found her voice. "I'm an innkeeper. You're
looking at the chief cook and bottle washer, not to mention concierge, bellhop, and sometimes chambermaid, of
the Darby Inn. I can do everything from type letters to

sew on buttons. In a pinch, I can even change an oil filter and unclog a drain."

Latrice chuckled. Erin had her attention now. "I see. And what brings you to New York?"

She explained the rather unusual circumstances that had brought her here. "I can't promise I'll still be around when the six months are up," she added, "but I *can* promise you'll get your money's worth until then."

Latrice seemed curious about the swap, and wanted to know what Erin hoped to get out of it.

"Answers, I guess." Erin crossed her legs, the run in her panty hose forgotten. She told Latrice about her long-ago dream to live in New York, and the tragedy that had changed the course of her life. "I've always wondered where that road would've taken me," she said. "This is my chance to find out."

Latrice smiled. "When I was growing up, I wanted to be an astronaut. I begged my parents to send me to space camp. That's what cured me. I couldn't see myself living off those little packets of dried food. Is it any wonder I ended up here?"

She informed Erin that she was still interviewing other candidates, but that she'd make a final decision by the end of the week. It wasn't an offer, but for some reason Erin felt optimistic as she strolled back to Jessie's apartment. Her mother used to say that if you cast your bread on the waters it would come back sandwiches, and Erin hoped it was true in this case.

She stayed busy the rest of the week, wanting to have

something lined up in case she didn't get the job at the Cooking Channel. Every morning she pored over want ads, circling restaurant jobs, most of which, it turned out, were for experienced waitresses and line chefs. It seemed there was about as much demand for country innkeepers in Manhattan as there was for Elvis impersonators in Willow Creek. She traveled from one fruitless interview to the next on the subway, where at peak hours it was standing room only, sweating profusely in her winter coat as she struggled to keep her balance with each lurch of the car that threatened to pitch her into someone's lap. Riding home at the end of one particularly grueling day, she felt something she thought was a briefcase poking her in the rear, only to turn around and find a leering man pressed up against her.

Each day, she returned home hoping to find a message about a job on the answering machine. But if there was one it was usually from Jessie, sounding as if she were on the verge of a nervous breakdown—her first day she'd nearly burned down the inn when she'd neglected to take the pancakes off the griddle before dousing them in Grand Marnier. No word from Skip. Would it have killed him to pick up the phone? Did she mean that little to him?

By Friday, when she still hadn't heard back from Latrice, despite several messages Erin had left on her voicemail, her proverbial sandwiches had begun to look more like day-old bread. She told herself there would be other opportunities, but she couldn't help feeling disappointed. The only thing she had to look forward to now was Drew's show. In anticipation, she'd bought a colorful silk scarf from a street vendor to spruce up her trusty black cocktail dress and splurged on a pair of black stilettos.

When Drew arrived to pick her up, he whistled appreciatively. "Wow. You look amazing."

"I wasn't sure what the dress code was, so I went for the Holly Golightly look," she said with a laugh, warming at the obvious appreciation in his eyes as they traveled over her.

"Well, Miss Golightly, it suits you." Drew wore faded jeans and a charcoal sport coat over a black T-shirt. When she glanced down at his trusty Converse sneakers, he explained with a smile that artists had to look as if they were above any petty, bourgeois concerns about actually selling their art.

As they walked the three long blocks to West Chelsea, the dark, near-deserted streets lined with warehouses made her glad she hadn't decided to go on her own. It was a pleasant surprise when they emerged from the shadow of an elevated track onto a brightly lit street where the warehouses had been converted into residential lofts and art galleries.

The gallery hosting Drew's show was in a former factory on the corner of Twelfth and Twenty-sixth. They rode the elevator up to the second floor, where they stepped out into a spare, cavernous space still smelling of fresh paint. The owner, a pale, skeletal woman in a black turtleneck and long black skirt, who looked in need of a blood transfusion, wafted over to kiss Drew on both cheeks before extending a bony hand to Erin. Leaving them to confer, Erin wandered off to take in the exhibit before the others arrived.

Drew's photographs were stunning in their simplicity. Erin had taken a photography class in college and though she hadn't pursued it, she knew enough to recognize talent when she saw it. She lingered before a photo of an empty, bare-walled room, its lines appearing to float in space. Beside it was a striking image of a cyclone fence forming a starkly geometric pattern against a cloudless sky. Other photos showed a more human touch, like the one of a homeless woman in line at a soup kitchen, looking more dignified than pitiful, and that of a Hasidic man striding jauntily down the street, his homburg set at a rakish angle on his head.

"What do you think?" Drew asked, slipping up alongside her.

"They're beautiful." Erin gazed raptly at a blown-up photo of a red scarf, caught by a breeze, swirling up into the sky like a cardinal in flight. "I had no idea you were this talented."

"Unfortunately, talent doesn't always pay the rent," he replied ruefully. "Sometimes I think I'd have been better off if I'd gone to law school like my parents wanted me to."

Abruptly, she turned to face him. "But it wouldn't have been what *you* wanted." Guilty, thoughts of Skip crept in. Shouldn't she have offered him the same encouragement?

"What do you want out of life, Miss Golightly?" Drew asked, his gaze locking with hers and touching off an answering ripple in the pit of her stomach.

"Right now, I'd settle for a job."

"In that case, you're in the right place." People had begun to drift in, and Drew pointed out a heavyset older man accompanied by a much younger woman. "That's Mort Zeigler. He owns half the real estate in New York." He identified an older, blond woman as the CEO of her own cosmetics company. Drew was taking Erin over to introduce her when he was waylaid by the gallery owner, who dragged him off to meet some friends of hers.

Before long the gallery was packed. At the buffet table, Erin sipped champagne and nibbled on canapés, eavesdropping shamelessly on the conversations around her. Listening to people drop the names of artists and photographers she'd never heard of, and discuss the merits of the Fellini revival at the Film Forum and the de Kooning exhibit at the Guggenheim, she felt outclassed, just another of the out-of-towners she'd been horrified to learn were referred to in some circles as the "flyover people." The closest thing to an art scene back home were the arts-and-crafts exhibits at the annual Heritage Days festival, where last year Homer Pucket's photo of his baby grandson was voted best in show.

An attractive, sharply dressed man wandered over to her. "You look a little lost," he said with a smile.

"This isn't really my scene," she confessed. "Where I come from, Friday night you have your pick between bingo and bowling."

He laughed, his brown eyes twinkling. "I'll let you in on a little secret: Most of us aren't from around here. If we have our noses in the air, it's really just to keep from being exposed as crass outsiders." He put out his hand. "I'm Eric Cohler, by the way. And you're . . ."

"Erin Delahanty."

"Can I get you a refill?" His gaze dropped to the empty glass in her hand.

"Sure, why not." She handed it to him.

No sooner had Eric headed off in the direction of the bar than Drew sidled up to her. "Do you know who that is?" he whispered. "Eric Cohler is one of the hottest interior designers around. He knows everyone who's anyone. If you play your cards right . . ."

Before he could finish, Drew was buttonholed by Mort Zeigler. Mort was interested in buying one of the prints, but he thought it might be too small for the spot in his living room where he wanted to hang it. Could Drew make him a larger print of the same image? Erin ducked away, leaving Drew to conduct what she hoped would result in a sale. Spotting Eric near the bar, drinks in hand, she began making her way toward him.

She was halfway across the room when the floor went skidding out from under her, and she flew backward to land with a *woof* of escaped breath on her rear.

The people immersed in conversation around her abruptly fell silent. Erin looked up to find them staring down at her. Hot shame spread through her along with the waves of pain radiating from her tailbone. *Oh, God, they probably think I'm drunk.*

Drew helped her to her feet, and Eric rushed over to

see if she was okay. But the damage was done. All Erin wanted was to escape. The gallery owner apologized profusely, explaining that the floor had been polyurethaned only last week, but Erin knew it was her new shoes that were to blame. She should have known better. In fact, she shouldn't have come at all. *Holly Golightly, my ass*, she thought. *More like Calamity Jane*.

"It could've happened to anyone," Drew consoled her as they walked home. "Besides, most people were so busy worrying about the impression *they* were making, I'll bet they didn't even notice."

"They weren't the ones flat on their asses," she moaned.

"By tomorrow, it'll be ancient history."

Erin wasn't sure which was worse, to be important enough to have every misadventure make the gossip columns, or to be a complete nonentity. She paused, turning to him. "Thanks. Though I wouldn't have blamed you if you'd pretended not to know me."

"Why would I do that? You were the prettiest girl there," he said gallantly.

"Pretty is as pretty does, as my mother always said. And so far all I've done is make a fool of myself."

"You could always get hired to entertain at parties," he teased.

"Very funny."

"Well, beating yourself up isn't going to help. You need to cut yourself some slack. In fact, I prescribe a weekend in the town. I'll bet you haven't done any sightseeing yet."

"Sure I have," she told him. "I've seen every subway station from here to Battery Park City."

"What are you doing tomorrow?"

"More of the same."

"Never mind that. I'm taking you on the Staten Island ferry. Best view of Manhattan, and it doesn't cost a cent."

"I really shouldn't."

He nudged her in the ribs with his elbow. "Come on, it'll do you good."

"All right," she relented. "But only if you let me buy you lunch. It's the least I can do." Drew had gone out of his way to be nice to her since she'd arrived. When he went out for coffee in the morning, he always brought her back a cup. He'd showed her on a map how to navigate the subway system, and had provided her with menus for all the best takeout.

He grinned. "It's a deal."

When they arrived back at the brownstone Erin was acutely aware of his hand lightly pressing against the small of her back as they mounted the steps. He lingered a moment at her door to say good night, but she was careful to give him only a chaste kiss on the cheek.

She was getting ready for bed when the phone rang. She dashed to answer it before the machine could pick up, certain it was Jessie. Who else would be calling at this hour?

"'Lo," she mumbled around a mouthful of toothpaste.

"Erin?"

She was so startled by the sound of Skip's voice, she

accidentally swallowed the toothpaste, and when she tried
to answer the words emerged as a strangled gulp. She
gave her mouth a backhanded swipe, sputtering, "S-Skip!
Is everything okay?" A host of dire emergencies flitted
through her head like images in a furiously spinning slide
carousel—Kayla sick or injured, the inn burned down, a
guest in the hospital with food poisoning. Why else would
he have called? It couldn't be because he missed her.

"Everything's fine." He paused, then added, "I just
called to see how you were doing."

"I'm good," she answered cautiously, relieved and at
the same time a little hurt by his nonchalant tone—as if
she were a casual acquaintance he was inquiring after.
She lowered herself onto the bed. "I still haven't found a
job, but other than that things are okay." She spoke
lightly, not wanting him to know how much she missed
him, how the mere sound of his voice was enough to set
her heart banging in her rib cage like a pesky salesman
knocking at the door. "What's up with you?"

"Nothing much." She could tell from his tone that he
was still angry with her. Even so, he was making an effort.
"Look, if you're low on cash, I have a little set aside . . ."

"I'm fine." She spoke more brusquely than she'd intended.

"Sure, whatever." She could tell he was offended.

Silence hung between them, as palpable as the light
snow that had begun to drift down outside. Erin found
herself remembering the old days, their meaningless little
exchanges as they were getting ready for bed—*Honey,*

would you pick up the dry cleaning when you're in town to-morrow? or *The car's making that funny noise again. We should have it checked out*—that she hadn't realized until too late had meant the world. Swallowing against the lump in her throat, she ventured, "How are you and Jessie getting along?"

It was the exact wrong thing for her to have said. "Jessie," he said with disgust. "Christ, it's not bad enough she messed up my brother's life, she had to screw with ours."

Erin felt a hot rush of blood to her head. "You think this is *Jessie's* fault?" Her voice rose a notch. "I wouldn't be here if you hadn't walked out on me."

"Goddamn it, Erin," he swore. "Don't make me out to be the bad guy. You *know* why I left."

"Yeah, I know. To punish me. But if you called to hear me beg your forgiveness, think again, buster. You made your bed, and you can damn well lie in it!"

"If you call the foldout sofa in my brother's den a bed."

"So now I'm supposed to feel sorry for you?"

"I'm not asking for sympathy."

"What the hell *do* you want then?"

"I was hoping—" He broke off. "Never mind."

"You were hoping *what*?"

"That I could get through to you. That there was still something left of the woman I married."

Erin sucked in a breath, doubling over as if she'd been socked in the stomach. "That was low," she said through gritted teeth.

"It's true: I don't know you anymore."

"Then we're even, because I never knew you were such a son of a bitch!" A silence louder than any words filled the gulf that with this latest salvo had widened into a canyon. In a voice quivering with emotion, she said, "Look, I have to go. It's late."

"Erin—"

She lowered the receiver into its cradle, cutting him off.

It wasn't how she'd wanted the conversation to go. What she'd wanted to say was how much she loved and missed him, that she longed for his touch, his head on the pillow next to hers. Falling flat on her ass tonight paled in comparison to how wretched she felt now.

When she finally crawled under the covers, she was aching all over. The room that had once seemed so cozy and cheerful, with its Florentine purple walls hung with Italian movie posters, its beaded lamps and embroidered pillows, now only served to remind her of how far from home she was. Lying on her back, staring up at the ceiling and listening to the creak of Drew's footsteps overhead, she thought of the line from the Hank Williams song, which summed up how she was feeling right now: so lonesome she could cry.

Chapter Six

Jessie rolled over in bed, batting blindly at the thing beeping in her ear. The alarm clock. Right. She hauled herself upright, peering into the darkness with one eye squinched shut. The shadowy terrain slowly materialized, and now she could make out the shapes of a dresser and chair, a mirrored armoire in which her ghostly reflection shimmered. The pale light seeping in through the shutters and distant crowing of a rooster told her it was morning, but her sleep-fogged mind refused to accept it as fact.

Yawning, she crawled out from under the covers. Forget any quaint notions she might've had about innkeeping. There was no such thing as sleeping in late; no reading the paper as you sipped your morning coffee. It was like being in the military: up at the crack of dawn every morning. In her case, to prepare a breakfast she could only hope would be edible, for anywhere from six to sixteen people. The rest of the day she spent racing from pillar to post until she collapsed in bed at an hour, in her former life, when she'd have been enjoying a drink with friends or sitting down to a late meal in a restaurant.

But once she was showered and dressed, Jessie could appreciate the lovely stillness that was like balm after years of being rudely awakened by the groaning of garbage trucks and shrilling of car alarms. With Kayla still snoozing down the hall, there was only the creak of her own footsteps and the sound of Otis padding at her heels as she made her way down the hallway and out the front door. On the porch, she lingered a moment, filling her lungs with the crisp, dry air as she watched the dog race out into the yard that separated the family quarters from the main building. At this hour, the land was awash in pale mauve light, clusters of white blossoms on the greasewood that grew wild everywhere standing out like snowflakes against the darker greenery. She was reminded anew of the skillful job Skip had done in landscaping it, leaving much of its wild state intact and planting hardy perennials, like flame-blossomed Mexican bird of paradise and purple ruellia, flowering cacti and succulents, that added splashes of color to the more muted natural terrain.

Skip. She felt a sense of loss, as always, at the thought of him. Once they'd been like brother and sister, but those days were long past. When she'd arrived, he'd been up on a ladder trimming some boughs off the olive tree out front. She'd waved to him, and he'd waved back, but he'd taken his time climbing down to greet her. It wasn't until she was inside, talking to Maria, that she heard the clomp of boots on the porch. He appeared in the doorway, eyeing her as if she were a door-to-door salesperson peddling something he had no interest in.

"Hey, Jessie," he said, none too warmly.

"Skip. Nice to see you. It's been a while." She put out her hand, and after a moment of hesitation he shook it. "How have you been?"

"I've been better." She noted the deep lines bracketing his unsmiling mouth.

"Well, you look great. As fit as ever."

He shrugged, making it clear she wasn't going to win him over with compliments. "Working two jobs keeps you in shape."

"I just made a pot of coffee," Maria told him. "Skip, why don't you come in and sit down? I'm sure you two have a lot of catching up to do." Her tone was purposefully upbeat, as if by sheer force of will she could singlehandedly get this lead balloon off the ground.

He turned to Maria, his expression softening, reminding Jessie of the way he used to look at her before he'd soured toward her. "Thanks, but I should finish up," he said. "I have to get back to work."

Jessie remembered that he was working for his brother. He must have come here on his lunch break. "Say hello to Mike for me," she called after him, as he sauntered off. After all these years, wasn't it time to put the past behind them?

He turned to give her a look that would have curdled milk. "I'll do that," he said.

Since then, she'd only caught glimpses of Skip in the early morning when he was outside tending the garden or cutting wood. Evenings when he came by to pick up Kayla, he honked his horn to let her know he was there rather than come to the door. Jessie knew he resented her, not just for what she'd done to his brother but because, as he saw it, she was the reason his wife was in New York. He probably assumed Jessie sided with Erin as well. But Jessie saw his side, too. Much as she loved Erin, she wasn't the easiest person to live with. Jessie knew it had to have been hard for Skip being married to a woman who saw foreclosure in every overdue bill and unexpected expense. Though she thought he'd have had a better understanding if he'd known Erin's parents, as she had. In Erin's house, every knock on the door was potentially bad news: someone from a collection agency, APS threatening to shut off their electricity, and once, scarily, a sheriff's deputy with a warrant for her father's arrest for some outstanding parking tickets.

Now, as Jessie walked along the path to the inn, listening to birds calling to one another—the distinctive *tiwee tiwee tiwee* of a towhee rose in the air, shimmering, like notes trilled on a flute—she realized that her coming back to Willow Creek wasn't so much a fresh start as the equivalent of cleaning out an attic jumbled with old, discarded stuff. She had a lot to wade through, and she'd have to get her hands dirty from time to time.

Her thoughts turned to Jonathon. She'd told him she was doing this mainly for professional reasons, but that she also thought the time apart would be good for them, give them both a chance to reassess their relationship. Calm, measured words when what she'd really wanted to say was, *Wise up, buddy, before it's too late*.

Apparently it was the wake-up call he'd needed. He was more attentive than ever, phoning her often, sometimes just to tell her that he missed her. For Valentine's Day he'd sent her an antique gold-filigreed locket that she'd admired in a shop window in Soho. And plans were in the works for him to fly out for a visit in a few weeks. She couldn't wait. Already she missed him terribly.

The time apart had given her some perspective as well. Now, when they spoke, she didn't feel so irritated when he went on and on about his kids. She could even sympathize to some extent. With the life he'd known in shambles, it was only natural that he'd cling to his children. He needed them as much as they needed him.

All quiet on the Western front, she thought, as she let herself in through the back door, Otis trailing after her. She flicked on the overhead light. The kitchen, with its gleaming copper pots hung in a row, its appliances awaiting the touch of a button, made her think of the one and only time she'd gone horseback riding, when she was twelve. Her mother had insisted she take lessons, no doubt envisioning the blue ribbons that would one day line her

walls. But from the look of disdain the horse had given
Jessie as she'd attempted to mount it, she'd known instantly
who was in charge. She felt that way now, as if the kitchen
were silently mocking her.

It's breakfast, not brain surgery, she told herself, as she
did every morning. With enough practice anyone could
learn how to cook. Though she didn't like to think about
what she'd have done without Maria's help those first
couple of weeks.

She scooped coffee beans into the grinder, then measured the ground coffee into the Bunn. When it was done
brewing, she poured some into a mug and sat down at the
table to page through the loose-leaf binder of Erin's
favorite recipes, each with notations in Erin's scrawled
hand.

To Jessie, it might as well have been the Dead Sea
Scrolls. The easiest ones, like French toast, she'd pretty
much mastered. Anything more complicated, she was like
a blind person behind the wheel of a car. Her near disaster with the Grand Marnier pancakes had taught her to
steer clear of pyrotechnics. Things made with yeast were
tricky, too—the cinnamon rolls she'd attempted could've
doubled as hockey pucks. Simple but hearty, that was the
key. Like the baked omelet with cottage cheese and
canned chilis that was on the menu for today.

She was cracking eggs into a bowl when she heard the
back door open. Thinking it was Kayla, she turned to
greet her, a smile forming. The smile froze when she saw
that it was Skip.

Jessie was so startled the egg she was holding slipped from her hand to land with a splat on the floor. She looked down with dismay at the slimy Rorschach blot at her feet, dotted with bits of broken shell.

"I guess I should've knocked," Skip said, eyeing the mess.

"You don't have to knock." She grabbed a wad of paper towels and bent to wipe the floor clean.

He gave in to a small, wry smile, glancing about the kitchen as if seeing it for the first time. "These days, I never know if I'm in the right place."

He was wearing his Sunday best: pressed khakis, a navy sport coat and tie. She remembered that he was taking Kayla to church today. "Kayla's not up yet," she informed him. "Do you want me to let her know you're here?"

"No, let her sleep. I have a few things to take care of first."

"Help yourself." She gestured toward the Bunn.

She was sure it would be his cue to leave, but he nodded and took a mug down from the cupboard, filling it with coffee. She thought he looked a bit haggard, as if he hadn't been getting enough sleep, though it only enhanced the spare angularity of his face. The tiny lines radiating from the corners of his eyes and the silver in his hair gave him a seasoned look that made him more intriguing than handsome—*Dawson's Creek* meets *Dirty Harry*. Jessie didn't doubt that the women in the congregation would be focusing more on Skip than on their prayers.

"How's it going?" He eyed the bowls and cooking utensils strewn over the counter, with something close to amusement.

"Let's just say I have yet to send anyone home with food poisoning. Though I came pretty close to burning the place down," she told him.

"So I heard." He blew on his coffee and took a tentative sip.

"Erin warned me, but I didn't realize it was such hard work."

"I don't see anyone holding a gun to your head."

Jessie sighed, folding her arms over her chest. "Look, Skip. I know this is hard for you. But I'm not the enemy."

He eyed her warily for a moment, then some of the tension went out of his shoulders, and he nodded wearily. "I know. It's just easier when you have someone to blame."

Someone besides Erin, that is. And possibly himself.

She went back to cracking eggs into the bowl. "How are your folks?" she asked, eager to change the subject.

"Both fine. Though Mom's convinced Dad's going to drop dead of a heart attack any minute. He says he can't remember the last time she cooked him chicken with the skin on. He sneaks off to KFC whenever he can. I'm pretty sure she knows, but she turns a blind eye."

"At least it's not another woman."

After a moment of awkward silence he cleared his throat, asking, "How's Erin?" She turned to find him leaning up against the counter with studied insouciance, his mug cradled in his hands.

"If it's any comfort, she's as miserable as you are."

"It hasn't been easy for either of us, I guess," he acknowledged grudgingly.

"You should visit her," Jessie urged, hoping she hadn't overstepped her bounds. It wasn't as if she'd discussed it with Erin.

He snorted. "She hasn't exactly sent me an engraved invitation."

"In that case, why don't you surprise her?"

He gave her a look that instantly put that idea to rest. "Thanks for the coffee." He dumped the rest into the sink, rinsing out the mug and placing it in the drainer. "When you see Kayla, tell her I'm out back," he said as he was letting himself out the door. "I want to make sure those ropes are secure."

"Ropes?"

"On the tent."

Jessie drew a momentary blank before realizing he'd meant the tent for the Travers wedding. She'd forgotten it was this afternoon—the caterer would be here in just a few hours. Just what she needed, a wedding to remind her that she wasn't likely to make a similar trip down the aisle anytime soon.

While the omelet was in the oven, Jessie set up the buffet on the long oak table in the breakfast room—a glass canister of Erin's homemade granola and bowls of sliced strawberries and oranges, yogurt from a local dairy, a selection of jams and preserves, and thermoses of coffee and hot water for tea. She was making another pot of coffee when Kayla wandered in through the back door dressed for church.

"What do you think?" She twirled in front of Jessie, showing off the wraparound skirt she'd bought yesterday when she was at the mall with Devon.

"You look gorgeous," Jessie told her.

"It doesn't make me look fat?"

"Not a bit."

Kayla eyed her skeptically. "You're just saying that."

"Then why ask my opinion?"

"*Now* you sound just like my mom." Kayla reached into the refrigerator to pour herself some juice.

The novelty of having her godmother around had worn off to some extent, and they'd settled into a routine. Weekday mornings, Kayla hung out with Jessie in the kitchen until the school bus arrived. In the evenings, when she was done with her homework, they played cards or watched TV. Sometimes they'd lie on the bed in Erin's room, gossiping and giggling the way Jessie and Erin had as teenagers. For Jessie, the best thing about trading places with Erin was the chance to spend unlimited time with her daughter.

Her thoughts turned to her own mother. Jessie had put off seeing her, using the valid excuse that she was too swamped at the inn. Naturally it wouldn't occur to Beverly to drive over to see *her*. Sooner or later, Jessie would have to pay her a visit; she'd just prefer that it was later.

Kayla was finishing her juice when Skip sauntered in through the back door.

"Morning, Pumpkin. You all set?" He slung an arm around her.

"Hi, Dad." Kayla leaned up against him, resting her head on his shoulder.

He peered down at her, frowning. "Is that makeup you have on?"

Kayla ducked her head, and pulled away from him. "*All* the girls wear makeup, Dad."

"Yeah, well, those girls aren't my daughter." He shot Jessie a reproachful look, as if it were her bad influence.

"I let her try on some of mine," Jessie explained, a tad defensively.

He ignored her, ordering Kayla, "Go wash your face. We don't want to be late for church."

Kayla groaned, but did as she was told. It looked as if Skip's and Erin's roles were reversed now that Erin was no longer laying down the law. Or was it that he wanted his little girl to stay just that for a while longer? Either way, by the time they left, Kayla's face was scrubbed clean, though she still wore a faintly sullen expression.

Jessie was taking the omelet out of the oven when she heard voices in the next room. She walked in to find Mr. and Mrs. Pritchard, a middle-aged couple from Baltimore, helping themselves to the buffet. Jessie couldn't help feeling a bit anxious as she lowered the steaming omelet onto the trivet, recalling yesterday's blueberry muffins, which had been a little salty. But when she returned a minute later with a basket of warm rolls, the Pritchards were seated at a table by the window happily tucking into their food.

Jessie felt herself relax. Okay. She could do this.

More guests trickled in, and Jessie was kept busy ferrying back and forth from the kitchen. The breakfast room looked out over what Erin referred to as the "north forty," where currently a large white tent was staked, and as Jessie moved from table to table, making sure everyone had what they needed, she marveled at the beauty of the manicured grounds and orchard beyond. Erin and Skip's achievement in making this such a fabulous getaway was nothing short of miraculous. She'd seen photos of the inn before they'd renovated it. At the time, it seemed impossible that a phoenix could ever rise from the ashes of such a wreck.

Now, instead of the dark, dingy room depicted in those photos, sunlight poured in through skylights, and French doors opened onto a patio in back. In place of the long trestle table that used to occupy the center of the room there were café tables draped in chintz, each with a bud vase holding a sprig of clematis from the garden. All that was left of the former dude ranch were the exposed oak beams and pine floor, sanded and polished so that it gleamed like honey, and the built-in cabinets displaying Erin's collection of lusterware.

Jessie stopped to chat with Mr. and Mrs. Kim, who told her about their hike up Chollo Ridge the day before. She was giving them directions to Sedona when Rona Tomlinson, a retired schoolteacher who was traveling alone, stopped to inquire about the best spots for bird-watching. Jessie found this to be the most enjoyable part of the job, since most of the guests were a pleasure to be around. Like that nice couple from Cleveland, the Morriseys, who'd gone out of their way to compliment her on the French toast that was slightly burned. And the Schmidts, who'd invited her to join them for dinner the other night.

Of course, there were things to watch out for. Last week, Maria had stopped her from committing what might have been a major faux pas as Jessie was about to mail back a nightgown Petra had found in one of the rooms after the guests had checked out.

"Trust me, you don't want to do that." Maria nodded toward the sheer black nightie Jessie was stuffing into a padded envelope. "How do we know for sure it belongs to *the* Mrs. Mancusso?" She told Jessie about the time she'd sent back a found pair of panties, only to have the husband call a week later, furious because his wife, who'd known nothing of the affair with the ersatz Mrs., was threatening to divorce him as a result. "If she wants it back, you'll hear from her."

It wasn't until the last of the guests had drifted off that the doubts crept back in. Jessie kept telling herself her reasons for being here were valid, that in terms of her career she hadn't really had a choice, but it didn't prevent her from feeling homesick. She missed her cat. She missed Essa bagels and Thai food and the fruit seller on the corner of Eighth and Twenty-third who always slipped her an extra banana or orange. She missed hanging out with Clive and Drew. Most of all, she missed Jonathon.

By the time she'd loaded the last plate in the dishwasher it was after eleven. With less than an hour before the caterer was due to arrive, she took advantage of the lull to slip away for a little breather. Minutes later, she found herself strolling along the path to the creek, the sun warm against her skin, the sky a cloudless sprawl overhead. She passed the garden, where the gazebo was festooned in garlands of baby roses and the satin bows marking the rows of folding chairs fluttered in the breeze. Beyond lay a meadow knee deep in wildflowers, bordered by woods. In New York, she'd still have been wearing her winter coat. But here there were signs of spring everywhere she looked: in the new grass rippling in green waves, in unfurling buds, and birds swooping low in search of twigs to build their nests.

When she reached the creek, where she and Erin used to swim as kids, it was a letdown to find that it had shrunk to little more than a trickle, its parched banks streaked with chalky bands of sediment. Slipping off her shoes and rolling up her jeans, she waded out into the middle. At its deepest, the water only came up to her knees.

"Careful, you might drown."

The coolly ironic voice seemed to come out of nowhere. Startled, Jessie spun around to see a figure emerge from the shadows of the trees: a man in faded jeans and a chambray shirt, now ambling toward her. His hair, the iridescent black of a crow's wing, fell thick and straight about his ears, and his skin was a dark bronze that didn't come from the sun. From the ease with which he negotiated the steep bank, skidding down it on the heels of his well-worn cowboy boots, it was clear he was no stranger to these parts.

"Must've been a dry year," she remarked when she'd waded back in to shore.

"No more than most." He explained that the man who owned the land a few miles north had leased bottling rights to the spring on his property to the bottled water giant, Sylvan Glade. The problem was that the spring tapped into the aquifer that supplied water to the entire county. "You're looking at the fallout," he said grimly.

"Isn't there a law against that?" she asked.

"Sure, if you can prove it. Even then, you're bucking up against politicians who have a vested interest in turning a blind eye. If we—" He broke off with a rueful smile. "Sorry. You didn't come here to be lectured." He put out a hand, callused fingers closing over hers. He had full lips and broad, planed cheekbones. His skin gave off a coppery glow in the sunlight glancing off the water. "Hunter George. I live just up the road."

"Jessie Holland." She had the oddest feeling they'd met before, but she'd have remembered.

"You staying at the inn?" He nodded in the direction from which she'd come. No doubt her city pallor had given her away.

"You could say that." Briefly, she explained the circumstances that had brought her back to Willow Creek, adding, "I grew up here, so it wasn't as crazy as it might seem."

"Still, it must feel strange after all these years," he remarked, eyeing her with interest.

She gazed about at the ancient trees bowed under the weight of their branches and the dragonflies skimming the water's surface, catching the sunlight in little rainbow flickers. "I'd forgotten how peaceful it is, for one thing," she said. She sat down, intending to slip her shoes on, but the sand was so warm and inviting she stretched out her legs instead. After a moment, Hunter joined her. "Have you lived here all your life?" she asked, turning to him.

He shook his head. "I grew up on the reservation." His father had been a Lost Bird, he said. "That's what we Navajo call the children who were stolen as babies and adopted by white families. It wasn't until Dad had kids of his own that he found out his true heritage. He wanted to know his real family, so we packed up and moved there from Seattle."

"What a terrible thing to do to a child," she said.

Hunter shrugged. "He had his reasons."

"I was thinking of your father. And all those other children." She'd heard of the heinous practice he was referring to, but didn't know much more about it than what she'd seen on *60 Minutes*.

"The white people believed it was for the children's benefit, that they were being saved from growing up to be ignorant savages," he said in a mild voice laced with irony.

"You don't seem bitter about it," she said.

"If I hated all white people, I'd be in big trouble," he said, explaining that his mother was white. "The lone *be-*

lagaana among a pack of Indians." He grinned, and Jessie
was uncomfortably reminded of the Westerns she used to
watch as a kid, in which pioneers in covered wagons were
besieged by savages in war paint—there'd never been any
question as to who the bad guys were. "Though being a
half-breed wasn't much better. The kids in school used to
call me Casper, after Casper the Friendly Ghost."

"It's hard being the new kid no matter what," she said,
thinking of how tough it'd been for her when she'd moved
here from Pasadena.

"What's weird is that after Dad died, Mom decided to
stay put," he said. "By then, it was home."

"What about you, do you ever miss it?" From what
little she knew about the Navajo culture, its ties ran deep.

"My friends and family, but other than that there's not
much to miss. Almost everyone I know is unemployed,
and the rest are scraping by on welfare or minimum
wage." He spoke without judgment, as if merely stating a
fact. "When I left for college, I never looked back."

"What brought you to Willow Creek?"

"I teach sixth grade at Yavapai Elementary."

"Oh, God. Don't tell me Mr. Brunswick finally retired."

"It *has* been a while." He sat cross-legged beside her, regarding her curiously, as if he sensed her reasons for being
here were more complicated than she'd let on. Jessie felt
her face grow warm, and she quickly averted her gaze.

"Do you enjoy teaching?" she asked.

"When I feel like I'm making a difference. Which

isn't as often as I'd like," he added ruefully. "At the moment we're studying the revised history of western expansion."

"Why revised?"

He smiled. "Let's just say we Indians have a slightly different take on how the West was won."

They chatted a while longer, and when Jessie finally glanced at her watch she was surprised to see that half an hour had gone by. "I should be getting back," she said. She slipped on her loafers and reluctantly pulled herself to her feet.

"I'll walk with you." He rose in a single, fluid motion.

When they reached the branch in the path, which presumably led toward his place, Hunter paused, turning to face her. "Listen, I know it's short notice, but we're holding a rally tomorrow night, at town hall." He explained that he was president of the Willow Creek Conservancy, which was fighting to protect the watershed. "We could use your support."

"Tomorrow? I'll be pretty tied up all day," she hedged.

He held her gaze, his dark eyes seeming to challenge her in some way. "Well, if you change your mind, let me know. I can swing by and pick you up on my way." He scribbled his number on the back of a card he'd pulled from his wallet.

I don't need this, Jessie thought, as she dutifully took the card from him, tucking it into her back pocket. She had an inn full of guests, a mother to whom she owed a long-overdue visit, not to mention a boyfriend in New

York who would wonder if her sudden bout of activism had less to do with a social conscience than with the handsome stranger leading the charge. Yet she remained motionless, fixed in place by Hunter's depthless gaze—his eyes, she saw in the sunlight, weren't really black, but a deep shale gray. After a long moment, she roused herself, and said, "I'll do my best."

The following afternoon, goaded by her guilty conscience, Jessie found herself on her way to her mother's. Driving through town, she was struck, as always after a long absence, by how little it had changed since she was a child. The green oasis of the town square was exactly as it was when she and Erin used to climb the statue of the Spanish-American War hero collecting bird shit by the old courthouse. Murphy's and the Silver Spur remained the last survivors of the stretch along Main Street formerly known as Whiskey Row. On the corner of Main and Montezuma, opposite the Victorian-era post office, Broken Arrow Arts still displayed souvenir dreamcatchers and kachina dolls in its window. And if she'd been so inclined, she could have stopped for a bite to eat at the Benjamin Franklin, where Frito pie and chocolate malteds were still on the soda fountain's menu.

She turned off Main Street onto Brookside, cruising along familiar streets lined with gracious older homes and well-established trees. Minutes later she was pulling up in front of her mother's. Except for a fresh coat of white paint, it looked the same as when she'd last visited—

square and unpretentious, the house equivalent of a solid citizen. She made her way up the brick path that neatly bisected the freshly mown lawn, and mounted the porch steps. There was the glider on which she'd whiled away afternoons as a girl, lost in books. On the front door hung a dried-flower wreath decorated with a little gingham swan that made her think of the decoys used by duck hunters. She took a deep breath and rang the doorbell, telling herself, *I'm thirty-five years old. She can't hurt me anymore.*

When her mother appeared at the door, a small, harmless-looking woman in pink slacks and a matching checked blouse, Jessie felt foolish for imagining she had anything to fear. They hugged, a strand of Jessie's hair catching on one of Beverly's earrings as she drew back. There was an awkward moment before she could disentangle herself, then she stepped back and smiled.

"You haven't changed a bit," she said. Beverly wasn't so much aged as *cured* from years of exposure to the relentless Southwestern sun, her hair an unnatural shade of red that could only be described as oxblood.

Beverly looked pleased. "You're looking well, too."

"Sorry I'm late," Jessie apologized, though she was only a few minutes behind schedule. "The guests I wasn't expecting until later this afternoon showed up early."

"It's just sandwiches, nothing fancy," Beverly said, as she led the way down the hall.

In the kitchen, Beverly poured them each a glass of iced tea, while Jessie looked around, noting that her mother had redecorated since her last visit. Gone was the old wallpaper with its pattern of trellised ivy interspersed with watering cans. The seventies avocado refrigerator had been replaced by a tan Sub-Zero that blended in with the new peach-and-aqua color scheme, as ubiquitous to the Southwest as rehab facilities and retirement villages. Where the old sunburst clock had hung was a wrought-iron Kokopelli, and a glass dinette had taken the place of the Formica one she remembered from childhood. It was set for two, on each plate a sandwich cut into neat triangles along with half a pickle and a handful of potato chips.

Jessie's gaze fell on the wine rack that had replaced the old pine china hutch. "When did you become a connoisseur?" she asked in amazement, wondering how a woman whose idea of fine wine was Asti Spumanti over ice had come to be collecting vintage labels.

"Oh, that. It was Gay's idea." Gayleen Whitehead was her mother's oldest friend, and the reason they'd moved here after Jessie's father died. "You know how she's always complaining about what a cultural wasteland this is. Well, the next thing I knew, she had us both signed up for this class. It's at a different house every week, and we all chip in for the wine. Our teacher is French," she said grandly. "His name's Jean Claude."

"Sounds like fun," Jessie murmured, taking a sip of her tea.

Over lunch, Beverly talked on and on, about the lump in her breast that had turned out to be benign, the new irrigation system being installed at the country club, and every thoughtful thing Gay's son and daughter had done for their mother lately. She didn't ask how Jessie was faring at the inn or about her life in New York. The man Jessie had met yesterday at the creek had seemed more interested in her than her own mother—a man who, irritatingly, had refused to fade from her mind like most of the people she met in passing. She was even seriously considering attending the rally.

It wasn't until she was helping her mother clear the table that Jessie managed to interject, "By the way, our first column in *Savvy* is coming out next week."

"Is that so?" Beverly had been skeptical when Jessie first told her about the assignment. She thought the title, "Life Swap," too suggestive.

"The biggest surprise was Erin. She wasn't sure how much she'd have to contribute, but now you can't shut her off. The first week alone she turned in twelve pages, which I had to boil down into four paragraphs," Jessie went on. "Between writing and running an inn, believe me, I have my hands full."

"I suppose I should be grateful you found the time to see me." A peeved note crept into her mother's voice.

Jessie felt the food she'd eaten congeal into a lump in her belly. Every walk down the garden path with her mother invariably led up to this point, with Beverly, obliquely if not overtly, letting Jessie know that she'd disappointed her in some way.

At the bottom of it all was the ultimate finger of blame: that of her father's death. The coroner had listed the cause as heart failure, but Beverly knew better: That day at the beach if seven-year-old Jessie hadn't disobeyed him and swum out past the waves, he wouldn't have been forced to go after her. He might still have had a heart attack, but he wouldn't have drowned as a result.

"Gay's eldest granddaughter is starting high school next year," Beverly informed her as she was putting coffee on.

"That's nice," Jessie replied listlessly, setting out cups and saucers.

"You should see her. She's the spitting image of Gay. Smart as a whip, too. Just like her brothers."

"Gay must be proud."

"With six grandchildren, counting Bobby's two, she says she's running out of room on her mantel."

"I suppose I should get married and have kids just so you'll have pictures of grandchildren to show off," Jessie said irritably, her patience worn thin.

Beverly cast her a wounded look. "You don't have to be snippy."

"I'm sorry." Jessie backed down at once, as always. "It's just that it's a sensitive subject."

"Pardon me for saying so, but if you're still single, you have only yourself to blame."

Jessie rolled her eyes. *Here we go again,* she thought. Her mother was never going to let her forget that she'd blown her one chance at happiness, in Beverly's view, by not marrying Mike. Never mind that they'd probably be divorced by now. "Did it ever occur to you that I might be perfectly happy with my life as it is?" Her words rang hollow even to her own ears. She thought of Jonathon, who'd had to cancel the visit he'd had planned for this weekend when Rebecca informed him at the last minute that she had a conference in San Francisco. It was too short notice to find a babysitter, so he'd had to take the kids. He'd promised to make it up to Jessie, but in her head she could hear Erin saying, *Talk's cheap, it takes money to buy whiskey.*

"If everything was so hunky dory, you wouldn't be here," Beverly pronounced, folding her arms over her chest.

Thanks for the insight, Dr. Phil, Jessie replied silently, but all she said was, "Can we please not have this discussion?" She massaged her forehead, which had begun to throb. "Trust me, when I'm ready to settle down, you'll be the first to know."

"I just hope I live that long."

Jessie sighed in defeat. "If you must know, I'm seeing someone. His name's Jonathon."

Beverly perked up. "Is it serious?"

"Too soon to say." Jessie chose her words carefully, not wanting to get her mother's hopes up. "He just went through a difficult divorce, so we're taking it slow." She didn't mention that Jonathon had kids and was in no hurry to start a second family.

From then on, Jessie stuck to safe subjects until she could politely escape. Beverly walked her to the door, where she hugged Jessie with uncharacteristic warmth, murmuring, "It's good to have you back." Jessie searched her mother's face when she drew back, but saw nothing in her smiling, clear-eyed gaze to indicate that her words hadn't been heartfelt. "Oh, I almost forgot," Beverly called to her as she was making her way down the steps. "Gay invited us to lunch at the club. Do you think you can get away one day next week?"

Jessie promised to let her know as soon as she'd checked her calendar. Gay had been like a mother to her after Beverly had more or less abdicated that role, and Jessie felt badly that she hadn't kept in touch. It wasn't that Jessie wasn't fond of her, just that Gay was a reminder of that terrible time in her life.

As she drove back to the inn, memories she normally kept at bay closed in on her. She saw herself at age seven, in her polka-dot swimsuit, racing down the beach, her father shouting after her to stay close to shore. Then the moment of terror when the first big wave snatched her off her feet and sent her tumbling over and over in the surf. The rest was a blur, except for a single image that stood clear: that of her father swimming toward her as she was being swept out to sea.

It was the last time she saw him alive.

It wasn't just Mike she'd run out on all those years ago, she realized. It was the guilt she felt whenever she looked into her mother's unforgiving eyes.

Jessie phoned Erin from the car. "Hi, it's me."

"What's up?" Erin asked a bit anxiously, like always, as if she half expected it to be bad news.

"Nothing much. I just came from my mother's, and I needed to hear a friendly voice."

"She give you a hard time?"

"No more than usual. But it's been a while since my last booster shot."

"You have five more months to build up an immunity." There was a brief pause, then Erin asked, "Everything okay on the home front?"

"I haven't set anything on fire lately, if that's what you mean."

"How's Kayla?"

"I don't know how to break it to you, but she's surviving just fine without you." Jessie made the turn onto the winding road that led to the inn. "She aced her last math test." Jessie had been tutoring her in geometry.

"Really? That's great! Tell her I'm proud of her." As if Erin wouldn't be telling Kayla herself before the day was out.

"How's the job search going?" Jessie ventured, knowing it was a sore subject.

Erin groaned at the other end. "I've been pounding the pavement so hard my blisters have blisters."

"Something's bound to turn up."

"It'd better be soon, or I'm looking at washing dishes for two-fifty an hour."

"At least you'd be getting paid for it," she joked in reference to her own, unpaid kitchen duty.

Not even a chuckle. This must be more serious than she'd thought; normally she could wring a laugh out of

Erin even in the bleakest moments. "If it weren't for Drew, I'd be tempted to call this whole thing off," she said. "He's been great."

"I'll bet. I saw the way he was looking at you."

"It's not like that—he's just being nice. Besides, I'm married."

"I believe the correct term is separated."

Erin asked caustically, "Speaking of the devil, have you talked to Skip lately?"

"Except for hello and good-bye, we've had exactly one conversation."

"And?"

"He misses you."

"He told you that?"

"Not in so many words . . ."

Erin gave a derisive snort. "I'll believe it when I hear it from his own mouth." In an obvious bid to change the subject, she inquired, "What about you? How's your love life?"

"According to my mother it's nonexistent."

"I'll be sure to let Jonathon, know," Erin said dryly. "I'm having dinner with him on Tuesday." Jessie had urged him to call Erin, figuring she could use the company. She had an ulterior motive as well: She wanted to know what Erin thought of him. "Should I tell him you're pining away, or do you want him to think you have some hot guy lined up?"

A mental image formed of Hunter standing on the creek bank. "I don't have time for a pedicure, much less a date," Jessie said. "The only thing I've been invited to lately is a protest rally." She told Erin about yesterday's chance encounter with Hunter George.

"You should go," Erin told her.

"Give me one good reason."

"For one thing, it's a good cause," she said. "Those of us who give a damn have just been pissing in the wind ever since Burt Overby sold out to Sylvan Glade. It wasn't until Hunter got people mobilized that we actually had a voice. Not that it's done much good so far, but if anyone can put a stop to this, I'm betting on Hunter George."

"He does seem pretty determined."

"He's a good guy. Not your type, though."

A guilty flush crept into Jessie's cheeks; it was as if Erin had read her mind. "What's that got to do with anything? Besides, if I *do* go, it won't be because of some cute guy."

"Oh, so you think he's cute?" asked Erin mischievously.

Jessie sighed. "Okay, you win. He's cute. End of story. You know perfectly well I have eyes only for Jonathon."

"Does that mean you're going to the rally?"

Jessie pondered for a moment. "Yeah, why not?" She still had the card with Hunter's number on it. She'd give him a call as soon as she got back.

Chapter Seven

"Not even an itty-bitty taste?" Clive gazed longingly at the pie in Erin's hands.

"The next one will have your name on it," she promised.

"Cruelty, thy name is woman." Jessie's landlord heaved a sigh of resignation. One of his more eccentric traits was dressing up in uniforms, of which he had an extensive collection. Today's was an Italian *garde*'s, complete with a crimson beret that sat at a rakish angle atop his ivory mane. Though with his blue eyes heavily lined in kohl the effect was more that of an aging silent film star. "Did anyone ever tell you you'd make a good dominatrix?"

"No. But if I don't find a job soon, it's something to keep in mind," she replied with a laugh.

The idea of making a pie in order to get her foot in the door at the Cooking Channel had come to her after yesterday's conversation with Jessie. She had nothing to lose, and though by now the position had surely been filled, there might be another opening down the line. She had the perfect recipe, too—the chilled white chocolate-raspberry pie that had won her a blue ribbon at last year's Heritage Days festival. Yesterday afternoon she'd baked the crust and made the filling, then this morning, after the pie had set in the refrigerator overnight, she put on the finishing touches: fresh raspberries arranged in circles, drizzled in white chocolate. She'd run into Clive in the hallway as she was on her way out to deliver it.

"By the way, how's our friend?" he asked, in a voice of hushed concern, as if Jessie had been unaccountably detained in some Third World country. "I can't help picturing her in a bonnet, digging for turnips with her bare hands." He shuddered theatrically.

Erin smiled at the image. In Clive's worldview, terra firma ended at the Hudson River; anything west of it was off the map. She didn't want to spoil the illusion by informing him that they had running water and indoor plumbing in Willow Creek.

"You'll read all about it in next week's issue of *Savvy*," she said, shifting the pie from one hand to the other as she edged toward the door.

"Give me a hint, at least," he pleaded.

"All I can tell you is that it involves bondage," she confided with a wink.

For once, Clive was speechless. Erin blew him a kiss on her way out, leaving him to wonder what she'd meant. Minutes later she was barreling down Tenth Avenue in one of New York City's infamous kamikaze cabs. The driver was so busy jabbering on his cell phone she didn't dare ask him to slow down; if she distracted him, she could end up splattered all over the backseat along with her pie.

She pictured herself comatose in a hospital bed, Skip at her side, tears running down his cheeks as he clutched her limp hand. *You've got to hang on*, he pleaded. *I can't go on without you. You're my whole life . . .*

Angrily she banished the image. Dammit, why should she have to be at death's door for him to come to his senses? Not, she was quick to remind herself, that she was exactly pining away. In some ways, she was enjoying her new freedom.

For one thing, it was nice having only herself to look after for a change. If she didn't feel like cooking, there was a stack of take-out menus to choose from. And instead of the daily round of chores, there was only the occasional straightening up around the apartment and her weekly trip to the Laundromat. Even grocery shopping was limited to what she could carry.

There were times she was homesick, sure. And she missed Kayla. But they talked on the phone every other day, and Erin had the consolation of knowing her daughter was better off not having to listen to her parents fighting all the time. Kayla had made it clear she was enjoying the break from Erin's constant nitpicking as well.

What Kayla didn't know was that Erin, far from having all the answers, often felt out of her depth. From the moment her daughter had emerged from the womb, the fearsome responsibility of raising a child had seemed one for which she wasn't remotely qualified. Part of the reason she was so strict was to make up for what she saw as her gross incompetence. That, and because she herself had hardly known a carefree moment while she was growing up; she knew all the things that could go wrong.

Coming to New York, however stressful in some ways, had reminded her that life could be fun. Like the day she and Drew had gone sightseeing, ending up on the Staten Island ferry; she recalled how she'd felt standing on the deck with the wind whipping her hair about her head, gazing up in wonder at the Statue of Liberty, like some mythical figure emerging from the mist, as they glided past. Her troubles and worries had seemed far away; she'd felt as if she were setting sail on a marvelous adventure.

At the Cooking Channel she informed the security guard at the entrance that she had a special delivery for Ms. Powers. "I'll see that she gets it," he said, putting his hand out to take the pie from her.

She stepped back, holding it out of reach. "I'd rather deliver it personally, if you don't mind."

He shook his head. "Sorry, Miss. We got rules. Nobody gets in without an appointment."

Erin was momentarily at a loss. Then she had a sudden inspiration, and flashed him her most winning smile, leaning in to confide, "It's from Mario." Let him wonder *which* Mario she was referring to.

He eyed her uncertainly, appearing to waver. But she'd guessed correctly that he wouldn't want to take the chance of pissing off a VIP, for minutes later she was being escorted up to the executive producer's office.

"I hope you like raspberries," Erin said, thrusting the pie into Latrice's hands.

Latrice contemplated it for a moment, as if not quite sure what to make of it. Then she let out a throaty chuckle. "You made this?" Erin nodded, and Latrice shook her head with regret. "I'm afraid you went to all that trouble for nothing. The job's been filled."

Erin's heart sank, but she mustered a crooked smile. "I figured as much. But I thought what the hell, it's worth a try. I've never been one to go down without a fight."

"You chose an interesting plan of attack."

"Anyone can type," Erin said. "But how many people can bake?"

"It certainly isn't a job requirement. But if this pie is as good as it looks, you could be raising the bar." She eyed Erin speculatively, then seemed to come to some sort of decision. "Actually, come to think of it, I may have something for you."

"Really?" Erin felt a surge of new hope.

"You've heard of the Singing Chef?"

"Who hasn't?" A failed Italian opera singer turned TV chef, he was famous for belting out arias as he whipped up delectable dishes on his top-rated show.

"Well, I just got off the phone with his producer. One of their PA's quit, and they need someone right away," Latrice explained. "I have to warn you, though, Robert's pretty demanding." In other words, he was the reason the erstwhile production assistant had thrown in the towel. "It can be a real pressure cooker—no pun intended."

Erin smiled to herself. Latrice couldn't know just how uniquely qualified she was. "When do I start?"

"Yesterday," Latrice answered, blowing out a harried breath.

They settled on the following morning at 8:00 A.M.; then Erin was dispatched to Personnel to fill out the requisite forms and get her security badge. Twenty minutes later she was making her way back downstairs in a kind of daze. Her mother had been wrong about one thing: It wasn't bread cast upon the water that came back sandwiches, it was pie.

"Here's to your new job." Drew lifted his glass.

"And to dusting off my little town shoes." Erin raised her own glass. "My mama always said I had more balls than a bowling alley, though I'm not sure it was a compliment."

"So you were like this even as a kid?"

"Worse," she said with a laugh. "I used to tap-dance on our coffee table at night in front of the living room window, just in case a Hollywood scout should happen to drive by."

He chuckled. "I don't know of anyone who got discovered that way."

"Me, either. Besides, I couldn't dance worth shit."

They were at the Rocking Horse Café, where he'd taken her to celebrate, and where Erin, sipping a margarita in a glass the size of a birdbath, was already feeling a little tipsy.

"There was one thing I was good at, though," she went on. "In my house, if you wanted something other than Hamburger Helper or Rice-a-Roni, you had to make it yourself, so by the time I was tall enough to reach the counter I knew how to cook." Erin could still remember the first meal she'd prepared all on her own: creamed tuna on toast. "My mom, as you've probably gathered, wasn't exactly Betty Crocker. Everyone loved her, though. All the regulars from the diner where she worked showed up at her funeral."

"How old were you when she died?" he asked, his smile giving way to an expression of sympathy.

"It was right after I got out of college." Erin felt a familiar tightening in her chest. "A drunk driver plowed into their car. She and my dad both died instantly. I was told they didn't suffer."

She gazed about at the fanciful *Dia del Muerte*–themed artwork decorating the sponge-painted walls: skeleton cutouts and colorful paintings of skull and bones. Over the years, she'd tried hard to find some meaning in her parents' deaths, but all she could see was the senselessness of it.

"It must have been hard for you."

"It was." But something good had come of it: She'd

gotten together with Skip—a silver lining that had become tarnished over time. But she didn't want to think
about Skip right now; it would only spoil the mood. She
forced a smile. "What about you? You haven't told me
much about your family."

He shrugged. "I was your typical suburban kid. Boy
Scouts and Little League, sleepaway camp in the summers. The most traumatic thing in my life was my parents
getting divorced when I was twelve."

"I hear there's a lot of that going around," she said,
lapsing back into unhappy thoughts of her own marriage.

She'd done some soul-searching these past weeks, and
though it pained her to admit it, Skip had been right
about one thing: She hadn't been the most supportive
wife. What stuck in her craw was that he hadn't given her
a chance to make it right. What did it say about a man
that he'd sooner give up than see a marriage counselor?

"At the time," Drew went on, "it seemed like the worst
thing that could ever happen. But it turned out to be for
the best. They're both remarried now and happier than
they've ever been."

"What about you?" she asked. "Are you happier?"

"I'm not scarred for life, if that's what you mean." His
easy laugh didn't fool her. She caught a flicker of old pain
in his eyes. "Though my mom seems to think it's the reason I'm still single. I keep telling her it's not that I have
anything against marriage in general, just that I haven't
met anyone I can see myself spending the rest of my life
with." He gave Erin a meaningful look. Or was it her imag-

ination—booze downed too quickly on an empty stomach?

"Not even close?" she asked.

She wondered what he would think if he knew that at night sometimes, when she couldn't get to sleep, as she lay in bed listening to the creak of his footsteps overhead, she imagined him crawling in next to her. The thought sent a rush of warmth to her cheeks.

"Well, there was my girlfriend in college," he said. "But after graduation, we sort of drifted apart. There've been a few others since then. No one that made me want to jump off a bridge when they took off after getting tired of waiting for me to pop the question." He slowly twirled his glass, gazing into it like a fortune-teller reading tea leaves. When he looked up at her, his face was flushed. "The thing is, I don't believe in settling. I've seen it with some of my friends. If they haven't met the woman of their dreams by the time they're in their thirties, they get to thinking maybe she isn't out there, that they should just go with the next best thing. Before they know it, they've got a mortgage and kids, and it's too late to back out."

"That's a pretty cynical view," she said.

"Is it? Look at you. You can't tell me you don't have regrets, that you don't wish things had turned out differently." He eyed her intently, as if he could see right through her.

Erin sensed that they were heading into dangerous territory.

"Maybe, but it's not as simple as that," she said. "When you've been married as long as I have . . ."

Their waiter appeared just then with their orders, saving her from having to wade in any deeper. Over dinner, they lapsed back into the comfortable rhythm of the past few weeks. Friends enjoying a night out, nothing more. By the time they left the restaurant, they were once more on safe ground.

The cold snap of the past few weeks had thawed, giving way to milder weather, and as they strolled toward home she saw signs of spring—trees beginning to leaf out, green spears pushing up in window boxes. They nodded pleasantly to old Madame Beteille, who scowled at them like the Wicked Witch of the West from her stoop. They were climbing the stairs in their building when Clive stepped out of his ground-floor apartment.

"What do you think? Isn't it just *too* Hemingway?" Resplendent in full toreador regalia, he twirled so his scarlet-lined cape flared out around him.

"The panty hose are a nice touch," Drew observed wryly.

Clive grinned. "Honey, they don't call them queen-sized for nothing." He flashed them a naughty grin as he headed back inside, calling, "Night night, kiddies. Don't stay up *too* late . . ."

Erin darted a look at Drew. Oh, God. Was it that obvious? She'd been so careful to treat him as she would any other friend it hadn't occurred to her that the only person she'd only been fooling was herself. At her door, she fumbled with her keys and it took several tries before she finally got it open. She was relieved when Drew, instead of accompanying her inside as he often did—to get a book she'd offered to loan him or to borrow something he was out of—only kissed her on the cheek, saying, "Good luck tomorrow."

She was so tired, she fell asleep almost as soon as her head hit the pillow. Hours later she was dreaming of Skip—they were making love in their bed at home—when she was roused by a loud knocking at the front door. She fought to hold on to the dream as it receded, but at last she had no choice but to drag herself out from under the covers to see who it was, cursing under her breath and sending Delilah, curled at the foot of the bed, leaping to the floor with a disgruntled meow.

But it was only Drew. She unlatched the chain and, with a yawn, opened the door wider, squinting at him groggily. "Jesus, do you know what *time* it is?"

"Your keys. You left them in the lock." He dangled them in front of her.

Erin went weak at the thought of what might've happened if it had been a burglar . . . or, God forbid, a rapist . . . who'd spotted them first. She might as well have put out a welcome mat.

"I would've waited until morning," he said, "but I figured you'd be leaving early for work."

"What are you doing up so late?" she asked.

"I couldn't sleep, so I went for a walk."

She stood there blinking at him, suddenly aware that

she was wearing nothing but an oversize T-shirt that barely covered her ass. Her dream . . . and the way Drew was looking at her . . . somehow they'd become tangled together in her mind. Before she knew it she was moving toward him as if in slow motion.

There was the momentary shock of his cold parka against her warm skin as she wrapped her arms about him, burying her face against his chest. Drew made a little groaning sound deep in his throat as he pulled her close. He smelled of the outdoors, a smell that made her think of Willow Creek, coming in from the cold to a crackling fire and a mug of hot cocoa. She tipped her head up, and their lips met. A kiss, tentative at first, then more urgent.

Wordlessly, he took her hand and led her back down the hall. *This isn't real. I'm still asleep*, she thought even as she climbed onto the bed, Drew snuggling up next to her. In the darkness, the hands caressing her might have been the ones she'd thrilled to in her dream. She gave herself over to the sensations. It had been so long. . . .

Warm lips brushed her neck and the hand on her belly moved lower. Oh, God. This was what she'd ached for. She reached down, easing open the zipper on his jeans and sliding her hand in. But everything about it—its shape, its texture—was so unfamiliar, so wrong somehow, she was shocked into full awareness of what she was doing. Abruptly, she drew back.

"What's wrong?" Drew murmured.

"I can't do this." She sat up, wrapping her arms around her knees as she tucked them in against her chest.

"Hey, it's okay. We don't have to." His voice was gentle.

"I . . . thought . . ." Her throat closed as she fought back tears. How could she tell him she'd wanted him to be Skip?

He sat up, putting his arms around her. "What?"

"It's not you," she said miserably. "It's just . . ." *I miss my husband.* "I'm married."

"A minor detail that had escaped my notice," he said wryly.

She twisted around to face him. "Don't joke. That only makes it worse."

"I wasn't trying to be funny."

"I know. It's my fault. I feel terrible."

"You didn't do anything wrong." He stroked her hair.

"You'll still respect me in the morning?" She made a weak stab at humor.

"Hey, you're talking to the guy who threw up all over his date's shoes at the senior prom. Now *that* is a deal breaker." He grinned, his teeth a flash of white in the darkness. "Look, this doesn't change anything. We'll still be friends."

She dropped her head onto his shoulder with a sigh. "Promise?"

In response, he kissed her on the cheek before getting up off the bed. "If you change your mind, you know where to find me," he bent down to whisper in her ear as he was leaving.

*   *   *

" . . . And I'll need copies of these on my desk by noon."
Erin's boss thrust a sheaf of papers into her hands. "Oh,
and for the record," he added testily, "it's *Robert*, not
Bob."

Erin couldn't recall having addressed him as anything
other than Mr. Hannigan. But she only shrugged and
said, "Yes, Mr. . . . um, Robert." She'd have no trouble
keeping his name straight, as there was nothing remotely
Bob-like about this Robert. With his arctic blue eyes and
satanic brows, his pointy goatee, he could have played the
devil in *Faust*.

Her number one priority she'd been told was tending
to the Singing Chef's every need. She was to run errands
and perform tasks like ironing his chef's whites and keeping his dressing room stocked with snacks and cold drinks.
All it would take was a single complaint, Robert had
made clear, and she'd be out the door. She hadn't even
met the man, and already she was in a cold sweat.

"Oh, and Elaine . . . ?" Robert called after her as she
was leaving his office. She opened her mouth to tell him
it was *Erin*, not Elaine, but he was shuffling through
some papers on his desk, not paying any attention to her.
He glanced up. "Coffee. You know how to make it, I
assume."

"I should hope so." She thought of the gallons consumed every week at the Darby Inn.

"Good. Because I could use some."

The coffee room down the hall was equipped with a
fancy espresso machine that took her several false starts

and a scalded finger to master. The rest of the morning she spent racing up and down the halls at warp speed, delivering cups of coffee and espresso to Robert and the rest of the senior staff, in between Xeroxing production notes and scripts, typing up a press release, and taking inventory of the props for the Easter-themed show that was being taped next week.

She quickly discovered that the junior staffer who'd warned that bathroom breaks had to be penciled in wasn't kidding. Lunch was a protein bar gobbled on the run. At two-thirty, one of the associate producers, a harried-looking woman named Trish, drafted her to help "load in" the audience for that afternoon's live-to-tape show. Erin tagged after her as she patrolled the outer corridor, where ticket holders had been waiting in line for hours. Trish checked off names on her list before handing out numbered tags that indicated where each person was to sit. It was Erin's job to usher them to their seats, which were arranged in tiers, with café tables in front for VIPs and those doing guest spots.

She made it a point to be friendly to everyone. Most of the people were from out of town, and she was reminded that it wasn't that long ago she, too, had been looking about in wide-eyed wonder, only slightly less clueless than the older, poodle-haired woman coming out of Tiffany's the other day whom she'd overheard mutter indignantly to her husband, "Well, if they don't serve food, why the heck is it called BREAKFAST *at Tiffany's . . . ?*"

When everyone had taken their seats, Trish instructed them to turn off their cell phones, stow their cameras, and spit out any gum they might be chewing. As if they were third graders on a field trip, Erin thought with amusement. Next came the warm-up, which consisted of another staffer, a plump frizzy-haired woman whose voice would have carried into the upper tiers even without a mike, telling jokes and whipping the audience into a frenzy of excitement.

By the time the Singing Chef came bounding out onto the set, amid cheers befitting a rock star, Erin was swept up in the excitement as well. He looked even larger in life than on TV, a huge rump roast of a man, with a gap between his front teeth and hair that stuck out like boar bristles from his head. As the band played, he mamboed across the stage leading an invisible partner, surprisingly graceful for a man his size.

Before long he was tossing ingredients into a sizzling skillet as he carried on a running monologue that had everyone, from the little children on their mothers' laps to the old folks who'd been bused in from a senior citizens' center in Passaic, as rapt as if he were speaking directly to them. Under the blaze of spotlights mounted to the grid overhead, surrounded by cameras, he might have been in his own kitchen, he appeared so relaxed, even breaking into song from time to time.

Erin, watching from the sidelines, thought, *This is what it's all about.* What she'd aspired to tap-dancing on the coffee table as a kid. So what if she'd never become famous? At least now she knew what it was like up at the top; she was breathing the same air.

At each of the commercial breaks, the culinary staff came swooping in like a task force to tidy up and replace whatever was on the stove or in the oven with the same dish in a more advanced stage of completion. Far from its spoiling the illusion, Erin felt as if she were being let in on a wonderful secret. She was spellbound until the final moment, when the cameras zoomed in for a tight shot of the Singing Chef passing out samples of the dishes he'd prepared to those seated at the café tables in front, and delivering his familiar sign-off, "We make beautiful music together, eh? Until next time, *arrivederci . . . !*"

When the cameras stopped rolling, he stepped out into the audience, moving among them with the ease of a politician, shaking hands and kissing cheeks, making one old lady blush like a schoolgirl. The only thing he didn't do was sign autographs; that would have taken all day.

Then Erin and Trish were herding the audience members toward the exits. When the studio had been cleared, Erin made her way backstage through a maze of industrial shelving, stacked with everything from power cables to plates and cutlery and ornaments for every season, down the corridor and past the green room to the Singing Chef's private dressing room. Her mouth was dry, and her heart beating much too fast, as she knocked on the door. Except for the concert back in the eighties when she'd caught a sweaty towel flung out into the audience by the bass guitarist from Depeche Mode, this was her first encounter with a celebrity. Not just any celebrity—one whose first impression of her could mean the difference between a paycheck and a one-way ticket back to Willow Creek.

A deep voice boomed merrily, "Come in! Come in!"

The first thing she noticed as she stepped inside were the chef's whites she'd ironed earlier in the day, now rumpled and stained, lying in a heap on the floor. The Singing Chef, looking equally rumpled in a tent-sized plaid shirt and chinos, was helping himself to a soda from the minifridge.

She stuck out her hand. "Hi, I'm Erin."

Before she could explain her presence, he said, his brown eyes twinkling, "Ah, my new handler." Her hand was engulfed in his gigantic bear's paw. "I hope you last longer than my previous one. She wasn't nearly as pretty, though it's hard to say, the poor thing was in tears most of the time." He spoke with a British accent that she would soon learn was the product of his having been brought up in London. The *paisano* act was just part of his *shtick*.

Erin grinned. "I'm a tough nut."

"Even tough nuts crack." He produced a bottle of Scotch from the cabinet below the minifridge and poured a healthy slug into a glass. "Drink?"

She shook her head. Robert wouldn't approve of her drinking on the job, even if it was in the interests of keeping the talent happy.

He shrugged, knocking back the contents of the glass. He was older than he appeared on TV—late fifties, she guessed—the heavy base covering his face caked in the creases around his eyes. "Have you peeked into Blue- beard's closet yet? Seen all the heads of your predeces- sors?" She must have looked worried, for he gave her shoulder a fatherly pat. "Don't worry. His bark is worse than his bite. And you know what they say about men who carry big sticks," he added with a suggestive wink.

She bit her lip to keep from laughing.

She was turning to go when he asked, "You like Ital- ian food?"

"My father was Italian." She didn't add that her dad's idea of Italian cuisine was Chef Boyardee.

He flashed her a grin that revealed the gap between his front teeth. "In that case, my dear, you and I will get along just fine."

The rest of the day went by in a blur. It was well after dark by the time Erin got off work. Stepping outside, she found the rain that had been threatening all day coming down in torrents. Naturally she hadn't brought an um- brella—it rained so infrequently back home, she'd gotten out of the habit. Not only that, there were at least three people on every street corner trying to hail cabs. Luckily she spotted one as it was making the turn onto Twelfth, and she sloshed her way through a puddle to grab it before anyone else could.

On the ride home, thoughts of Drew that had been circling all day moved in for the kill. How could she face him again after last night? *Maybe I should have slept with him*, she thought. But she knew why she hadn't. *If I cross that line, it'll mean my marriage is really, truly over.* And she wasn't ready to accept that. Not yet.

She wondered if it was too late to reschedule her dinner with Jonathon. All she wanted tonight was a long soak in a hot bath. But she didn't want to disappoint Jessie, who was anxious for her to meet him. Also, if she stayed home, Drew might drop by. Eventually she would have to face him, but right now she didn't want to think about last night and what it implied: that her wedding vows weren't as sacred as she'd always believed.

Patsy's restaurant was something of an institution. As soon as Erin walked in she could see that it wasn't just hype. Autographed eight-by-tens of famous faces covered the walls by the entrance, and the well-heeled crowd at the bar let her know that its glory days weren't just in the past. Yet there was nothing snooty about the place. The owner, an older man who introduced himself as Joey, welcomed her as if she were a guest in his own home. After taking her coat, he personally escorted her to Jonathon's table.

Jonathon rose, smiling. "Erin. I've heard so much about you. I can't believe I'm finally meeting you."

She took the hand he extended toward her. "I've heard a lot about you, too." He was even handsomer in person than in his photos. More like one of the famous faces on the walls than someone who might one day be her best friend's husband. "Jessie talks about you all the time."

Their waiter brought a wine list and menus, and

Jonathon, after ordering a bottle of Merlot, chatted with him briefly, asking after his wife and children.

"You must eat here a lot," she observed.

"At least twice a week." Jonathon explained that the CTN newsroom was in the building across the street. "If I can't get away from my desk, they send something over. After 9/11, when we were all working around the clock, Sal—Joey's son, he's the chef—kept the entire newsroom fed. And Rose"—he gestured toward the owner's bubbly wife, manning the coat check at the door—"is like my Italian mama."

"I didn't know you were Italian," she teased.

He brought a finger to his lips. "Shhh. Don't tell my mother."

"Why, would it upset her?" She went along with the joke.

He rolled his eyes. "You don't want to know."

"So it's true what they say about Jewish mothers."

"Ever heard the joke about the Jewish mother who buys her son two shirts? Kid tries one on, and she says, 'So what's wrong with the other one?'"

Erin chuckled, but she was remembering Jessie's not-so-funny tale about her disastrous visit with his parents. "Is your mom like that?"

"Not since she stopped buying me shirts."

"So she wouldn't mind if you married someone who wasn't Jewish?" A loaded question if there ever was one, but Erin had to know if he was serious about Jessie or if she was merely wasting her time.

His smile faded. "I gather you've heard—my parents didn't exactly roll out the red carpet. It wouldn't have been so bad, but my kids weren't on their best behavior either." He sighed. "I just wish Jessie hadn't taken it so personally. They're just *kids*."

"I know. I have one of my own," Erin said.

"It's nothing against her," he went on. "They'd have a problem with anyone I was seeing. But I'm sure once they get to know her . . ." He let the rest of the sentence trail off, looking vaguely defeated for a man who spoke with such optimism.

"That'll be kind of hard with her in another time zone," Erin observed dryly.

His shoulders sagged. "You're right. What the hell was I thinking? That she'd wait patiently in the wings until I got it all sorted out? I just hope it's not too late to make it up to her."

"Phone sex can only get you so far. If I were you, I'd hop on a plane."

"Believe me, I'd like nothing more. But something always seems to get in the way."

A red flag went up. If he was so crazy about Jessie, Erin thought, wouldn't he move heaven and earth to be with her?

Over dinner, they talked about other things. He told her about his kids and wanted to know all about Kayla. There were war stories, too, from when he'd first started at CTN, as a reporter, like the time he'd come within inches of getting shot during a hostage negotiation. By the end of the meal, she was won over. Almost. Jonathon was a good guy, but that didn't necessarily make him right for Jessie.

When the table had been cleared, Joey brought them dessert menus. Erin patted her stomach saying, "I'm afraid I'm going to have to pass. I couldn't eat another bite."

"You sure?" Joey urged. "It's on the house."

"Just the check," Jonathon told him.

Joey beamed at him as if he were a son. "Tell your friend," he said to Erin with a wink, "that if she knows what's good for her, she won't leave this guy on his own for too long." He gave Jonathon's cheek a fond pat. "All the ladies want to know if he's up for grabs."

"I'll tell her myself when I see her," Jonathon said.

You'd better make that sooner rather than later, Erin thought, remembering the excitement in Jessie's voice when she'd talked about last night's rally and how impressive Hunter had been.

The rain, she saw when they stepped out of the restaurant, had tapered off some. Jonathon walked Erin to the corner, where he hailed her a cab. "I don't remember when I've had such a good time," he said, smiling as he held open the door for her. "You're exactly as Jess described you."

"You, too. You're everything she said you'd be," Erin told him, standing on tiptoe to kiss him on the cheek. *Only handsomer,* she added silently, a bit dazzled by such close proximity to a man who could literally have made most women swoon.

Handsome is as handsome does, she could hear her mother's voice in her head, as she rode home in the cab. The question was what, exactly, he was going to *do* about Jessie.

JESSIE:

My first week as a country innkeeper, here's what I learned: a) what I'd previously thought of as night-time is when some people actually get up to go to work (yawn) b) when dousing pancakes in Grand Marnier, it's a good idea to first remove the pan from the flame c) people in other parts of the country are no less kinky than in Manhattan; they're just better at disguising it.

I discovered this while learning to use a gadget that no one who would ever sink to buying Cool Whip could possibly know about. It's called the Miracle-Pro. It whips cream inside this nifty stain-less-steel canister. All you have to do is insert a car-tridge that pressurizes it. What I learned the hard way is that before unscrewing the cap, the canister must be empty, or you'll end up with whipped cream all over the walls and ceiling, not to mention yourself.

It was while I was on a stepladder scraping bits of cream from the cupboard doors that I was summoned upstairs. Mr. and Mrs. X had checked out earlier that morning, and one of the maids, while cleaning the room, had discovered something unusual: the sashes from the complimentary bathrobes tied to the bed-posts. I could only assume it was evidence of some sex play. Which illustrates something I've long suspected:

164

That often it's those you'd least suspect of having sex for any reason other than procreation who have secret lives rivaling anything in the Kama Sutra. Who'd have thought a mild-mannered Iowa accountant and his wife would be into bondage? It's kind of liberating, when you think about it. Hey, maybe there's another use for that Miracle-Pro. . . .

From "Life Swap"

Chapter Eight

"Let's hope he doesn't own a shotgun," Jessie muttered.

"I don't know of a rancher in these parts who doesn't," Hunter said. "I wouldn't let it worry you."

They were making their way up a forested slope, the crunch of their footsteps the only sound in the predawn stillness. Now she paused to look at him. "Worry?" She gave a dry laugh that sent a plume of breath out into the chill air. "When you said we might run into a little trouble, I thought you meant something *really* dangerous— like a rabid squirrel or poison oak. I don't suppose you noticed all those signs." Prominently posted around the perimeters of Burt Overby's property, they warned of dire consequences to trespassers.

"Look at it this way: If we're dead, they can't prosecute us."

Jessie shot him a dirty look, wishing she'd thought twice before agreeing to this harebrained scheme. The trouble was that when she was around Hunter she was so spellbound—by the fire that had lit up the whole auditorium the night of the rally, by the passion with which he'd spoken at the Conservancy meeting she'd attended the following week—it was only when they were apart that she was left wondering: *What the hell am I getting mixed up in here?* The latest involved her pitching *People* magazine (her idea, actually) for an article on the water war. When Hunter had suggested that she see Burt's operation for herself, reasoning that it would give her a better understanding of what they were up against, it had made sense at the time.

That was before she'd discovered that the road to the spring was heavily guarded, because of threats Overby had received, and that the only other way to it was on foot by way of trespassing. Jessie had heard enough stories about the cantankerous old man to know that her fears of what might happen if he caught them on his property were justified.

From the way Hunter was acting, though, you'd have thought that this was just an innocent nature hike. Only the alertness of his gaze and coiled tension in his body gave him away.

Jessie hugged herself against the chill. She didn't know if she was shivering from the cold . . . or from the close proximity to this man to whom she found herself strangely drawn. They'd met several times for coffee since the night of the rally. Each time, she'd told herself she was merely conducting research for the piece she hoped to write, and each time she'd come away with a smile on her lips and a bounce in her step, along with a little tremor in her belly like she got when she was in a high place looking down.

"I just hope it's worth the trouble we'll be in if we get caught," she told him.

"I'm a lot more concerned with what's going on just over that ridge." He nodded in the direction of the tree line, through which the sun's first rays glimmered.

Jessie instantly felt ashamed for being such a scaredy-cat.

"It's been a while since I've done an investigative piece," she confessed. "I just hope I can do it justice." Her last one, five years ago, on corruption at the Board of Education, had led to the firing of several officials. She felt something stir in her now at the prospect of actually making a difference.

She'd contacted the editor at *People* for whom she'd done articles in the past. He'd seemed interested, but only if she could place it in a larger context. Once she'd done a little digging, she'd discovered there were other towns, in various parts of the country, at war with corporations over water rights. Bottled water was a multibillion-dollar business, the sales of which had tripled in the past two decades. It had given her some idea of the scope of what they were up against.

"If nothing else, it's material for your next column."

"Thanks, but I already have enough to fill a book," she said. Within hours, every copy of this week's issue of *Savvy* had been sold out at Miller's Drugs, and everyone in town, it seemed, was talking about "Life Swap." "People I barely know have been coming up to me on the street, telling me their life stories, no doubt hoping I'll write about them."

"With me, it's the opposite," he said. "People I've known for years cross the street when they see me coming." He was referring to those, mainly business owners, who were profiting in some way from the boost to the local economy brought by Sylvan Glade. Clay Jenkins, from whom Sylvan Glade leased the bottling plant, was his most outspoken opponent.

Hunter, though, appeared unfazed. "It doesn't bother you?" she asked.

He flashed her a grin that went through her like a shot of whiskey, warming her insides and bringing a flush to her cheeks. "I enjoy a good fight," he said.

They'd reached the top of the rise, and now he paused to look around. The sky was lightening, the sun visible over the horizon. The only sounds were the breeze rustling in the pines and the cawing of a jay somewhere deep in the woods. He turned to her, putting a finger to his lips, then motioned toward the stand of trees below. Amid the branches, water glinted darkly, like tarnished silver. Her pulse quickened.

They started down the slope. They hadn't gone more

than fifty feet when he came to an abrupt halt, reaching
for her hand and gripping it so tightly she winced. That's
when she heard it: dogs barking in the distance. The tiny
hairs on the back of her neck stood up.

"I have a bad feeling about this," she muttered under
her breath.

"Yeah, me too."

From the set of his jaw as they stepped cautiously
from the underbrush onto a reedy bank, it was obvious he
wasn't referring to any danger they might be in. His steely
gaze was fixed on the opposite shore, where a cyclone
fence topped with razor wire enclosed the pumping station and two mammoth holding tanks.

This was no small-time operation. She'd learned from
the pamphlet put out by the Conservancy that water was
being pumped from this spring at the rate of two hundred
gallons a minute. If the hemorrhaging didn't stop, it
would mean the death of Willow Creek as they knew it.

Jessie thought of a quote from Mark Twain that she'd
come across in her research: *Whiskey is for drinking, and
water is for fighting.* If that was true, Hunter was in for the
fight of his life.

He wanted to get some close-range shots with his
Nikon, so they began making their way around to the opposite shore, climbing over rocks and ducking under low-
hanging branches. As they approached, the barking grew
louder, and Jessie's nerves quivered at the breaking point.
If not for Hunter leading the way, calm and steady, she
might have bolted.

At the same time, despite her panic, or maybe because of it, she felt more alive than she had in years, every sense alert and everything around her strangely magnified—the dew sparkling on the leaves and the sunlight glinting on the water, bright and sharp as shards of glass; the taut muscles in Hunter's shoulders under his denim shirt, and the sheen of sweat on the back of his neck. She could almost feel the heat coming off him, though he appeared cool as the shimmering surface over which his reflection glided.

As they neared the pumping station, she could see the graveled road leading up to it, where a tanker was parked, the muddy area around it gouged with tire ruts. Nearby stood a double-wide trailer that looked to be a field office. When they were close enough to get an unobstructed view, Hunter dug out his camera and began firing off shots.

He was tucking it back into its case when the silence was shattered by a shotgun blast. Ducks exploded into the air, squawking wildly, and Jessie's heart seemed to soar up along with them while the rest of her remained frozen in place, like Lot's wife. In the eerie stillness that followed the blast, she felt a strange, almost ethereal calm steal over her.

The next thing she knew, Hunter was yanking her to the ground.

"Come out, you tree-hugging son of a bitch, before I blow you to kingdom come!" bellowed a voice she recognized from the rally as Burt Overby's.

Hunter and Jessie remained pressed to the ground, the tall grass around them providing only the scantest of cover. The smell of wet earth rose around her, a smell that never failed to trigger a specific memory: that of her father being lowered into his grave. She began to tremble.

Hunter lifted his head to murmur, "He's only trying to scare us."

"Guess what? It's working," she replied in a panicked whisper.

She wondered if there was any truth to the rumor that Burt had a body or two buried on his land. But before she could give serious consideration to the strong likelihood that they would soon be joining those nameless victims, Hunter grabbed hold of her wrist and rose to a crouch, dragging her along with him as he made a break for the trees. Another shotgun blast rang out, and a strange heaviness descended over her, making her clumsy. She stumbled over a tree root and would have fallen if Hunter hadn't been propelling her along—she might have been a kite in tow for all that it slowed him down.

They were deep in the woods before he finally drew to a halt. Jessie doubled over, gasping for breath, a hand pressed to the burning stitch in her side. But when she looked over at Hunter, poised like a buck at the edge of a clearing, looking back the way they'd come, he seemed barely winded.

Satisfied that Overby was no longer in pursuit he relaxed his stance, giving her the all clear signal. It seemed an eternity nonetheless before they finally emerged from the trees onto the grassy berm bordering the highway. Hunter's Pathfinder was parked a short distance down the road, and when they reached it he had to give her a boost as she climbed in, her legs were so wobbly.

"You could have warned me," she said, anger taking the place of panic, now that the danger had passed. "I'd have worn my bulletproof vest."

"At least now you know what we're up against." His clothes were filthy, and streaks of mud stood out on his face—Geronimo meets Rambo. She could only imagine the state she was in.

"A lot of good it would've done if we'd been killed."

He didn't respond. He just sat there, his gaze fixed on her with an intensity nearly as unnerving as the scare they'd just had. He might not have been breathing, he was so still, the only movement the leafy shadows playing over his face. She could see the variegated hues in his eyes, like flaws in a gem. Eyes that seemed to challenge her, as they had that first day at the creek. When it grew unbearable she turned toward the window, feigning a sudden interest in the scenery.

At last, he said, "That was just the tip of the iceberg. It'll get uglier. I won't hold it against you if you decide to bail out."

She brought her gaze back to him. He was looking at her in a way that made her distinctly aware that whatever she felt for him, it wasn't one-sided. Also, of how far she was from Jonathon, and not just in terms of distance. A lazy warmth uncoiled in her chest and traveled down through her belly and below. When his hand floated up to pluck a foxtail—from her hair—it felt more intimate than if he'd kissed her.

Her voice emerged as a rusty croak. "I'm not a quitter."

"Good. That makes two of us."

His smile broke as slowly as the sunrise, hovering about his lips before spreading up into the creases around his eyes. The smile that had gotten her into this and that was about to get her into even more trouble if she didn't watch out—mysterious, seductive, irresistible. Even with all that she'd been through, she was helpless to keep from smiling back.

He pulled a handkerchief from the back pocket of his jeans and gently wiped the dirt from her cheeks. Jessie hadn't had anyone do that for her since she was little, and she was unexpectedly moved almost to tears. The warmth from his hand glowed like a sunburn on her skin. She closed her eyes, and after a moment she felt his arms circle her and the firm pressure of his mouth against hers. A kiss as direct and sure as the man himself—as if he understood things about her that she was only just beginning to know herself.

Somewhere in the depths of her mind a protest was trying to form, like some clumsy creature swimming to the surface; but she ignored it, opening her mouth to meet the thrust of his tongue.

She breathed in the resiny scent of pine sap mingled with the good masculine scent of his sweat. She pushed her hand up into his hair, which slid like warm oil through her fingers. Most men had only one gear: forward. But Hunter's kisses were a subtle dance, switching from forceful to gentle, then back again. When he caught her lower lip lightly between his teeth, running the tip of his tongue along its underside, the sensation was like an electrical shock.

She pulled back with a sharp intake of breath, thinking, *What the hell am I doing?*

For a long moment neither of them spoke. They just sat there eyeing each other, both a little dazed by what had just happened and not quite sure what to make of it.

Then, in a slightly unsteady voice, he said, "I could use a cup of coffee. How about you?"

She nodded mutely.

He started the engine, and they headed back toward town. As if nothing were out of the ordinary, as if she hadn't been turned inside out like a pocket full of loose change. She stared out the window, struggling to pull herself together. It wasn't as if she hadn't seen it coming. What she hadn't anticipated was the brute strength with which it would overtake her. If they hadn't been out in the open, heaven only knew where it would have led.

The realization left her profoundly shaken. She'd always thought of herself as a moral person. She'd never cheated on a boyfriend, even the ones who'd ultimately proven unworthy of her loyalty. It rocked her to the very core that she could have this strong a reaction to a man she hardly knew while still being in love with Jonathon. What kind of woman *was* she?

"What time do you have to be back?" he asked, as they were nearing town.

She glanced at her watch, surprised to see that it was only a little past eight—it felt as if a whole day had passed. "I'm in no rush. Why?" She'd left Maria in charge at the inn.

"The least I can do is buy you breakfast," he said, "after nearly getting you killed."

She realized suddenly that she was starving. "Do you know a good place?" Not much was open at this hour.

"Trust me," he said, tipping her a wink. "I won't lead you astray."

Too late, you already have, she thought.

They turned off the highway, leaving behind the fast-food franchises and strip malls that had metastasized along this stretch in recent years. The two-lane blacktop they were on now was lined with older, mom-and-pop businesses, many of which had been around since she was a kid, like Ferguson's Lumber and Jewell's Juntiques.

As they drove past the Sunrise Motel, she thought once more of how close she'd come to letting things get out of hand with Hunter. Even now, a part of her wanted nothing more than to tumble into bed with him, to feel his hands against her bare skin, his naked body pressed up against hers. She felt a pang of regret as the motel faded from view.

If you don't nip this in the bud, she told herself sternly, *you'll be even sorrier.*

*   *   *

His whole life, Hunter George had wondered what it would be like to inhabit a place the way you did your own skin. Growing up on the rez, he hadn't felt at home in either. There, he'd been more white than Indian; on the outside, more Indian than white. If there was a special category for half-breeds, it wasn't one anyone in their right mind would chose.

Every summer, as part of a church-sponsored program, he'd been sent to stay with a different Anglo family, presumably so he could see how the other half lived. At first, eager to fit in, he'd done his best to ingratiate himself. Not until the summer he was fourteen, when seemingly overnight he'd turned from a cute little Indian kid into a hulking adolescent with a voice like some mischievous *yei* that had taken up residence in his throat, did he realize that, while he could escape the rez, there was no escaping the color of his skin.

That summer he'd been staying with the Tilsons, who had a daughter his age. It had started innocently enough, with Marcy taking every opportunity to accidentally on purpose brush up against him when her parents weren't looking. It progressed to stolen kisses, then to necking. One day they were making out on Marcy's bed when Mr. Tilson walked in on them. They'd been fully clothed and not doing anything that would have earned more than a stern lecture had Hunter been a clean-cut white boy. But Mr. Tilson had flown into a rage, accusing Hunter of taking advantage of his daughter, even threatening to have him thrown in jail. The only thing that had kept him from being killed, Hunter was sure, was that it would have meant everyone's knowing what Marcy had been up to and with whom. Instead, he'd been on the next bus home.

He'd been with other Anglo women over the years. Some had seen him as a walk on the wild side; with others he'd enjoyed more meaningful relationships. He didn't know which category Jessie fit into. She wanted him as much as he wanted her, that much was clear. What he didn't know was where it would lead, and that made him nervous. He liked knowing where things stood, and right now all he knew was that there was nothing casual about the feelings she stirred in him.

He thought of how she'd looked the night of the rally, in her designer jeans and sleek leather jacket, with a haircut that had probably cost more than most of the people there earned in a week. Among the crowd milling about outside town hall, she'd stood out like a BMW in a parking lot full of Buicks. Even Jessie had seemed unsure of what she was doing there.

At one point during the meeting, which had quickly disintegrated into a shouting match, elderly Pearl Langley had struggled to her feet, wheeling her oxygen tank up the aisle. The crowd fell silent as she spoke haltingly into the microphone about her well running dry and the hardships she'd faced as a result. By the time she shuffled back to her seat, Pearl looked on the verge of collapse. Before anyone else could come to her aid, Jessie jumped up and rushed over to her. Hunter, watching her guide the old woman toward the exit, an arm around Pearl's waist, had guessed that this wasn't the last he'd see of Jessie Holland.

When she showed up at the Conservancy meeting the following Thursday, the older members had eyed her warily, no doubt wondering what this city slicker was doing in their midst. But she'd quickly won them over with her charm and her genuine interest in the cause. Before the meeting was out she'd become the heroine of the hour by volunteering to use her contact at *People* to get them national attention.

Their growing friendship was an added bonus. Hunter enjoyed spending time with her—even when he wasn't thinking about ripping off her clothes. They liked the same things and laughed at the same jokes. He'd quote a line from a book or a movie, and she immediately got the reference. And she was the only other person he knew of besides himself who could take the heat in the Iron Skillet's chili-laced omelet without batting an eye.

But after their kiss yesterday in the car, he'd realized he was in deeper than he'd thought. He hoped to get married someday and have kids, but he was in no rush. Lately, though, his formerly nameless, faceless future wife had begun to look a lot like Jessie, and it scared him. He knew that she had a boyfriend back home and that she was only here for a short time. After a sleepless night of wrestling with it, he'd decided it would be best to maintain a friendly distance.

Which was why, at two o'clock the following afternoon, when he found himself driving to the inn, a large bouquet of peonies on the passenger seat beside him, he felt like the world's biggest fool headed for a fall. He hadn't intended to buy her flowers, but earlier, when he'd been walking through the farmer's market, the peonies had jumped out at him, pink and white blossoms the size of small cabbages. The next thing he knew he was scooping up every peony in the flower seller's stall.

When he reached the inn he had a moment of indecision, but it was too late. Maria happened to be outside greeting some early arrivals, and she waved before walking over to his SUV. She eyed the bouquet, smiling as if she knew the score.

"She's in the basement," Maria told him, hooking a thumb toward the inn.

Shyness wasn't in his nature, but he suddenly felt as he had in the fourth grade on his way to present his teacher, Miss McCutcheon, on whom he'd had a crush, with a pinecone turkey he'd made for her. "These need to be in water," he said, noting that a few of the peonies had started to wilt.

Maria laughed. "Oh, there's no shortage of that around here."

He saw what she'd meant as soon as he descended into the basement to find it flooded. Jessie, in man-sized rubber boots, her hair disheveled and splotches of water standing out on her jeans, looked up from the washing machine she was struggling to wrestle away from the wall. She turned bright red. "Oh, God." Her hands flew up to rake her fingers through her hair. "I must look like a mess."

"You look beautiful," he said.

She turned even redder. "I wasn't expecting company."

He looked down at the inch or so of water covering the concrete floor. "What happened here?"

"That's what I'm trying to figure out." She eyed the washing machine in despair. "I'm pretty hopeless when it comes to appliances."

"Let me have a look."

As soon as he'd pulled the machine away from the wall he saw what was wrong. "The hose is loose," he told her. A few turns with a wrench did the trick. He pushed the washing machine back into place. "There. That should hold, at least until it's not your problem anymore."

She set it for the wash cycle, and when it started churning she sloshed over to the staircase and sank down on the bottom step. Her gaze fell at last on the bouquet in its paper cone, atop a stack of boxes marked XMAS DECORATIONS. "Flowers . . . how lovely." She picked them up and buried her face in the bright, nodding blooms, inhaling deeply. "You shouldn't have." She was smiling, but he had the sense that she meant what she'd said.

"I wanted to make up for yesterday."

"Really, it wasn't necessary."

"It's not much." Suddenly he didn't know what to do with his hands.

"You came at the right time, though. I don't know what I'd have done if you hadn't showed up when you did. Try finding a repairman on Sunday."

He leaned up against the banister, looking down at her. A hank of her hair had slipped down over one cheek. He fought the urge to reach down and tuck it back behind her ear. "In that case, I'm glad I could be of service."

"I don't want you to think of me as a damsel in distress. I'm usually pretty self-reliant."

"I can see that."

"I don't mean just today," she said, referring to yesterday's near miss.

"You had every right to be scared."

There was an awkward moment in which he sensed she was thinking the same thing he was: That Burt Overby's chasing them wasn't the only close call. Then Jessie cleared her throat. "Look, Hunter, I'm not . . ." She caught her lower lip between her teeth, and he remembered the feel of its soft underside against the tip of his tongue. "I don't usually go around kissing men that I'm not . . . involved with—romantically, that is."

He shrugged. "No harm done." His tone was light, but in his mind he was seeing Mr. Tilson's furious red face. *What's wrong? Aren't I good enough for you?* he wanted to cry. But the rational part of his brain knew this wasn't about the color of his skin or the fact that he'd grown up on the rez.

She looked up at him, as if appealing to him. She wasn't wearing any makeup, and it made her appear vulnerable somehow. His heart caught. "In another time and another place maybe," she said with what sounded like genuine regret. "I'm sorry if I gave you the wrong impression, but Jonathon and I . . ." It was the first time he'd heard her refer to him as anything other than "my boyfriend." "We're still very much together."

"It won't happen again," he said as if it were no big deal.

Her face relaxed. "Thanks for being so understanding."

"What are friends for?"

She found a couple of mops and a bucket, and he helped her mop the floor. They were finishing up when a voice called from above, "Aunt Jess! Phone!"

Jessie craned to look up at the girl who'd appeared at the top of the stairs; Hunter recognized her as Erin's teenage daughter, Kayla. "Who is it?" she called up to her.

The washing machine kicked into the spin cycle just then, drowning out Kayla's response. "Who?" Jessie called again, louder this time, and when Kayla shouted the name it seemed to echo off the walls and still-glistening floor like yesterday's shotgun blast.

"Jonathon!"

Jessie waited until that evening to call Erin, after she'd finished locking up for the night and was luxuriating on Erin's bed, a mound of pillows at her back, sipping a glass of sherry from the decanter in the great room.

"What a day," she said, blowing out a breath.

"What now?" Erin asked.

"The basement flooded, for one thing."

"Welcome to my world," Erin said with a laugh. She sounded remarkably unconcerned for someone who, just weeks before, had fretted over every little household crisis.

"It turned out to be a loose hose on the washer. Hunter fixed it."

"That was neighborly of him," Erin said. Jessie thought she detected a wry note in her voice.

"He just happened to be here. He was dropping something off." Jessie was quick to downplay it, not wanting Erin to get the wrong idea. Yesterday, when Jessie had given her an account of the hair-raising brush with Overby, she'd left out the part about Hunter's kissing her afterward. She was doing her best to pretend that it hadn't happened, and she knew that Erin would never let her forget it.

"How convenient." Erin managed to inject volumes of meaning into the observation. "What was he dropping off?"

Jessie hesitated, then confessed, "Flowers."

"Really?" Erin sounded more amused than surprised. "What kind?"

"Peonies," Jessie said impatiently. "What difference does it make?"

"A lot," Erin said. "Roses are the obvious choice. Any guy could've thought of that. Peonies, on the other hand—a guy who'd bring you peonies is a guy who knows what he's doing."

Jessie didn't know if it was the sherry or the disturbing

turn the conversation had taken that was making her feel warm inside and out. "Funny, I seem to recall your saying he wasn't my type. Anyway, what about Jonathon?"

"What about him?"

"I thought you liked him."

"I do. It's just . . ." Erin was breathing hard as if from exertion, and Jessie could hear traffic sounds in the background. She pictured Erin striding along the sidewalk at her usual breakneck pace. "I'm not sure if he's right for you."

Jessie thought back to his untimely phone call earlier in the day. It turned out he was free the weekend after next, and he'd wanted to know if that was a good time for him to visit. Of course, she'd said yes. So why wasn't she more excited? Instead, all she could think about was Hunter. She'd replayed his kiss in her mind a thousand times, burning at the memory—not entirely from shame. She thought about it in the shower with the warm water trickling over her breasts. At night, she tossed and turned, unable to sleep. She was hoping a long weekend with Jonathon would cure her of the fever and banish any doubts she was having.

"You only had dinner with him once," Jessie reminded her.

"True, so let's just say the jury is still out. Anyway, I'm the last person who should be handing out advice. Ann Landers would have a field day with me." Erin sighed.

"It could be worse." Jessie was relieved to be changing the subject. "Skip might have his head up his ass, but there's at least one man who isn't immune to your charms." She was referring to Drew, who was clearly smitten with Erin, even if she chose to ignore that fact—leaving aside her momentary lapse, which, according to Erin, would never be repeated.

Erin groaned. "If you mean Drew, you can forget it. It's not going anywhere. Whatever I might think of Skip at the moment, the fact is I'm . . . *Shit*. I stepped in something." There was a pause, and Jessie heard the sound of Erin attempting to scrape whatever it was off her shoe. "Just my luck. I'll show up at Enzo's smelling like dog poop."

"Enzo, is it?" Jessie teased. Erin and Lorenzo Carrera, otherwise known as the Singing Chef, had become quite chummy in the short time she'd been working at the Cooking Channel.

"It's a cocktail party," Erin was quick to inform her. "Lots of other people are going to be there. Besides, he's old enough to be my father."

"From what I've read in the tabloids, that doesn't seem to stop him."

"Don't believe everything you read."

"That reminds me, any more feedback on our column?" In Willow Creek, they'd become overnight celebrities, but she knew that with media-bombarded New Yorkers it might take a while to catch on.

"Clive still can't stop talking about it, of course. But except for the few people who came up to me at work, most either haven't connected the dots, or they're not all that interested. We're just little fish in a big pond."

"Here, we're the catch of the day," Jessie informed her. "The other day Nellie Harris at the A&P asked me for my autograph." At the moment she didn't miss the bustling anonymity of New York, where celebrities and A-listers were a dime a dozen. It was kind of nice being the flavor of the moment, even if it was the only flavor Willow Creek had.

"What was Skip's reaction?" Erin was trying to be nonchalant, but Jessie heard a little flutter of anxiety in her voice.

"I wouldn't know. He hasn't said a word to me. Why don't you ask him yourself?"

Jessie smoothed a hand over the quilt that covered the bed, one that Erin had fashioned out of scraps from old clothes—patches of corduroy from the Oshkosh overalls Kayla had worn as a toddler, soft as velvet, and ones of faded denim from jeans that might have been Skip's; flowered remnants from Erin's Laura Ashley phase, and snippets of lilac taffeta from a long-ago bridesmaid dress; what was left of the green velveteen elf costume Kayla had worn in her fourth-grade Christmas play. A collection of memories from happier times that seemed especially poignant in light of how things had played out.

"He never gives me a chance. Whenever we talk, it's strictly business." Erin sounded more sad than bitter.

"Well, at least you're talking."

There was a brief pause, in which Jessie could hear traffic sounds and the bleating of car horns. "How'd it go at the bake sale?" Erin shifted gears, becoming purpose-fully upbeat.

Last Friday, Kayla's freshman class had held a bake sale to raise money for one of their classmates, a boy with leukemia, and Kayla had asked Jessie to help out. Now she rolled her eyes, and said, "I was the only one there without a wedding ring. I felt like Rip Van Winkle." The mothers at the bake sale had been nice, but the main topic of conversation had been their husbands and kids. "At the rate I'm going, if I ever have a kid, I'll be paying for diapers out of my Social Security check."

"You're not alone. The other day, I complimented this gray-haired lady on her cute grandbaby. You should've seen the look she gave me."

Jessie smiled knowingly. In Manhattan, first-time moms over the age of forty were commonplace, but in Willow Creek, they were the exception.

"How's work?" she asked.

"Still crazy, though not as bad as the first week. And my boss is a prick. But Enzo's great. He's been teaching me the tricks of the trade—it's like a master class for one." Jessie could hear the excitement in her voice. It was what Erin had always dreamed of.

"I'm glad it's going so well."

"It's not all truffles and caviar."

"But you don't regret it?"

"No," Erin said, though Jessie thought she detected a note of wistfulness in her voice.

"Me either." Despite kitchen disasters and malfunctioning appliances.

They shared a moment of silent communion, then Erin said, "This looks like the right address. I'd better go. I'll call you tomorrow, okay?"

Jessie mulled over the conversation as she was brushing her teeth before bed. Funny how Erin hadn't seemed the least bit interested in how things were going at the inn. She used to grill Jessie constantly. Was she so preoccupied with her new job, or was it just that Jessie was giving her less to worry about these days?

It occurred to her, not for the first time, that when the six months were up Erin might very well decide to stay on in New York. And if so, was it completely out of the question that Jessie might do the same—opt to remain in Willow Creek? The bottom dropped out of her stomach at the thought, but she instantly dismissed it as ridiculous. There was about as much chance of that happening as of her running off to Vegas with Hunter George.

ERIN:

The weird thing about being "famous" is that you don't actually have to be a celebrity to have people think you're somebody. Let me back up a little. Okay, so there I am in my third week as a production assistant at the Cooking Channel, keeping an eye out from the wings for disruptive audience members while The Singing Chef *show is being taped, when suddenly I hear the man himself call out my name—my Robin Quivers moment. I look up and there's my face on the monitor overhead, like a deer caught in headlights. I don't remember what I said, but it must've been something clever, or maybe it was just the goofy grin on my face, because the audience cracked up.*

Since then it's gotten to be kind of a semiregular thing. The Singing Chef *will toss me a line, and I'll toss one back. Why me? I'm not really sure. But I guess for every Howard Stern there has to be a Robin Quivers—it's like a law of nature, or something. Now when I'm out and about in the world I occasionally get recognized. The other day, a waitress at the Tick-Tock Diner said she'd seen me on TV, though she couldn't think where. Then her face lit up, and she said, "You're Courtney Cox, aren't you?" (I take that as a compliment, though I'm not sure Courtney would agree.) When I politely informed her that she was mistaken, she scratched her head and asked, "Are you sure?" And the other night I went to this glitzy benefit, where the Singing Chef was signing copies of his latest cookbook. I happened to be the first one out of the limo, and suddenly there I was, surrounded by paparazzi, all those flashbulbs going off at once, everyone shouting at me to smile for the camera, even though not a single one of them knew who the hell I was. . . .*

From "Life Swap"

Chapter Nine

Six months ago, had anyone told Erin she'd one day be doing a guest spot on *The Singing Chef* show, she'd have said they were nuts. The way it came about was as a result of a simple twist of fate. The guest booked for that day's segment, the pastry chef from the hot new restaurant Forte, had canceled at the last minute due to a sudden illness, which had thrown Robert into a swivet. Enzo was to prepare Cornish hen *en croute*, and the puff pastry was a key element of the demonstration. If they couldn't find a replacement, the entire show would have to be restructured, with less than an hour to spare. Erin walked into a staff meeting to find her boss stomping about, hurling abuse at everyone, which he was in the habit of doing whenever anything went wrong, and before she knew what she was saying, the words were out of her mouth.

"I know how to make puff pastry."

Robert stopped his pacing to stare at her. "And why exactly," he asked in a voice dripping with scorn, "should that be of the slightest interest to *us*?"

Bile rose in Erin's throat. She'd had all the bullying she could take from him and was on the verge of telling him to put it where the sun don't shine when Andrea Fowler, one of the associate producers, piped meekly, "I don't see why she couldn't fill in for Claude. She's good on camera, and the viewers are familiar with her."

Erin flashed her a grateful look, and Andrea offered her a tentative smile in return, one that withered instantly in the death-ray beam of their boss's glare. Then someone else— Gil Dyson, whose job it was to book the guests and who clearly had an enlightened self-interest in all this—chimed in, "Why don't you run it by Enzo, see what he has to say?"

A hush fell over the room, then in a cold, bright voice Robert replied, "Now why didn't *I* think of that? Oh yes, let's *do* see what Enzo has to say. I'm sure he'd be thrilled to have a *PA*"—he spat out the title as if it were a dirty word—"cohosting his show."

To prove his point, he grabbed the phone and punched in the number for Enzo's private line, putting him on speakerphone so they could all hear him laugh at the absurdity of the idea. Instead, to Robert's utter amazement, Enzo embraced it as enthusiastically as if Erin weren't a poor second but his first choice.

Erin wasn't as surprised as everyone else. From day one, Enzo had taken her under his wing, going out of his way to instruct her in everything from how to make the perfect *beurre blanc* to the most flattering camera angles. Erin, not wanting to stir up jealousy among her coworkers, had kept the special nature of their relationship to herself for the most part. Only a few people on the culinary staff, as separate from the "back of the house" where she worked as church from state, knew about the time she spent in the prep kitchen with Enzo after-hours.

She was nonetheless panic-stricken at the thought of being on camera. Tossing off a line or two from the wings was one thing, but this—how on earth was she going to pull this off? As the hour approached, she became a nervous wreck. Her hands wouldn't stop trembling, and she was sweating so much that Vivian, in makeup, had to powder her face before she could apply a coat of base. When Vivian was done working her magic, one of the sound technicians clipped a lavalier mike to the chef's whites Erin had buttoned on over her dress.

She spent the next ten minutes pacing nervously backstage, awaiting her cue. When she heard her name announced onstage, she froze. It was a moment before she could collect her wits and walk out onto the set to the accompaniment of polite applause and a drumroll from the band.

At first there was only a hot blaze of lights. She stood there, paralyzed, wearing a stupid grin, unable to think about anything but all those people watching her, not just the studio audience but the millions of TV viewers who'd be tuning in when the show aired. Then Enzo caught her eye and winked, and she felt the bolts holding her limbs locked in place loosen a half turn. She remembered his advice: to just be herself. It was okay if you were a little nervous, he'd said, people could relate to you that way.

Turning to the audience, she said, "I'm new to all this, folks, so bear with me. I'm just a country innkeeper, and the only other time I was on TV was when one of our guests got his big toe stuck in the bathtub spigot, and a news crew showed up along with the paramedics." KPNX, out of Phoenix, happened to be in town covering another story at the time.

The audience chuckled appreciatively. It had the effect of a drug, bringing a rush of exhilaration. *I can do this*, Erin thought. All she had to do was forget about the cameras, and she'd be fine. Soon she found herself—the Erin that had once tap-danced on the coffee table in her parents' living room—chatting easily with Enzo while tossing together the ingredients set out in transparent glass bowls, in what she hoped would be a decent *choux*.

It wasn't all that different from what she did at the inn. Often a guest would wander into the kitchen while she was cooking, then hang around to schmooze. And growing up, she'd learned from the best—her mom. Erin used to watch her with the regulars at the diner, doling out a teasing remark here and a swat on the hand there when one of the guys got too frisky, making it seem like a big, fractious family she was feeding rather than a job that left her with swollen feet at the end of the day.

When the Cornish hens *en croute* emerged from the oven, their crusts perfectly browned, it seemed that only minutes had elapsed instead of the better part of an hour. After the guests at the café tables in front had sampled the food, making the usual appreciative noises, the band struck up, signaling that it was time for the sign-out. The audience applauded Erin warmly, and roared when Enzo threw his head back and broke into an aria from *The Barber of Seville*. It wasn't until the lights went down and the cameras stopped rolling that Erin felt the surge of energy that had sustained her on the set drain from her as if she, too, had been switched off. She wobbled offstage, her knees threatening to buckle with each step.

The crew members gathered around to congratulate her. Minutes later, in the staff room, even Robert looked pleased, though naturally he was hogging all the credit, as if it had been his idea all along.

The following day Erin was called into the executive producer's office. "Nice going yesterday," Latrice complimented her. "You clearly have a knack for this."

"Beginner's luck," Erin replied with a shrug, not wanting Latrice to think she'd gotten a swelled head.

"You're a little rough around the edges, but that's only natural considering it was your first time. With practice you'll be fine," Latrice went on. "In fact, I have a proposition for you. How would you feel about taking over for Kendra while she's on maternity leave?"

Kendra Shaw hosted *Sugar & Spice*, which aired in the 7:30 A.M. slot. Erin was so stunned, it was a moment before she could stammer, "I . . . I don't know what to say." Yesterday's stunt had been the equivalent of lifting a car off someone trapped underneath, a heroic effort she wasn't confident she could repeat.

Latrice reminded her that Kendra's show was straight to tape, which meant no live studio audience, thus less pressure. It was twenty segments that would air in June; she'd tape two a day over the next couple of weeks.

"You don't want me to audition?" Erin asked, still thunderstruck.

Latrice broke into a wide grin. "Honey, you just did." She plucked a videocassette from her desk and handed it to Erin. "Study it. See where you can improve. In the meantime, I'll have Harvey draw up a contract." She went on to explain that the standard fee was five thousand a segment. Not all in a lump sum, of course—still, an amount so staggering to Erin, for whom two-ply toilet paper had once been a luxury, she was left momentarily speechless.

Staring at the cassette in her hands, she knew just how Aladdin must have felt, rubbing his magic lamp for the first time. What she didn't know was if this would turn out to be a dream come true . . . or a case of being careful what you wish for.

Later, back at the apartment, she played and replayed the tape until she had it memorized. At first, she couldn't believe that was *her* up on the screen. Who was that woman looking so at ease? Then she'd begun picking out the flaws. The hems and haws, the sheen of sweat on her forehead, the awkward moment when she fumbled with one of the bowls and almost dropped it. Her voice sounded nasal like it did on answering machines, and what was with that thing she did with her upper lip when she laughed? She took notes and practiced in front of the mirror. She paced the room with a book on her head to improve her posture.

At last, she collapsed on the sofa. Her reward was the video that had come in that day's mail. When she and Kayla had first talked seriously about her going to New York, Erin had agreed to it on one condition: That each week, in addition to regular phone calls and emails, Kayla would send her a videotaped message so Erin wouldn't feel so homesick. Now she drank in the sight of her daughter seated cross-legged on her bed, Otis stretched out beside her, Kayla filling her in on everything that had happened since last week. Most of which Erin already knew from talking to her on the phone: Kayla had dropped out of the glee club and was thinking of running for student council, which would look better on her college résumé; she and her classmates were organizing a car wash to raise more money for Phillip Drobowski, who needed a bone marrow transplant; and the other day Aunt Jess had taken her shopping and bought her this awesome sweater. Erin could barely concentrate on what she was saying, though; she was too fixated by Kayla's appearance: Her fourteen-year-old daughter was wearing makeup, and her formerly honey blond hair was at least three shades lighter.

As if on cue, Kayla moved in closer, grabbing a handful of her hair to show off its new highlights. "Oh, and check this out. Didn't Aunt Jess do the most *amazing* job? Practically professional." She sat back. "Well. That's about it. I hope everything's okay with you." Almost as an afterthought, she added, "I miss you, Mom."

Erin felt suddenly and uncharacteristically furious with her best friend. For weeks it had been Aunt Jess this, Aunt Jess that. It seemed Jessie was a guru in everything from fashion to the latest music trends, where Erin was apparently clueless about such matters. Normally, Erin didn't mind too much—it was easy to remain on a pedestal when you weren't the one making the rules—but this time Jessie had gone too far. *I'm her mother, damn it,* she silently cursed. Jessie could have at least asked her permission. What was next—a pierced navel, blue hair?

At the same time, she realized that part of the reason she was upset was because Kayla was growing up. Without her. Erin had watched her take her first steps. She'd dried Kayla's tears after every crushing disappointment and expired pet, and had been there for every bump and bruise and doctor's appointment. Now, her child was moving into adulthood, and Erin could only watch from a distance.

She was getting up to punch the rewind button when a scene from one of their home movies jumped to life on the screen—Kayla must have accidentally taped over it. Erin watched, transfixed, as a much younger Skip, bare-

chested and wearing baggy shorts, swooped three-year-old
Kayla up into the air while she crowed with delight. Erin's
younger self stood off to one side, grinning as she looked
on. Her hair had been longer then and her skin deeply
tanned from working in the yard, but the most striking
thing about her was how happy she'd looked. As if the
thought that her husband might one day leave her were as
remote as that of him sprouting wings and flying off.

They'd been having a barbecue that day to inaugurate
the newly installed pool. There was a blurry sequence of
Skip jumping in with a huge splash, followed by a drip-
ping-wet Erin playfully batting him over the head with one
of Kayla's inflatable water wings while Skip tried to snatch
it from her hands. Off camera, she could hear Mike's
voice—he'd been the one filming them—call laughingly,
"Hey, cut it out you two, before I call the cops. . . ."

We were good together, she thought, her eyes welling
with tears. It hadn't always been a battleground. She recalled the time, after a sweaty morning of hauling rocks
up from the creek for the retaining wall, they'd taken off
all their clothes, right there in broad daylight, and gone
skinny-dipping. Afterward, they'd made love under the
lacy tent of a weeping willow.

Then there was the time she'd been in the hospital
after her appendix was taken out, more miserable over the
fact that she was missing out on the first spring blossoms
than that she was stuck in bed. Skip had surprised her
with Polaroids he'd taken of their fruit trees in bloom.
Long after the flowers sent by well-wishers had withered

and died, those photos served to remind her, not just of the season, but of her husband's love.

She remembered, too, Skip's reaction when she'd told him she was pregnant. She'd still been reeling from the news herself and had expected him to be equally shocked and upset—they'd only been seeing each other for a few months, marriage the furthest thing from either of their minds. Instead he'd put his arms around her and held her for the longest time. When at last he drew back, he was smiling. "I love you," he'd said. Just that, nothing more. Three weeks later they were exchanging vows at the courthouse.

Erin, wiping a tear from her eye, reached for the phone and, before she could change her mind, punched in Mike's number. After several rings, Mike's deep voice answered, "*Playboy* mansion."

An old joke worn thin, which now carried a worrisome connotation. Mike was always ribbing Skip about being a family man, as if to remind him of all the pleasures, carnal and otherwise, that he was missing out on. Now she wondered if he'd taken it a step further, if he were introducing his brother to the freewheeling bachelor life he so enjoyed.

"It's me, Erin," she said.

There was an awkward pause before Mike said, "Hey, sis. How's life in the big, bad city?"

"Believe it or not, I'm still in one piece."

"Seriously, everything okay?" The laughter went out of Mike's voice.

"Everything's fine. How about you?"

"Same old, same old. Working too hard, and not getting any younger."

"Aren't we all." She paused a moment before asking as casually as she could, "Is Skip around?"

"He just walked in." Mike pulled the receiver away from his ear to yell, "Dude! It's your wife!"

A moment later Skip's voice came on the line. "Hi," he said cautiously. "What's up?"

"Nothing much. You just get off work?" She maintained a casual tone despite her heart racing. On the TV screen, the younger Skip, still dripping from the pool, was chasing her around the patio as she squealed in mock panic. It seemed a cruel joke.

"I got off a couple of hours ago," he said. "I was helping Kayla with her homework. By the way, she's thinking of running for student council."

"I know. She told me."

He chuckled softly. "She's going places, that girl."

"You were like that at her age, as I recall." In high school, in addition to being on the football team, Skip had been on at least four committees.

"Yeah, and look at me now—hanging Sheetrock for a living," he said with a bitter laugh.

"It's nothing to be ashamed of." Even as she spoke, she knew how hollow her words must sound. She wanted to tell him how sorry she was that she'd prevented him from fulfilling his dream, that not a day went by when she didn't replay it in her mind—the afternoon he'd come back from town brimming with excitement over the opportunity to buy out his former boss—and wish it had come out differently.

"It pays the bills," he said curtly.

Desperate to change the subject, she asked lightly, "You and Mike getting on each other's nerves yet?"

There was a brief pause, then he said in a low, cautious voice, "Actually, I'm thinking of getting my own place."

"I see." Suddenly she was having trouble breathing.

"I wasn't going to say anything until I had something lined up," he went on. "I haven't even told Mike." As if that was supposed to make her feel better.

"So I guess this is it," she said in a queer, flat voice. "You're not coming back."

"I think it's for the best. For now, at least."

"Just like that? Without even discussing it with me?"

"I think we've said everything there is to say."

Oh, no, we haven't. Not by a long shot. Anger swelled in Erin like waves from a storm far out at sea, but she struggled to rein it in. She'd eat a little humble pie if need be to keep from losing Skip. "I was thinking we could talk it over when I got home," she said as evenly as she could.

"And just when will that be?" he asked coolly.

"Not long. A few more months." Surely, he could wait until then.

"So, let me get this straight. I'm supposed to put my life on hold until *you* decide to come home?"

"It's not like that. You know as well as I do—"

"All I know," he broke in, "is that I'm here busting my butt while you're drinking champagne and riding around in limos."

So that's what's eating him, she thought. He'd clearly formed the mistaken opinion, from reading about her exploits in "Life Swap," that she was living the high life, her husband the furthest thing from her mind. Erin might have seen it as a hopeful sign—at least he cared enough to be pissed off—if he weren't acting like such a jerk.

"I wouldn't even *be* here if it weren't for you!" she cried.

"You don't seem to be suffering any," he observed coldly.

It was the same old carousel going round and round. She desperately wanted to get off, but she didn't know how. Instead, she found herself saying in a sarcastic tone, "Amazing, isn't it? I didn't fall on my ass." Well, except for that one time. "As a matter of fact, things are going so well, I'm thinking of making it permanent!"

If Skip could have seen the horrified look on her face just then, he'd have known she didn't mean it, that she'd only said it to get back at him. The thought *had* crossed her mind, sure, but she'd never seriously considered it. Her home, her life, was in Willow Creek.

There was a long silence at the other end that spoke louder than any words. Then, in a voice of cold indifference that chilled her to the bone, he said, "Do what you like, but Kayla's not going anywhere."

Wounded, Erin snapped, "Doesn't she get a say in this?"

"I'm warning you, Erin. Don't put any ideas into her head."

"Or what? You'll take me to court?" As soon as the words were out, Erin wanted to snatch them back. Would she ever learn to *think* before opening her big mouth?

"You got that right," he said.

Erin took a deep breath and counted to ten the way she'd been taught to do as a child. "Look," she said, struggling to keep her voice even. "I didn't call to pick a fight. I just wanted—" She broke off. If she were to tell him the real reason she'd called, because she'd been remembering the good times, wishing they could find their way back to that, would it change anything? The realization that it might not gave way to a crushing sense of despair.

Skip let out a breath at the other end. "I don't want to fight either. I know you didn't mean what you just said, so let's leave it at that, okay?"

She heaved a sigh, her gaze straying to the TV screen, where five-year-old Kayla sat at a picnic table holding a huge slice of watermelon, more dirt on her face than on the ground. "Remember the summer we went camping at Eagle Lake?" she asked softly.

"How could I forget? It rained for three days straight. I thought we'd never dry out."

"You made up for it by taking me out to dinner when we got home. We both drank too much champagne, as I recall." She smiled at the memory.

"I sobered up fast when I saw the bill."

"Oh, Skip." Her voice cracked.

"We had some good times," he acknowledged, sounding wistful.

Suddenly she wanted to take it all back, every harsh word. Was it too late to start over? Maybe not, but at the moment the enormity of the task seemed overwhelming. Unable to voice what was in her heart, she drew in a trembling breath and said, "Listen, I should go. . . ."

She yearned for him to say the magic word: *Don't.* Then she'd have known there was still a chance. But it seemed the young husband who'd filmed her asleep on the screened porch of the cabin they'd rented when their campsite washed out, moving in for a close-up of her sleeping face, had been replaced by an angry, embittered man who'd risk losing everything rather than forgive her.

Erin mentally kicked herself as soon as she'd hung up. If he hadn't forgiven her, maybe it was because she hadn't *asked* him to. She could have told him how sorry she was, that she'd acted out of old fears that had nothing to do with him. Maybe then they could have put all this behind them and moved on.

Desperate at the thought of the long, lonely night ahead, she reached for the phone and started to punch in Drew's number. Then she thought better of it and lowered the receiver into its cradle. If Drew came over, it might lead to something she wasn't ready for. And before she climbed into bed with him again she had to be sure her marriage was really over.

If it isn't already, she thought bleakly.

*   *   *

"Dude, you okay?"

Skip, staring sightlessly at the receiver in his hand, dragged his head up to meet his brother's concerned gaze. "I'm fine," he answered in a strange, hollow voice.

"The old lady giving you grief?"

Skip shook his head. "Nah. She just called to see how I was doing."

"Yeah, right." Mike gave a snort. "I'll bet she was checking up on you, making sure you weren't out getting laid."

"Thanks for the insight," Skip replied sarcastically.

"Trust me, I know women."

"All you know," Skip said, "is where to put it."

Mike grinned as if it were a compliment. "Something you, my man, have clearly forgotten."

Skip watched his brother cross the living room on his way into the kitchen. The house, in one of the newer sub-divisions Mike had built, was decorated in what Skip could only have described as Early Bachelor, epitomized by the brand-new, top-of-the-line leather recliner nestled beside the hand-me-down sofa from their parents' den. On the wall above the sofa hung Mike's most prized possession: a framed poster from the first Woodstock concert, which he was too young to have attended but which held an almost mystical draw for him. Mike might be a harddriving contractor whose partying was limited to a beer or two in the evening, but somewhere on his soul was etched the sixties anthem: drugs, sex, and rock and roll.

He hadn't always been like this. In high school, he'd been a little wild, sure, but once he and Jessie got serious he'd settled down and started thinking about the future. Something in him was irreparably broken the day she walked out on him; he was never the same after that.

Skip watched his brother moving about the kitchen that opened onto the living room. Mike grabbed a beer from the fridge, popping the top with the bottle opener bolted to the wall beside it. He took a long swallow before pausing to regard Skip across the butcher-block counter, with the air of a guru about to impart some life-changing piece of wisdom.

"My advice is, don't show all your cards," he said. "You want to keep her guessing. Nothing like a little uncertainty to bring a woman to her knees."

Skip couldn't remember a time when his older brother hadn't known what was best for him. *Go for it, dude, you know you want it,* Mike would urge when Skip, as a teenager, was reluctant to make a move on a girl . . . or flash a fake ID . . . or cut school. He'd rarely followed that advice, yet at some level hadn't he envied his brother's freewheeling ways? There'd been no wife to remind Mike of his responsibilities when he decided to go into business for himself. And look at him now, so busy he was turning away work.

"The last time I took your advice," Skip reminded him, "I ended up with eighteen stitches in my head." He fingered the scar over his right eyebrow, a legacy of the time, when he was ten, he'd popped a wheelie, at Mike's urging, and gone flying over the handlebars to land on his head on the pavement.

Mike padded back into the living room in his stockinged feet, beer in hand. His curly brown hair, bleached to a lighter shade by the sun, was speckled with plaster from the house they were framing up on Las Cruces. He was muscular from a lifetime of hard physical labor, but Skip couldn't help noticing the inch or so of gut pushing out over his belt—the years of frozen pizzas and FritoLays were finally catching up with him.

Mike paused to look down at Skip pityingly. "I mean, for all you know she could be getting some herself."

Skip felt something twist in his gut. "Watch your mouth."

But Mike wasn't letting up. "No disrespect, you know how I feel about Erin. Don't forget, I was the one who stuck up for her when Mom and Dad were all set to run her out of town. But the plain fact is *you* were the one who walked out. And I've never known a woman who didn't see that as license for some serious payback."

Skip abruptly rose from his chair and stalked into the kitchen. The groceries he'd bought on the way home were still in their sacks on the counter, and he began putting them away, wrenching cupboards open and slamming them shut hard enough to rattle the dirty dishes in the sink.

Mike looked on with the expression of a benign parent whose patience was wearing thin. "I know it's not what you want to hear," he said, "but I think you *both* owe it to yourselves to see what else is out there."

Skip crammed a bag of nearly melted french fries into the freezer. "I get it, Mike. Now will you shut the fuck up?" His brother, he'd noticed, had been increasingly outspoken on the subject of his marriage ever since Jessie had taken up residence at the inn. Mike hadn't seen her, and he had no intention of seeing her—he avoided the inn like it was Chernobyl—but she was having an effect on him nonetheless.

"Dude, if ever I saw a man in desperate need of a lay, it's you," Mike went on, undeterred.

"I mean it, Mike." Skip spoke in a low, warning voice.

"Jeannie Rivington, runs that art gallery over on Mesa? You'd have to be blind not to have noticed the way she was checking you out the other night at the Spur. I'm telling you, dude, all you'd have to do is—"

Skip swung around, fists clenched. "Back. Off."

"Okay, okay. I can take a hint." Mike threw up his hands in mock surrender, giving him a look that seemed to say, *You know I'm right, even if you won't admit it.*

"We're having problems, sure, but it's got nothing to do with either of us wanting to fool around," Skip informed him coldly. At the same time, his brother had planted a seed of doubt. Skip's gut gave another viscious twist at the mental image of Erin in bed with another man.

"All I'm saying is, maybe it's time to move on," Mike said, with the faintly injured air of someone who'd only had his brother's best interests at heart.

Skip stood with his head low and his palms flat against

the counter, elbows locked. He took slow, deep breaths until he'd regained sufficient composure to bring his head up to meet his brother's gaze. "You're right. It *is* time to move on."

Mike got his meaning, and his face fell. "That not what I meant."

All at once, Skip felt the anger go out of him. If it weren't for Mike, he wouldn't have a job and a roof over his head. "I've overstayed my welcome as it is," he said more gently. He could crash at the inn, the attic room reserved for overflow, until he found his own place. He'd be closer to Kayla, but far enough removed so that he and Jessie wouldn't be in each other's hair.

"Suit yourself," Mike said with a tight shrug.

Skip had a sudden revelation: *He doesn't want to be alone*. It made sense, when he thought about it. All of Mike's buddies from high school were married with kids. They were always joking about how lucky Mike was to have escaped "the noose," but that didn't change the fact that he was the odd man out. Nights could get lonely when you had nothing to come home to but a cold beer. Even lonelier, in Skip's view, was the interchangeable lineup of women, who seemed to get younger with each passing year.

"Don't tell me my being here hasn't cut into your action," he said in an attempt at levity.

Mike grinned, but it seemed more of a reflex than anything. "Don't sweat it. Half of what I get is more than you'll ever see."

When he'd finished putting away the groceries, Skip walked back into the living room and retrieved his jacket from the chair it was slung over, shrugging it on as he headed for the door. "I'm going out for a little while," he announced.

Mike followed him to the door, looking faintly woebegone. "You're not still pissed at me, are you?"

"Nah." Skip paused to clap a hand over Mike's shoulder. "I know you're only looking out for me, bro."

He had no particular destination in mind, but within minutes of turning out of the driveway he found himself en route to the inn. Houses and strip malls gave way to densely packed trees as the road climbed, becoming more mountainous. A short distance from the turnoff to the inn, he pulled over onto the shoulder and rolled his window down, letting in the scent of newly mown grass mingled with a trace of woodsmoke. A wave of intense homesickness washed over him. He'd been so busy telling himself what a relief it was to be free of its endless demands that he hadn't acknowledged just how much he missed the old place.

From where he sat, Skip had an unobstructed view of the inn, perched on the hill above, every window ablaze, the smoke from its chimney a dark smudge against the twilit sky—like something out of a storybook. He recalled what it had looked like when he first saw it, the floor rotted through in places, its rafters home to mice and squirrels. Money had been tight so he and Erin had done a lot of the work themselves, laboring side by side, often long after the workmen had left for the day. When Kayla came, she slept in a portable crib or in her Snuggli, oblivious to the sawing and hammering going on around her. At the time, it had seemed more hard labor than a labor of love, but looking back he couldn't recall a single accomplishment he was prouder of.

And Erin—he'd never seen anyone work so hard, harder than any man. Yet she'd somehow juggled it with the demands of a newborn without losing her sense of humor. When they weren't sanding floors or painting walls, they were haunting flea markets and antique shops and stores that specialized in vintage plumbing fixtures. The day the inn finally opened for business, it had seemed almost anticlimactic. The real satisfaction, he saw now, was in making it happen.

With the daily grind had come a restlessness that spilled over into his marriage. Things he'd once shrugged off began to irritate him: Erin's coolness toward his parents and how quick she was to judge his brother; how she fretted over every little purchase, often accusing him of spending too much. And no one was more stubborn than Erin. When she dug her heels in, it was like a Chinese finger puzzle: The harder you tugged, the tighter she held on.

Their daughter was another bone of contention. He thought Erin was too strict, and she thought he was too lenient. He recalled when Kayla had been teething. She'd wake screaming in the night, and Erin, after walking the floor with her for an hour or more, to no avail, would insist on putting her back in her crib simply because some child-care expert had said she'd become spoiled otherwise. They were all unhappy about it, Kayla most of all. But Erin was adamant. It was as if she'd been afraid to trust her own instincts.

But the list of things he loved about her was longer. If she was less than kindly disposed toward his parents— who, in all honesty, deserved it—she was passionate about those she loved. Even her penny-pinching, he had to admit, wasn't always a bad thing. It was the main reason they weren't more in debt. And who could argue that Kayla was anything other than the product of a loving home?

A mental picture formed of Erin at the kitchen stove, dressed only in a T-shirt of his that hung down past her knees (for some reason, she had an aversion to nightgowns and pj's). They'd just made love, which always gave her a ferocious appetite, and although it was the middle of the night she'd been scrambling eggs. Looking so deliciously sexy in her bare feet, with her hair mussed, he'd wanted to take her all over again.

An invisible hand closed around his heart.

How had it come to this? These past months he'd begun to see that it wasn't all Erin's fault. If she had a temper, it was usually over in a flash, while he tended to let things simmer until they came to a boil. And except for grumbling from time to time, he hadn't really shared with her just how unhappy he was playing innkeeper. How was she to have known what a lifeline Coburn's offer had seemed? When he'd blown up at her, it had probably seemed to Erin like it was coming out of nowhere.

Skip threw the truck into gear and continued on up the hill. As he approached the gated drive, he noticed that the sign was crooked—he'd missed it somehow when he'd been by earlier to do his chores. He added it to his mental punch list. When he reached the inn, he pulled around in back and parked. He was nearing the house when the firefly glow of a cigarette amid the shadows of the porch caught his eye. It cut a slow arc, and now he could make out a seated figure faintly illuminated by the light from inside.

Jessie. Who was responsible for his wife's being in New York, and before that for breaking his brother's heart. Could he learn to forgive her just a little? He'd been civil to her, for Kayla's sake, nothing more. Now he had to swallow his pride and ask a favor of her.

"Hey, Jess," he called softly.

She shot to her feet, a hand to her chest. Then he stepped into the light and she saw that it was him. She let out a breath. "Jesus, you almost gave me a heart attack."

He climbed up onto the porch. "I didn't know you smoked," he said, eyeing the cigarette in her hand.

"I don't. I gave it up years ago." She dropped it, crushing it under her heel.

"This place is finally getting to you, huh?"

"Worse than that, it's growing on me."

He smiled crookedly. "You can take the girl out of the country . . ." He didn't finish the sentence. It was clear from the look on her face that now wasn't the time to re-mind her of her origins.

She sank back down in her chair. He noticed that she was wearing cowboy boots. It seemed her city wardrobe had found a permanent home in the back of the closet; these days he rarely saw her in anything other than jeans and T-shirts. In the dim light, she looked the way she had in high school. He wondered if she'd suspected back then that he'd had a crush on her. If she hadn't been his brother's girlfriend . . .

"If you're looking for Kayla, she's at Devon's," she in-formed him. "They're working on a science project, so I said it was okay if she spent the night." The last bit she added somewhat defensively, as if half expecting him to give her heat about it being a school night.

"I didn't come to see Kayla," he said. "I came to see you."

"Oh." Jessie looked startled, and a little apprehensive.

He felt himself tense. He hated having to come to her hat in hand when if anyone had no right to be here, it was Jessie. But there was no sense getting into all that other stuff; he had more pressing concerns at the moment. "I was wondering how you'd feel about me bunking at the inn for a little while, until I find my own place."

"Why, is Mike kicking you out?" she asked teasingly.

"Nah, nothing like that." Skip didn't feel comfort-able discussing his brother with her. However much a pain in the ass Mike could be at times, it would've felt disloyal.

"Sure," she told him. "I mean, of course you can stay here. It's your place."

"It used to be. I guess it still is, but you can't hang your hat on a deed." He glanced about, drawing in a breath of the clean mountain air before sinking into the wicker chair next to hers. Inside, Otis was snuffling at the door, whining to be let out. Skip gave in to an ironic smile. His wife might have moved on, but it was reassuring to know his dog still wanted to be with him. "Kayla tells me your boyfriend's coming out for a visit," he remarked, wanting to start off on the right foot. If they were going to be living side by side, he'd have to make peace with her.

"Huh? Oh, yes . . . yes, he is." She seemed distracted.

"It's none of my business, but you don't seem too thrilled about it."

"It's not that. It's just . . ." She spread her hands in a helpless gesture. "It's been a while, and things were sort of up in the air when I left."

"I know the territory," he said, thinking of Erin.

"At first, I thought it was because he was so wrapped up in his kids. But lately I've been wondering if the reason I was attracted to him in the first place was because he was unavailable. One way or another, I seem to keep running from the altar." She sighed, giving him a rueful look. "I know what you're thinking—par for the course, right?"

He smiled. "Actually, I was thinking about the time we all went fishing, and you caught the biggest fish." This was the most in-depth conversation they'd had in more than a decade, yet he fell easily into the old rhythm. "As for you and Mike," he said, "I was more hurt than angry, though at times it was hard to know the difference. Besides," he added, "at the moment I'm not exactly in a position to judge."

"Still, I owe you an apology." He felt her light touch against his wrist. "I should have told you good-bye at least. You were my friend, and I let you down."

"You were more than that to me," he confessed. "I was a little bit in love with you."

"Oh." From the astonished look she wore, it was obvious she'd had no clue. "I don't know what to say. I'm flattered, I guess." She peered at him. "Does Erin know?"

"I told her when we first started going out. She said she didn't blame me, that any guy in his right mind would be in love with you."

Jessie looked touched, but she shook her head, saying, "I can't believe she didn't tell me. I guess even best friends don't know everything there is to know about each other."

He looked up. The stars were so close that if he'd climbed his ladder he could have plucked them right out the sky. He looked back at Jessie to find her regarding him somberly. "You miss her, don't you?" she said. It wasn't a question.

He felt himself start to close off again. What right did she have to stick her nose into his business? If it hadn't been for her, Erin would still be here, where she belonged, and they might've had a shot at working things out.

But the person he was really angry at, he knew, was himself. Jessie was just a scapegoat. After a moment, he sighed, and said, "Yeah, I miss her." There was no use denying it.

"Tell her," she urged. "One of you has to go first, and you know it won't be Erin."

A corner of his mouth hooked up. "I think that's a pretty safe bet."

Jessie smiled and shook her head. "When we were kids, I used to feel like such a wimp next to her. If someone gave her a hard time, she'd fight back. I think it was because nothing ever came easy to her."

"I never met them, but from what Erin's told me, I gather her parents were kind of flaky."

"They *adored* Erin." Jessie clearly didn't wish to speak ill of the dead. "But they both worked long hours, and she had a lot of responsibility from a really young age. She got used to doing things her way. It's a tough habit to break."

Skip nodded slowly. "I'm not the easiest person to live with either."

"We all have our faults." Jessie was quick to let him off the hook, and he was grateful for that.

"Still, I could've handled things better," he admitted.

Jessie gave him a long, searching look. "She needs to know you feel that way."

"At this point, I'm not sure she'd want to hear it."

"Try her."

He smiled, thinking of his brother. "Why is everyone suddenly an expert on my love life?"

Jessie snorted. "Please. I'm still trying to figure out my own."

They lapsed into companionable silence. The only sounds were the chirping of crickets and an occasional low, doggy whine from inside the house. When Skip finally got up to leave, Jessie rose with him, walking him to his truck.

"I'll be by tomorrow with my things," he told her.

He felt lighter, as if some of the burden he'd been carrying around for weeks had lifted. The prospect of sharing quarters with Jessie didn't seem so fraught anymore.

Not until he'd driven halfway back to his brother's did it occur to him that he probably should have run it by Erin first. She might read more into it than she should, and he wasn't prepared to take the leap of moving back in for good. Not until he was sure it wouldn't bite him in the ass.

Chapter Ten

All morning Jessie had been a nervous wreck. Jonathon was due to arrive in just a few hours, and the thought brought a sweet-sick clutch of anticipation each time it surfaced. At breakfast, as she refilled the thermoses and juice pitchers, she pictured him walking in through the door, and wondered how she'd feel when she saw him. Overjoyed? Or guilty because he wasn't the only man on her mind?

Last night, she'd attended the Conservancy's regular Thursday night meeting. Their civil case was going to court in a matter of weeks, and as she listened to Hunter address the gathering of a hundred or so, laying out the particulars of the case, Jessie had been reminded of what she'd spent the past week trying to forget: That he was a force to be reckoned with. She couldn't deny her attraction any more than she could justify it.

Following the meeting, the officers—veterinarian Jeff Carmody, and Roger Munsey of Mile High Towing; Janet Olshefsky and her husband Mark; Michelle Young who owned the Flower Mill out on Route 6—got together at Murphy's for drinks, and Hunter invited Jessie to join them. An hour later, she glanced around in surprise to find that it was just the two of them. She'd scarcely noticed as the others had drifted off one by one.

They finished their drinks and headed out back to where their cars were parked. "I hope we didn't bore you," Hunter said, as they strolled along, their elongated shadows angling across the blacktop. "We tend to forget that not everyone's been in this as long as we have."

"Not at all," she said. "I always learn something new." She hadn't known, for instance, that at least two species of native birds were endangered as a result of the streams drying up. "I just hope I can condense it all into a couple of pages." *People* magazine had given her the green light, and now she was faced with the challenge of writing an article that would stir up public indignation. The best-case scenario would be Sylvan Glade's parent company, Federated Foods, pulling the plug on Overby's operation to avoid consumer backlash. If that happened, it would save the Conservancy months, maybe even years, of battling it out in court.

"At the moment, you're our best bet." He didn't have to remind her that the outspoken editor in chief of the

Willow Creek Mercury, Link Woodhouse, had been banging the drum since day one, without much success—he was mainly preaching to the converted. Exposure on a national level would change everything.

"If it's true that the pen is mightier than the sword, we should see a few heads roll."

He turned to her, smiling as if he understood her in a way only those closest to her did—he would never mistake her quiet nature for passiveness. When she spotted Erin's Toyota, Jessie was grateful for the excuse to rummage in her purse for the keys so he wouldn't see the emotions she felt sure were written all over her face. She glanced up to find him leaning against the hood, watching her with a bemused expression.

"What?" she said.

"Nothing." His smile widened. "I was just thinking that you're a woman of contradictions."

"How so?"

"Well, you strike me as pretty independent, but you're sentimental enough to wear a heart-shaped locket with your boyfriend's picture in it." His gaze dropped to her neck.

Jessie's cheeks warmed, and her hand crept up to finger the locket. How had he known about the photo? Was it just a lucky guess? A little defensively, she countered, "Why is that a contradiction? I want the same things everyone wants."

"Such as?"

"A home and family. Good friends. A meaningful career."

A pickup truck cruised slowly past, its headlights briefly playing over Hunter's face, highlighting its beveled planes, his glittering anthracite eyes. "What about children?" he asked.

"That, too." Uncomfortable with the direction this conversation was taking, she added in a more lighthearted tone, "In the meantime, my cat satisfies my maternal instinct."

"I didn't know you had a cat."

"Her name's Delilah."

"You must miss her."

She nodded. "Especially at night." She missed Delilah purring on the pillow next to hers. "Not that I don't love dogs, but try sleeping with a golden retriever."

"I had a dog once. His name was Blaze."

Something about the distant, faintly pained expression he wore prompted Jessie to ask, "What happened to him?"

"My dad shot him."

Jessie was aghast. "Why? Was he hurt?"

The muscles in his jaw tightened. "Dad was drunk at the time, and Blaze wouldn't stop barking. The next morning he didn't even remember shooting him. But I guess it was the wake-up call he needed, because after that he started going to AA meetings. Never touched another drop. He said he wanted to die sober, and he got his wish." His father had died two years ago after a long battle with cancer, he told her.

She thought of her own father. "I lost my dad when I was eight."

"How did he die?"

"According to the autopsy, it was a heart attack, but . . ." She shivered in the chill air that had found its way through her jacket. "We were at the beach that day. I got caught in the undertow, and he was swimming out after me. He never made it back to shore."

He was giving her that look again, as if he'd peeled back her layers and could see what was underneath. "My people believe that if you watch someone die, you're haunted by their spirit—their *chindi*."

"Is that necessarily a bad thing?" She found the idea of her father's spirit hovering over her strangely comforting.

"It is, if it's holding you back in some way."

"Supposing it's true, how would you get rid of this spirit?"

"A medicine man—a *hataali*—would perform a cleansing ceremony," he informed her. She must have looked skeptical, because he smiled. "You don't believe in spirits?"

She shrugged. "It's enough just dealing with the living."

"Anyone in particular?" he asked.

"My mother, for one."

"I see." He nodded slowly.

"Even if I could forgive myself, she never would. She blames me for what happened to my father."

He looked puzzled. "But you were only a little girl."

"A little girl who disobeyed."

He did something unexpected then: He laughed. "Come to my classroom someday, and you'll see true disobedience. Believe me, even at your worst, you'd have looked like an angel next to some of the kids I've had to deal with."

She gazed past him, pondering his words. All these years her guilt had grown along with her. Now, with a single whack, Hunter had cut it back down to size. She saw her eight-year-old self through his eyes, and had a sudden impulse to console that little girl. She hadn't meant any harm. She didn't deserve to be punished for the rest of her life.

The evening scene at Murphy's was winding down— week nights in this town they rolled up the sidewalks after dark—and the parking lot was empty except for a handful of cars. Just then, the rear exit opened and light spilled out onto the pavement. A couple strolled out, hand in hand, laughing and jostling each other. From inside came the sound of the jukebox, a country western tune— a song about heartache. Jessie thought of Jonathon and his impending visit, and felt a swarm of conflicting emotions.

"I should be going," she told Hunter. "I'm afraid it's past my bedtime."

Hunter, leaning up against the hood of the car, made no move to leave. She was acutely aware of him watching her with those depthless black eyes, and it made her uneasy. What was he waiting for? What did he want from her?

But Jessie knew perfectly well, and it was all she could do to keep from closing the three or four feet that separated them. Only this time it wouldn't stop at kissing. She turned to unlock the Toyota, but her fingers had grown clumsy all of a sudden, and the keys slipped through her fingers, landing with a jingle on the pavement. She bent to retrieve them, but Hunter was quicker. He scooped them up, pressing them into her hand. She could feel the warmth from his touch all the way up her arm. "You're sure you don't want me to drive you home?" he teased. As if she'd had anything stronger to drink than a Diet Coke.

"I'm sure." She was glad it was dark, or he'd have seen the flush on her cheeks. Only the thought of Jonathon propelled her into the driver's seat.

She was backing out when he tapped on her window. She rolled it down. "Listen, I'm driving up to the reservation on Saturday," he said. "If you don't have any plans, why don't you come with me?"

Her heart leapt. Then she remembered that Jonathon would be here this weekend. "Another time maybe," she said, with genuine regret. "I have a . . . a friend coming from out of town." Immediately she kicked herself for not telling him it was her boyfriend. What did she have to hide?

Hunter shrugged. "Sure . . . another time." He ran his knuckles lightly over her cheek, igniting it with a trail of fire. "Good night then." He sauntered off, leaving her to the storm of emotions that roiled inside her as she drove back to the inn.

This morning, after a restless night, she was still in turmoil. Had she avoided telling Hunter the whole truth because, at some level, she was keeping her options open? Talk was cheap, and she wouldn't know until she and Jonathon had spent some time together whether he'd had a real change of heart, or if he was just telling her what she wanted to hear.

She got through the rest of the morning somehow. She saw guests off on various expeditions, clutching their maps and brochures, and inspected a leak in one of the bathrooms that turned out to be a loose pipe fitting, easily fixed with a wrench. She was in the office poring over a stack of receipts when Maria poked her head in through the door to inquire, "This boyfriend of yours, he wouldn't happen to have a twin brother, would he?"

"No, why?" Jessie glanced up distractedly.

Maria pointed toward the window. "Because if that's not who I think it is, tell me now so I can give him my phone number."

Jessie looked out the window to find Jonathon striding up the front path carrying his battered Mark Cross suitcase. The doubts she'd been having flew out of her head, and she let out a whoop as she jumped to her feet, knocking a pile of papers off the desk in the process. Then she was dashing out into the hall to fling open the front door.

She was in his arms before she'd even had a chance to say hello. They hugged each other tightly, and kissed until she remembered where they were. "God, I can't believe it. You're *here*," she said, when they drew apart at last.

"I know, I can hardly believe it myself." He grinned.

She grabbed his hand, tugging him inside. "Come on. Maria's dying to meet you."

Maria behaved herself for the most part, except to arch a brow the moment his back was turned, as if questioning Jessie's sanity in leaving a man like Jonathon alone in a city full of single women. Looking at him now, Jessie wondered the same thing herself. Even rumpled from his flight, he was handsomer than any man had a right to be.

After she'd given him the full tour, they settled out on the patio under the shade of the cabana. Luckily, there were no guests around at the moment, so they had it all to themselves.

"I see the appeal," he said, looking around appreciatively.

The area surrounding the patio was landscaped with native plants and trees—bush anemone and purple-flowered ruellia, flame-colored Mexican bird of paradise, with palo verde trees providing shade. Even the swimming pool was cleverly designed to look like a product of nature, with its waterfall that trickled over artfully arranged rocks. Off to one side was a *kiva* where guests could warm themselves on cold evenings.

"It *is* lovely, isn't it?" she said, seeing it anew through his eyes.

"If I were you, I'm not sure I'd want to go back to New

York." He spoke lightly, but she heard the question in his voice.

"It's fine, as long your taste in food is limited to pizza and burgers," she said. "Or if your idea of *haute couture* is Thelma's Threads." The truth was, she'd grown used to the slower pace in Willow Creek and saw its unspoiled beauty as a fair trade for whatever she might be missing out on in New York, but Jonathon didn't need to know that.

"So it's fancy restaurants and Saks Fifth Avenue you miss?" he said, turning to her with a smile.

"Let's not forget the Popover Café. And Barney's warehouse sale."

His expression turned serious. "God, I missed you. You have no idea."

"I missed you, too," she replied more airily. Something was causing her to hold back. She didn't know if it was because of Hunter, or if she still didn't quite trust Jonathon. Politely, she inquired, "How are the kids?"

"They're great." His eyes lit up. "Did I tell you Sara's taking French? She really seems to love it—already she's angling for a trip to Paris. And Zach's team won the intramural championship."

"That's wonderful," she said sincerely. "You must be so proud." Jessie had done a lot of thinking over these past months and had come to the realization that if they were to make this work, she was going to have to meet Jonathon halfway, which meant accepting, even embracing, his children. "Speaking of kids, Kayla can't wait to meet you."

"I feel like I know her already," he said. "Erin talks about her all the time." They'd met several times since their dinner at Patsy's, Jessie knew. She saw it as a good sign that he was taking the time to get to know her closest friend.

At the same time, she felt a little stab of envy. The one thing Erin and Jonathon had in common that was outside Jessie's realm of experience was that they both had kids.

When Kayla arrived home from school, it was immediately apparent that she was captivated by Jonathon. Instead of disappearing into her room as she usually did, she became wonderfully helpful. While Jessie was making dinner, she emptied the dishwasher and set the table. Throughout the meal, when Kayla wasn't peppering Jonathon with questions, about his work and his kids, she hung on his every word.

"He's totally hot," she pronounced, as she and Jessie were washing up, after he'd gone off to unpack.

"Not to mention he has excellent taste in jewelry." Jessie eyed the silver charm bracelet from Tiffany's that dangled from Kayla's wrist, thinking that he couldn't have chosen a more perfect gift.

"That, too." Kayla lifted her arm to admire the bracelet. "Seriously, Aunt Jess, if you don't marry him, you're crazy."

Jessie plunged her hands into the sinkful of suds. "You're forgetting one tiny detail: He hasn't asked me yet." The memory of the one and only time she'd raised the subject, on the drive back from his parents', was still painfully fresh in her mind. "Anyway," she teased, "if you like him so much, maybe we should keep him on ice until you're old enough to marry him yourself."

Kayla made a face. "Ewww, gross."

"Didn't you just tell me he was hot?"

"I meant for a guy his age."

In Kayla's view, anyone over thirty was practically middle-aged. Jessie smiled. "So I guess this means Brett Conners"—a boy in her homeroom class whom Kayla had confided she was interested in—"won't have to worry about competition."

Kayla blushed and began applying herself with renewed vigor to the pot she was drying.

Later, alone with Jonathon, Jessie wondered if Kayla was right, if she'd be crazy to let him go. She was getting undressed before bed when he came up behind her, wrapping his arms about her and burying his face in her hair. She felt something release in her like an exhaled breath.

"You smell good," he murmured. "What's that perfume you're wearing?"

"Lemon Pledge." She informed him that she no longer had the luxury of dressing up and putting on perfume. "I'm lucky if I have time to take a shower in the morning."

"Well, you've never looked more beautiful," he said, swiveling her around to face him. "Whatever you're doing, it's clearly having a positive effect."

Meeting his open, smiling gaze, she felt a twinge of

guilt. He'd done nothing to be ashamed of—she could see it in his eyes. While she . . .

She burned at the memory of Hunter's kiss.

When they were both naked under the covers, Jessie took her time reacquainting herself with Jonathon's body. She ran her fingers over his chest and the trail of fine hairs along his belly. She sank her teeth lightly into his shoulder, tasting him. When the thought of Hunter intruded, she pushed it away. She didn't want anything to spoil this moment.

As they made love, she thought, *What could another man give me that Jonathon can't?* He knew her body better than anyone. He knew what pleased her, where she liked to be touched. When they came together, it was like an affirmation. Jonathon must have felt it, too, for afterward, as she lay snuggled in his arms, he breathed in her ear, "Marry me."

Jessie grew very still. "Was that a proposal?" she asked, fearing it had been nothing more than a postcoital slip of the tongue.

"It was indeed." He propped himself up on one elbow, looking deep into her eyes. In a clear, resonant voice, he asked more formally, "Jessie Holland, will you marry me?"

Jessie didn't know what to say. It was what she'd longed for. But she still had lingering doubts. Not just about him, but whether or not it was what *she* wanted.

Nonetheless, a giddy joy rose in her, a joy that possessed a mind of its own. "I never thought I'd be proposed to in the altogether," she said with a breathless laugh.

He smiled down at her languidly. "Would you rather I'd waited until you were dressed?"

"That depends on whether or not you were planning to seduce me again," she said, tracing the whorls of hair on his chest with her finger.

He grinned. "Give me a minute, and I may take you up on that." She subsided onto the mattress with a sigh, and was snuggling in his arms, gazing stupidly up at the ceiling, when he said, "We'll shop for a ring when you get back. I didn't want to get you one you wouldn't like."

Jessie felt a tiny stab of disappointment. As if she could possibly have disliked any ring he'd picked out for her!

But it was childish to let such a little thing matter. What difference did it make?

It wasn't until after they'd made love again that she realized she hadn't told him yes, exactly, not in so many words. She was drifting off to sleep when she heard him ask, "So was it worth it?"

"What?" She lifted her head to squint at him.

"Did you find what you were looking for?"

It took a moment for her to realize he'd meant the swap with Erin. "I'm not sure if I even know what I was looking for," she replied sleepily. She certainly hadn't expected the grass to be greener. "But . . ." She recalled the wonder on Kayla's face as she'd gazed in the mirror, seeing herself in makeup for the first time, a look worth all the shops, museums, and three-star restaurants in Manhattan. She thought, too, of how peaceful it was in the early-morning hours when the house was so still you could hear the birds cheeping in the eaves, and of the people she wouldn't have met otherwise, from all parts of the country and all walks of life. " . . . whatever it was, it found me."

"Does that mean you're having second thoughts about marrying me?" he teased.

"Just because I'm not miserable without you every second of the day doesn't mean I haven't missed you something fierce," she told him.

"I was thinking of Christmas," he said, as she was nodding off again.

"Hmmm?" She struggled to keep her eyes open.

"That might be a good time for the wedding."

"We don't have to set a date just yet, do we?" She was thinking of how difficult it would be for Erin and Kayla to get away that time of year.

"Of course not. There's plenty of time," he said. "It's just a thought."

"When do you plan on breaking it to the kids?" she asked cautiously.

"I thought we'd wait until you got back."

They'd welcome the news like an outbreak of anthrax, she knew. His parents, too. But why worry about that now? She was determined not to let anything or anyone spoil this moment. Whatever was in store down the line, she'd face it when the time came.

*   *   *

The following morning Jonathon helped serve breakfast—to the delight of the inn's female guests. Afterward, leaving Maria in charge, they headed off for a hike up Thumb Butte. They made it all the way to the top before the day's heat sent them staggering back to the air-conditioned cool of the car, then spent the rest of the morning strolling around downtown, Jessie pointing out the various sights—the imposing nineteenth-century courthouse built of native granite, the candy pink Victorian trimmed in gingerbread that'd been a brothel in the boomtown days, the firehouse with its antique hose cart that every year was trundled out for the annual Fourth of July parade down Main Street.

They had lunch at the Dinner Bell Café, stopping afterward for ice cream at the Sundae Times, then they crossed the street, licking their cones, to settle on a bench in the town square. Watching a group of children chase each other around the fountain, Jessie smiled, imagining what it would be like when she and Jonathon had children of their own. Which reminded her, she'd promised her mother they'd stop by after lunch so she could meet Jonathon.

She hoped she wouldn't live to regret it.

But when they arrived, Beverly was at her most charming. She seemed quite taken with Jonathon, and at one point Jessie could have sworn she was actually flirting with him. As they relaxed in rattan chairs out on the porch, sipping glasses of Equal-sweetened lemonade, Beverly told them all about her and Gay's wine-tasting tour of Napa. "Though I honestly don't know what I could've been thinking, buying a whole case of champagne," she said, shaking her head. "It's silly, really. I don't entertain much these days."

Jessie hadn't yet broken the news about her engagement. She waited until her mother had finished her story, then said, "Uh, Mom? Jonathon and I . . ." All at once the memory of her long-ago flight from the altar rose up to choke off the rest of the sentence. She recalled how furious Beverly had been when Jessie finally got up the nerve to phone her, how she'd threatened everything from disownment to the early demise that was sure to befall her, Beverly, as a result of Jessie's selfishness. *You're killing me, just like you killed your father!* she'd screamed. When Jessie had finally hung up, she'd looked as if she'd literally seen a ghost, according to Erin.

Jonathon, sensing her distress, came to the rescue. "We're engaged," he announced with a grin, reaching for Jessie's hand.

Jessie nodded mutely, squeezing his hand.

"We haven't set a date yet," he went on. "We thought we'd check with you first."

A dazed smile deepened the creases in Beverly's face. "Oh, my. A wedding." She brought a hand up, absently fiddling with the collar on her blouse, as if not quite daring to believe it—her errant daughter getting married after all these years. "I know! I'll throw you a party. An engagement party. It's short notice, but I'm sure my friends won't mind canceling any plans they might have, and I have the champagne."

"Jonathon's only here until Monday," Jessie reminded her.

"In that case," Beverly said, "we don't have any time to lose. What about tomorrow evening?"

"We've already made plans for tomorrow." Jessie didn't stop to think how ungracious it would sound.

Beverly's smile faded. She looked hurt. "What could be more important than this?"

Jessie felt guilty and at the same time resentful. Whenever she was around Beverly, she reverted to about ten years old, hating her mother and at the same time wanting desperately to please her. But there was no pleasing Beverly. Even when Jessie was giving her what she wanted, it was never enough.

"It's not that we don't appreciate the offer," she said, with a stiff formality that did nothing to appease her mother.

Beverly looked as if she were about to give Jessie a piece of her mind when Jonathon once more came to the rescue. "It's sweet of you, Mrs. Holland, but I know my family would want to be there, and I'd hate for them to be disappointed. Can we take a rain check?"

Beverly looked somewhat mollified. "Yes, of course. I wasn't thinking of your family. How silly of me."

Jessie felt herself relax. A scene had been averted, if only narrowly.

In the car on their way back to the inn, Jonathon observed, "Don't shoot me for saying so, but I liked her. She certainly wasn't the ogre I was expecting."

"Well, the feeling was clearly mutual," Jessie said, somewhat peeved that he'd won her mother over so quickly, when it had taken her years merely to achieve a cease-fire.

There was a pause, then he chided gently, "It wouldn't have killed you to give in to her, you know. She meant well."

"She only wants to throw a party so she can show off to her friends. It has nothing to do with me—or *you*, for that matter."

He raised an eyebrow. "Isn't that kind of harsh?"

Jessie fell silent. *He's right*, she thought, feeling suddenly small and mean-spirited. "I guess I could've been a little nicer," she conceded grudgingly. Jonathon might bring out the best in Beverly, but Beverly brought out the worst in her.

"We'll make it up to her." He reached over and patted her hand reassuringly.

Jessie flashed him a grateful smile even as she was thinking, *Whose side are you on?*

The following morning they left early for Sedona, arriving two hours later to find the rustic town she recalled from childhood awash in tourists and tacky souvenir shops. They stopped only long enough to pick up some sandwiches in town before hitting the back roads that wound through the rugged red rock country, which thankfully remained unspoiled, where they picnicked on a bluff overlooking a canyon gloriously painted in shades of umber, orange, and magenta.

It was well after dark by the time they got back to the inn. Tired and sunburned, Jessie wanted only to climb into bed, but the moment she walked in and saw Maria's grim face she knew she wasn't going to have that luxury anytime soon.

Maria motioned her into the office and shut the door. "I tried reaching you on your cell phone, but I couldn't get through." From the worried look she wore, it was obvious this was more urgent than a burst pipe or downed power line. "Hunter's been arrested."

"*What?*" Jessie stared at her in disbelief.

There'd been an explosion over at Burt Overby's pumping station, Maria informed her. Thankfully no one had been hurt, but the blast had been intentional. According to investigators, the evidence pointed to Hunter.

"That's ridiculous!" Jessie cried.

Maria obviously shared her outrage. "I know, but it looks bad for him. According to my sister"—Jessie recalled that Maria's sister, Jennifer, was a police dispatcher—"they found footprints at the scene that match his."

Jessie felt her knees give way, and she sank into the nearest chair. "Oh, God." She was thinking of the day they'd traipsed all over Overby's property. Had it rained since then? No, she'd have remembered. This time of year they got only the occasional downpour.

When she could stand without her knees buckling, she headed off in search of Jonathon. She found him in the kitchen pouring himself a glass of milk. "Something's come up that I need to take care of," she told him. "Do you mind? I won't be long."

"Anything I can do to help?" he asked.

"No, it's best if I go alone." She was grateful when he didn't press for details. He probably figured it was some urgent matter involving one of the guests. "I'll tell you all about it when I get back," she promised as she was heading out the door.

Twenty minutes later she arrived at the normally sleepy police station to find it humming with activity. Several squad cars idled at the curb, bubble lights flashing, and at least a dozen of Hunter's friends and fellow activists, many of whom she recognized from Conservancy meetings, had gathered on the steps out front. She buttonholed Link Woodhouse as he was stalking away in a huff from what appeared to have been a heated exchange with one of the policemen.

"What's going on?" she asked.

"I was just telling that young whippersnapper"—Link, hawk-nosed, with snowy hair that floated about his head like down from a torn pillow, hooked a thumb in the direction of the scowling cop—"that it would've served the old bastard right if he'd been blown to smithereens. The only reason I thank God he wasn't is because it'd be just one more thing they'd try to pin on our boy."

Link, she imagined, had seen every variety of human foible in his forty years as editor in chief of the *Mercury*, but nothing that had gotten him more fired up than this. He filled her in on what little he knew: The explosion had been triggered by a timed device, the work of some-one familiar with explosives. That alone ruled out Hunter, in Link's opinion. What didn't look so good for him was that Overby was claiming to have caught him trespassing on his property a few weeks back.

Jessie grew warm, reliving her role in that incident. "He'll need a lawyer."

"Stu's on his way over now."

Stu McCall was the attorney handling the civil suit. "I just hope Stu won't be in over his head," she said, thinking that a criminal lawyer might be more like it.

But Link replied with a glint in his eye, "Hunter can take care of himself. In fact, I wouldn't put it past him to turn this to his advantage."

As he headed off to the parking lot, muttering under his breath, she pushed her way through the crowd milling near the entrance. Inside, the policeman at the front desk, paunchy with graying muttonchop sideburns, was busy scribbling something on a form. "You his lawyer?" he asked in a bored voice, barely glancing up at her, when she put in a request to see Hunter. She told him no, and he grunted, "Sorry, Miss. Can't help you."

Jessie was momentarily at a loss, then her journalistic instincts kicked in. She leaned in to confide, "Listen, I'm a reporter. I'm doing an article for *People*." *Now* she had his interest. She dug into her purse, pulling out a notepad and pen. "Would you mind giving me your name, Offi-cer? I want to make sure it's spelled correctly."

His indifference gave way to the look of a man who

can hardly believe his good fortune. "Purdy," he said, sitting up straight and throwing his shoulders back. "Thomas Jefferson Purdy, but everyone calls me Jeff. *People* magazine, huh? Jeez. Wait'll the wife hears about this. . . ."

The next thing she knew she was being personally escorted by Officer Purdy down a fluorescent-lit corridor lined with cells, all of them empty except for the one at the far end. Hunter, stretched out on his cot, jumped to his feet as she drew near. "You got company," Purdy announced as he unlocked the door to Hunter's cell, allowing her inside.

"I came as soon as I heard," she told him.

He nodded, seeming glad to see her. He gestured toward the cot, and she sank onto it. Hunter sat down beside her.

"Are you all right?" she asked, touching his hand to reassure herself that he was in one piece.

"I'll live." He shrugged, but she saw every minute of the ordeal etched on his tired face.

"I still can't believe it," she said, shaking her head.

"Me either."

"It doesn't make any sense."

"Actually, it makes perfect sense when you think about it." His mouth stretched in a mirthless smile. "I'm the ideal fall guy. In fact, I wouldn't put it past the old man to have staged the whole thing just so he could pin it on me."

"You really think he'd go that far?" She lowered her voice so Purdy, standing guard outside the cell, wouldn't overhear.

Hunter's shoulders slumped. "No." For the first time since she'd known him, he looked dispirited.

"Do you have any idea who *is* responsible?"

He shook his head. "Not a clue. The only ones crazy enough to pull something like this is ELF." The Earth Liberation Front was known for its terrorist tactics. "But as far as I know there's no connection."

"So what happens now?"

"I'll know more when my lawyer gets here."

"Do you think he'll be able to get you out on bail?"

"Maybe, but it's a moot point because I'm staying put." Hunter's jaw settled into the stubborn lines she recognized as his fight mode. "Don't look so worried," he said, with the touch of a smile. "I've been doing some thinking, and I'm wondering if this isn't a blessing in disguise. You need a hook for your article, and what could be better than this? The noble Indian fighting for his land, accused by the White Man of a crime he didn't commit."

He was smarter than even Jessie had given him credit for. There was just one catch. "What if John Q. Public doesn't buy that you're innocent?"

"I'll take my chances."

Something else occurred to her. "The article won't be out for another few weeks. Do you plan on staying locked up that long?"

"After a few days of protestors, not to mention Link's muck-raking, they'll be throwing me out of here." He grinned. "In the meantime, if we play our cards right, we'll have every newspaper, radio, and TV station west of the Mississippi, on this, as Link would say, 'like a tick on a deerhound.'"

"By 'we,' I'm assuming you mean you and me," she said dubiously.

"Weren't you the one who was saying the pen is mightier than the sword?"

"I wouldn't stake my life on it, if I were you."

"There's a lot more at stake here than my noble red skin."

"You're crazy, you know that?" she said, shaking her head.

"So I've been told."

Officer Purdy cleared his throat loudly, and when she glanced up, he pointed at his watch to let her know her time was up. "I have to go," she told Hunter, reluctant to tear herself away.

"Yeah, I know, you don't want to keep your boyfriend waiting."

He spoke lightly, but she felt a guilty warmth travel up her neck and spread across her cheeks. Of course, she thought. It didn't take a genius to figure out that Jonathon was her "friend" from out of town. What embarrassed her, deeply, was that now he knew she hadn't been honest about her feelings, either. A woman who withheld such pertinent information was a woman who was keeping her options open.

"I should have told you. It's just that—" She broke off, realizing she was only making it worse.

"You don't owe me an explanation." He sounded more resigned than bitter.

As she walked away, Jessie realized she wasn't being entirely honest with him even now. She'd neglected to mention the most important detail of all: that she and Jonathan were engaged.

Chapter Eleven

The first week of taping was so hectic Erin didn't have time for stage fright. Each morning she did two back-to-back segments, then, after a break for lunch, she spent the rest of the afternoon meeting with the show's producer and then with the point person on the culinary staff, to go over the following day's segments. Monday she made her signature lemon ricotta pancakes, which always wowed her guests at the inn, and for the second segment, banana-nut bread. Tuesday it was her aunt Sally's apple pie, the secret for which was a tablespoon of molasses, then Skip's favorite chocolate cake. Wednesday she whipped up a batch of spoon bread, then one of oatmeal-chocolate chip cookies, which came with the story about the time she'd mistakenly made them with, instead of flour, the diatomaceous earth that was used in the pool filter—the barrels they were stored in were identical—and they'd been literally hard as rocks.

By the end of the week she'd hit her stride. Cooking in front of cameras seemed as natural as cooking in her own kitchen. It wasn't about being glamorous or accomplished, she realized, it was about being accessible and about having *fun*. Even Latrice seemed pleased; she gave Erin a few suggestions, but she told her she was on the right track. On Friday, Erin headed home at the end of the day feeling tired, but more upbeat than she had been since arriving in New York.

She was rounding the corner onto her block when she noticed a man seated on the steps of her building, a duffel bag at his feet. She couldn't see his face—it was obscured by the map he was studying—but there was something familiar about him. Oh, God, could it be? Her heart kicked into high gear. She broke into a run and went flying down the sidewalk. When she was close enough to see that, yes, sweet Jesus, it *was* him, she cried out his name.

"Skip!"

He lifted his head and, as he rose to his full height, she recognized the long-sleeved checked shirt he had on as one she'd ironed any number of times. "What are you doing here?" she gasped, when she'd caught up to him. "Why didn't you let me know you were coming?"

He cast her a sheepish smile. "I was afraid you'd tell me not to."

"You're right, I probably would have. But that doesn't

mean I'm not glad to see you." She was grinning help-lessly. It was all she could do not to throw her arms around him. "How's Kayla?"

"Fine. She sends her love."

Erin stood there looking up at him in wonder, still finding it hard to believe that it was Skip, not some hallu-cination brought on by her overwrought brain. What had they been so mad at each other about? All of that seemed insignificant at the moment.

Skip broke the spell by saying, "Aren't you going to ask me in?"

Erin led the way up to Jessie's apartment. As she showed him around, she was careful not to appear propri-etary in any way. She even made a little joke about how different Jessie's style was from her own, not wanting him to know that she'd made this her own little nest. His only comment was that it must seem small compared to what she was used to. It wasn't until he spotted Jessie's cat, curled asleep on the bed, that he showed any interest in his surroundings. "Ah, the lady of the house," he said, picking up Delilah and rubbing her behind the ears as she purred loudly—yet another female to fall under his spell.

"How's everything back home?" she asked, when they were settled on the sofa with glasses of wine.

"As good as can be expected," was his measured re-sponse.

It was odd to see him in this setting. Amid the jumble of embroidered pillows, ethnic rugs, and wall hangings, he might have been a cowboy who'd stumbled into a Turkish bazaar.

"What did Kayla say when you told her you were coming to see me?"

"That she hoped we didn't kill each other."

His tone was wry, but Erin saw nothing to smile about. She thought of the heated arguments Kayla had witnessed and the tense meals at which Erin and Skip hadn't been speaking to each other. The worst thing about all this, she thought, was that she'd unwittingly exposed her daughter to the very thing she'd vowed to protect her from: harm.

But that was then, and this is now, she told herself. Sitting beside her husband in a strange city far from home, it was possible to believe they could start over.

She was about to tell him about her new gig as substitute on-air chef when she became aware of the muffled sounds of angry voices next door. Jessie's neighbors, the Hendersons, whom she'd privately nicknamed the "Bickersons," were at it again. Erin jerked a thumb in the direction of the wall through which the noises were emanating. "The only time they're not at each other's throats is when they're both at work," she told Skip.

"What do they fight about?" He lowered his voice as if they might hear.

"It's always the same thing." She'd caught snatches here and there, just enough to get the gist of it. "From what I can gather, she's insanely jealous. She accuses him of flirting with other women. He denies it, of course. He says she's being paranoid."

"Now where have I heard that before?" He spoke teasingly, but Erin bristled.

"I never accused you of being unfaithful. I only *asked*. There's a difference."

"My memory must be playing tricks on me then." He smiled, as if to let her know there was no malice in his words. "I seem to recall a certain someone coming after me in Murphy's, accusing me of all kinds of terrible things."

"*You* came after *me*. I was headed out the door."

Skip's smile fell away, and he set his glass down on the coffee table. "Erin . . ." She stiffened at his somber tone. *Please, don't say it,* she pleaded silently. If he were to confess that he'd slept with another woman, there would be no wiping the slate clean. " . . . the reason I came all this way to see you is because there are some things you can only say face-to-face. What I wanted you to know, now that I've had time to think it over, is that"—he broke off, clearing his throat, his eyes unnaturally bright—"I'm not ready to throw out the whole thing just because part of it's broken."

"Oh, Skip." It was as if a tight bandage wound around her rib cage had eased, allowing her to breathe again. "I've thought about it, too. I wanted to tell you, but whenever we talked on the phone . . ." He reached out to take her in his arms, but she gently pushed him away. "No. You need to hear this. I was an idiot for standing in your way. I had my head so far up my ass, I couldn't see what was right in front of me—that you'd make a success of anything you set out to do. There hasn't been a day since you left that I haven't wanted to take it all back, every damn word." A sob rose, but she bit it back.

"We were both pigheaded."

Erin gave a teary little laugh. "So now we're going to fight over who's the most pigheaded?"

He took her hands in his, their familiar warmth like finding some valuable keepsake she'd thought was forever lost. "There's something else I want you to know," he said, his shining blue eyes fixed on her. "I never stopped loving you. I know it got kind of buried under all that other stuff, but there was never any doubt in my mind about that."

Tears spilled down Erin's cheeks. She was too choked up to speak.

"You know how you used to joke that if we ever got divorced, I had to take you as part of the settlement?" he went on. "That's how it felt. Like you were with me even when you weren't." His fingers tightened around hers. "Can we get back to the way it was in the beginning? Do you think that's possible?"

The lengthening shadows had deepened into twilight, and outside the streetlights had come on. It was so quiet, it was as if the world had taken a breath: For once there were no traffic sounds, no voices drifting up from the sidewalk. Even the Bickersons were silent.

Skip rose to his feet, pulling her with him. At first, when he drew her into his arms she felt as if she were butting up against him, all elbows and knees. Then, like pieces of a puzzle falling into place, they came together as one. He cupped her head, tilting it back and threading his fingers through her hair as his mouth closed over hers. The very first time he'd kissed her, she'd known he was The One—her body had responded as if Mission Control were clearing it for blast-off—and the same tingling rush swept through her now. Only now there was a sweet ache at the center of it, like a bruise on a perfect piece of fruit. They'd hurt each other. Badly. It would take time to heal.

His lips traveled down her throat, the tip of his tongue tracing the hollow at its base. He knew every tender nook. The spot on her rib cage where she was ticklish, and that she loved being kissed behind her ears. Some of Erin's married friends had confided to her that they'd grown bored with their sex lives, but for Erin it was just the opposite: With each passing year the sex had gotten better as they became more adept at pleasing each other and in taking pleasure. Even when she was mad at Skip, she never stopped wanting him.

They made their way down the hall, breathless as teenagers, pausing every few feet to kiss some more. When they finally reached the bedroom, small heaps of discarded clothing littered the floor in their wake. They tumbled into bed, and he sucked in a breath at the shock of her cold feet. One of the things she loved about Skip, that made her love him now beyond all measure, was that, instead of recoiling, he let her warm her feet against his, which were always toasty even in the dead of winter. They lay still for a minute, tangled up in each other, Skip lightly stroking her back, Erin with her head against his chest breathing in his familiar scent, as familiar as home itself. Then he began kissing her again, and she was once more lost.

She couldn't remember when they'd last made love with such urgency. Like when they were first married, when they couldn't keep their hands off each other, when an hour was too long to wait—one time they'd done it in his parents' guest bathroom with Hugh and Paula down the hall getting dinner on the table. Now, when she came, it was with a queer sense of loss. She'd wanted it to last a little longer, for this feeling to never end.

Afterward, she burst into tears.

"Shhh . . . it's okay. I'm here," Skip soothed.

But she couldn't seem to stop crying. She wept for all the cruel things they'd said to each other and all the time they'd wasted being apart; she wept for the lonely nights she'd lain awake wondering if he would ever come home; she wept with relief, too, knowing it wasn't too late, that God had given them another chance. When she finally ran out of tears, she gave a last convulsive shudder and fell still. A sweet calm stole over her then, and she thought that this was how she must have felt as a baby in her mother's arms.

"I'm sorry," she said. "I don't know where that came from."

"I have a pretty good idea." He gently dried her cheeks with a corner of the sheet.

"How long can you stay?"

"Just for the weekend. I fly back on Monday," he said.

"Mike's giving me a couple of days off as it is. I don't want to push my luck."

"You two getting along okay?" When she'd learned that Skip had moved out of Mike's and was staying at the inn, she'd been cautiously optimistic. Now she needed to know if he'd still be there when she got back.

"Yeah. I mean, we have our moments, but he's my brother—we're supposed to get on each other's nerves."

"You still thinking of getting your own place?" She held very still, scarcely daring to breathe.

There was a long silence, then he answered cautiously, "I'm holding off on that for now. I'm hoping I won't have to."

It occurred to her that he needed reassuring too. "Me too," she said.

"It won't be easy." He didn't have to add that there was more to it than picking up the pieces. They had to figure out a way to put those pieces together again so that they fit.

"I know," she said, and sighed—partly with relief, and partly because she knew it was going to be a long, uphill climb.

Minutes later she drifted to sleep, spooned against him, knowing she was safe . . . for now at least.

They spent most of the following morning in bed. It was almost noon by the time they ventured outdoors to find it a beautiful spring day, the kind of day New Yorkers dream about all winter. They took the subway down to the Village, where they lunched at a sidewalk café, then strolled around taking in the sights. This was Skip's first visit to New York, and he was fascinated by everything he saw: the old row houses narrow as chimneys along the equally narrow cobbled streets, the skyscrapers towering in the distance, the mind-boggling array of shops offering every kind of ware, from vintage posters to sex toys. He paused in front of a store window on Eighth Street, shaking his head in bafflement at its display of S&M gear, saying, "I feel like Jon Voight in *Midnight Cowboy*."

"Minus the cowboy hat," she said, tugging on the Yankees cap he'd bought from a street vendor.

They might have been any couple out sightseeing. No one would have believed, seeing them strolling about hand in hand, that less than twenty-four hours ago they'd been headed for divorce.

That night, long after Skip had dropped off to sleep, Erin lay awake listening to him snore. At home, his snoring used to drive her to distraction. She would poke and prod him in a mostly futile effort to get him to stop. But tonight she found it comforting, for some reason. *You don't know what you're gonna miss till it's gone*, she thought.

In the morning, she slipped out while he was still asleep to pick up some croissants at the corner bakery. On her way back, she ran into Drew on the stairs. "You're up early," he said. "I figured you guys would be sleeping in." His tone was carefully neutral.

Yesterday, she and Skip had run into him on their way

out. When she introduced them, Drew had looked like a little boy whose favorite toy had been snatched from him, though he'd quickly regained his composure. She felt badly that she hadn't had a chance to warn him that Skip was coming.

"I bought extra," she said, holding out the bag of croissants.

He shook his head. "Thanks, but I'm meeting a friend for breakfast." She noticed that he hadn't mentioned whether the friend was male or female, and wondered if it was on purpose. "What are you two up to today?"

"More sightseeing."

"Well, if you're not doing anything later on, why don't you come up for a drink? I have a wedding this afternoon, but I should be back around six."

She promised to give him a call, but she had no intention of taking him up on the invitation. The last thing she needed was for Skip to pick up on any weird vibes with her and Drew.

She walked in to find Skip in the kitchen pouring himself a cup of coffee. Seeing him standing there in nothing but his boxers, looking more delicious than anything in her bag of goodies from Le Bergamot, she wanted to drag him back to bed.

"Who was that?" he asked casually—*too* casually?

"No one. Just Drew." He must have heard them talking in the stairwell. She popped the croissants into the toaster oven. "He invited us for drinks later on, but I told him we'd probably be busy. I didn't think you'd want to go."

Skip surprised her by saying, "Why not? He seems like a nice guy."

"He is, but I figured since we only had the weekend, you wouldn't want anyone else horning in on our action." She spoke lightly, keeping her back turned so he wouldn't see the guilt she was sure was written all over her face.

"We could spare half an hour or so, just to be neighborly."

Something told her there was more to this than a desire on his part to be sociable. Had he sensed something? She suspected, too, that Drew's invitation wasn't as offhand as he'd made it sound. Probably it was nothing more than alpha males circling each other, but either way she wanted no part of it. Still, she couldn't think of a way out that wouldn't arouse suspicion, so she said, "We'll see how we feel when we get back."

After breakfast, they walked to the Empire State Building. Normally Erin would have minded the long line, but not today—every moment with Skip was precious, even if it was standing in line. Then it was off to Chinatown and lunch at a hole-in-the-wall noodle shop, where they stuffed themselves for a grand total of twenty dollars. The last stop was Ground Zero. As they stood gazing at the enormous crater where the Twin Towers had once stood, she glanced over to find Skip with his head bowed and his lips moving, as if in prayer. *This is the man I want to spend the rest of my life with,* she thought. There would never be anyone else.

She had forgotten all about Drew's invitation until

Skip suggested, when they were back at the apartment getting dressed for dinner, "What do you say we take your neighbor up on that drink?"

Erin froze in the midst of tugging on her panty hose, nearly losing her balance. She tried to think of a way out, but it was only a little past seven, and their reservation at Le Madri wasn't until eight, so she had no choice but to reply, "Sure, why not?"

She told herself that she had nothing to hide . . . not really. Even so, she felt distinctly uneasy as they climbed the stairs to Drew's apartment. Her fears were soon put to rest, though. Drew greeted her warmly but not too warmly and struck just the right note with Skip.

"Make yourselves comfortable." He gestured in the general direction of the living room that doubled as his studio, which, as usual, was strewn with contact sheets and assorted camera equipment. "Beer okay?" he called from the kitchen. "I seem to be out of everything else."

"Beer's fine," Skip called back.

Drew reappeared a few minutes later with three Heinekens and a bowl of tortilla chips. He set the chips down on the coffee table and handed them each a beer. "You enjoying your stay?" he asked Skip, sinking into the chair opposite the sofa where they sat.

"It's been quite an experience. I don't know when I'll ever be back, but it sure was worth the trip." Skip darted Erin a meaningful look—she had to bite down on the inside of her cheek to keep from smiling—before glancing around the room at the blowups mounted on foam core, mostly of New York City street scenes, that covered every available inch of wall space. "Nice stuff," he said. "Erin told me you were talented. She wasn't kidding."

"Drew's last show was almost sold out," she said.

"I'm still a long way from being able to hang up my tux," Drew said with a laugh, helping himself to a handful of chips. He explained that weddings and bar mitzvahs were still the main source of his income.

"You do what you gotta do." Skip took a pull off his beer, and sat staring off into space for a moment, as if thinking that he and Drew had that in common, at least.

"There are worse things," Drew said, "than taking pictures of people on the happiest days of their lives."

So far, so good, Erin thought, feeling herself relax.

They'd finished their beers and were getting up to leave when the phone rang. Drew dashed into the next room to answer it, and while they waited for him to return, Skip wandered over to the drafting table where Drew did most of his work—she'd known him to spend hours at a stretch poring over contact sheets with his magnifying loupe. On the wall above it was a corkboard that held more contact sheets and dozens of prints, some beginning to curl at the edges. She watched as Skip leaned close to peer at them.

All at once he grew very still.

Even before she got up to see what he was looking at, Erin sensed something wrong. The photos seemed to jump out at her as she drew near: Shots of her sprawled barefoot on the grass in Central Park, her head thrown back in laughter; several of her mugging for the camera with Drew's leather bomber jacket draped over her shoulders; and one that Kate had taken, the day they'd all gone shopping in SoHo, of Drew with his arm around her in the slinky red cocktail dress she'd been trying on at the time. All perfectly innocent . . . except in the eyes of a husband who had every reason to doubt her.

She could see from the set of Skip's jaw that he wouldn't be buying any explanation she cared to give. And what could she say? Would he want to hear that she'd almost slept with Drew, but that she'd thought better of it before they could go through with it?

Still, she couldn't let him go on thinking something that wasn't true. Or at least, not entirely true. She loved *him*, not Drew. As soon as they were back in Jessie's apartment, she put a hand on his arm, entreating him, "Skip, it's not what you think. If you'll just let me explain . . ."

"Don't bother." He jerked his arm away. "I may not be the smartest guy around, but I'm not stupid either. I can put two and two together. Obviously, you and your buddy Drew are a lot cozier than you led me to believe. And you know the old saying: Two's company, three's a crowd. So if you'll excuse me, I'll go pack."

"You're leaving?" She stared at him, dumbfounded.

"I can't think of a reason to stick around, can you?" he said with cold fury.

He spun on his heel and stalked off. When she caught up to him, he was in the bedroom, stuffing clothes into his duffel bag. A horrid sense of déjà vu washed over her. All of a sudden she had trouble catching her breath.

"But your flight isn't until tomorrow," she managed to croak.

"Whatever." He gave her a look that said he'd rather spend the night on a hard bench at JFK than with her.

"Skip, this is crazy. Drew and I are just friends."

"*Good* friends, from what I can see."

"It's not like that."

"All right then, let's hear it." He swung around to face her. "Look me in the eye and tell me he never laid a hand on you."

"Nothing happened, I swear."

"You swear on your parents' graves?"

She must have hesitated a beat too long, for he nodded in grim satisfaction. "Just as I suspected."

Maria had once joked that Erin was the forward to Skip's reverse, and now she could feel the gears gnashing as she fought to regain the ground that had been so hard won. But her temper got the best of her. "You're one to talk!" she hurled at him. "I catch you falling all over some woman in a bar, and you have the nerve to point a finger at *me*?"

But this time he didn't bite. He just stood there shaking his head, looking at her as if he didn't even know her, as if she were some bothersome stranger he'd had the bad luck to get stuck with in an elevator. "Nuh-uh, no way," he said, almost as if he were talking to himself, not to her. "I'm not gonna get sucked in this time. I'm through."

"Just like that? Without even giving me the benefit of the doubt?"

"It'd be more than you ever gave me."

"What's *that* supposed to mean?"

"Talk's cheap, Erin. It's easy for you to say you would've backed me up, but the fact is you didn't."

"Oh, so we're back to that again. You're never going to let me forget it, are you? Well, let me tell you something, Mister . . ." She pulled herself up to all five feet four inches of her height, bristling like a cat. But she was stopped cold by the look on Skip's face: that of someone who wasn't interested in getting the last word, who just wanted out. The fight drained from her, and she sank onto the bed.

When he'd finished packing, he brushed past her without so much as a glance in her direction. She flinched when she heard the front door slam shut down the hall. Each muffled thud of his footsteps descending the stairs was a punch in the gut. Then . . . nothing. For the longest time she sat staring sightlessly into space. Then with an arm that seemed to float up of its own accord, she reached for the phone to cancel their dinner reservation.

JESSIE:

Long-distance relationship . . . now there's an oxymoron. How can you be with someone when you're nowhere near that someone? The only one who comes out ahead, in my experience, is the phone company. My monthly cell phone bill (unlimited weekend minutes will only get you so far) would cover the rent on a double-wide trailer at the Heavenly Haven Trailer Park, here in Willow Creek. This I know because Emma Coombs, who manages the park, is friendly with the postmistress, Louanne Weedman (Miz Lou to the folks around here), who tucked my most recent Sprint bill into Emma's box by mistake. Now it seems that everyone in town knows what it costs me per month to conduct my long-distance relationship. . . .

From "Life Swap"

Chapter Twelve

"Honestly, I don't know how Skip and Kayla would have managed without you."

Skip's mother smiled up at Jessie, her eyes the blue of the ceanothus sprig in the bud vase in the center of the table at which she and her husband sat having breakfast with Skip and Kayla. No one would have guessed this was the same woman who'd made Erin's life miserable.

"Believe me, it wasn't easy getting Erin to agree to it." Jessie was quick to set the record straight. "I was the only girl in our class who flunked Home Ec. She was afraid I'd turn this place into a disaster zone."

Hugh chuckled, while Paula only murmured non-committally.

Earlier in the week, when Skip had informed Jessie

that he'd invited his parents for breakfast on Sunday, she hadn't known what to expect. She hadn't seen either of them since the wedding that never was, and she couldn't imagine their being too kindly disposed toward her. The warmth with which they'd greeted her had come as a mild shock.

"By the way, Mom sends her love," Kayla told her grandparents with a cheeriness that seemed strained.

"You must be looking forward to seeing her." Hugh patted her arm.

"Yeah, I can't wait. It'll be so awesome." Kayla's eyes lit up. She was counting the days until her trip to New York, as soon as school let out.

"Don't forget to send us a postcard," Paula said.

Skip said nothing. He merely stared down at his plate.

"These are delicious," Paula said, taking a bite of her pancakes.

"Not as good as Erin's, I'm sure," Jessie said.

Hugh got the message and said with false heartiness, "Of course, we're very proud of her. Being on TV, and all. It's really something. Son, would you pass the bacon?" Skip's father had grown portly with age, his sizeable belly earning him a sharp look from his wife as he reached to take the platter from Skip, helping himself to several more strips.

"She's a natural, all right," Jessie said. The first of Erin's segments on the Cooking Channel had aired earlier in the week, and it was clear from the moment she'd appeared on the screen that a star had been born.

"I remember the first time I performed onstage. . . ."

Skip's mother launched into a tale about her reign as Miss Arizona 1958. She'd kept her figure, and except for her silver hair and her skin that had begun to sag, ever so genteelly, like a delicate silk undergarment that had lost its elasticity, it wasn't hard to imagine her in a swimsuit before a panel of judges.

When she was done, Skip pushed his chair back, asking, "More coffee, anyone?"

"I'll get it." Jessie seized the excuse to slip away.

The inn was fully booked, and every table filled. Her and Erin's fifteen minutes of fame had proved an unexpected boon for the Darby Inn; a number of first-time guests had commented that they'd wanted to see for themselves if it was as quaint as Jessie had made it sound. She was kept so busy running back and forth from the kitchen, she didn't have a chance to speak with Skip's parents again until they were leaving.

"Such a treat, my dear. And so wonderful to see you," Paula said.

"My pleasure." Jessie kissed Paula's proffered cheek.

Paula's hand lingered on her arm. "Why don't you come for dinner one night? It'd be just like old times."

Paula and Hugh exchanged a meaningful glance. They clearly had an ulterior motive. Jessie recalled Skip's mentioning that his parents' one remaining wish in life was to see their older son married. Could they be plotting to get her and Mike back together? If so, it would explain their apparent, and somewhat baffling willingness to let bygones be bygones.

She felt flustered all of a sudden. "That's nice of you, but I'm not sure if . . ." she started to say.

Skip, sensing her discomfort, stepped up alongside her to announce, "Mom, Dad, I don't know if you've heard, but Jessie's engaged."

Paula's jaw dropped. "Engaged?"

Jessie nodded, wearing a strained smile.

"Congratulations, my dear." Hugh recovered his manners, and asked with forced politeness, "Who's the lucky man?"

"His name's Jonathon. Jonathon Silver. He's the New York bureau chief for CTN," Jessie informed him.

"He's really hot," Kayla piped.

Paula colored slightly, and took her husband's arm, saying, "Hugh, we should go. We don't want to be late for Mindy's party."

Watching them go, Jessie secretly felt like a fraud, acting like the proud fiancée when the truth was she'd been having second thoughts. After Jonathon had gone back to New York, the initial excitement had worn off and doubts had crept back in. She'd begun to wonder if she hadn't been a little hasty in accepting his proposal. After all, what assurance did she have that things would be different when she got back?

There was also the matter of Hunter George. He was like an itch she couldn't scratch—maddening and at the same time tantalizing. The best remedy would be to avoid him altogether, but right now that wasn't feasible. He was the focal point of her piece—the public outcry that had greeted his arrest was just as he'd predicted, and even now that he was out on bail, the media was heralding him as a martyr. The photographer assigned by *People*, a stringer named Andrea Haynes, was driving down from Phoenix on Friday to do the shoot, which meant that Jessie and Hunter would be spending the better part of the day together.

Jessie turned to Skip, and said, "Thanks for rescuing me. Somehow I don't think Erin would have appreciated my getting chummy with your folks."

"I didn't do it for Erin," he said, his jaw tightening.

Jessie knew his trip to New York had ended disastrously. Erin had called in tears the day after he'd left to tell her all about it. Had they finally run out of road? Jessie hoped not. The more she was around Skip, the more she saw how right he was for Erin, despite their obvious differences—she was the yang to his yin, the vinegar to his oil.

"It's not just them, you know," he said, gazing out the window, watching his parents make their way down the walk. "She hasn't made it any easier."

"Can you blame her?"

He brought his gaze back to Jessie, looking so morose it was all she could do not to place a comforting hand on his arm. "It wasn't that they didn't like her. Christ, they barely knew her. They still hadn't gotten over you and Mike, and suddenly there I am announcing that my girlfriend's pregnant. They didn't know what hit them."

"It was a hard time for Erin, too. She'd just lost her parents," Jessie reminded him.

He nodded slowly. "I know, that's what made it so tough. I see both sides."

Jessie could only hope he'd find it in his heart to forgive Erin now.

"Almost there!" Hunter shouted above the roar of his SUV's engine as they bumped their way up the steep incline.

The narrow dirt lane they were on led to the long-defunct silver mines, a once-busy thoroughfare of horse-drawn carts and mules, from the sepia photos in the museum, now so rutted and overgrown it was accessible only by four-wheel drive. Jessie had no idea where he was taking her; he'd been mysterious about the purpose of this particular destination, the last in a long afternoon of traipsing over the countryside, with Andrea Haynes taking shots of muddy flats where streams had once flowed and of grim-faced homeowners posed beside cracked foundations; and, even more dramatically, of Hunter, posed on the courthouse steps looking as if he were facing down a cavalry charge. Now they were on their way up Miner's Hill, Andrea bringing up the rear in her Explorer.

It wasn't until they reached the summit and Hunter pulled over that Jessie understood why he'd brought them here. Climbing out of the Pathfinder, she was met by a view of the once-pristine forest marred by great swaths of brown where the trees were either dead or dying.

"My God, what happened?" she asked softly, in dismay.

Hunter waited until Andrea had caught up with them before offering an explanation. "Beetles. They do more damage than the logging everyone was so fired up about a few years back." Trees produce a natural insect repellant, he said, and when they don't get enough water, they're vulnerable to infestation. To prove his point, he bent to pick up a piece of bark riddled with holes, crumpling it in his fist like so much Styrofoam.

Andrea, whom Jessie had pegged as the no-nonsense type, a single woman in her late forties with a brisk air about her and graying brown hair that was strictly wash and wear, looked skeptical. "Isn't drought responsible for some of it?" she asked.

They'd had a few dry years, sure, Hunter acknowledged. But even in times of drought the trees' taproots went deep enough to reach the water table. Only when it dropped below a certain level did they suffer the kind of damage in evidence now. "I'm surprised it hasn't burned down," he said, gazing out at the ravaged landscape, his face curiously expressionless, like storm shutters battened against a brewing storm.

Jessie was sickened by what she saw. What had begun as a sense of civic duty, and a desire to have something more to show for her time in Willow Creek than learning to make waffles and to do hospital corners, had steadily grown into a sense of moral outrage.

Andrea fired off more shots before finally calling it a day. As she was packing up her gear, Hunter turned to Jessie, asking, "Ever been up to the mines?" She shook her head, and he said, "It's a nice hike. If you're not in any hurry to get back, I could take you up there."

"With our luck, we'd probably get attacked by a bear," she said with a laugh.

He grinned. "More likely a skunk."

"In that case, you're responsible for my dry-cleaning bill." Was she actually agreeing to this insanity? The real danger wasn't from wild animals, she knew. It was from being alone in the woods with this man. She hadn't forgotten the last time, when they'd come close to discovering just how creative two people could get in an SUV.

At the same time, with the sun shining and the rest of the afternoon to herself—Maria wasn't expecting her back until that evening—Jessie couldn't think of anything else she'd rather do.

After seeing Andrea off, they set out along the trail. It was so overgrown in spots it was hard to make out, but Hunter, leading the way, didn't miss a step. "Do you come here a lot?" she asked, when the trail widened enough to allow them to walk side by side.

He nodded. "It's a good place to clear your head."

"You must have a lot on your mind these days." He was scheduled to be arraigned on Monday. If his lawyer couldn't get the charges dropped, which appeared unlikely at this point, Hunter would be looking at a trial.

But if he was worried, he showed no sign of it. "You know what I'm thinking right now?" he said. "That Mother Nature is one tough broad." He glanced up in appreciation at the dense canopy of leaves overhead—this part of the forest, untouched by infestation, was still lush and green.

"You're not worried about your court date?"

"Not particularly."

"You could go to prison," she reminded him.

He flashed her a smile, alternate patterns of light and shadow flickering over his face as they strolled along the path. "I'm flattered that you're so concerned about my welfare, but I don't think that's what's really bothering you," he said, holding a branch aside so it wouldn't swat her in the face as she stepped from the shade into the sunlight of a clearing.

"What makes you think something's bothering me?" she asked.

There was a swishing noise behind her as he released the branch. "You've been preoccupied all day."

She frowned. "What gave you that idea?"

"For one thing, you kept calling that poor woman Alicia."

"I did?"

"Also, after lunch you walked off without your credit card."

Jessie stopped in her tracks, swinging around to face him. "Why on earth didn't you say something?"

"You were nice enough to pick up the tab. I didn't want to embarrass you in front of Alicia." His smile widened as he dug into his back pocket and pulled out her Visa card.

"Thanks." She snatched it from him, her cheeks burning.

In the cathedral-like hush of the forest, broken only by the rusty cawing of a blue jay, she was acutely aware of Hunter's presence—the measured crunch of his footsteps and his sleeve brushing against her, electrifying the tiny hairs on her arm. Several more minutes passed before he inquired casually, "Did you have a nice visit with your boyfriend?"

She hadn't yet gotten around to telling him that her boyfriend was now her fiancé, and she wondered again why she was witholding the information. "Very nice, thank you," she replied somewhat primly.

"Must be tough, being so far apart."

"We manage. Jonathon's very supportive."

Hunter shot her an odd look, but didn't respond.

"Actually, I think the time apart's been good for us," Jessie went on, frowning down at the ground as she walked. "It's given us both a chance to put things into perspective."

"How so?"

"We were having some problems," she admitted. "I guess it comes with being older—we all have our baggage. He's divorced with kids, and I . . ." She hesitated, thinking of her less-than-stellar history with men. "I've lived on my own for so long, I've gotten kind of set in my ways. It's a matter of striking a balance between your expectations and what's real."

"You make it sound like a negotiation."

"In some ways, it is."

"To me, it's pretty simple," he said with a shrug. "Either

you love someone enough to take them, warts and all, or you don't."

"That's a little naive, don't you think?" A note of irritation crept into her voice.

He looked at her with those cool, assessing eyes, as if to say, *Maybe you've never been in love.*

He hadn't spoken it aloud, but Jessie found herself growing indignant nonetheless. What right did he have to make such assumptions? Anyway, what did *he* know? She didn't see a ring on his finger.

A few hundred feet or so ahead, the trail ended on the bank of a dry gorge littered with the remains of a footbridge that must have been washed out in a flash flood. She was about to suggest they turn back when Hunter began picking his way down the steep slope, leaving Jessie no choice but to follow. She was halfway down when she lost her footing and, with a yelp, went skidding the rest of the way on her backside to land at the bottom amid a hail of loose dirt and pebbles.

She looked up to find Hunter peering down at her with concern. "Are you okay?"

"I think so," she said, as he helped her to her feet. "Nothing seems to be broken."

His dark eyes remained fixed on her even after he'd let go of her, and for several long moments they just stood there facing each other, still as a held breath, the dust settling around them. When he reached for her hand once more, drawing her close and wrapping his arms around her, she didn't resist.

As his mouth closed over hers, she parted her lips and felt the tip of his tongue against hers, soft and seeking. His hands moved down the small of her back, sliding into the back pockets of her jeans and pulling her in so they were hip to hip. *This isn't supposed to be happening*, she thought. But an odd, heat-stunned lethargy had settled over her, and while mentally a part of her stood off to one side, looking on in silent disapproval, she twined her arms around Hunter's neck, kissing him deeply as she arched into him.

They found a sandy spot ringed with boulders, and he took off his shirt, spreading it over the ground for them to lie on. Seeing him kneeling before her bare-chested, she thought she'd never known anyone so magnificent. His skin, polished with sweat, gleamed a deep bronze, streaks of dirt standing out on his thickly muscled arms. Yet there was none of the subtle preening she'd noticed with other men—the pose held a second too long, the oh-so-casual movement designed to show off all those hours at the gym.

When they were both undressed, he took his time getting to know her body. He cupped her breasts, running his thumbs lightly over her nipples before bending to kiss, first one, then the other, reverentially almost, the ends of his hair brushing over her skin. Light touches alternated with more insistent ones as he explored, not just with his hands, but with his mouth. Jessie grew faint with desire. Even with Jonathon, she'd never felt anything this intense.

He shot her a questioning look, and she murmured she was safe—she'd been tested and she was on the Pill. He slipped into her then, and she tightened her legs about him. Drugged with heat, their bodies slick with sweat, they rocked together in a languorous rhythm. She came with a sharp cry. He came moments later, making no sound at all, but with a convulsive shudder that gripped her to her core.

They lay still for a bit, then he drew back to kiss her softly on the lips. "Better?"

"Much." Her mouth curled in a little cat smile.

"At least you know I wasn't planning to seduce you." Otherwise, he said, he'd have come prepared.

She laughed. "Fat chance."

Though she wasn't entirely sure she wouldn't have thrown caution to the winds nonetheless—he had that effect on her. Look how easily she'd given in to him, without so much as a whisper of protest. Hardly the behavior of an engaged woman! But those thoughts only flitted through her head without landing, like the gnats hovering over them, attracted by their sweat. At the moment, it seemed she hadn't a care in the world. They lay on their backs, gazing up at the blue denim sky, where the sun had passed its zenith and a hawk wheeled in lazy circles.

She must have dozed off for a bit, because when she opened her eyes she saw that shadows had slipped out from under the surrounding boulders. On the ridge above, the setting sun glinted gold amid the treetops. Groggily, she pulled herself upright and began tugging on her clothes.

They didn't speak until they were heading back along the trail, and then it was only small talk—talk that did little to obscure the question looming large in Jessie's mind: *What now?*

With the lengthening shadows had come the chill of realization: She'd cheated on Jonathon. Even if he never found out, it was something *she* would have to live with. Worse was the niggling suspicion that it hadn't been just an itch needing to be scratched, that whatever she felt for Hunter was more than mere animal attraction—a thought more troubling than what had happened back there in the gorge.

She wondered if what Hunter had implied was true: that she wasn't in love with Jonathon, not really. Was it even possible to love someone that much, to be able to walk down the aisle on your wedding day without any doubts or fears, knowing there could never be anyone else? Look at Skip and Erin, whom she'd once thought the most happily married of couples. If they were anything to go by, it was proof that happily ever after existed only in fairy tales.

They stopped at the Sunoco station for gas on their way back into town. Hunter had filled his tank and gone inside to pay when a yellow Dodge Ram, the door on the driver's side bearing the logo MILE HIGH CONSTRUCTION, pulled into the next pump. The driver hopped out, a tall, well-built man in paint-spattered jeans and a red baseball cap with the same logo as his truck—a man she recognized with a small shock as Mike Delahanty.

The timing was almost eerie. What was this, the Ghost of Failed Relationships come to warn her against repeating the same mistake?

She shrank down in her seat, but it was too late. He caught sight of her and, after a moment's hesitation, began walking toward her. He came to a halt a few feet from her open window.

"Jessie, hey. Long time, no see." In the lowering sun, the brim of his cap cast a wedge of shadow over his face. All she could see was his mouth curled in an ironic little smile.

"Hi, Mike." Her own smile felt glued on.

"I heard you were back in town."

An understatement—according to Kayla, he'd been going out of his way to avoid her. "You heard right," she said in the same relaxed tone. Two could play at this game.

"You look good."

"So do you."

An awkward silence fell. Mike glanced over at Hunter, who was still inside, chatting with the kid behind the counter. "What're you doing mixed up with *him*?" he asked.

She bristled. "Who said I was mixed up with anyone?"

"Look, it's none of my business, but I'd watch out if I were you. That kind of trouble has a way of rubbing off."

"Thanks for the warning," she said stiffly.

"Hey, it's no sweat off me."

It was obvious the statute of limitations hadn't run out on her crime, at least not as far as Mike was concerned. But could she blame him? What she'd done to him was unforgivable.

She quickly changed the subject, remarking, "I understand you've done well for yourself." She glanced toward his truck, its bed piled with ladders and tools. "Skip tells me you're so busy, you're turning away business."

He nodded. "You haven't done too badly yourself, from what I hear."

"It's a living," she said with a shrug.

"You're being modest." His smile widened into a grin that made her think of a dog baring its teeth. "The guys tell me it's all their wives talk about—that 'Wife Swap' column of yours."

"It's 'Life Swap,'" she corrected him.

"Yeah, whatever." His smirking grin let her know there was no distinction as far as he was concerned. "You know, there's talk that old Skip's part of the bargain. Him moving back in and all, you have to admit it looks kind of fishy. And he always did have a thing for you." He pushed his cap back, and she saw the cold, unsmiling eyes above his grin. It was more than that he hadn't forgiven her; he was out for blood.

"There's nothing going on between me and Skip," she informed him coolly.

"If you say so." He leaned in, resting his elbows against the open window, his face inches from hers. She noticed the puffiness under his eyes and the slight sag under his chin—Mike was still handsome, but he wasn't aging as well as Skip. "On the other hand, I don't know why I should take your word for it, given that your word doesn't count for much."

"Mike, please . . ." Jessie lowered her voice. "I don't want a scene. If you have something to say to me, just say it."

He gave a harsh laugh. "Don't flatter yourself—I got over you a long time ago, lady. In fact, you did me a favor. It looks like us Delahanty boys aren't the marrying kind after all. Good thing my brother finally wised up."

Just then, she caught sight of Hunter walking toward them. He assessed the situation at once, asking, "Is there a problem?" He spoke calmly, but she heard the note of warning in his voice.

"No problem," Mike answered, that smirking grin never leaving his face. "Jessie and I were just catching up on old times."

Hunter cast her a questioning look, and she said weakly, "I don't know if you've met Skip's brother."

"We've met," Hunter said flatly.

"I was just congratulating Jessie here on being the toast of the town," Mike went on, his good-old-boy drawl becoming more pronounced with every word. "She sure knows how to get people talking. In fact, I'd have to say that if there was one person guaranteed to make waves, it's our Miss Jessie—soon to be Mrs. Somebody-or-other. By the way"—he paused to tip his hat to her—"congratulations on your bee-trothal." He drew out each syllable.

"I'm sure you'll make him a happy man. That is, if you don't end up leaving him at the altar."

Hunter took a step toward him, hands balled into fists. "That's enough."

Jessie, panicking at the thought of a fight, cried softly, "Hunter, no, it's all right. . . ."

"You better listen to the lady," Mike mocked. "Aren't you in enough trouble as it is?"

"I only go looking for trouble when it's worth my while," Hunter replied, eyeing Mike as if he were of no more consequence than a squashed bug on the windshield. "Now, if you'll excuse us . . ." He walked around to the driver's side and climbed in, starting the engine.

Jessie, unnerved from the encounter, stared sightlessly out the window as they pulled out of the station and headed down the road. *I should never have come back*, she thought. She should have let sleeping dogs lie. Mike hadn't forgiven her, and neither had her mother. Maybe she didn't deserve to be forgiven. Look at her now, still making a mess of things.

As if echoing her thoughts, Hunter remarked coolly "So you're engaged? Funny you didn't mention it. Something like that, I don't see how it could have slipped your mind."

"I was going to tell you, before we—" She broke off, growing warm at the memory.

"Does he know?"

"About us?" Her voice rose to a panicked squeak. "No, and there's no reason he has to."

"Assuming it was just a one-time deal." His voice was flat.

She grew even warmer. "I didn't expect this to happen. It just . . . happened."

He cast her a bemused glance that didn't disguise the hurt in his eyes. "Sort of like the weather, huh? You're walking along enjoying the sunshine when all of a sudden it starts to pour."

"I didn't say that. You're putting words in my mouth."

"What *are* you saying then?" His tone remained mild, but she noticed that his grip on the steering wheel had tightened.

She sighed. "I don't know. Can we take it a step at a time?"

Hunter didn't answer right away. He kept his eyes on the road, his knuckles standing out like knots on a rope, he was gripping the wheel so hard. "What happened up there on the mountain," he said at last, "it felt more like a leap than a step."

Make that a trip to the moon, she thought. She reached out to touch his arm. "I'm sorry. I should've told you about Jonathon. The reason I didn't is because I'm a little confused at the moment. In fact, if I were you, I'd be running in the opposite direction. You saw what happened back there with Mike. It's been more than fifteen years, and he's still pissed at me. That's how royally I screwed up."

"Looks to me like you'd have made a bigger mistake marrying him."

"True," she acknowledged. "But that doesn't change the fact that I handled it badly."

"What happened? You never told me."

"I just woke up one day and knew I couldn't go through with it."

"Cold feet?"

"More like hypothermia." She was quick to add, "It's different with Jonathon. I went into it with both eyes wide open."

"And now?"

Jessie felt a sudden, queer lightness in the pit of her stomach that was part excitement and part fear, like when she used to coast downhill on her bike as a kid without holding on to the handlebars—usually when Erin had dared her to. Was she willing to take a risk now, with Hunter?

She gazed out the window, so heavily coated with dust that in the last slanting rays of the setting sun the houses and lawns skimming past seemed tinted in sepia—as if this were a dream sequence in a movie. "I'll let you know as soon as I know," she said.

Jessie walked in to find Maria assembling the evening cheese plates. Maria glanced up at her. "There you are. I was beginning to think something had happened to you."

Something did happen, Jessie thought. Something a lot bigger than engine trouble or a flat tire. "Sorry. I should've phoned. Everything okay?"

"All quiet on the Western front," Maria reported. She

was slicing strawberries and arranging them in little fans on each plate. "Oh, before I forget, Mrs. Dawson called to say their flight was delayed; they won't get in until after midnight. I told her where we keep the spare key."

"I don't mind waiting up," Jessie said. She might as well; she wouldn't be getting much sleep tonight as it was.

Maria cast a pointed glance at Jessie's arm. "You should put something on that sunburn." Jessie looked down and saw, on her right arm just above the elbow, the pale imprint of Hunter's fingers standing out like a brand against the angry pink of the surrounding flesh—his hand must have been resting there when she'd dozed off. She felt herself flush. Maria giggled. "Talk about being caught red-handed."

"I guess it wouldn't do any good to make up an excuse about why I'm late?" Jessie said sheepishly.

"Nope. Consider yourself officially busted." The smile flickering at the corners of Maria's mouth burst into a full-fledged grin.

Jessie sank down in a chair at the table. "God, what a mess."

"Yeah, tough break." Maria shook her head in mock sympathy. "Two gorgeous men, and you can only pick one. It's like *The Bachelorette*, when it's down to the final rose. Who'll be the lucky one? Who gets sent home?"

Jessie groaned. "This isn't a reality show. It's my life."

"Once this gets out, the women who can't even get a date will run you out of town on a rail," Maria predicted cheerfully.

"Right now, I wouldn't mind."

"Of course, whoever you *don't* pick, I'd be happy to volunteer as consolation prize." Maria struck a coy pose, looking so comical as she batted her Betty Boop eyes, her dark ringlets bouncing about her head, that Jessie gave in to a laugh.

"I don't know what I'm going to do," Jessie moaned. "In fact, I don't even know how I got into this mess in the first place. I thought Hunter and I were just friends."

"Are you kidding? Practically every woman I know wants to jump that man's bones. Why should you be any different?"

"Because I'm taken, that's why." The thought of Jonathon brought a fresh stab of remorse.

"You're sure about that?" Maria arched a brow.

Jessie sighed. She'd thought so . . . until now.

"It could be worse," Maria said. "You could be in Erin's shoes."

"I thought I *was* in her shoes," Jessie said, gesturing around her. Then, noting Maria's serious expression, she asked, "What? Is something wrong?"

Maria hesitated before answering. "The other day I saw Skip coming out of Jack Flagler's office." She dropped her voice to add, "Jack's the one who handled Cricket's divorce."

A little alarm bell went off in Jessie's head, but she was quick to reply, "It doesn't necessarily mean anything." As far as she knew, Jack Flagler didn't specialize in family law.

Still, she couldn't rule out the obvious: that Skip was lining up his ducks.

Maria nodded, and said, "You're probably right. It's just that I can't help wondering if . . . you know."

Jessie nodded, feeling sick inside. "It would kill Erin."

"Should we say something to her?" Maria eyed her anxiously.

Jessie shook her head. "We don't know anything for sure." First, she would see what she could find out from Skip. Until it was confirmed, Erin was better off being in the dark.

"I just hope she knows what she's doing," Maria said. "A guy like Skip . . . let's just say he wouldn't have to place a personals ad. I'm sure the line is already forming to the left."

"Even if she flew home tomorrow, it wouldn't automatically solve everything," Jessie pointed out.

Maria shook her head. "Poor Kayla. She's the one I feel sorriest for. She never asked for any of this."

Jessie caught a movement in the hallway out of the corner of her eye just then, but when she turned to look, the hallway was empty. Probably just Otis wandering around looking for handouts—guests were always slipping him treats. She thought nothing more of it as she reached for a knife and began cutting the Brie on the cheese board into wedges.

ERIN:

I talked to this homeless man on the street the other day. I gave him a dollar, he gave me the story of his life. I was amazed to learn he'd been an economics professor, before drink got the better of him, as he put it. We talked about the state of the economy, and how it would be affected if the current interest rate went up. In the grocery cart that held his worldly belongings were yellowing copies of the Wall Street Journal. It was the only paper worth reading, he said. The rest, he told me with a disdainful flick of his wrist, were just garbage.

This man's whole life had been nuked, and yet inside that bombed-out shell he was still intact. His intelligence. His humanity, for lack of a better word. It made me wonder how this experience has changed me. Am I any different? Or am I just the same person in a different setting? Are the new friends I've made any better than the ones I left behind? All I know is that my favorite meal is still macaroni and cheese. I still get teary-eyed over Hallmark commercials and chick flicks on Lifetime. And I have yet to see a painting at the Metropolitan Museum that moved me as much as the drawings my daughter used to bring home from school. . . .

—From "Life Swap"

Chapter Thirteen

The first week in June, Erin subbed for Modou Nyambe, the hot new Nigerian chef, who was on tour promoting his new cookbook—her first experience with live-to-tape since she'd gotten her feet wet on *The Singing Chef*. She'd been a little nervous at first, but it had gone okay, and by Thursday, when she was summoned to the executive producer's office, she expected nothing more than a pat on the back for a job well done. Instead, Latrice announced, "I just got out of a meeting with Randy." As in Randall Freeman, the network head. "We're putting together the fall lineup, and we'd like you on it."

"You . . . you mean my own show?" Erin heard herself stammer.

"If you're interested."

For once, Erin was speechless. She hadn't allowed herself to believe this whole thing was anything more than a fluke. Now her boss was telling her that it was only the beginning. She shook her head in wonderment. "I don't know what to say."

Latrice smiled. "I hope you'll say yes."

"It's a big step," Erin said. "Can I get back to you?" Kayla would be arriving tomorrow for a weeklong visit; Erin needed to discuss it with her before she could make a decision. There was so much at stake. . . .

"Take your time," Latrice said airily. But Erin knew that time in this universe was relative; they'd need an answer by next week at the latest.

Latrice sketched out a rough outline for the show. It would be more down-home than haute cuisine, along the lines of what Erin had already been doing. Thirty segments to start with, and they'd build from there if it netted a good audience share. Latrice didn't have to add that a hit show like *The Singing Chef* could spawn an entire industry—Enzo, in addition to half a dozen cookbooks, had his own cookware line, bottled sauces, DVDs and video-on-demand, even a chain of restaurants of which he was part-owner. If you were a household name, Erin knew, there was millions to be made in ancillary profits alone. It was mind-boggling. . . .

When the meeting was over, Erin floated to her feet, surrendering her hand to Latrice's executive grip. It was too much to take in all at once. She'd need the weekend just to process it.

She wondered what Kayla's reaction would be. Something this huge that involved her daughter couldn't be Erin's decision alone—not if she wanted to remain on speaking terms with Kayla. How would Kayla feel about moving to New York? It would mean changing schools and saying good-bye to her friends, most of whom she'd known since kindergarten. It would also mean visits with her father being limited to summers and school breaks.

And Skip? Erin knew that if she accepted this offer, it would be the start of a whole new life, but it would also mean the death to her old one. It might already be too late for her and Skip, but if there was even a thread of hope left she'd be severing it.

That evening, when Drew invited her to join him for a bite to eat, Erin jumped at the chance—if she'd had to sit alone in her apartment one more minute, with her brain running in circles like a caged squirrel, she'd have been climbing the walls. Minutes later they were in a cab, on their way to her favorite Italian eatery in the East Village, one that Enzo had turned her on to.

It was a warm night, so they chose to sit out on the patio, an ivied grotto strung with fairy lights. Over a bottle of Pinot Noir, as they caught up on things, she felt herself gradually unwind. She hadn't seen much of Drew since that awful business with Skip. The truth was she'd been avoiding him, which she felt badly about—none of this was Drew's fault. But in the wake of her husband's abrupt and angry departure, while she'd still been licking her wounds, Drew had been too painful a reminder.

"You'll need an agent," he said, when she'd told him about Latrice's offer. "I know a few people. I'll make some calls first thing in the morning." His eyes shone with excitement, as much for himself as for her, she suspected. If she moved to New York, they'd be doing more than dancing around the edge of the volcano.

"Whoa. I haven't even given them an answer yet." She was quick to put on the brakes. "First I have to talk to my daughter. Also—" She broke off before she could add, "my husband." "There's a lot at stake. I might be biting off more than I can chew. Maybe I'm too old to start from scratch."

"Since when does thirty-five qualify as old?" he teased.

"Easy for you to say," she said. "You can pick up and go anytime you want. It's different when you're a parent."

"I thought you said your daughter loves New York."

"To visit. I'm not sure she'd want to live here."

"We'll, you'll have the whole week to sell her on the idea. I'll even do my bit by showing her around while you're at work."

"That's nice of you, but . . ." Erin hesitated. "Let's see how it goes, okay?"

Drew captured her hand, lacing his fingers through hers. "Of course, I have an ulterior motive. You've spoiled me forever for takeout. If you leave, who'll feed me?"

She laughed, withdrawing her hand as soon as she could without it seeming abrupt. "I guess it's true what they say about stray cats—a saucer of milk, and they're yours forever." She could see from Drew's expression that he wasn't fooled by her lighthearted tone; he knew she was avoiding the real issue.

"What about your husband?" he ventured at last, as they were tucking into a platter of antipasto. "Where does he figure into all this?"

"I haven't discussed it with him," she said, adding with a sigh, "At the moment, we're not on speaking terms."

"Uh-oh. That doesn't sound like a recipe for domestic bliss."

She sighed again. "You don't know the half of it."

"He seemed kind of upset when he left. Was it something I said?" Drew looked genuinely concerned, and she knew it wasn't just an act. She felt a surge of affection for him.

She rushed to assure him, "No, nothing like that." She explained about the photos.

"Erin, I'm so sorry," Drew said. Clearly he hadn't intended for this to happen. "I shouldn't have left them out where he could see them."

"You had nothing to hide," she told him.

"Still, he must have been thinking, where there's smoke, there's fire."

He wasn't wrong about that, Erin thought. Except the fire had been stamped out. If he'd stuck around long enough, if he'd bothered to *listen* to her, he'd have seen that for himself.

Erin, distracted by her thoughts, barely tasted the rest

of her meal. It wasn't until they were back home, climbing the stairs, that she realized how she must've come across to Drew; she hadn't spoken more than two words to him since they'd left the restaurant. To atone for her bad manners, she insisted that he give her his blazer, which he'd spilled wine on at dinner, to spot-clean. Stains she could deal with; they didn't require guesswork or soul-searching.

"You sure you don't mind?" he asked, slipping off his jacket at her door.

"Not at all. The trick is to soak it in milk—the stain comes right out."

She was reaching into her purse for her keys when he leaned in to kiss her on the cheek. But instead of pulling back, he moved in closer, his arms circling her. As his mouth closed over hers, Erin sagged against the doorframe, her purse slipping from her hand along with his jacket and dropping to the carpeted landing with a muffled thud. It was like a drug taking effect, rolling through her in warm, rippling waves, bringing the heady rush of realization that there was at least one man on the planet who didn't find her intolerable.

After a moment, he drew back to murmur, "Should we take this inside?"

Erin was sorely tempted. It would be so easy—as easy as turning the key in the lock.

What's stopping you? urged a voice in her head. For all she knew, Skip could have cheated on her by now. From his perspective, she hadn't given him a reason not to.

She bent to retrieve her purse, rooting in it for her keys. No, not *her* keys—*Jessie's*. For the first few months Erin had felt as if she were living Jessie's life as well. But that was no longer the case. Whatever happened from now on, it would be of her own making.

Her fingers closed over the keys, tightening until she could feel them digging into her palm. She stood there with her head bowed, as if concentrating hard . . . or praying. At last she looked up at Drew, and slowly, regretfully, shook her head. "I'm sorry. I'm not ready."

She saw a flash of disappointment in his eyes, but all he said was, "I can wait." Maybe not forever, but at least until she'd decided what her next move would be.

Moments later she heard him whistling on the landing above as he let himself into his apartment. Not like a man who'd been rejected—twice. More like he knew something she didn't.

"Does your neck ever get sore?" Kayla asked, craning to look up at the tall buildings around her.

Erin smiled. Not so long ago she'd been the one with her head constantly tipped back in openmouthed wonder. "You get used to it," she said.

She hadn't broken the news yet about her job offer. They'd been having such a good time, Erin hadn't wanted to spoil it. The evening before, they'd gone straight home from the airport, where they'd caught up on all the latest gossip. This morning they'd gotten up early to go sightseeing. So far, they'd been to St. Patrick's and

Rockefeller Center. They'd had tea at Burberry's, and Kayla had tried on practically everything in her size at H&M. Yet apparently she wasn't too grown up for FAO Schwarz, where she'd squealed with delight at its vast menagerie of stuffed animals.

Now they were strolling along Fifth Avenue on their way to the Empire State Building. Kayla had always wanted to see the view from the top, but both times she'd visited Jessie the weather hadn't cooperated. Today it was sunny skies; they'd be able see all the way to the Jersey skyline and beyond. They paused on the corner of Thirty-fourth Street to buy soft pretzels from a street vendor, munching on them as they stood in line at the Empire State. Before long, they were riding the elevator up to the observation deck.

"Wow. Everything looks so small from up here." Kayla gazed in wonder at the city spread below; the buildings that had seemed so tall from the street looked like alphabet blocks.

"I remember the first time I came here, with your aunt Jess—we weren't much older than you. I had the bright idea of tossing a note off the deck." Erin smiled at the memory.

"What did the note say?" Kayla sounded intrigued.

"Nothing much. It was just to let whoever found it know that we'd been here—Erin and Jessie, two girls fresh out of college ready to set the world on fire."

Kayla giggled. "It sounds like something you'd do. It's funny, though, how Aunt Jess stayed, and you went back."

Kayla knew the story of how her plans that long-ago summer had been tragically cut short by her grandparents' deaths. Erin was opening her mouth to tell her that she'd been given the chance to turn the clock back when Kayla wandered over to the next lookout.

"Isn't that Rockefeller Center?" She pointed at the glittering plaza off in the distance, the size of a postage stamp from here.

"Looks like you know your way around," Erin observed.

"It's easy. Aunt Jess showed me on the map how it's all laid out on a grid."

Erin, looking at her daughter leaning into the wind, a leggy young beauty in her jean jacket and ruffled miniskirt—she'd lost a few pounds since Erin had last seen her—felt her heart swell with love. As much as she hated to admit it, the time apart from her had been good for Kayla. She'd matured in ways she might not have with Erin constantly looking over her shoulder, second-guessing her every move; she seemed more self-possessed, more confident. Erin realized that her little girl was growing up, faster than she could keep up with, and she didn't want to miss a single minute more.

"Could you see yourself living here?" she asked.

Kayla turned slowly to face her. From her expression, it was clear she knew that Erin hadn't been referring to some vague time in the distant future. She peered narrowly at Erin through the storm of hair the wind was whipping about her head, asking warily, "Does this have anything to do with you and dad?"

"In a way, I guess." She took a deep breath, and said, "They offered me my own show."

Kayla blinked, her mouth falling open. "Seriously?"

Erin nodded. "I know. I can't believe it either."

"Wow." Kayla shook her head, as if struggling to digest it.

"I haven't given them an answer yet. I wanted to talk it over with you first," Erin hastened to add. Shivering, she leaned up against the granite barrier that, even with the sheet of Plexiglas above it, did little to shelter them from the wind. "It would mean us moving here."

"Us?"

"You and me."

"What about Dad?"

"I'm not sure your father and I—" Erin broke off, not knowing quite how to phrase it. Gently, she said, "If things don't work out, I have to start thinking ahead."

"You mean if you get divorced." There was a brittle edge in Kayla's voice.

"No one said anything about divorce." Erin spoke a bit too sharply, but she knew as well as Kayla that that was where this road was leading.

Kayla glanced at the other tourists huddled in small groups along the deck. She wasn't far past the age when just being seen in public with her parents was a source of embarrassment. "What do you know? When was the last time you even *talked* to Dad?" Kayla demanded in a low, angry voice.

"We haven't talked in a while, but . . . sweetie, what is

it, what's wrong?" Tears were running down Kayla's cheeks. Erin reached to comfort her, but Kayla ducked away.

"I heard Maria and Aunt Jess talking," she said in a choked voice. "Maria said that Dad had gone to see a lawyer."

Invisible fingers closed around Erin's heart. It was all she could do to maintain a neutral tone as she replied, "People see lawyers for all kinds of reasons."

"That's what Aunt Jess told Maria."

Erin, struggling to contain her emotions, gazed out at the city she'd come to love, at the toy cars moving in neat stitched lines down streets that appeared no wider than her thumbnail. Why hadn't Jessie told her? Erin felt betrayed, even though she knew deep down that Jessie was only trying to protect her. Mainly what she felt, though, was sad. "I never expected it to turn out like this," she said.

She hadn't realized tears were running down her own cheeks until Kayla hugged her, and said, "Don't cry, Mom. Maybe Aunt Jess was right, maybe it didn't mean anything."

Erin straightened and forced a smile. "Either way, you didn't come all this way for a pity party. We're supposed to be having fun. What do you say we head back down? There's loads more to see."

Kayla drew back to fix her with the somber gaze of the young woman she'd become in Erin's absence. "Mom," she said in the exact same tone Erin had used with her when she was little and needed reassuring, "I didn't come to see the sights. I came to see you."

Chapter Fourteen

Jessie arrived at the courthouse the morning of Hunter's preliminary hearing to find news vans double-parked along the curb and reporters jostling for space with the crowd of protestors on the steps out front. It was just as Hunter had predicted. Her story in last week's *People* had stirred a public outcry and made him an overnight cause célèbre. There had been a slew of calls from environmental groups offering their assistance. Don Sidwell, the Democratic congressman from their district, had issued a statement decrying "the pillaging of our nation's precious resources for profit." And, of course, the Navajo tribal council had weighed in, in support of one of their own. As Jessie drew nearer, she spotted Hunter's boyhood pal, Art Begay, whom she'd met at the arraignment, along with at least a dozen more of Hunter's friends and relatives from the reservation, all chanting and waving placards. It was several more minutes before she was able to make her way through the crush to the courtroom on the second floor, where the hearing was scheduled to take place.

She found Hunter at the defendant's table seated next to his lawyer, an older man with bright blue eyes that peered up at her puckishly from under squirrelly white brows. "Mornin,' darling," Stu greeted her in his down-home drawl. It didn't fool her any more than did his suspenders and bola tie: Stu had gotten his degree from Columbia Law and could hold his own with any top-notch city lawyer. "You get a load of our welcoming committee? You'd think this fellow here was a rock star." He clapped a hand over Hunter's shoulder.

"I just hope we haven't created a monster." Jessie cast a wry glance at Hunter as he rose to greet her. He was conservatively dressed, for him, in a charcoal blazer, white oxford shirt, and pressed chinos. She fought an urge to run her fingers through the damp comb tracks in his hair—God, would she ever stop feeling this way when she was around him, like a teenager who'd just discovered sex? "Next thing you know he'll be posing for GQ."

"I promise I won't let it go to my head," he said, smiling. He appeared relaxed, but his gaze was alert as he scanned the faces of the people filing into the courtroom. It was one thing to recognize the publicity value of a media circus, another to be facing a possible prison term.

She felt jittery herself, and not just from the three

cups of coffee she'd downed on an empty stomach (she'd been too nervous to eat breakfast). According to Stu, there was little chance of the charges against Hunter being dismissed; the footprint matching his that had been found near the scene was enough on its own to warrant a trial. Which meant there was a chance he'd be found guilty. At the thought, Jessie's stomach executed another twisting half gainer.

It was all so surreal, like those movies in which the heroine's life plays out on dual tracks. There was the Jessie Holland in New York, who right now would be at Tiffany's, with Jonathon, shopping for a ring . . . and the Jessie Holland taking her seat in the courthouse in Willow Creek, fretting over her lover's fate.

Lover. Even the word seemed alien as she turned it over in her mind. If Jonathon knew, he'd be devastated. Though maybe not as much as she'd thought at first. Ever since they'd gotten engaged he'd reverted back to his old ways, as if, now that he had her sewed up, he didn't have to worry anymore. He didn't call as often, and whenever they did talk he seemed harried or preoccupied. His excuse was that they were short-staffed in the newsroom, but if that was true, why did he seem to have all the time in the world for his kids? Listening to him talk about the fun they'd had at the Bronx Zoo and at Chelsea Piers, she couldn't help feeling . . . left out. Which she knew was ridiculous and unfair, given that she was sleeping with another man. But wasn't that the main reason she *was* cheating on him?

In contrast, she thought about how she'd felt the other morning waking early to the sight of Hunter's boots on the floor beside his bed, the quiet joy that had filled her, a joy as uncomplicated as that which she'd felt as a young child waking up on Christmas morning. And how, after they'd made love, she'd lain in his arms feeling more content than she ever had with anyone, even Jonathon. Simple pleasures made her happiest: drinking coffee with him on the porch, watching the birds flock about the feeder in his yard—he could identify each of the species, and had even tamed a towhee he'd named Calamity to eat out of his hand—and going on long walks. One day last week they'd explored the old copper mining town of Jerome. The evening before they'd danced around his living room like a couple of teenagers, Springsteen's "Born to Run" blasting from Hunter's stereo.

Her lighthearted mood had given way to a more somber one since then. She glanced around the courtroom, which was rapidly filling up. Hunter's friends and fellow activists packed the benches in front, among them the Conservancy's treasurer, Jeff Carmody, who liked to joke that his title was nominal since there was never enough money to keep track of, and Art Begay, in an ill-fitting suit with his hair slicked back. Plump Norma Gleason, from the Dancing Crane bookshop, sat wedged in next to Link Woodhouse from the *Mercury*; directly behind them, sitting ramrod straight, was the town's postmistress, Miss Lou, accompanied by her longtime companion, Cora Halsey.

The reporters were clustered in back, where they could exit quickly to file their reports. Jessie could only hope the tide wouldn't turn after they'd heard whatever trumped-up evidence the DA was presenting. With the media, she knew, hard facts often took a backseat to entertainment value, and today's hero could be tomorrow's dangerous fanatic.

Jessie had no sooner lowered herself into the seat that Art had saved for her when the bailiff boomed, "All rise! The court is now in session, the Honorable Judge Ernesto Sanchez presiding!"

The judge, a middle-aged man with a wrestler's compact build and wavy black hair that was in stark contrast to his iron gray mustache, strode through a side door into the courtroom, black robe fluttering at his heels. Jessie remembered him from the arraignment; he'd seemed tough but fair. She could only hope the assesment proved correct.

When the formalities were dispensed with and the charges read, Stu McCall unfolded leisurely from his chair at the defendant's table. "Your Honor, let me just say this," he drawled, "if suspicion was all it took to hang a man, there wouldn't be enough rope to go around." He looked around the courtroom, smiling in a way that caused a few people to shift uneasily in their seats. "My client's only crime, if you want to call it that," he went on, fixing his gaze on a glowering Burt Coffey, who sat with the spokesperson for Sylvan Glade, "is ruffling a few feathers."

A ripple of laughter went through the courtroom. The district attorney, a pale, red-haired stork of a man, looked less than amused when it was his turn to address the bench. The evidence, he held forth, though admittedly circumstantial, would show that the defendant, Mr. George, was guilty of the crime with which he'd been charged. A crime, he added, his reedy voice rising, that might well have resulted in the deaths or severe injury of Mr. Coffey and his employees.

The first witness for the prosecution was a young security guard named Kenny who stated that he'd seen an SUV the same color as the defendant's parked down the road on the day in question. It was only under cross-examination that Kenny was forced to admit that it had been too far away to see what make it was. Nor could he positively identify the "Mexican-looking guy" he'd seen drive off in it later that day as the defendant.

"Well, now, that's understandable," Stu remarked amiably, "being as all Mexicans look pretty much alike."

The irony wasn't lost on the judge, who shot Stu a warning look. He'd cautioned both attorneys at the outset that he had no tolerance for grandstanding and cheap tricks.

Next up was Burt Overby himself, a red-faced bulldog of a man who stood with his legs apart and his jaw thrust out, as he was being sworn in, as if daring the bailiff to take a punch. He testified that he'd chased the defendant off his property on numerous occasions, grousing, "Son of a bitch is like poison oak—the more you cut it, the faster it grows." He also claimed to have received threatening letters from Hunter. But when the DA read one aloud, Jessie thought it could just as easily have been interpreted as a threat of legal action.

The lone piece of physical evidence besides the footprint, it turned out, was a matchbook from Murphy's, where Hunter and the Conservancy officers often met to strategize, that had been found in the vicinity of the destroyed pumping station. But since Murphy's was a local watering hole frequented by nearly everyone in town, it could have fallen out of the pocket of anyone in the courtroom, Stu McCall was quick to point out. Even the judge looked skeptical.

What was becoming increasingly clear, not just to Jessie, judging from the looks of bald disbelief on the faces around her, was that the prosecution had no real case. It might stick in a small town where deals were cut in smoky back rooms, but it wouldn't hold up under the kind of scrutiny that had been generated by the article in *People*. In the glare of the public spotlight, with reporters poised to pounce at the slightest whiff of impropriety, there could be no cutting of corners or fudging of facts, no quietly looking the other way.

Jessie felt some of the tension go out of her. She wouldn't relax until all this was over, but the odds of Hunter ending up in prison had decreased dramatically, in her opinion.

When the hearing came to a close Hunter's supporters crowded around him, practically sweeping him out of the courtroom. She caught up with him on the steps outside, where he was giving his statement to the press, amid a lightning storm of camera flashes and whirring shutters. "First, let me say that I don't condone violence of any kind," he said into the microphone the reporter from CTN had shoved into his face, adding that he hoped they caught whoever *had* committed the crime. "But we can't lose sight of what's at stake here—this land. *Our* land." He threw out an arm, gesturing to include his cheering constituency. "If we let people whose only interest is in making a profit take what belongs to *all* of us, we'll lose more than our water. Our jobs will be next, then our homes, and the schools that depend on tax revenue from tourism. . . ."

Poised on the steps, bathed in the glow of handheld lights, he looked as if he could lead a nation into battle. A loud cheer went up from the crowd. Just then he turned, and his gaze locked with Jessie's. She felt as if she were being lifted up, her chest expanding with something lighter than air. As she pushed her way toward him through the thicket of jostling elbows, she thought that if he asked her to run off to Argentina with him right now, she'd go in a heartbeat.

When she finally reached him, he crushed her to him, lifting her off her feet and swinging her around. Whatever the outcome of the trial, he'd achieved what he'd set out to, which in itself was cause for celebration.

"Next thing you know, they'll have you running for office," she teased.

"First, I have to win this case." But he, too, must have concluded that the prosecution didn't have a leg to stand on, because he didn't sound too worried.

"Okay, we'll hold off on the champagne for now. In the meantime, would you settle for a beer?"

He grinned. "You're on, lady."

The following Saturday Jessie rose earlier than usual. One of Hunter's cousins was getting married, and Hunter had invited her along to the wedding. She wanted to have breakfast laid out by the time Maria arrived, as it was a good four-hour drive to the reservation, with the ceremony, in keeping with Navajo tradition, set to take place at sunset.

It was late afternoon by the time they turned off the highway onto a dusty road lined with buildings in various stages of disrepair. They passed several churches, and a row of sad-looking storefronts. The cars parked along the side of the road were mostly older models, those big gas guzzlers that had gone out with the Reagan era and that these days you seldom saw in any number outside of Third World countries.

"Welcome to Many Farms," said Hunter, with a note of irony.

She gazed out at the bleak landscape. "Where are the farms?"

"Good question," he said. In other words, there weren't any.

They turned onto an unpaved road, and after miles of

teeth-rattling washboard, where the only things moving were the clouds of dust boiling in their wake, they reached a cluster of buildings that appeared to be some sort of community center. Hunter pulled up in front of the ceremonial hogan, a large, circular adobe structure. The yard was packed with cars, and people were milling around outside, calling out greetings and slapping each other on the back. Under the primitive *lattia* cabana out back, long tables were laden with covered bowls and casserole dishes. It was traditional, Hunter informed her, for the bride's family to provide the wedding feast, and the women had spent days preparing it, while the men had done their part by digging a barbecue pit. The smell of roasting meat wafted toward her, reminding her that she hadn't eaten lunch.

Inside the hogan, rugs were spread over the floor in lieu of chairs, on which adults sat cross-legged chatting with one another while young children scampered about. The lone piece of furniture was a table in the center of the room that held an earthenware jug. "Come on, there's someone I want you to meet," Hunter said, taking her hand and guiding her over to where an older woman sat, deep in conversation with the man beside her. At their approach, she leapt to her feet, throwing her arms around Hunter with a cry of delight.

Before he could introduce her to Jessie, the woman put out her hand. "I'm Naomi, Hunter's mother. And you must be Jessie." She was handsome in a Georgia O'Keeffe kind of way, with skin like a brown paper bag that had

been crumpled, then smoothed out, stretched over promi-
nent cheekbones. With her long, white hair in a braid,
wearing a traditional velveteen skirt and embroidered
blouse, she might have been mistaken for a Navajo
woman, except for her eyes—they were the pale green of
new leaves. Eyes now fixed on Jessie with frank interest.
"I'm glad you could make it. Is this your first Navajo wedding?"

My first, and probably my last, Jessie thought, but she
only nodded, and said, "I was raised Presbyterian. Where
I'm from, the couple on the wedding cake only comes in
one color."

Naomi chuckled knowingly. "The first time my parents came to visit after we moved here, I thought they
were going to tie me up and drag me back to Muskogee,"
she recalled.

Hunter slipped an arm around Jessie's shoulders.
"Don't scare her off, Mom. She just got here."

"She doesn't seem the type to be scared off easily," observed Naomi, her frank, assessing gaze seeming to say, *I
hope I'm not wrong.*

Hunter's uncle Yazzie had saved places for them and
they lowered themselves onto the floor. The sun was low
in the sky, but there was no sign yet of the bride or groom,
or their families. Hunter explained that, before the ceremony could take place, the bride's family had to approve
of the gifts that had been given to them by the groom's. If
they were deemed inadequate, the wedding would be
called off. Though Hunter assured her that there was little

danger of that happening; these days, it was only a formality.

The light had begun to fade by the time the groom, Hunter's cousin, a ruggedly handsome man about Hunter's age, appeared at the entrance to the hogan accompanied by a white-haired man who looked to be his father. They were followed by the bride, a pretty, dark-haired young woman in a full white skirt and turquoise velveteen blouse that went with the groom's white jeans and darker turquoise shirt. She carried a large woven basket, and an older man, presumably her father, walked at her side. The other family members filed in, taking their seats near the center of the hogan. From their beaming faces, it appeared the gifts had been satisfactory.

The bride and groom took turns pouring water from the ceremonial jug over each other's hands. Then the ancient *hataali* sprinkled some sort of powder over the wedding basket while uttering chants in a low, cracked voice—Hunter whispered in Jessie's ear that it was corn pollen, which represented fertility. After the bride and groom had each dipped their fingers into the basket to sample its contents—what appeared to be cornmeal mush—it was then passed among their family members, each of whom took a taste.

As the *haatali* performed the rest of the ceremony in his cracked singsong, Hunter translated softly, "He's telling them to treat each other with respect, that love and acceptance must go before selfish desires. He's asking that they be blessed with many children."

Jessie briefly allowed herself to imagine that it was her and Hunter in the center of the hogan, the *haatali* passing his knotted-rawhide fingers over their bowed heads. She guiltily replaced it with one of her and Jonathon under the *chuppah*, but the image wouldn't stay in focus. How could she marry Jonathon now? He deserved better than a wife whose heart was divided.

You deserve better, too, whispered a voice in her head. Jonathon had promised her that things would be different when she got back, but she wasn't confident that would be the case. He was taking her for granted like before—at least that was the way it seemed. Was she merely looking for an excuse to justify her betrayal?

Only time would tell. And time was something she was quickly running out of. Her six months were almost up.

When the ceremony was over, they all sat down to a feast that included everything from traditional fry bread and Navajo stew made with sweet potatoes to more commonplace dishes, like hamburger pie and tuna-and-potato-chip casserole. The goat that had been roasting on a spit since that morning was carved up and passed around. Jessie found it to be delicious. She ate every scrap on her plate, sucking the small bones and licking her greasy fingers when she was done.

Afterward there was dancing and singing, followed by numerous toasts. The bride's grandfather's was the most eloquent. "You have lit a fire that must never go out," he said, directing his sober gaze at the newlyweds. "Tend it well, and it will make your new life together a long and happy one, and bless you with many children. It will keep you fed, and it will warm you when the winter winds come. It will go on burning even after death."

Jessie found herself blinking back tears and, when she glanced over at Hunter, she saw that his eyes were suspiciously bright.

It was close to midnight by the time they said their good-byes. Neither of them felt up to the long drive home, so they opted to stay at a motel and get an early start in the morning. Entering their room at the Dew Drop Inn, Jessie looked around at its faux wood-grain walls and Day-glo orange bedspread, its painting of a lighthouse hanging crookedly on the wall, commenting dryly, "Now I know what it's like to have an illicit affair."

Hunter put his arms around her, murmuring, "Isn't that what this is?"

She felt a fresh stab of guilt. And the thought surfaced, as always: *What kind of woman sleeps with another man when she's engaged?* It went against every grain of her being, and yet . . . strangely, it seemed right. "I'm half expecting Norman Bates to walk in right now," she joked in an attempt to ward off the chill that went through her.

"Don't worry, I'll protect you." His arms tightened around her.

Jessie, her head buzzing pleasantly from the wine she'd drunk, whispered back, "Yes, but who'll protect me from *you*?"

He kissed her, and for a long moment they stood that way, locked in each other's arms, swaying on their feet as if slow dancing. At last, he drew back and, holding her lightly by the wrist, guided her over to the bed, where he slowly removed each item of clothing as if it were something to remember her by. When they were both undressed, he folded back the quilted spread, and they climbed in between crisp white motel sheets smelling faintly of bleach. He nuzzled her neck, nipping an earlobe, before kissing her again on the mouth. Lightly at first, then with more urgency, his hands moving over her naked body. *We could lie here all night, just kissing,* Jessie thought swoonily, *and it would be enough.*

After a few minutes, he rolled onto his back, allowing her to explore him, as if he knew she needed to memorize every inch, from the crooked little toe on his right foot to the scar on his chin from a boyhood fight. His skin, in the lamplight, was the color of strong tea, and when she ran the tip of her tongue over it she could taste its saltiness. When he could no longer bear it, he pulled her on top of him and entered her. She gave a sharp gasp of pleasure. However many times they'd made love, each time was like the first.

Or the last, she thought.

Afterward they lay motionless amid the tangled sheets, Hunter sprawled on his back and Jessie with her head nestled in the crook of his elbow. As his chest rose and fell, his heartbeat a muffled thudding against her ear, she sensed him working up the courage to say something. But whatever it was, he kept it to himself. Jessie was relieved, for had he voiced the question that hovered over them like *chindi*, she wouldn't have known what to tell him.

Chapter Fifteen

"I'm bringing potato salad," Beverly informed Jessie over the phone.

"Mmm," Jessie murmured distractedly, the receiver wedged between her shoulder and ear as she carefully lowered the vase of fresh flowers she was holding onto the front hall table.

"Just in case you were planning to make it, too."

Jessie tried to focus on what her mother was saying, but the least of her concerns right now was what to bring to the Frontier Days potluck tomorrow. "I was thinking of making cookies," she said. "Do you still have that recipe for Snickerdoodles?"

"Somewhere. I haven't made them in years." Beverly sounded pleased that she'd remembered. They chatted for a few more minutes, then just as her mother was about to hang up, she said, "Oh, I almost forgot, would you mind picking me up tomorrow? My car's in the shop."

"What about Gay, isn't she going?" Jessie asked, surprised that Beverly wasn't catching a ride with her best friend, who lived only a few blocks from her.

There was an audible exhalation at the other end. Jessie waited for Beverly to say something snippy like, *If it's too much trouble, don't bother.* But all she said was, "If you must know, Gay shouldn't be driving—her eyesight isn't what it used to be."

Jessie recalled that Gay wore glasses. "Maybe she just needs a new prescription."

"I'm afraid it's more serious than that—she has glaucoma."

"Oh." Jessie sank down on the deacon's bench in the hallway. "Poor Gay." She thought about how Gay had looked after her and Beverly in those first terrible weeks after her father died, insisting they eat even when they weren't hungry, forcing them to go on walks and, when all else failed, pulling out a deck of cards and saying brightly, *Who's up for a game of gin rummy?* With her son and daughter living far away, who would look after her?

"None of us is getting any younger," her mother said, with a sigh.

"What will she do when—" Jessie broke off, not wanting to say the words, *when she goes blind?*

"We'll cross that bridge when we get to it." Beverly

was as good a friend to Gay as Gay had been to her. Whatever the challenge, they'd face it together.

Jessie spent the rest of the morning clearing off her desk. She recalled how tedious the work had seemed in the beginning, all those accounts and receipts. How she'd let it pile up, and how her head would swim at the end of each day with the myriad of details to keep track of. Now she could practically do it in her sleep. Even the cooking no longer fazed her. She wouldn't win any awards, but it was good to know that she could throw a meal together in a pinch.

By noon she was on her way to pick up Kayla at the airport. Originally the plan had been for Skip to go, but Jessie had volunteered, thinking the drive home would be the perfect opportunity for a heart-to-heart with her goddaughter. She knew from talking to Erin that Kayla wasn't interested in moving to New York, and Jessie wanted to be sure she understood just how much it would mean to Erin—an opportunity like this might never come again. Kayla needed to know, too, that there was a whole world beyond Willow Creek, one with unlimited opportunities for her as well. If Jessie had been given that advice when she was Kayla's age, she wouldn't have had to run off on the eve of her wedding like some fugitive; she'd have waited until she was old enough to know what she was doing before she got engaged.

Am I still running? she wondered. There were times the thought of staying in Willow Creek was tempting, mainly because of Hunter, other times when the old panic would grip her, and she'd feel as if she were in quicksand being slowly dragged under. She thought about all the things she'd miss—Carnegie Hall and Shakespeare in the Park; dressing up for parties and dining al fresco at outdoor cafés; the Christmas tree in Rockefeller Center, and the leaves changing in the fall.

It wouldn't be like it was before she'd left. Thanks to "Life Swap," she was in fairly good shape financially. And it looked as if her own star, not just Erin's, was on the rise. Both the *Post* and the *Times* wanted interviews, and they had several TV talk show appearances lined up. There'd been nibbles from book publishers as well, which could mean a whole new direction for her. *Face it,* Jessie thought, *staying in Willow Creek would be career suicide.*

She tried hard not to think about what she'd be giving up in return.

At the airport, Jessie waited outside the security gate, scanning the disembarking passengers as they streamed past. When she finally spotted Kayla, in new low-rise jeans and a wraparound top that showed a stripe of tanned belly, she almost didn't recognize her.

"Love the outfit," Jessie said.

"Mom got it for me." Kayla twirled around. "Cool, huh?"

"Way cool."

In the car, Kayla told Jessie all about her trip. She'd *loved* Clive, and Drew was a cool guy—he'd taken her to a matinee of *The Lion King,* and afterward for a carriage ride in Central Park. She'd been to every department store and tons of shops, including one that sold ladies' clothes to men—Clive, she said, had wanted to show her a side of New York that most tourists didn't get to see.

At the same time, Jessie sensed she was holding back. Kayla didn't say a word about the talk she'd had with her mother, and when Jessie gently broached the subject, she lapsed into silence—not the moody teenage kind that meant she wanted you to pry it out of her, but as if she simply saw no point in discussing it. It was obvious something was eating at her. Even her lively chatter seemed to mask some deep melancholy. It was as if Kayla had come to the conclusion that her parents weren't running the show anymore, that from now on she'd have to look out for herself.

"Well, I'm glad you're back," Jessie said, trying a different tack. "The house was pretty empty with just me and Otis rattling around in it."

"I've only been gone a week," Kayla reminded her.

"I know, but it made me think about how hard it'll be when I have to go back to seeing you just once every other year."

Kayla smiled the way adults did at a child's attempt to manipulate them. "I know what you're getting at, Aunt Jess," she said, "and it won't work. I'm not moving to New York."

Jessie spotted the exit for Willow Creek and eased into the right lane. "You won't even consider it?"

Kayla shook her head, turning to gaze out the window.

"I know you think I'm being selfish, but the way I see it, this whole thing is just another excuse for Mom and Dad to get into it. And I'm sick of being in the middle. Whatever they decide, I want to be left out of it."

"I know it's been hard on you," Jessie said. "But maybe a fresh start—"

Kayla turned away from the window, and the look of heartbreaking resignation on her face caused Jessie to break off in midsentence. "I don't want a fresh start," Kayla said. "I want us to all be together like it used to be. But I don't think that's going to happen."

"Your mom—"

"Mom doesn't think so, either."

"You don't know that for a fact," Jessie said. "They love each other. They wouldn't be so mad at each other if they didn't. There's still a chance."

But Kayla only shook her head, her mouth turning up in a sad little smile. "That's only in movies," she said.

The following morning, Jessie pulled up in front of her mother's promptly at eleven and was about to tap on her horn when Beverly stepped out of the house carrying a large Saran-covered bowl. As Jessie watched her make her way cautiously down the walk, the bowl cradled in her arms, she was struck by how frail her mother seemed. *She's getting older*, Jessie thought, feeling a little inner lurch. All these years, she'd seen her mother as all-powerful. Now she would have to shift gears and see her as someone to be looked after rather than to defend herself against.

Beverly lowered herself into the passenger's seat, placing the bowl in her lap. Jessie could see that she'd been to the beauty parlor; her hair, instead of its usual henna, was more of a Rita Hayworth russet. "You look nice, Mom," she said. "I like what you did with your hair."

"Do you?" Beverly patted its bulletproof waves, but she seemed preoccupied. It wasn't until they were halfway down the block that she remembered to thank Jessie for the ride.

Jessie assured her it was no trouble at all, adding, "Let me know when your car is ready. I'll give you a lift to the garage."

Lately she and her mother had been getting along better, and though Jessie suspected it was mostly to do with her having fulfilled Beverly's fondest wish by getting engaged, she was anxious to maintain the fragile peace. She'd begun to realize, too, that she hadn't made it any easier all those years. If Beverly pushed her buttons, it was because Jessie had enough of them to equip NASA Control.

Beverly looked blank for a moment, then she said, "Thank you, dear, but that won't be necessary. Mr. Gustavo said he'd have one of the boys drop it off."

"It's nothing serious, I hope."

"What?"

"Your car." Had her mother become hard of hearing? "Those repairs can be expensive."

Beverly shrugged, and said, "It's only money."

Jessie couldn't believe what she was hearing. Her father used to joke that Beverly could squeeze a nickel until the buffalo farted. What was up with her?

They were turning up the hill to the fairgrounds when her mother remarked out of the blue, "It's a shame you have to leave so soon. It seems like you just got here."

Does this mean she'll miss me? Jessie wondered. "Seems that way to me, too. I honestly don't know where the time went," she replied lightly, when she'd recovered from her shock.

"You must be anxious to get back."

"Actually, I've gotten kind of used to country life."

"Home is where the heart is," Beverly said, as if she'd coined the phrase.

Hunter came to mind, but Jessie knew that Beverly was referring to Jonathon, so she replied dutifully, "Of course, I can't wait to see Jonathon." And it wasn't a lie. She *would* be happy when she saw him in person, when he wasn't just a disembodied voice over the phone . . . at least, that's what she kept telling herself.

"I remember when your father was overseas," Beverly mused aloud, gazing out the window, as if addressing the faint ghost of her reflection in the glass. Jessie's father had fought in Korea; his medals were displayed on the wall in the living room, yet Beverly mentioned him so rarely, he'd come to seem as distantly iconic as the framed photo of JFK that hung alongside them. "It seemed like he was never going to come home."

"That was before you were married, right?" Jessie knew the answer, but she was anxious to keep her mother talking—Beverly hardly ever spoke about their life together before Jessie was born.

She nodded, wearing a faraway look. "We'd only been engaged a few weeks when he got his orders to ship out."

"If someone else had come along, someone you . . . had feelings for, would you have waited?" She'd been careful to keep her relationship with Hunter under wraps, but suddenly it seemed important that she connect with her mother on this one level.

Beverly turned toward her, looking surprised that she would have to ask. "There was never anyone but your father," she said, with such conviction that Jessie didn't doubt it was the truth.

Yet Jessie's memories told a different story. Even at a young age, she'd known her parents weren't happy. It wasn't one thing she could point to—she'd never heard them exchange so much as a harsh word—but they didn't act the way her friends' parents did. They were polite the way people were when walking on eggshells. They didn't go out in the evenings, to dinner or a movie, and Jessie couldn't recall their ever going on a trip together without her. More often, it was Jessie and her father going off on their own. Sundays, if the weather was nice, he'd take the top down on the Cadillac, and they'd drive to the beach in Santa Monica, or go to the A&W for root beer floats. He was careful to invite Beverly along, but she'd always say she had too much to do around the house. It hadn't occurred to Jessie then that her mother had stayed home because she knew they were secretly hoping she would.

"To me, it always seemed like you were in your own separate worlds," she said as delicately as she could.

She expected her mother to insist that theirs had been a match made in heaven, but Beverly only said, with a sigh of resignation, "I suppose we were, in a way."

"Were you happy with Dad?"

"Happy? We didn't think like that in those days. It was what it was, and if there was something you didn't like, you learned to live with it."

"But it wasn't always like that, was it?"

Beverly shook her head, wearing a sad little smile. "I didn't even know we'd drifted apart until you came along." Jessie felt her defenses go up, but there was no accusation in her mother's voice. "Your dad was so over the moon — we'd been trying for years, and had just about given up. I thought it was sweet at first; he was like any new father. It wasn't until you were a little older that I realized . . ." She paused, as if trying to find the words to express what she'd so long denied, probably even to herself. " . . . you were giving him something I couldn't." She let out another sigh. "It was never the same after that. I couldn't be around you two without feeling like a third wheel."

Jessie had turned into the parking lot across the street from the fairgrounds, and now she pulled into an empty space. The shady ones were all taken, and she knew that the Toyota would be an oven when they returned later in the day. Already it was stifling, even with the windows rolled down. Yet neither of them made a move to get out.

"I always wondered why you didn't like me." It felt

strange to say the words Jessie had carried inside her for so long, like a thorn in her heart, and at the same time liberating.

Her mother shook her head. "It wasn't you," she said, bringing her fingertips to rest briefly on the back of Jessie's wrist—a touch so light, it might have been the brush of her sleeve. "I just felt . . . excluded. It wasn't just that he loved you more. You loved *him* more."

Jessie stared down at her lap. How could she deny it? "It felt like the end of the world when he died."

"For me, too," Beverly said.

They sat in silence for a moment, the only sound the ticking of the engine as it cooled. Across the street, a line had formed at the gated entrance to the fairgrounds, where the elderly Hathaway sisters, Mabel and Mavis, sat at a picnic table under a large, striped umbrella, taking money and tearing tickets off large rolls. At last, Beverly rallied, and said briskly, "Well! We'd better get a move on. I just hope Lolly remembered to bring her cooler. I don't want this sitting out in the sun any longer than it has to." She glanced dubiously at the bowl of potato salad, as if it might already be teeming with bacteria.

Jessie, desperate to hold on to the fragile bond they'd forged, placed a hand on her mother's arm as she was opening her door to get out. "I'm glad you told me. About Dad. I'm curious about one thing, though. Why didn't you tell me before?"

Jessie longed to hear her say something meaningful like, *These past months we've grown so much closer*, or *I*

*didn't want you to go back to New York without setting the
record straight.* But her mother only shrugged, and said,
"It never came up."

Stepping through the gates onto the fairgrounds was like a
trip back in time. Familiar smells from childhood wafted
toward her, Philly steaks and funnel cakes, cotton candy
and kettle corn. The annual Frontier Days festival, a week
of festivities commemorating the date the town was
founded, in 1863, was just as Jessie remembered it: Carnival rides, and booths selling everything from cheap toys
and trinkets to the chance to win a prize; rodeo and 4-H
events, along with musicians who'd be performing
throughout the week. Even the tradition of the scarecrow
contest had been carried on, she saw, smiling as they
passed the grand-prize winner—a large straw-stuffed pig
in bib overalls, brandishing a pitchfork.

Jessie deposited her mother, along with the Tupperware container of Snickerdoodles she'd baked the night
before, at the tent where the potluck—a church fund-
raiser for which an extra ticket was required—was being
held. The minister's wife, Mrs. Stanton, thanked her for
the cookies and urged her to stay, but Jessie excused herself, saying she had to meet someone. She'd promised
Hunter she'd stop by the Conservancy booth.

She hadn't seen him in over a week. It was high season for weddings at the inn, and she'd scarcely had a
moment to herself. For his part, he'd been tied up with
his court case; it wasn't going to trial until September,

but he and his lawyer had a lot of groundwork to do before then. With the days dwindling before she was to return to New York, Jessie realized she could no longer put off the conversation they'd both been avoiding. Hunter, she knew, was hoping she'd change her mind and decide to stay. She was going to have to tell him that, however torn, she couldn't bring herself to abandon her life back home. It wasn't just Jonathon; it was everything she'd built up over the past fifteen years. How could she walk away from that?

At the same time, she thought, with a pang, *How can I walk away from* him?

Inside the exhibit hall, she wandered up and down the aisles in search of his booth. In the section where the horticultural entries were displayed, she stopped to admire the roses, in every sunset hue, and a pumpkin the size of a footstool, as well as some freakishly shaped zucchinis that resembled science projects. A glass bakery case at the far end of the aisle showed off the baked good entries—homemade brownies, peanut butter cookies, and coconut snowballs that sat proudly alongside the more ambitious cakes and confections. Jessie was sampling a cube of the banana bread set out on a paper plate when she spotted Gay.

Her mother's friend, standing out like a billboard in lime green slacks and a scoop-necked pink top, greeted her as if it'd been years, not weeks, since they'd last seen each other. She gave Jessie a warm hug. "Hi, honey. Where's your mom? I've been looking all over for her."

"She's at the potluck," Jessie informed her.

"Which I'd have known," Gay said, "if she'd stop being so stubborn and get a cell phone like everyone else. Lord, you'd think it was the Stone Age to listen to her talk. Email? You might as well ask her to run for Congress." She shook her head in fond exasperation before leaning in to ask, in a hushed voice, "How's she holding up?"

"Fine," Jessie said, puzzled by Gay's solicitous tone.

"She didn't seem down in the dumps?"

"A little preoccupied maybe, but other than that she seemed okay." What was this all about? If anything, Gay should've been the one who was down in the dumps.

She tried to think of a delicate way of telling Gay that she didn't have to put up a brave front for her sake, but before she could say anything, Gay went on, "That's Bev for you. If she was trapped under a car, you wouldn't hear a peep out her. Though I know it hasn't been easy for her, being so active and all. I'm sure you've been a real comfort to her."

Suddenly it all fell into place: Beverly's needing a ride, and how vague she'd been about her car being in the shop: It wasn't Gay's eyes that were going; it was her mother's.

Jessie did her best to keep the shock from showing on her face, managing to stammer, "I—I just wish there was something I could do." Mentally she grasped at straws. A specialist in New York? Some experimental drug or cutting-edge technology?

But Gay was shaking her head. "It's old age, hon.

Nothing you can do about that." Her sad expression gave way to one of forced cheer. "Don't you worry, though, I'll take good care of her," she promised. "She'll be dancing at your wedding."

After Gay had hugged her good-bye, Jessie wandered off in a daze. God, her poor mother. How long had she been keeping this from her? Weeks? Months? Had Beverly hoped to spare her, or was it merely that she hadn't wanted to appear vulnerable? Over the years, Jessie had run through the gamut of emotions where her mother was concerned, but there was one she'd missed: pity. This was the first time she'd felt sorry for her mother.

There *had* to be something she could do. She'd call Kate as soon as she got back to the inn; her editor knew all the best doctors.

At the Conservancy booth, she found Hunter and two of his officers, Roger Munsey and Janet Olshefsky, seated at a table stacked with brochures and Xeroxed copies of articles, including the one from *People*. Mounted on the particle-board partition behind them were blown-up photos of dry streambeds and dying trees, and one with a fish belly-up on a muddy bank.

"We wanted something cute and cuddly," Hunter explained, following her gaze, "but the only thing we could find was a possum that'd died trying to find its way out of Art's basement."

Art, perched on the other end of the table, offered cheerfully, "Stunk like hell."

Jessie fished a lapel button from the plastic bin on the

table, printed with the slogan OUR WATER, OUR FUTURE. Conservancy T-shirts were for sale as well; it looked as if they'd been doing a brisk business, judging from the limited supply left.

"Anything I can do to help?" she asked.

"Yeah, get him something to eat." Art hooked a thumb in Hunter's direction. "He's been at it all morning like a monkey on meth."

"When it rains it pours," Hunter said, gesturing toward the new member sign-up sheet. He informed her that more people had signed up in the past few hours than in the last two months combined, adding with a chuckle, "Goes to show what a little notoriety will do."

Together he and Jessie strolled out into the sunshine. The new worry about her mother had pushed thoughts of her impending departure to the back of her mind, but now they rose up again, and she wondered anew how she could bear to say good-bye.

The fairgrounds were more crowded than when she'd arrived. Everywhere she looked, she saw the happy faces of children, and not a Gameboy in sight. At the food stalls, they bought grilled shish kebab and roasted corn on the cob, and large cups of ice-cold lemonade to drink. Balancing their cups and paper plates, they made their way over to the bleachers that'd been set up near the makeshift stage, where a bluegrass trio was warming up for their first set.

"You're awfully quiet. Something on your mind?" Hunter asked after a bit, when he noticed that she wasn't eating.

Jessie told him about her mother. "It hasn't quite sunk

in," she said, shaking her head. "I've never thought of her as someone needing to be taken care of."

"It does complicate things," he agreed, nodding in sympathy.

"I know I'll feel guilty for leaving her."

"So stay."

"You make it sound so simple," she said, frowning.

"I didn't say it was simple."

Suddenly she wished it *were.* She wished she could turn the clock back, the way she'd adjusted her watch to the three-hour time difference when she'd first arrived, only she'd go all the way back to the moment she'd stepped off the plane. If she had this to do all over again, she wouldn't have wasted so much time; she'd have spent every spare minute with Hunter.

"I didn't arrive here on a half shell. I have a whole other life in New York," she said, somewhat irritably.

"Not to mention a fiancé." His tone was mild, but she caught an undercurrent of something darkly primitive: She didn't doubt that in another time and place, if he and Jonathon were locked in mortal combat, he'd have fought to the death. The thought scared her . . . and at the same time made her wonder if she was an idiot for walking away from a man who loved her as much as that.

"I know how it must seem to you," she said. "If I'm so crazy about him, what am I doing with you?"

"The thought had occurred to me," he said dryly.

"All I know is that I owe it to myself, and to him, to find out if we have a future together."

"And I'm supposed to wait around until you do?" He arched a brow.

"I'm not asking you to wait," she said. But, of course, that's what she *was* asking. Or at least hoping.

Slowly, he shook his head. "Good," he said, "because I don't intend to." Hunter wasn't a man who was used to being second in line or to taking no for an answer. With him, everything was clear-cut; no blurred lines, no maybes or we'll-sees.

She felt a sudden, desperate urge to throw all caution aside and leap onto the back of his white charger, but she forced herself to say, in the measured voice of an adult who'd paid the price for her rash actions in the past, "I'll understand if you want to break it off."

Suddenly his hard mask fell away, and she saw the raw emotion underneath; it was like looking straight into the sun, at once glorious and blinding. "That's not what I'm saying. I'm asking you to marry me."

Jessie's heart soared, then plummeted. Oh, God. How could she give this up? How could she *live* without this man? It took every ounce of willpower she possessed to answer, "I can't. I'm sorry." There was no sense in even discussing his moving to New York; it would be like transplanting a mature tree and expecting it to thrive.

His eyes glittered with unshed tears. "I'm sorry, too."

Envying him his certainty, she cried in frustration, "How can you be so sure I'm the one you want to spend the rest of your life with? You've only known me for a few months."

"I've known you longer than that," he said, a corner of his mouth turning up in a sad little smile. "The only thing I didn't know, until we met, was that the woman I'd been looking for all these years was you. Corny, but true." He took her hand. "Jessie Holland, if I didn't say it before, I'm saying it now: I'm crazy about you. And I think you'd be crazy to say no to this."

Jessie could only stare at him with a mixture of elation and anguish. Anything she could have said would have spoiled the moment—a moment at once perfect and perfectly awful. She allowed herself to fantasize for a moment about taking a chance, just as she'd urged Erin to do, and as Erin used to urge her to do when they were kids, whenever Jessie hung back, fearful of taking that last leap when crossing a stream or of climbing to the highest branch of a tree. But she wasn't a kid anymore; there was too much at stake.

"I have to go back," she said at last, in a voice choked with tears. "For now, at least. In a few months . . ." She let the rest of the sentence trail off. Would anything be different in a few months? Even if it didn't work out with Jonathon, her life was in New York, not here.

Now it was Hunter who was shaking his head, his mouth pressed into a firm line. "This is a one-time-only offer. Take it or leave it."

"You're asking too much!"

"I know what *I* want. If you don't, we should end it now, before somebody gets hurt even worse."

She knew he'd meant that that somebody would be

him, but Jessie was hurting, too. Just because she couldn't bring herself to take such a leap of faith, to throw away everything she'd worked for all these years, it didn't mean she loved him any less than he did her. A long time ago, she'd nearly made the mistake of marrying the wrong man. She didn't intend to make the same mistake again. With Jonathon . . . or with anyone. If Hunter couldn't wait long enough for her to sort it all out . . .

Her thoughts were interrupted by a familiar voice calling out her name. She looked down to find Skip standing below, peering up at her under the brim of his cowboy hat. "You seen Kayla?" he called through cupped hands.

"Not since this morning!" she called back, glad for the distraction. Another minute, and she'd have been in tears.

Skip climbed up to where she and Hunter sat. He looked flushed, and he was breathing hard. "She was supposed to be at the rodeo—her friend Brett's competing in the barrel race. I've looked everywhere for her, and no one's seen her."

"She'll turn up eventually," Jessie assured him, none too concerned. There was only so much trouble you could get into at a small-town fair.

"Yeah, you're probably right." He looked dubious even so. "It's just that she's been acting kind of funny since she got back. I've been a little worried about her, to be honest."

"I've noticed it, too," she told him. Jessie had a pretty good idea why Kayla was out of sorts, but now wasn't the time to get into it. "How did she seem on the ride over?"

Skip frowned, looking puzzled. "I thought she rode in with you."

Jessie felt a little pulse of alarm. "She told me you were taking her." When Jessie was leaving, Kayla had still been in her room. She'd called through the door, asking if she wanted her to wait, and Kayla had called back that her dad was picking her up.

Jessie and Skip stared at each other for an instant as the full realization sank in. Kayla had lied to them both. But why? What had she hoped to gain?

Jessie felt a steadying hand on her arm. "I have a suggestion," Hunter said. "Why don't we have them make an announcement over the PA system? Like they do for lost kids."

"Kayla's not—" Jessie broke off. Lost? No, she was too old to be lost. A kid? She wasn't that either. Just a confused girl trying to find her place in a world full of equally confused adults.

They all headed off to the lost-and-found booth. Jessie imagined how embarrassed Kayla would be when she heard her name called out, like some four-year-old's, how she'd berate them later on for humiliating her. The thought was comforting almost, because it meant that she *would* turn up, that she hadn't done something stupid like . . .

Run away.

But Kayla didn't turn up when she was paged. Nor was she at the house. Maria reported that the last time she'd seen her was several hours ago, when Kayla was leaving the house. Maria had assumed that she was on her way to the fair. The only thing she'd thought a little odd was that Kayla had been toting her backpack.

By midday, when it became clear that none of Kayla's friends had seen her all day, Jessie grew truly concerned, her head filled with dire thoughts of what happened to runaways. She berated herself for having told Kayla about the time she and Erin had hitchhiked to Phoenix. The world was more dangerous now than when they'd been growing up. She could only pray that the grim scenarios playing through her mind were more the stuff of urban myth than of headlines. The only thing that kept her from phoning Erin was the expectation that Kayla would turn up any minute; that, and knowing there was nothing Erin could do, that it would only worry her.

Darkness fell, and Mike and several of Skip's buddies, along with Hunter and Art, joined the hunt. While Skip and his brother and friends fanned out to check every conceivable place Kayla might have gone, Hunter and Art traversed the roads and highways in the slim hope that they would find her trying to thumb a ride.

Hours later Jessie was in the kitchen making coffee when a grim-faced Skip tromped in through the back door to announce, "That's it, I'm calling the police."

Chapter Sixteen

"Someday I may regret this," Erin told Kate that night over dinner at L'Impero, "but I know I'd regret even more not being there for my daughter." She'd managed to stall the Cooking Channel for over a week, but they were getting antsy, and she'd promised to have a decision for them first thing on Monday morning.

Kayla needed to know that there were still some things she could count on. Erin wanted to be there, too, those last years before Kayla went away to college. She couldn't imagine not seeing her daughter all dressed up for her proms, not being there to applaud her at school concerts, or to help pick up the pieces when her heart was broken by some boy she liked, as it inevitably would be.

As tough as it was, Erin knew that she was making the right decision in passing up this opportunity.

"You're doing a good job of selling me on all the reasons not to get married and have kids," Kate said, only half in jest. "Have you stopped to think that this could be an amazing opportunity for her as well? For one thing, she'd get a great education. One of my closest friends is the admissions director at Dalton. I'd be happy to have a word with her. . . ."

Erin shook her head, unshaken in her resolve. "It's not just Kayla. The truth is . . . I'm a little homesick." When she'd first arrived here she'd been so caught up in pounding the pavement, she hadn't had time to dwell on being homesick. She'd been like someone clinging to a small raft, tumbling over the rapids. And there'd been Drew to keep her from feeling too lonely. But now . . . "I miss my house, and my dog. I miss walking barefoot through the grass, and seeing other kinds of birds besides pigeons. I miss watching the sun come up over the mountains and falling asleep at night to the sound of crickets."

"You should be writing for *Arizona Highways*," Kate observed wryly. "You're a good advertisement for country living."

Erin took a sip of her wine. "Don't get me wrong, I love New York." There was no place like it on earth. "But it's not home."

"Home, in my experience, is vastly overrated." Kate

twirled a strand of linguine around her fork before delicately sucking it into her mouth.

Erin smiled. Kate had grown up in Greenwich, Connecticut, a stone's throw from Manhattan. Clearly she had no idea what Erin was talking about. "It's not so much where you live, it's who you *are*." She glanced around at the other diners: ladies in fashionably wrinkled linen and whisper-soft silk, men in summer-weight suits, sporting Hamptons tans. "At crosswalks? I'm the only one who waits for the light to turn green. And the other day in D'Agostino's, all I had was a quart of milk, so I very nicely asked the woman in front of me if I could cut ahead of her in line. You'd have thought I'd asked her to donate a kidney from the look she gave me."

Kate laughed her velvety Upper East Side laugh, in which Erin could hear limos and expense account meals and weekends in Sag Harbor. Erin didn't hold it against her. Kate was more than an editor—she'd become a real friend—and she was trying to see Erin's point of view, but she was one of those New Yorkers, like Clive, who can't envision life beyond the Hudson or East Rivers, who'd feel seriously deprived if she had to go without fresh bagels or her monthly appointments with her colorist. "A kidney? That's nothing," she said. "I know people who'd sacrifice a limb to be first in line in Zabar's."

Erin smiled, and said, "Well, Zabar's."

Kate gave her a look that seemed to say, *How can you go back to the land of iceberg lettuce after Zabar's?* But all she said was, "All right, I respect your decision. But know this:

If down the line, you change your mind, there's no going back. As far as your boss is concerned, you'll have ceased to exist. She won't even return your calls."

Erin felt a pang at the thought; Kate would never know how tempted she'd been by Latrice's offer. "Where I come from, it's the opposite. No one ever forgets, and you never live anything down," she said, with a small, ironic smile. Like when she'd been the girl from the wrong side of the tracks, the time she'd overheard a neighbor of the St. Clairs, the family she used to babysit for, say to Mrs. St. Clair, *Who knows what kind of dirty habits that girl's picked up?* No, this wasn't about some rose-colored vision of Willow Creek. What it boiled down to was that there were some choices you could live with, and others you couldn't. "Look, I know what I'm passing up," she added, eyeing Kate soberly, "When I was twenty-one, I'd have killed for a chance like this. The trouble is, it came too late."

She thought of what else it might be too late for: any chance of salvaging her marriage. Passing up this opportunity didn't guarantee that she'd get her husband back in return; in fact, in some ways it might make things more difficult. She couldn't run away from her problems; she'd have to confront them head on.

That, she thought, was the ultimate sacrifice.

When she arrived home, she saw that the lights were on in Drew's apartment. Erin knew it was time she told him of her decision; she'd put it off long enough. She climbed the stairs, her heart heavy as she knocked on his door. Moments later the door swung open to reveal Drew, naked except for the towel around his middle, his hair standing up in wet spikes.

"Erin." He looked surprised to see her; it had been a while since she'd popped in on him unannounced.

"Late date?" she asked. Obviously he'd just stepped out of the shower.

He gave her a mock injured look. He'd made no secret of the fact that he was holding out until she came to her senses and realized she'd be a fool to pass him up. Now she was going to break his heart.

"I just got back from the Meyer girl's bat mitzvah," he explained.

"How was it?" she asked, sinking down on the sofa.

He rolled his eyes. "If your idea of chasing after a bunch of giggling thirteen-year-olds while having your eardrums blasted is fun, it was a ball."

"We were thirteen once, remember?"

"Vaguely. All I remember is thinking I was never going to get a girl to kiss me, much less get laid." He glanced down at the towel that was the only thing covering him. "Speaking of which, I should throw something on. I don't want you to get the wrong idea." Drew's way of handling any awkwardness between them was to joke about it. Which only succeeded in making Erin feel worse.

He disappeared into his bedroom and minutes later reappeared wearing jeans and an Old Navy T-shirt. "So," he said, flopping down next to her on the sofa, "what have you been up to?"

"Not much. I just got back from dinner with my editor."

"Kate?"

She nodded. "She took me to L'Impero."

"As well she should. You and Jessie must have boosted circulation by at least one zero. Which reminds me," he said, "I found the perfect agent for you. He handles mostly broadcasters—his biggest client's an anchor on ESPN—but he comes highly recommended. Hold on, I have his number. . . ." He jumped up and began rummaging among the papers strewn over the table that served as his desk.

"Drew . . ." At her tone, he froze, and turned slowly to face her. "I won't be needing that number," she told him.

"So . . . ?"

She nodded. "I've decided not to accept the offer."

His face fell. He looked so crushed, she wanted to put her arms around him and console him, but she knew that would only make it worse. "I can't say I didn't see it coming, but oh hell, Erin . . ." He sank down heavily in a chair at the table. "I really thought . . . at least, I hoped . . ."

Erin got up and went over to him, placing a hand on his shoulder. "I'm sorry, Drew. It wasn't an easy decision, if that helps. But I owe it to my daughter—she's been through so much already." She swallowed against the knot in her throat. He'd been a good friend to her. He might have been more than that, if not for Skip. Knowing she'd be going home to an empty bed only made it harder.

He tipped his head up, wearing his old, easy-come-easy-go smile, which in light of the current circumstances only succeeded in making him look more woebegone. "Well, I guess my loss is your husband's gain."

"This isn't about Skip," she said, her hand dropping from his shoulder.

But Drew knew better. He withdrew an eight-by-ten glossy from the slew of prints spread over the table, and held it up for her to see—a shot of a bridal couple posed against the stone facade of a church or synagogue. "They look happy, don't they? You'd never guess she was just diagnosed with MS. She found out right after they got engaged. She offered to let him out of it, but he told her he loved her enough to marry her anyway. He said he'd rather have her, in a wheelchair, than any other woman on earth. That's love." He looked up at her. "I just hope your husband realizes how lucky he is."

Erin hoped so, too. But it wasn't a realistic hope, more the hope-springs-eternal kind that was like a stubborn blade of grass pushing up through a sidewalk.

She went to hug Drew as she was leaving but he stepped back, putting a hand out to stop her. "I'm a nice guy, but I'm not that nice. I'm not going to pretend this doesn't suck," he said, with tears in his eyes and a crooked smile trying to form. "Let's just say I wish you all best."

"Erin, it's me." Jessie's voice penetrated the mists of Erin's sleep-fogged brain.

Erin groaned, squinting at the clock on the nightstand.

It was one in the morning. "What is it?" she mumbled through what felt like a mouthful of marbles.

"It's Kayla."

Erin was suddenly wide awake. "What happened? Is she okay?"

"I'm sure she's fine. It's just that at the moment . . ." Jessie faltered before continuing, "We don't know where she is."

Jessie's words went through her like a low-voltage current. She bolted upright, her heart racing. "Have you tried Devon's?" Whenever Kayla didn't show up on time, she could usually be found at her best friend's.

"We checked. She's not there." Jessie spoke with exaggerated calm, as if trying to reassure a hysterical passenger on a plane that was going down. "The guys have been out looking for her since this afternoon, and Maria and I have called everyone we could think of. I'm sure she's okay," she repeated. "It's just . . . well, I thought you should know."

Don't panic, Erin told herself, taking slow, deep breaths. *There has to be a simple explanation.* At the same time, something was buzzing inside her head, like a bee bumping about frantically in a jar: the thought she didn't dare let loose, or she'd scream, that some terrible harm might have come to her daughter.

"I'm on my way," she said, throwing back the covers and leaping out of bed.

Jessie didn't argue with her. She knew Erin too well. Erin checked online and booked the earliest available flight, the 4:20 A.M. out of Newark. Not bothering to shower, she threw on some clothes, then scribbled a note to Clive, asking him to feed Delilah while she was away. Within minutes of slipping the note under his door, she was in a cab hurtling down Ninth Avenue on her way to the Holland Tunnel.

Jessie was waiting at the airport in Phoenix when the plane landed. Hugging her, Erin felt herself go weak with relief. She drew back to eye Jessie anxiously. "Any news?"

Jessie shook her head. She looked tired, her eyes bloodshot from lack of sleep. "They put out an Amber Alert," she informed Erin, taking her arm as they made their way out of the terminal—Erin hadn't bothered to pack a suitcase, so there was no need to stop at baggage claim. "I'm sure we'll hear something soon, if she doesn't show up before then. My guess is the fun of being on her own has pretty much worn off by now." She mustered a small smile that seemed more for Erin's benefit than anything. "Remember, this is the same kid who thinks MTV and Häagen-Dazs are major life necessities."

Erin clutched Jessie's arm. "How do we know she wasn't kidnapped? Did she leave a note?" All morning, visions of Kayla being snatched by some crazed psycho had been running through her head on a continuous loop.

Jessie shook her head. "We searched her room. We didn't find one."

"She keeps her babysitting money in her top dresser drawer. Did you notice if it was missing?"

"I checked her drawers. I didn't see any money."

Erin felt some of the tension go out of her. The likelihood that Kayla had run away was small comfort, but it was preferable to the alternative.

"You look different," she observed, when they were in the car.

"Yeah, I know. I look like shit." Jessie ran her fingers through her unkempt hair.

"I mean in a good way."

In New York, Jessie wouldn't have dreamed of setting foot outside her apartment without makeup, and even when she wore jeans it was with stylish boots and a leather jacket, a crisp blouse unbuttoned at the throat to show a string of pearls. Yet she looked more beautiful now than ever. Even tired and rumpled, she glowed. Erin had noticed, too, when Jessie hugged her, how strong she'd become, no doubt from hauling suitcases up and down the stairs. It was clear, to Erin at least, that Jessie was thriving in Willow Creek.

Soon they were on I-17 headed north. "You're probably wondering why Skip didn't call," Jessie said, somewhat apologetically, aware that it was a sensitive subject. "He was going to, but he was afraid he'd lose it. I've never seen him this upset."

Funny, it hadn't occurred to Erin until now that Skip should have been the one to phone her. At the moment, such petty concerns were the furthest thing from her mind. "That makes two of us," she said.

Jessie reached over to squeeze Erin's hand. "She'll

turn up, you'll see. In fact, I wouldn't be surprised if she's there when we get back."

Erin drew no solace from her words. "It's all my fault," she said, staring bleakly out the window. Without meaning to, she'd forced Kayla to make a decision no child should have to make, one that had placed her in an impossible situation. Running away must have seemed the only solution.

"It's *not* your fault," Jessie said sternly. "If anyone's to blame, it's me. *I'm* the one who pressured her about moving to New York." Her voice caught. "I should've known better."

Erin sighed. "With kids, you're flying blind most of the time. You take your best shot, then cross your fingers and hope it turns out all right."

"I'm beginning to see that with my mother. She did her best, even if it wasn't good enough."

Erin was surprised that Jessie was so forgiving of her mother—obviously her time here had benefited her in more ways than one. "I heard someone say once that we're all raised by amateurs," she recalled, with a small smile. "You don't know how true that is until you have kids of your own."

Jessie fell silent, perhaps wondering if that day would ever come for her.

Erin went back to gazing out at the seared brown hills rolling by. She'd forgotten what it was like to look out at such emptiness—vast stretches without a single building or tree in sight. She rolled her window down, letting in the dry, sage-scented air: the smell of home. Though she never could have imagined a homecoming like this.

Two hours later, they were turning up the steep road to the inn. Erin was struck by how little had changed in the months that she'd been away. At the Lazy Q, the horses munched contentedly on hay in their paddock, and the Millers' border collie was in his usual sentry post at the head of their drive. After New York City, where nothing stood still, and you never walked down the same street twice, the peace and quiet was almost a shock to her system.

The inn welcomed her like an old friend. Making her way up the path, she noticed things that she wouldn't have if she'd been rushing from pillar to post: the paw prints embedded in the cement from when Otis had wandered onto it while it was still wet, the nasturtiums spilling from the planters on either side of the porch steps. She was climbing those steps when the front door opened, and Otis came bounding out with a high, excited bark.

Erin crouched down, wrapping her arms around his neck and letting him shower her with doggy kisses. "Hey, old boy. Did you miss me? I sure missed you."

She looked up to find Maria standing in the doorway, her eyes swollen as if she'd been crying. Carefully, like an old woman or someone in considerable pain, Erin drew herself up to her full height, her anxious gaze communicating what she didn't dare voice.

Maria shook her head. "Still no word."

Erin felt relieved, even so. At least it wasn't bad news. "Where's Skip?" she asked, glancing past Maria as she stepped into the house.

"He and Mike are putting up flyers all over town," Maria informed her. "I just finished running off another batch." She gestured toward the stack on the hall table.

Erin picked up the top one off the pile, a grainy Xerox of last year's school picture, Kayla smiling with her mouth shut to keep her braces from showing. The word MISS-ING was printed in large, bold letters across the top, the vital information in smaller print below. She felt the air leave her lungs and her knees start to buckle. All those photos of missing children, on kiosks and on milk cartons, hadn't prepared her for this.

In the kitchen, she lowered herself into a chair at the table. Jessie was eyeing her with concern, as if Erin were just out of the hospital, and it was Jessie's job to nurse her back to health. But she only said, "You must be hungry. Why don't I fix you something to eat?"

Erin had no appetite, but she didn't protest. It would be something to do, at least. Watching her friend bustle about the kitchen, she felt like a stranger in her own home. She was taking careful sips of the soup Jessie had heated up for her when she heard a car door slam outside, then the clicking of bootheels on the concrete walk. Moments later the screen door swung open, and Skip stepped inside. He froze when he caught sight of Erin. After a moment she rose, weightless, and floated over to him. Wordlessly, he took her in his arms.

She pressed her face into the folds of his striped shirt, which smelled of sweat and the cigarettes his brother smoked, and of Skip's own scent, which she'd know blindfolded. His arms, strong and steady, anchored her against the panic that rose like floodwaters, threatening to swamp her. When they drew apart, she saw that his face was drawn and his eyes shadowed with exhaustion. He shook his head, letting her know there was still no news.

They'd put up flyers all over town, he informed her, and search parties were combing the area. Right now, he was on his way down to the VFW hall, where volunteer headquarters had been set up. He'd only stopped by to see how she was doing and to let her know that everything humanly possible was being done.

"I'm coming with you," Erin said as he was leaving.

Skip placed his hands on her shoulders, saying gently, "No, stay here and get some rest."

"I can't—"

"You should be here in case she calls," he insisted.

"We're making coffee and sandwiches to take down to the VFW. You can help with that," Maria told her.

Reluctantly, Erin gave in. "All right. But promise you'll call as soon as—" She broke off, scenes from the evening news, of dead bodies in shallow graves, flickering through her head. She shivered, hugging herself as she willed away those grisly images.

She closed her eyes as Skip bent to kiss her on the forehead. He hadn't shaved, yet his beard stubble grazing her skin might have been the tenderest of caresses for the

warmth that flooded into her, bringing her numb hands
and feet back to life. "My cell phone's on if you need to
reach me," he murmured in a voice scratchy with exhaustion.

When she opened her eyes, he was gone.

It was well after dark by the time the men trooped in
like weary soldiers from the battlefield: Skip and his
brother, followed a short while later by Hunter George.
They hadn't turned up anything yet, Skip reported, but
the search parties still had plenty of ground to cover.
They'd get a fresh start first thing tomorrow morning, as
soon as it was light out.

Hunter hung back, not saying much, as if aware of the
fact that he wasn't a family member. Erin studied him out
of the corner of her eye as she set out plates and forks for
the casserole Jessie had warmed up. She realized that despite his being her closest neighbor, and that practically
every time she opened the *Mercury* he was being quoted,
she didn't know him all that well. Which made her that
much more grateful for everything he was doing for them.

She walked over and put a hand on his arm. "You'll
stay for supper, won't you?"

"I don't know about supper," he said, "but I could use
a cup of coffee." His gaze slid past her, seeking out Jessie.
As if asking her permission to stick around, given how uncomfortable things were with Mike. They exchanged a
meaningful look, one that seemed to communicate volumes.

Anyone with eyes in their head could see that it was

Hunter, not Jonathon, Jessie was in love with, and that the feeling was mutual. Obviously he wasn't happy about the fact that she'd soon be leaving; he wore the look of someone who, if it weren't for Kayla, wouldn't be anywhere near here, having salt rubbed in his wounds.

For the next hour or so, they sat around the kitchen table discussing various plans of action. Kayla had been missing less than forty-eight hours, so thankfully they hadn't run out of options. Tomorrow they would widen the search to include the outlying communities.

Finally, Maria pushed herself to her feet, yawning. "I don't know about you guys, but if I don't get some sleep, one of you will have to carry me to bed." Mike flashed her a grin, as if to say he'd be more than happy to volunteer, but it was Otis who followed her to the door, his tail wagging. She paused in the doorway, clearly reluctant to leave. "You'll call if anything comes up? Even if it's the middle of the night?" They all nodded wearily in response.

For several moments after Maria left there was only the sound of Otis whining softly, as if he sensed something amiss. At last Skip said, with a sigh, "We should all get some sleep. Nothing more we can do tonight." He sat there for another minute or so, staring into his empty coffee mug, before pushing his chair back and hauling himself to his feet.

Hunter rose, too. "I'll walk you to your car," Jessie told him, leaping to her feet. The look he gave her contained a world of hurt and longing, but he didn't protest; he only shrugged and held the door open for her.

Mike waited a few more minutes before saying his good-byes. "Sure there isn't anything more I can do?" he asked, lingering at the door.

"I'm sure," Skip said. "Go get some shut-eye. I'll see you in the morning."

Mike darted a sheepish look at Erin on his way out. Knowing him, he'd probably been dragging his brother off to bars and strip clubs, and now he was feeling a twinge of remorse. For some reason, the thought didn't bother her as it once had. If Skip had stepped over the line, so had she.

At last, they were alone. Erin got up and walked over to him, instinctively reaching for his hand. "Tell me it's going to be okay. Even if it's just to make me feel better."

"It *is* going to be okay." His fingers wrapped about hers, squeezing tightly. "I truly believe that."

In that instant, looking into his eyes, Erin could believe it, too. Then the fear came rushing back in. "If anything happens to her, I'll never forgive myself." Her voice grew choked. "If I hadn't tried to talk her into moving to New York . . ."

Skip's face turned hard. "So is it true? You're going?"

She stared vacantly into space for a moment, then brought her gaze back to him and shook her head. "No."

"You're sure this is what you want?" he asked. She nodded, and he squeezed his eyes shut. When he opened them, they were wet with tears. "So you and Drew, you're not . . . ?" He didn't finish the sentence.

She was careful to look him in the eye when she answered, "I told you, we're just friends." *We came close to being more,* she added silently, *but you were always there in my heart to stop me.*

He went on eyeing her uncertainly, but he must have decided that she was telling the truth because his face relaxed.

"What about you?" she said. "I bet Mike was only too happy to share the wealth."

A corner of Skip's mouth turned down in a tiny smile of acknowledgment. "I won't deny he offered."

"You weren't tempted to take him up on it?"

"At one point, yeah. I was mad enough to do it just to get back at you," he admitted. "In the end, though, it didn't seem like a good enough reason. Besides, anyone I went to bed with, I'd've been thinking of you the whole time. It wouldn't have been fair."

"To her, or to me?"

He shook his head, smiling. "You never give up, do you?"

Erin had always seen their clashes as being about their differences; now, she was realizing that they were a lot more alike than not. "I'm just wondering what happens when a rock meets a hard place," she said. "Do they bash each other to pieces, or do they find a way to compromise?"

"I don't know, but we could find out." They gazed at each other, Erin hardly daring to breathe, as if to keep a guttering flame from going out. Then he slipped an arm around her waist, and said, "Come on, I'll tuck you in."

Erin hesitated, swaying slightly on her feet. Until now, she hadn't given a thought as to where she would sleep. Then Skip was leading her down the hall toward the staircase, and she knew that she would be sharing his bed tonight.

Together they made their way up the stairs, which creaked softly under their weight, Erin trailing her hand along the tongue-and-groove oak wainscoting, remembering when she and Skip had painstakingly stripped and varnished it.

It wasn't until years later that they'd gotten around to fixing up the attic room. There was never enough money, and something else was always in need of repair. In the end, Skip had done most of the work himself, stripping the paint from the old wooden sashes and refinishing the pine floorboards, wallpapering the slanted ceiling and walls. They used it only on the odd occasion when they were overbooked, as the nearest bathroom was on the floor below, so it was strange to see Skip's shirt draped on the chair by the closet, his change scattered over the dresser.

She undressed and climbed into the brass bed, so tired she could barely keep her eyes open. She was only dimly aware of Skip moving about the room: the thunk of his boots hitting the floor, the sound of dresser drawers pulled open and shut.

Then he was sliding in next to her. He pulled her to him, stroking her hair. As if they'd never been apart, as if this were just one of the thousands of nights they'd lain together like this. She fell asleep almost at once, tumbling gratefully into oblivion. She didn't know how long she slept, but it was still dark when she woke with a sharp intake of breath, jerking upright. Skip stirred and mumbled something in his sleep, then he opened his eyes to peer at her with concern. "What is it?" he asked in a groggy voice. "What's wrong?"

"A nightmare. I dreamed—" She broke off, realizing that her nightmare about Kayla was, in fact, a reality.

"We'll find her," he whispered, drawing her back into his arms.

His lips brushed over her cheek, her neck, the hollow of her throat—kisses meant only to calm and reassure her, she knew, but she found herself clutching onto him, as if for dear life. She kissed him back, on the mouth, wrapping her legs around him. He groaned, and she felt his muscles contract, as if he were struggling against his natural impulse.

But she didn't want him to hold back. She wanted . . . needed . . . oh, God . . . to lose herself in him. She touched him, feeling his hardness, letting him know with her fingers that it was okay. His breath quickened. She urged him on, kissing him more deeply, opening her legs and tilting her hips to take him in. The sealing of their bodies seemed an unspoken pact, a bargain that they were making with the gods to ensure that their daughter be returned safely to them.

They made love, not with the efficiency of long-married couples, but with the greediness of new lovers.

Afterward she gripped him tightly with her legs to keep him from slipping out of her, not wanting to be plunged back into the darkness that lay beyond his embrace.

Skip seemed to understand. Ordinarily he'd have been the first to fall asleep. It was one of the things she'd always envied about him: On nights when she tossed and turned, he'd be peacefully snoring. Now, though, his breathing was shallow and even, and his muscles lightly tensed. She knew that this time he wouldn't fall asleep until she did.

She dreamed that she was aboard a ship. It was nighttime, and moonlight glittered on the sea that rose and fell in gentle swells. The only sound was the rhythmic thumping of pistons below deck. Faint at first, but growing increasingly louder. The noise dragged her from sleep even as she fought to stay in the dream. When she could no longer resist the pull, her eyes at last fluttered open to find the room awash in pale sunlight.

Someone was pounding on the door.

"Erin! Skip!" It was Jessie. She sounded frantic.

Skip leapt out of bed, and was across the room before Erin could disentangle herself from the sheets. He paused only long enough to yank on his jeans before throwing open the door. Jessie lurched into the room, her hair wild and her cheeks flushed. She thrust a folded note into his hand. "I went through her room again and found this under the bed. It must have slipped between the mattress and headboard," she explained in a breathless rush. "I can't think how else we could've missed it the first time."

Erin let out a small cry and staggered over to them, still swaddled in the bedsheet. *Dear Dad,* the note read, *I'm writing this to let you know I'm okay. Please don't worry. And DON'T tell Mom. I just need to get away for a little while. I hate being in the middle, feeling like I have to choose. No offense, but right now I don't want to be with either of you.*

Love,
Kayla

Adrenaline surged through Erin, clearing her head of the last fragments of sleepiness. She thought of something then. Something that probably would have occurred to her yesterday if she hadn't been too exhausted to think straight. She looked up at Skip. "Have you checked to see if any of the camping gear is missing?" she asked. Every summer since Kayla was old enough to spend the night away from home, Skip had taken her camping up in the mountains for a long weekend, just the two of them. She knew those woods like the back of her hand.

Skip stared at her for a moment. His eyes were puffy with sleep, and a red stripe stood out on one cheek where it had been pressed against the folds of the blanket, but he'd never looked more alert. Then all at once he was flying out of the room. Erin threw on her clothes and went racing downstairs after him. She caught up with him in the garage out back, where he was frantically pulling away the folded lawn furniture stacked against one wall, trying to get to the camping gear stowed in cardboard cartons underneath.

After a thorough inventory, they discovered that a backpack, sleeping bag, and nylon pup tent were missing. Skip put a call in to the police, and minutes later, as deputies were being dispatched to check out every campground within a thirty-mile radius, Skip and Erin were in his truck heading up to Black Arrow Ridge, where he and Kayla had gone camping last summer. They were more than halfway there when the call came over Skip's cell phone that Kayla had been found—asleep in her pup tent, in the woods out near Deer Creek.

Skip and Erin arrived back at the inn to find her, dirty and disheveled, hunched over a steaming mug of cocoa at the kitchen table. She raised her head just enough to peer up at them apprehensively, as if not knowing whether to expect a hug or a royal reaming.

Erin swooped across the room to gather Kayla in her arms. "Thank God," she choked, hugging her tightly. "We thought . . ." She broke off, unable to finish the sentence.

"I'm sorry, Mom." Kayla sounded on the verge of tears herself. "I didn't mean to scare you."

Erin gave a short, sharp laugh. "You only took, oh, ten or twenty years off my life."

"Which is nothing compared to how long you'll be grounded, young lady," Skip growled, doing his best to look angry despite the huge grin he wore.

"I left you a note. . . ." Kayla cast a look of appeal at

Jessie, who stood at the stove poking with a spatula at strips of bacon sizzling in the skillet, but Jessie pretended not to notice. "I . . . I didn't mean to cause all this trouble," she finished in a small voice, bringing her gaze back to Erin. "Or for you to come all this way."

"You can't imagine what we've been through," Skip said sternly. Kayla looked down at the table, her lower lip trembling, and he added gently, "But we're glad you're okay."

"Yeah, except I forgot to pack mosquito repellant." Kayla scratched her arm, which was covered in reddish bumps. "And I kind of ran out of food."

"I'm fixing her something to eat," Jessie called over her shoulder.

The smell of frying bacon made Erin's stomach growl. "I hope you're making enough for all of us," she said.

Jessie smiled. "Are you kidding? There's enough here to feed the entire Western Hemisphere."

Watching her, Erin couldn't help marveling once more at the change in her. Jessie, who in her former life couldn't make toast without burning it, was whipping up a full breakfast with the ease of a farmwife.

Erin sank into a chair, feeling wonderfully useless.

Skip poured them each a mug of coffee before pulling up a chair. "So this wasn't some plan you cooked up to get us back together?" he asked Kayla.

"No way." Kayla shook her head emphatically before cracking a hopeful smile. "Why, did it work?"

Erin blew on her coffee, glancing at Skip out of the

corner of her eye. He was staring down at the tabletop, tracing the whorled oak grain with his fingertip. At last, she set her mug down, and said, "Right now, it's enough that you're home safe and sound. Let's not push our luck, okay?."

Chapter Seventeen

Another in a seemingly endless procession of perky young production assistants poked her head in to ask, "You okay in here, ladies? Anything you need?" This one wore olive drab cargo pants and a ribbed tank top, her brown hair twisted up in back with a barrette, the ends sticking up like plumage. Jessie, recalling her days as an editorial assistant, when that kind of attire would've earned you a pink slip, felt old by comparison.

"Are you kidding? I'm ready to move in," Erin joked.

When Erin and Jessie had arrived at the ABC studios in New York for their appearance on *The View*, instead of the ubiquitous green room, they'd been ushered into a private dressing-room-cum-suite complete with sofa and chairs, minifridge, and built-in dressing table with a mirror flatteringly lit to make even the most tired face look daisy-fresh.

The girl flashed them a bright smile, the laminated badge on a cord around her neck identifying her as Stacy Wisniewski. "Well, if you think of anything, let me know," she said. "I'll be back in a bit to take you down to hair and makeup." She added confidentially, "Oh, and don't be nervous about Barbara. She's a real pussycat once you get to know her."

Barbara Walters had been called many things, Jessie was sure, but the word "pussycat" wasn't one she imagined even Barbara's closest friends would use to describe her.

"If one more person tells us to relax," Erin muttered after Stacy had left, "I'm gonna start thinking we have reason to be nervous."

"What do you mean? You're an old pro at this," Jessie reminded her.

Erin leaned back on the sofa, tucking a leg under her. In her fitted red pantsuit and black silk shell, the Prada slingbacks Jessie had insisted on buying her when Erin had refused to take more than a modest cut of the book deal, she looked like a younger, sexier sister to the woman who'd stepped off the plane at JFK seven months ago.

"That was different," Erin said. "Back then my biggest worry was keeping crepes from sticking to the pan while trying not to sound like an idiot on camera. I didn't have to defend my entire lifestyle."

In their last interview, with Fox *News*, the thirtysomething blond anchor had put it to Erin with a bluntness that bordered on rudeness. "You chose your family over a shot at fame—something most people would *kill* for. Any regrets?" Which had placed Erin in the awkward position of having to admit that, while she had no regrets, it wasn't exactly *Return to Walton's Mountain*, either, that she and her husband were currently in counseling.

"You don't owe anyone an explanation," Jessie said, though she understood why Erin was so defensive. Judging from the letters to the editor, the majority of *Savvy* readers, most of them career women, saw Erin's as the oldest story in the world: a woman who'd had the brass ring within her grasp but had been pressured by her husband into relinquishing it. The real story, of course, was more complex, one that couldn't be told in sound bites.

With Jessie, it was the opposite—the response had been overwhelmingly positive. Single women in search of a mate had gobbled up her story, with its fairy-tale ending. Jessie had ventured into the wilds of rural America, and returned home to a six-figure book deal and a man who, in addition to being successful and drop-dead gorgeous, had loved her enough to wait. What no one knew, except Erin, was that the fairy tale wasn't all it appeared to be.

For one thing, Jessie hadn't even seen Jonathon since she'd gotten back. Two days before she was due to arrive home, he'd been called overseas to temporarily replace CTN's London bureau chief, who'd dropped dead suddenly of a heart attack. Naturally he felt terrible about it, but in a way Jessie had been relieved. It had saved her from a potentially uncomfortable situation, with her feelings for Hunter still so raw.

Hunter, who seemed to have taken up permanent residence in her mind and heart. Whole hours would go by when she didn't think of him, then without warning, while she was flossing her teeth or feeding Delilah or watching TV, he'd pop into her head. She'd picture him hiking up Miner's Hill, his hair gleaming like a raven's wing in the sunlight, or seated across from her in their booth at the Stage Stop diner sipping coffee. Or naked, in bed, making love to her.

She'd even arranged to have Erin send her copies of the *Mercury* so she could keep abreast of his court case, which had been headline news when it went to trial. After less than an hour of deliberation, the jury had come back with a verdict of not guilty. Jessie had been so relieved she'd immediately called to congratulate him. The conversation had been brief; he'd been pleasant, nothing more. She'd hung up feeling deflated, wondering if he'd moved on already. If so, she had only herself to blame.

"Believe me, I'd like nothing more than to wrap it up neatly and tie it with a bow," Erin said, echoing Jessie's thoughts. "But in real life it doesn't work that way. More like you slap it together and hope it sticks." The counseling sessions with Skip, she'd confided, were more like peace talks between warring nations—a rehashing of every grudge and hurt feeling, every word hurled in anger. They were hanging in there, but it was tough. Though at least Skip had officially moved back in.

Jessie got up and wandered over to the fruit and cheese platter that had been set out—enough to feed them for a week in the event of a hostage crisis. "Well, one thing you count on," she said, popping a grape into her mouth. "If you ever *do* decide to come back, New York will always be here."

Erin shook her head, and said firmly, "It was fun while it lasted, but I'm where I belong."

"Me too," Jessie said, with less conviction. An image formed of Hunter spooned up next to her in bed, an arm slung over her middle.

She quickly banished it. She couldn't afford to moon right now, just before she and Erin were to go on the air. The public didn't want messy real-life endings, they had enough of those in their own lives; they wanted happily ever after.

"My only regret is Drew," Erin said, with a sigh. "I never meant to hurt him."

"I know," Jessie said gently. She wondered whether it would've worked out in any event. Drew was funny and charming and sweet, but she couldn't quite picture him as a family man. And Erin, whose childhood had been fraught with uncertainty, needed that kind of stability the way she needed oxygen. For her, family wasn't optional.

In the end, whatever ideas she and Erin might have had about changing course they'd both come full circle. The only difference was that Erin was certain she'd made the right choice, while Jessie was still betwixt and be-ween.

Stacy reappeared just then to whisk them down the hall to hair and makeup, gushing, "I just know you guys'll be great. I mean, wow, your story is so amazing. Not that *I* could ever do what you did," she was quick to add. "This job? You know how many girls would be lined up to replace me? I mean, come on. It's insane. Last week we had Colin Farrell. The week before it was Brad Pitt." She glowed, still twinkling with stray molecules of stardust. "Here we are." She led the way into a narrow room heated to sauna warmth by the hair-dryers droning away and the dozens of lightbulbs ringing its mirrors. Promising to return shortly, she left them in the hands of a plump, honey-skinned woman named Rosa, who was putting the finishing touches on one of the other guests— a gorgeous, size two blonde.

"Is that who I think it is?" whispered Erin.

"If it isn't, it looks exactly like her," Jessie whispered back.

Rosa shifted to one side just then, giving them a better look at the woman in the chair. "Omigod, it *is*," Erin hissed. "It's Jennifer Aniston!"

Jennifer must have overheard, for she turned her head to smile at them. Jessie introduced herself and Erin, who stood there grinning like an idiot, too starstruck to speak. Now it was Jennifer's turn to cry in recognition, "I know you. I've read every one of your columns. I can't believe I'm actually meeting you guys."

"*You* can't believe you're meeting *us*?" Erin squeaked.

Within minutes, they were chatting like old friends.

Jessie and Jennifer reminiscing about the Emmy Awards Jessie had covered one year for *Savvy*, the year Jennifer had won Best Actress for her role in *Friends*.

After Jennifer had been escorted out by her personal publicist, it was Jessie and Erin's turn to have makeup brushes, hot combs, and hair spray launched at them like surface-to-air missiles. By the time they were done, Jessie hardly recognized herself. She looked like Tammy Faye Bakker, and Erin like a soccer mom turned showgirl. But Jessie by now knew that a strange alchemy took place on camera, and that to the millions who'd be watching them on TV they'd look perfectly normal.

They were escorted backstage, where a sound technician fitted them with lavalier mikes. From onstage came the roar of cheers and applause, followed by Barbara Walters's inimitable voice launching into the intro. "Many of you have probably wondered from time to time what your lives would be like if you'd taken a different path," she began. "If you'd chosen a husband and kids over a career . . . or if you'd climbed the corporate ladder instead of marrying your high school sweetheart. Well, you're about to meet two very special ladies, best friends since childhood, who swapped lives for six months to find out if the grass really *is* greener on the other side. Now they're here to tell us their story. Please give a warm welcome to Jessie Holland and Erin Delahanty. . . ."

Another round of applause. Erin and Jessie exchanged a look.

"It's showtime," Erin said, her eyes shining.

Jessie grinned, and said, "Break a leg."

Together they strode out onto the set.

"There's just one thing I'm curious about," Kate said tipsily. "Does the engagement count if you're not wearing a ring?" She swayed forward on her barstool to squint at Jessie's naked left ring finger. "Or is it sort of like a tree falling in a forest with no one to hear?"

She and Jessie and Erin were at the bar in the SoHo Grand Hotel, drinking Cosmopolitans. Only Kate had had too many, and now she was making Jessie wish she hadn't stopped at one; the subject was too sensitive to face sober. In an attempt to deflect Kate, she answered lightly. "A diamond didn't stop me from backing out the last time, so I thought I'd try a different approach."

"What is this, the sixties?" Kate said. "Next thing I know, you'll be telling us you want to get married on the beach and recite passages from Kahlil Gibran."

"It's not tying the knot that counts," Erin said, "It's *keeping* it tied."

"Is there such a thing as wedded bliss?" Jessie wondered aloud. "I mean, seriously," she turned toward Erin, "is there ever a day when you wake up next to your husband and think, 'my life with this man is perfect, I wouldn't change a single thing'?"

Erin snorted. "If that ever happened, I'd know I was still dreaming."

"What if things don't work out with you two?" Kate asked Erin.

"That's something I'd just as soon not think about." Erin looked distinctly uneasy.

"I mean, there's no going back, is there?" Kate plowed on. She sighed and shook her head. "And to think you could've been the next Martha Stewart."

"Yeah, but look what happened to her," Jessie was quick to point out.

"No one's perfect," Kate said.

Suddenly Jessie had an idea. In fact, she didn't know why she hadn't thought of it before. "Why couldn't you do the show from the inn?" she asked.

Erin looked at her as if she'd lost her mind. "For one thing, the Cooking Channel is *here*, not in Willow Creek."

"They could hire a local crew," Jessie went on. "TV stations do it all the time."

Now Kate's head was bobbing with drunken authority. "She's right. Whether or not they'd go for it is another matter though. But it's certainly worth a try. Why not run it by them?"

Erin perked up for a moment, then her shoulders slumped. "Weren't you the one who told me they wouldn't return my calls?" she said to Kate.

"Since when has a little thing like that ever stopped you?" Jessie said. The word "no" wasn't in Erin's vocabulary.

"Good point," Erin said.

The idea had taken hold and was percolating in 'essie's mind. "Think of it. You'd be in your natural habitat," she said, growing more excited by the minute. "You wouldn't just be doing cooking demonstrations, it'd be a day in the life of an innkeeper, that sort of thing. You'd give the viewers the feel of actually *being* there."

"It doesn't sound very cost-effective," Erin said, frowning.

Jessie smiled to herself. That was Erin for you, always thinking of the bottom line.

"Whatever it costs," Kate slurred, "you're worth it."

"I guess it wouldn't hurt to at least float the idea. The worst that could happen is they'll say no." Erin chewed on her lower lip, her frown deepening. "Though I'm not sure how Skip would feel about it."

"Why don't you ask him?" Jessie glanced at her watch. It was still early enough in Willow Creek for Erin to call.

Erin shook her head, looking troubled. "I'll wait until after I've talked to Latrice. No sense rocking the boat if it turns out to be over nothing."

They were on I-17, on their way home from the airport, before Erin finally got up the nerve to broach it to him. She'd been bursting with excitement ever since her meeting with Latrice yesterday, at which her former boss had agreed to run her proposal by the executive board. Latrice was too good a businesswoman to show her hand, but Erin hadn't missed the gleam in her eye.

Now she listened to Skip vent about the custom house he and his brother were building up on Las Cruces, how they'd had to rip out half the wiring because of some pissing match between Mike and the building inspector. The more he talked, the guiltier she felt. It wasn't that long ago he'd come to her with a proposition of his own. Now, because of her shortsightedness, he was working for his brother when he could've been his own boss—someone else had made an offer on Red Rock Landscaping after Skip passed on it. Still, maybe it wasn't too late. The money she'd earned at the Cooking Channel had gone into a college fund for Kayla, but with the extra income she'd be bringing in with her own show he could start his own business. . . .

"I saw my old boss while I was out there," she ventured at last.

"Don't tell me you've changed your mind about moving to New York?" Skip joked nervously.

"No, of course not." She hesitated before going on, thinking of the counseling sessions where every accusation and grudge had been like a match tossed onto a pile of kerosene-soaked rags. "It's just . . . well, I had this idea . . . actually, it was Jessie's . . ." She saw his eyes narrow, and immediately kicked herself for having dragged Jessie into this. But he was at least listening. She told him about her idea and the meeting with Latrice, hastening to add, "I don't even know if anything will come of it. At this point, it's pretty much a long shot." She cast him a nervous sidelong glance. His gaze remained fixed on the road ahead, but she could see a muscle flickering in his clenched jaw. Erin felt herself break out in a sweat. "The only reason I didn't talk it over with you first was because

I didn't see the point in getting all worked up if it turned out to just be pie in the sky."

"I see," he said.

"Look, I know how it must seem to you, after the way I acted about your buying out Coburn," she went on. "I also know that I can apologize until I'm blue in the face, and it won't change the fact that I screwed up. So if you think this is going to screw up things even more, just say so. Because nothing's more important to me than you and Kayla." When she paused to draw in a breath, she found that she was shaking all over.

Skip didn't respond and, as the silence stretched out, Erin's nervousness slipped over into panic. When he abruptly pulled over onto the shoulder, the truck skidding to a stop in a plume of dust, she thought, *This is it.* Last stop on the divorce express.

"You honestly think I'd have a problem with that?" he demanded, twisting around to face her.

"You don't?" she asked in a small voice.

"No. In fact, I'm all for it," he said, almost angrily.

Erin blinked at him. "You're not mad?"

"Should I be?"

A helpless grin spread across her face. "I thought—"

He didn't let her finish. "Woman, if you'd stop trying to read my mind long enough for me to *tell* you what I'm thinking, you'd know how I feel. Fact is, I'm proud of you—it's not every guy who gets asked for his autograph on account of his famous wife." Now he was grinning, too. "The only thing I've ever been afraid of was losing you."

"You came pretty damn close," she said.

His grin faded. "I know we still have some rough road ahead of us," he said, "but I want you to know I'm in this for the long haul. So can we agree on one thing at least— to stop walking on eggshells?" She nodded, too choked up to speak. "Besides," he added, his grin resurfacing, "I have some news of my own. I heard from Coburn while you were gone. Seems the buyer's financing fell through at the last minute. He wanted to know if I was still interested."

"What did you tell him?"

"That I'd get back to him as soon as I'd talked it over with you."

This time, Erin didn't hesitate. "Tell him yes."

"You're not worried about the money?"

"We'll manage."

Skip's face relaxed, but she could see that he wasn't ready to get excited just yet. "It's more than we'd talked about," he said. "Coburn's offering me the same deal, but the rent's gone up on the space. I looked at one over on Cortez that's a little more affordable. It's still more than I wanted to spend, but the landlord's prepared to be flexible."

She reached for his hand, squeezing it hard. "Why don't we stop on our way into town? I'd like to have a look."

"We could lose everything," Skip warned, his eyes searching her face.

"If we do, we'll start over from scratch." Erin was

pretty sure it wouldn't come to that. She had a good feeling about her prospects, about Skip's too. But if neither panned out, they'd still have each other, and if she'd learned anything from these past months, it was that it was never too late for a fresh start.

He put his arms around her and held her tightly, his cotton shirt, washed so many times it was the texture of flannel, soft against her cheek, his chin resting atop of her head. He'd come straight from work to pick her up, and his clothes smelled of a mixture of pitch and sawdust and sweat. Skip stroked the back of her head, his fingers tangling in her hair. "There's just one more thing. . . ." His voice rumbled up from his chest. "I'm not sure it can wait until we get back."

She tipped her head up to look at him. "What?"

"This." He pressed her hand to his crotch, grinning.

"Oh." She laughed, remembering the time, right after they were married, they'd been driving along this particular stretch of highway late at night and she'd gotten frisky, only to look up at one point and find a trucker leering down at them from the cab of his ten-wheeler.

"There's a motel just ahead," he reminded her. "What do you say?"

Erin lightly sank her teeth into his neck, murmuring, "I thought you'd never ask."

Chapter Eighteen

September slipped over into October with scarcely a ripple. Even with Jonathon in London, Jessie was so busy, the days flew by. She'd spent Labor Day weekend in Nantucket, with Kate, whose parents had a house there. From there, she'd flown straight to Boston to speak at a writers' conference. The following week she'd had back-to-back interviews, including one she and Erin did for a feature in *More* magazine, on women who'd realized their dreams by pursuing unusual paths—something that Erin could now boast as well, with her show for the Cooking Channel currently in preproduction.

It wasn't all work. With the advance on her book contract, Jessie was able to do things she couldn't have afforded before, like shop for new clothes and eat out at nice restaurants. She splurged on a shearling coat at Cole Haan and on a photo of Drew's that she'd always admired—a Central Park winter scene—and that she'd refused to let him give her. On Drew's birthday, she treated him to dinner at Nobu in an effort to cheer him up. He was having a hard time getting over Erin, and she knew exactly what he was going through—she felt the same way about Hunter. Jessie wouldn't have admitted it to anyone, not even to Erin, but she missed him more than she did Jonathon.

The second week in October, shortly before Jonathon was due back from London, Jessie's mother, accompanied by Gay, flew in for her appointment with the eye specialist Jessie had lined up. After a battery of tests, Dr. Berkowitz concluded that she was a good candidate for a clinical trial he was running. With her spirits boosted, Beverly and Gay were able to enjoy the rest of their stay. The three of them took the train up to the Bronx Botanical Gardens one afternoon, where Jessie and her mother, wandering amid the lush tropical growth, reminisced about the garden they'd had in Pasadena and the orchids Beverly used to raise. The following evening they all went to a concert at Carnegie Hall. When it was time for Beverly and Gay to return to Willow Creek, Jessie was genuinely sorry to see them go.

As luck would have it, Jessie came down with a raging case of the flu the day before Jonathon arrived home. She was too sick to even contemplate going to bed with him, which would only have complicated matters at the moment, while she was still so conflicted. It was bad enough that he was being so nice; with every container of chicken soup from Zabar's, every book and magazine he brought her to read, her guilty conscience grew. Friday of that week, when he asked sheepishly if she'd mind if he spent the weekend with his kids, she was quick to give him her blessing.

The following week she was feeling well enough to attend the party CTN was hosting at the Four Seasons on Wednesday. It was the kind of party she used to dream of being invited to when she was growing up, back in the days when she and Erin used to pore over magazines like *Vogue* and *Glamour*, picturing themselves in those elegant clothes, going to all those glittering events. But tonight, for some reason, Jessie felt listless as she put on her new, emerald chiffon cocktail dress from Searle and fastened the pearl necklace Jonathon had given her for her birthday last year. She told herself it was because she was still weak from the flu, but she knew that wasn't the only reason.

Jonathon was waiting when her cab pulled up at the entrance to the Four Seasons. "Did I tell you this was going to be an A-list event, or what?" he murmured, gesturing discreetly toward the black Mercedes SUV idling at the curb. A burly bodyguard wearing an earpiece with a coiled cord that disappeared into his collar stood guard as a gray-haired man, whom she recognized at once as the mayor, climbed out.

They followed the mayor inside, trailing after his phalanx of aides and bodyguards, but Jessie had eyes only for Jonathon. He looked handsomer than ever—the only person she'd ever known to have returned from London with a tan. In his dark blue Armani suit, he was the portrait of success, and she no doubt the envy of every woman eyeing them as they made their way through the Grill Room on their way to the Fountain Room in back, where the party was being held.

They stepped into a sea of reporters, all firing off shots of the mayor as he stood chatting with Brad Hensley, the head of CTN. Jonathon snagged two flutes of champagne off a passing tray and steered her over to the area by the podium, where the mayor would be speaking in a few minutes. Before long, he was surrounded by colleagues, everyone wanting Jonathon's take on the British government's role in the Middle East. With each new person who squeezed in to have a word with him, quite a few of whom, Jessie noticed, were women, she found herself pushed farther away. At last, she gave up and wandered off.

A waiter passed by with a tray, and she helped herself to a canapé before making her way around the swimming pool–sized fountain that occupied the center of the room, to the raw bar—great mounds of shelled lobster and crab, plump prawns and oysters on the half shell, four different kinds of seviche. There'd been a time in her life when such bounty, and all these A-listers circulating about would have reminded her of why she'd moved to New York and made her feel as if she'd truly arrived. Now all she could think about was how she'd rather be with Hunter right now, drinking beer instead of champagne. As she stood nibbling on a shrimp and watching Jonathon, across the room chatting with Judy Douglas, who coanchored CTN's evening news, she wondered what Hunter was doing, and if he was missing her, too.

"Lookit, Mr. George! Lookit what I found!" Billy Manfredi dashed over to Hunter, nearly tripping over his shoelaces in his haste. He thrust out a grubby fist, uncurling his fingers to reveal a flat, jagged stone. "It's a arrowhead, just like the pichers you showed us!"

Hunter took his time examining it, turning it this way and that, though he'd known at a glance that it wasn't an arrowhead. He handed it back to Billy, one of his slower pupils, saying, "Not quite, but good try, Billy. Keep looking. Guys!" he called to the rest of the class, who were scattered over the stream bank searching for treasures of their own. "Remember what we talked about. Stay where I can keep an eye on you!" Getting this field trip organized had been difficult enough without his having to launch a search party.

Most of the permission slips had been promptly returned, but there were kids, like Billy, who seemed to have black holes in their backpacks into which homework assignments and report cards and permissions slips regularly disappeared. Hunter had had to phone each of those parents, which had led to lengthy conversations about how well, or not well, their child was doing, a job that had taken up the better part of every evening last week.

"Gold! Whooee, I'm rich!" Skinny, spiky-haired Jordan McAuliffe came thrashing out of the stream, his jeans rolled up to his knees and his pockets bulging. He grabbed Hunter's hand and dragged him over to show him something glinting below the water's surface.

Hunter suppressed a smile. "Sorry, Jordan, but you're going to have to wait a while longer to buy that Cadillac. That's fool's gold." He explained the difference between pyrites and precious metals, but the boy's attention, he could see, was wandering. He and the other kids were too revved up. Soon Jordan was darting off to join his classmates.

Hunter waited until they'd burned off most of their energy before he gathered them together for the picnic lunch he'd packed. After they'd finished eating and had gathered up all the trash, he took them on a little expedition, pointing out various plants and insects along the way while he reviewed the history of the region. In class, they'd learned about the Yavapai, the region's earliest settlers, and the Navajo, who occupied the area to the north known as Four Corners. Their class project had been a diorama of a Navajo village, which had led to Hunter's telling his students some of the stories he'd loved listening to as a child, like the one about Mother Earth and Father Sky, and their daughter, Changing Woman, who was born every spring and who died an old woman every winter, only to be born anew the following spring.

Now, he spoke to them about the more recent battle to reclaim this land. The Conservancy had just enjoyed an important victory when the state appellate court had ruled in their favor, temporarily shutting down Burt Overby's operation until further environmental testing could be done—a victory far greater, in Hunter's opinion, than the verdict in his own case. He explained, in terms they could understand, about how this land, with its precious resources—the water and air and plants and animals and insects all around them—belonged to *them*, not just to a chosen few or to a corporation, and that if they wanted to hold on to it, they'd have to fight for it after he was gone.

Thoughts of Jessie crept in as he spoke. If he'd fought harder for her, would she have stayed? For the longest time he'd held out the hope that she would come back. At night, when he was drifting off to sleep, images of her would play across the blank screen of his closed eyelids. The way she'd looked first thing in the morning without makeup, her hair, a dozen shades of gold and red, spilling over the pillow next to his—like a sunrise. The way she'd throw her head back in a belly laugh, the way children did. The look in her eyes when they made love—Jessie was the only woman he'd ever known who kept her eyes open throughout, as if not wanting to miss a single thing.

If I got hurt, he told himself, *I have only myself to blame.* He'd walked into it with his own eyes wide open, knowing full well that she was promised to another man.

When it was time for them to head back, he had the children scour the area for any stray pieces of trash they might have missed. Some of the kids grumbled, and

Hunter had to remind them of the motto he'd had them memorize: *Take nothing, leave only footprints.*

As they started back along the trail, Hunter thought about the day he and Jessie had hiked up Miner's Hill. How they'd made love out in the open, under the sky that God seemed to have unfurled for the occasion. And how afterward he'd known that his life would never be the same. His throat tightened at the memory.

Take nothing, leave only footprints. Advice he'd have been wise to heed himself.

An hour into the party, after the mayor and Brad Henley had given their speeches, Jessie went in search of Jonathon. She found him in a huddle with Brad—standing with their heads together, one dark, the other burnished silver, the two might have been father and son. Jessie could well imagine Jonathon taking over when it was time for Brad to retire. It wasn't just that he was smart and had paid his dues; he had the same luster that Brad did, a glow that didn't come just with success, that was God-given.

Jessie knew she ought to consider herself lucky that Jonathon had chosen *her*, of all the women he could have been with, to be his wife. She knew, too, that if she walked away, dozens of those women would line up to take her place. Women more beautiful and accomplished than she. Women who wouldn't resent the time he spent with his kids, and who'd probably win over Zach and Sara in no time.

But suddenly Jessie knew without a doubt what her heart had been telling her all along: Jonathon could never love her the way she deserved to be loved—wholeheartedly, above all else. Hunter had shown her what real love was, and now there was no going back.

Jessie waited until Jonathon had finished talking to Brad before tapping on his arm to get his attention. An attractive brunette had zipped over to fill Brad's place at Jonathon's side, and she looked faintly irritated at the interruption, but Jonathon didn't seem to notice as he excused himself and slipped away, an arm around Jessie's waist.

"I'm feeling a little under the weather," she told him. It wasn't a lie—she still felt weak, also a little sick to her stomach at the thought of what she was going to have to tell him. "Would you mind if I ducked out early?"

He eyed her with concern. "Do you want me to come with you?"

"No, I'll be fine," she assured him.

He felt her forehead, and frowned. "You're a little warm. Are you running a fever?"

She shook her head. "Really, Jon, I'm all right."

"You're sure?"

"Go on," she gave him a little nudge. "Have fun. I'd feel even worse knowing I'd made off with the most popular man here."

He arched a brow. "More popular than the mayor?"

"*Especially* the mayor." She didn't doubt that if Jonathon were to run for office, he'd win by a landslide.

"Well, in that case. . . ." He glanced past her, already eager to get back to his networking. She kissed him on the cheek. "Call me in the morning. I should be back from the dead by then."

"You think you'll be up for dinner tomorrow?"

"I'll see how I'm feeling," she told him. The last thing either of them needed was for her to break up with him somewhere as public as a restaurant. "Why don't you come by after work? We don't have to go out."

"Fine. See you then." He'd started to walk away when he turned, and said, "Damn, I almost forgot. I promised Sara I'd pick her up from school. Something about a class project she wanted to show me."

"No problem," Jessie said. "We'll do it another night." Once it might have bothered her, but at the moment she was remarkably unaffected by her second-fiddle status; all she felt was sad that things hadn't worked out the way she'd hoped.

Three days later Jessie was on a plane to Phoenix. She arrived at the inn to find it decked in seasonal finery, even with Thanksgiving still weeks away. A pair of huge pumpkins flanked the front entrance, and a festive wreath woven out of corn husks and dried chili peppers hung on the door. In the entryway stood an orchard basket heaped with apples and, on the drop leaf table beside it, a copper vase filled with pussywillows and fall leaves. A fire crackled in the fireplace in the great room, where thermoses of mulled cider and hot chocolate had been set out along with bowls of Erin's homemade sugar-and-spice nuts.

"It looks like a stage set," Jessie said, as she surveyed the room. Certainly it had never looked this good when she'd been in charge. Every surface gleamed, from the furniture to the glass panes on the bookcases. A heaping basket of pinecones on the slate hearth let off a faint woodsy scent.

Erin laughed her throaty laugh. In a loose-fitting sweater and jeans, her hair tousled and her cheeks rosy as if she'd just come in from the cold, she looked more like herself than she had in New York. "That's because it is," she said. The pilot for her show, appropriately titled *Down Home with Erin*, was being shot the following Monday, she explained, and would air the day before Thanksgiving. She'd spent weeks preparing. "You can't imagine how crazy it's been. Would you believe we're already in production for the Christmas show." Erin had been so busy lately, their exchanges had been limited to emails that read more like telegrams. Jessie realized how much she'd missed her.

Which was why she'd turned down Beverly's invitation. She opted to stay at the inn instead, in the attic room that had been Skip's. Though, of course, Hunter's living just down the road had something to do with it. The mere thought of him, just a ten minute walk away, sent Jessie's heart into her throat, where it remained throughout lunch, like something she'd swallowed that wouldn't go down.

Later that evening, after the guests had gone off to their rooms and Skip and Kayla to bed, Jessie and Erin finally had a moment alone. Erin poured them each a glass of sherry from the cut-glass decanter in the great room, and they settled on the sofa in front of the fire.

"So? How'd it go with Jonathon?" From the eagerness in her voice, it was obvious she'd been dying to know all day. They hadn't talked since Jessie had confided that she planned to break up with him.

"Terrible." Jessie took a large, medicinal swallow of sherry. "It wasn't that he made a scene—that's what made it so awful. It was as if he'd known all along, deep down."

"Does he know about Hunter?" Erin asked, all ears.

Jessie shook her head. "What would've been the point of telling him? It was bad enough as it was."

"You poor thing." Erin scooted over, putting an arm around Jessie's shoulders. "I can only imagine how you must feel."

"You went through it with Drew," Jessie reminded her, careful to keep her voice low, even though Skip was nowhere within earshot.

"I wasn't engaged to Drew. I wasn't in love with him, either."

Jessie sighed. "I'm not sure if I ever really loved Jon— I think I was more in love with the *idea* of him. When it started to fall apart, I thought Hunter was the reason. But now I know it was the other way around—I never would've gotten mixed up with Hunter if I hadn't been conflicted in the first place."

"You weren't getting what you needed from Jonathon." Erin was quick to add, "Don't get me wrong. He's a nice guy, but he just wasn't willing to go that extra mile." Erin smiled to herself, as if thinking about all the miles she'd traveled with Skip. "Which brings me to my next point," she went on. "I know a certain somebody who'd walk over hot coals to be with you, though luckily he lives just down the road, so he doesn't have far to go."

Jessie's heart began to pound. "How do I know he'll even want to see me? He didn't seem too happy to hear from me the time we talked on the phone."

"Give the poor guy a break. You tell him you want nothing more to do with him, and then he's supposed to be thrilled when you call to tell him, not that you've had a change of heart, but to congratulate him on winning his case?"

"I never said I wanted nothing more to do with him." Jessie stared into the flames crackling in the hearth, frowning.

"You might as well have," Erin said. "Hunter's a proud man. What did you expect him to do? Throw himself at your feet?"

"He could be seeing someone else by now."

"Or not."

Jessie brought her gaze back to Erin, who wore a sly mile. "Do you know that for a fact?"

"More or less." Erin sipped her sherry, as if taking pleasure in drawing this out. "I happened to run into Link Woodhouse the other day. I told him I had this friend I'd like to fix Hunter up with, if he thought Hunter would be interested."

"You didn't!" Jessie stared at her, aghast, then leaned forward to ask breathlessly, "What did Link say?"

"He gave me this funny look." Erin didn't have to add that, in addition to being one of Hunter's oldest friends, Link was a veteran newsman who could sniff out a hidden motive quicker than a hound dog could a possum, as Link would've put it. "Then he sort of winked, and said that he knew there was one special lady Hunter had his eye on, even though he wasn't officially taken."

Jessie, seeing where Erin was going with this, felt herself flush. "What makes you think he was talking about me?"

"It's pretty obvious, isn't it?" Erin was giving her that look again—the look that said she was on to Jessie and that she wouldn't stand for any more evasions. "But if you don't believe me, I suggest you go find out for yourself. Tomorrow's Sunday. Why don't you pay him a visit?"

The following morning Jessie rose while it was still dark, a habit she'd formed during her brief, inglorious career as an innkeeper that she had yet to break. Downstairs, in the kitchen, she made coffee. And because she had nothing better to do, and because it would help take her mind off the thoughts that had kept her up half the night, she started a batch of biscuits. She was rolling out dough when Erin walked in through the back door, yawning. She didn't seem surprised to see Jessie up so early. Instead, she smiled as if she'd expected to find her best friend in an apron, rolling out dough, at six o'clock on Sunday morning.

"You couldn't sleep, huh?" she said, reaching for a mug to pour herself some coffee.

Jessie shrugged. "Must be the time difference."

"Must be," Erin said, as if she didn't know better. Her gaze fell on the dough Jessie was now cutting into rounds. "I'll finish that. Why don't you take Otis for a walk."

"Otis doesn't need me to walk him," Jessie said, centering the biscuit cutter over an uncut portion of the dough.

"It'll do you both good to get some fresh air," Erin insisted, reaching for an apron and elbowing Jessie aside. She whistled for Otis, who was sound asleep in his box by the stove. He leapt up, tail wagging.

Jessie opened her mouth to protest, but Erin was already untying her apron and pushing her out the door. Moments later Jessie was jogging after Otis as he lunged ahead of her down the path. She didn't stop to catch her breath until she'd reached the end of the drive, where it emptied onto the main road. Otis was nowhere in sight. Then she spotted him up the road, loping off in the direction of Hunter's house. He paused and gave a high yip, urging her to follow him—as if he, too, were part of the conspiracy.

The sun was coming up when she rounded the bend and Hunter's house came into view—a modest split-level set well back from the road, partially screened by trees.

Seeing his Pathfinder in the driveway, she felt her heart start to race.

She noted, too, the smoke rising from the chimney, which meant he had to be up and about. She shouldn't have been surprised when the front door opened and he stepped out, but it was a mild shock even so. He was wearing jeans and a faded navy sweatshirt and the same beat-up cowboy boots he'd had on that first day, at the creek, when he'd come skidding down its bank and into her life. It was as if she were reliving that moment all over again, only her heart was beating much faster now than it had then; it felt as if it were going to knock a hole through her chest.

Watching him walk toward her, she felt shy all of a sudden, and remained rooted to the spot. Otis had no such reservations. He went bounding down the path to jump up on Hunter with a woof of recognition. Hunter paused to ruffle the dog's ears before continuing on. He stopped a few feet short of Jessie, as if unsure of himself.

"I didn't know you were in town," he said.

"I just got here." Her face felt warm, as if she'd been standing too close to a fire.

"You look good."

"Thanks, so do you." Her gaze travelled up. "You cut your hair." Where it had come down past his ears, it was now clipped close to his head.

"One newspaper described me as a latter-day Geronimo. I figured it was time for a new look," he explained with a self-conscious laugh.

"It'll take some getting used to," she said, warming further as the implication of her words sank in — words that would sound presumptuous if he'd already moved on. Which led to another, more disturbing thought: What if the reason he'd come outside to meet her instead of waiting for her to knock was because he had company — *female* company? She took a step back, crossing her arms over her chest. "So how have you been?"

"Not bad. You?"

Tell him, urged a voice in her head. *Tell him you can't go another day, another minute without him.* But all she said was, "I'm getting over the flu, but other than that I'm okay."

"You here on family business, or just for a visit?"

"A little of both."

She had yet to break the news to her mother about her engagement being called off, something she needed to do face-to-face — it was only fair, after what she'd put Beverly through the last time. But that wasn't the real reason Jessie was here. *I came because of you,* she cried silently as she stood there, helpless to speak the words aloud. *I needed to see you, to touch you, to hear your voice.*

He glanced down at her hand, the hand that should have had a ring on it. "You here with your . . . fiancé?" His tone was mild, but his gaze was dark and unblinking.

She shook her head, asking, no, pleading, "Can I come inside? We need to talk."

He hesitated just long enough for her to wonder again if he had company, if at this very moment there was a woman in his bed who was just now waking to the sight of clothing crumpled on the floor and to the smell of woodsmoke from the fire he'd built. But he nodded, and said, "I was just putting on a pot of coffee. You look as if you could use a cup."

Jessie was shivering as she followed him up the walk, Otis trotting happily alongside her. The house, when she stepped inside, was as orderly as she remembered. Hunter wasn't the typical bachelor in that sense; he'd liked things where he could find them. What was missing, to her huge relief, was any evidence of a woman's presence. No little mementos, no stray lipstick tube, no jacket too small to be his on the coatrack by the door. The kitchen was equally neat, the dishes from last night in the drainer by the sink, the only thing out of place the open bag of coffee on the counter.

She sank into a chair at the Formica table. Watching him grind the beans—Nescafé, the beverage of choice on the reservation, had left him with a deep appreciation for the real thing—Jessie was reminded of mornings past when she'd sat like this, wrapped in his blue terry robe watching him make breakfast. In one sense, it was as if no time at all had passed since she'd last seen him. And yet everything had changed.

When the coffee was done brewing, he carried two steaming mugs over to the table and sat down across from her. She told him about Jonathon then, that it was over between them. Hunter didn't say anything at first, he just sat there without moving a muscle, his hands loosely cupped about his mug, wisps of steam rising about his face.

"No regrets?" he asked at last.

She shook her head. "Only that I waited as long as I did."

A corner of his mouth hooked up in a little smile. "I know the polite thing is to say I'm sorry, but I'm not."

"Not what? Polite, or sorry," she joked feebly.

"Neither. In fact, if you knew what I was thinking right now, you wouldn't have to ask. Let's just say polite isn't a word I'd use to describe it."

"What *are* you thinking?"

"That I'd like to drag you back to bed with me."

Jessie felt the guttering flame of hope inside her flare. When Hunter pushed aside his mug and reached across the table to take her hand, she asked, "So what's stopping you?"

Half an hour later, they lay snuggled together in bed, spent from lovemaking. "Does this mean you'd consider marrying a broke-ass Indian living off a teacher's salary?" he teased, one bare leg hooked over hers as he wound a hank of her hair about his finger.

She gave a nervous laugh as she disentangled herself and sat up. "I just got out of one engagement. Give me a chance to catch my breath."

He rolled onto his side, his head propped on one elbow as he looked up at her. "What sort of arrangement did you have in mind then?"

"I don't know." Jessie hadn't really thought it through;

she'd been too caught up in the moment. "How would you feel about living in Manhattan?" Before he could answer, she was shaking her head, saying, "No. Scratch that idea." Hunter could no more move there than could the mountains or the trees.

"On the other hand, you could live here," he said. "With me."

"I could," she said slowly. "But I'd miss New York. I can't imagine not spending at least part of the year there."

"That's always an option."

She eyed him in confusion. "What are you saying?"

"That I have summers off. Plus spring and winter breaks," he said. "Besides, I've always wanted to see Manhattan. I hear the Museum of Natural History alone is worth the trip."

"You mean it? You'd do that?" she asked, hardly daring to believe what she was hearing.

"When have you ever known me to say something I didn't mean?"

"I suppose it could work," she said cautiously. If she lived with Hunter, she could afford to keep her apartment. "Of course, we'd have to make some adjustments if—" She broke off, realizing they'd never discussed kids.

"What?"

"How do you feel about children?"

"Given that I have twenty-five of them, I think it's fairly safe to say I'm fond of them," he said, his lips twitching with a smile trying to break loose.

"I wasn't referring to your students," Jessie said, frowning to let him know this was serious.

He drew her toward him, giving her a lingering kiss on the mouth. "I've always wanted kids. In fact, we could start right now, if you like." His hand traveled over her hip, dispelling the last of her concerns along with any thoughts she might've had about leaving any time soon.

Just then Otis gave a polite bark, letting her know he was ready to go, even if she wasn't. Reluctantly, Jessie withdrew from Hunter's embrace. "I should be getting back. I promised Erin I'd help with Thanksgiving dinner."

He looked puzzled. "But Thanksgiving's not until next month."

She explained about Erin's show, which was being filmed tomorrow. "In fact, why don't you come over afterward? There'll be plenty of food for everyone, even with the crew."

"I'd love to," he said, as they climbed out of bed and began putting on their clothes. "As long as you promise to let me cook for you on the actual day. If you've never had a Navajo Thanksgiving, you're in for a treat."

"I didn't know you could cook." The only thing she'd ever seen him do was scramble eggs.

"I'm full of surprises," he said with a wink, tugging on his boots.

Jessie felt a touch of uneasiness. She was heading off into the unknown, where not all the surprises would be good ones. But there was no such thing as a storybook ending. And even if there were, wouldn't that take all the fun out of it? Even as a child, "happily ever after" had struck her as a bit of a cheat: Wasn't that where the *real* story began?

At the door, Hunter snagged his jacket from the coatrack, saying, "I'll walk you back." She must have looked relieved—she didn't want to be apart from him any longer than was necessary—for he teased, "You think I'd let you go on your own? How do I know a bear won't come after you? Or a crazed gunman?"

She arched a brow. "Or a 'broke-ass Indian' who's up to no good?"

"That, too." He slipped an arm about her waist, and they started back toward the inn.

Author's Note

I love hearing from readers. It's you who make those long nights when I'm burning the midnight oil, racing to meet a deadline, worthwhile. Your comments reassure and uplift me when I'm alone at my desk wondering if anyone will read what I've written. I welcome even the helpful ones that point out errors—it saves me from making the same mistake twice—though I think it's worth noting that for every error that slips through the cracks, there are dozens more that I and my eagle-eyed editor and copy editor *do* catch. So if you'd like to get in touch, you can email me via my website at: www.eileengoudge.com

"Sounds like fun," said Jay's wife, seated at the kitchen table in their Flatiron District loft, where her husband and his three closest friends had gathered for the post-mortem on their college reunion. She leaned back in her chair, hands folded over the swell of her pregnant belly. "Though I can't say I'm sorry I didn't go. Even if I'd been up to it, I would've felt like a fifth wheel." Her tone was matter of fact, even amused. Vivienne had never been the least bit bothered that her husband's best friends were female.

Franny wondered if it was because she was European, or because she was way too gorgeous to be threatened by another woman.

"It was fine until I ran into one of my old boyfriends," she said.

"Who offered to put a bun in her oven," said Stevie. She sat with one leg pulled up to her chest, a small bare foot propped on the chair, her toes peeking out under the ragged cuff of her jeans.

"It gives new meaning to the words old flame," teased Emerson.

"Maybe I should've taken him up on it. God knows I'm desperate enough," Franny said morosely, taking a sip of her ice tea. "Though it's too late now."

"Why is that?" asked Vivienne.

"I told him I was doing the honors," Jay answered for her, with a grin. "Only to get Franny off the hook, of course," he was quick to add.

Vivienne smiled, as if she found it amusing.

"What about Chris? He still on the fence?" asked Emerson. She might have been sipping tea at Buckingham Palace, her posture was so erect. Everything about her, in fact, was perfect, from her sleek blond hair to her French-polished nails—a Mayflower descendent whom only her best friends knew felt more closely affiliated with the *Titanic*.

Franny snorted at the mention of her most recent ex. "If he was on the fence, I think he climbed over it. I haven't heard from him in over a month." For a time, she'd thought he might be The One, but after six months of living together he still couldn't make up his mind about having a kid. Over a romantic candlelight dinner, she'd tried to get him to agree to it on a trial basis; if things didn't work out, she'd told him, she'd be perfectly happy to raise it on her own, no hard feelings. He wouldn't even have to pay child support. He'd agreed to give it some thought, but said he needed his space; it was too much pressure. He'd moved out the next day, and she hadn't heard from him since except for a few cursory e-mails.

Vivienne pushed herself out of her chair and padded over to the fridge, retrieving the pitcher of ice tea. "I never thought I'd find someone I wanted to marry, much less have kids with, until I met Jay," she said, her hand resting on his shoulder as she refilled his glass. They already knew their baby was a boy. They were naming him Stephan, after Jay's grandfather.

Franny felt a fresh stab of envy, though she was happy

for them, truly she was. She also didn't doubt that Vivienne, a former model, had had her pick of suitors. She was darkly exotic in a way that olive-skinned Franny, with her Grandpa Herman's nose and curls that wouldn't stay put, could never aspire to. The product of a French father and a Lebanese mother, Vivienne's hair was like silk damask and her skin the color of crème de caramel. And while Franny was lucky to fit into a size twelve on her best day, Jay's wife was so slender that you wouldn't have known she was almost four months pregnant.

"The truth is, she felt sorry for me," Jay said, tilting his head to smile up at his wife. "It was my first shoot, and when the photographer said something about a barn door, I didn't know he was talking about a piece of equipment. I thought he was taking a potshot at me."

Vivienne ruffled his hair. "I *did* feel sorry for you. You were like a stray puppy nobody wanted. I thought the least I could do was feed you." She spoke with a French accent that always had the effect of making Franny feel coarse, a peasant woman in *shmatas* next to a princess.

"It was all a ploy. I was really a wolf in disguise." Jay bared his teeth in a villainous grin that on him—the boy from Grant's Pass, Wisconsin, with his swoosh of wheat-colored hair and blue eyes the color of a prairie sky in haying season—looked more silly than anything.

"More tea?" Vivienne asked, moving around to where Franny sat.

"No thanks, I'm fine." She'd have preferred plain old Lipton's to Vivienne's strange-tasting herbal concoction.

Glancing across the table, she saw Jay flash her a knowing look. Since his wife had become pregnant, black tea had given way to chamomile and mint and linden flower. Vivienne ate only organic food and sushi was *verboten*. These days Jay had to stop at Starbuck's on his way to work for his coffee fix. Otherwise, he'd confided to Franny, he would have felt as if he were tainting the atmosphere somehow. When she'd replied laughingly she'd that she'd never heard of being poisoned by second-hand caffeine, he'd rolled his eyes and said, "Believe it." Among the many reasons he was counting the days until this baby was born was that it would mean no more sneaking off like a crack addict to his pusher.

"Seriously," Vivienne said, wearing a thoughtful expression, "Jay *would* be the perfect father for Franny's baby."

Franny felt a little jolt, her cheeks warming with what she was sure was a tell-tale flush. If only Jay knew how often she'd fantasized about it. And here was Vivienne actually *suggesting* it. It was too good to be true. Even so, she laughed, saying, "Come on, get real."

"It's the two-hundred pound gorilla we've been ignoring," Vivienne went on. "Tell me it hasn't at least occurred to you."

"Well . . ." Franny darted a furtive look at Jay. "It did cross my mind once or twice."

Emerson and Stevie exchanged a look, but offered no comment.

Vivienne stared pointedly at her husband, until he

threw up his hands with a half-baked smile, "Hey, I'm a guy. It's the male instinct to want to propagate the species."

"Well, we know everything's in good working order," Vivienne said, stroking her perfect little bump of a belly, wearing a dreamy expression. It was a purely Western notion, she said, that a man couldn't have children with more than one woman at the same time; her Lebanese great-grandfather, in fact, had fathered sixteen children with three wives. She wasn't suggesting anything as radical as that, of course, just that Jay spread the wealth a bit. "And," she added on a more practical note, "if Franny gets pregnant right away, Stephan will have a baby brother or sister."

"Whoa." Jay looked alarmed. "Don't I get a say in this?"

She shrugged. "It's your sperm."

"What about my *life*? How would we explain it to our kid, for one thing."

"Kids," Emerson corrected.

"See, that's what I mean. I could get complicated . . .and weird." He darted frantic glances around the table, as if beseeching his friends to toss the cold water of reason over his pregnant wife's newest bout of madness.

"On the other hand, it could be the best thing ever," Emerson weighed in at last. "Besides," she added, with a twinkle in her eye, "what are friends for?"

"Don't look at me. I'm the last person to give advice on having kids," said Stevie, when he turned to her in mute appeal.

Franny, for her part, was lost in a vision of all four of

them gathered around this table—her and Jay and Vivienne and their children. One big happy family. She thought of the Thanksgivings and Christmases and birthdays they would celebrate together. Who better to father her child than her dearest friend in the world? And Vivienne would be like a second mother.

Okay, so it would be a little weird, but weird wasn't necessarily bad. Besides, in this city they'd be just one more blended family. And in time, if she met someone and fell in love . . .

She brought her gaze back to Jay, a helpless grin spreading across her face. "You still have that turkey baster?"

Five months later . . .

Franny was on her way to a staff meeting in the boardroom when her secretary, Katrina, called after her, "Franny! It's Jay. He's calling from the hospital."

Franny raced back into her office, and snatched up the phone. But Jay wasn't calling with happy news. Vivienne was in labor, he informed her, but there was a problem—the baby's heart rate had dropped. They'd just rushed her into the OR for a C-section.

"I'll be right there," Franny told him, slamming down the phone.

Poor Jay. She'd never heard him sound so agitated. Growing up on a farm, he'd attended more deliveries than most midwives, so normally stuff like this didn't faze him. But this wasn't livestock, it was his son. What if something were seriously wrong with the baby? Franny grew cold at the thought, instinctively placing a hand over her own three-months'-pregnant belly. In the cab on her way to the hospital, she prayed that when she got there she'd find little Stephan safe and sound in his mother's arms.

Minutes later she walked into the visitors lounge, on the fifth floor of Beth Israel, to find Jay hunched over a Styrofoam cup of coffee, staring down at the floor.

"Jay."

He looked up at her, his mouth stretching in a mirthless smile, then he lowered the steaming cup onto the floor and rose to greet her. He looked like he had in college after a week of cramming for finals, pale and undernourished, his eyes bloodshot and his hair uncombed. Anyone would have thought it was Jay in need of medical attention.

Wordlessly, she took him in her arms. He smelled of sour sweat and too much caffeine. "How is she?" she asked when he drew back.

He shook his head. "I don't know yet. She's still in surgery."

Normally fathers were allowed into the OR, Franny knew. If Jay wasn't with Vivienne, it meant something really serious was wrong with her or the baby. But Franny couldn't let him see how worried she was. "It'll be fine. Don't forget what great shape she's in," she reminded him. "All that health food and yoga, the kid's gonna be a Ninja warrior."

Jay gave a hollow laugh. They'd often joked about the extremes to which Vivienne had gone while pregnant, but at the moment it seemed more ironic than amusing.

They sat in silence for the next fifteen minutes or so, Jay gripping tightly to Franny's hand, until the doctor appeared. An older gray-haired man in scrubs, he looked grim as he took Jay aside. From where Franny sat, she couldn't read Jay's expression as the doctor filled him in, but she could tell by the slump of his shoulders that the news wasn't good.

When Jay returned, she could see that he was in a state of shock, his eyes vacant and staring, his face drained of color. "Vivienne's fine," he reported in an odd, flat voice.

Franny sucked in a breath. "And the baby?"

"He didn't make it."

Franny felt as if she were in an elevator plummeting downward. "Oh, God. Oh, Jay." She didn't what to say. How did you console someone after such a loss?

He didn't cry or rail. He just stood there staring at nothing, his chest rising and falling in rapid, shallow breaths. "I should go to her," he said at last, in the same dead voice.

Franny touched his arm. "I'll be here you get back."

With what appeared a heroic effort, he straightened his shoulders and set off down the corridor.

Jay felt as if he were moving underwater. Hospital personnel floated by, the blatting of the PA system like the roar ing of distant surf in his ears. *It's got to be a mistake,* he told himself. *The doctor got Vivienne mixed up with another patient. Happens all the time.* When he got there, she'd be holding their son in her arms, beaming.

But he stepped into the recovery room, there was no baby. Just Vivienne, lying there looking like a casualty of war, her skin the color of tallow, her eyes staring like a madwoman's from bruised-looking sockets. She began to weep as he gathered her in his arms, clutching at him as if she were drowning. The sounds emerging from her throat didn't sound human; they were those of a wounded animal. It was all Jay could do to remain strong, for her sake, not to collapse under the weight of his own shock and grief.

"Tell them," she begged in a ravaged whisper. "Tell them our baby isn't dead. *Please.* They won't listen to me."

"Shhh. You should get some rest," he soothed, his voice breaking.

"They won't let me have him." Vivienne was growing increasingly hysterical. "Please. I want my baby!" She broke off, heaving with sobs. When at last she raised her head, he found himself looking into the face of a woman who'd lost all touch with reality. "Bring me my baby!" she cried. "*I want my baby!*" She began beating at Jay's chest with her fists, blows that might have been pebbles flung against a windowpane, he was so numb.

A nurse came running, and together she and Jay struggled to subdue Vivienne, who was shrieking now at the top of her lungs. The doctor was paged, and he gave her something to sedate her. But Vivienne wasn't going gently into that twilight. She continued to fight and rail until the sedative took hold. Even then, with her eyelids drooping, she went on beseeching him in a shrill whisper, "Please, Jay. You have to tell them."

"Later," he whispered, stroking her hair until she drifted off.

He looked up to find the nurse, a heavyset black woman with elaborately braided hair, eyeing him with compassion. "Would you like to see your son?" she asked. "Usually families want to say their good-byes, but we didn't know if this was the right time. Your wife was so upset."

Jay shook his head. When Vivienne woke up, they'd face it together. Right now he didn't think he could cope with it.

How had it come to this? Everything had been going so smoothly, Vivienne's labor as textbook as her pregnancy. She'd been in the final stage, doing her Lamaze breathing while he massaged her lower back, when things had begun to go horribly awry. The next thing he knew, a doctor was taking over from the nurse-midwife and Vivienne was being whisked off to the OR. Jay would never forget the look on her face as they were wheeling her away. She'd looked more shocked than scared. She'd had done everything right. This wasn't supposed to be happening to *her*, of all people.

But all those measures, he realized now, had been about as much use as the amulet Vivienne's Lebanese grandmother had sent her to ward off evil spirits.

Making his way back to Franny, Jay could see her at the other end of the corridor, a beacon in her red dress, her curly hair glowing under the fluorescents as if electrified. He felt a wave of relief crash over him. As if he were far out to sea, struggling to stay afloat, and had spied land.

"How is she?" Franny asked. Though at the moment it was Jay she was most worried about: He looked close to the breaking point.

"They gave her something to help her sleep," he said in a hollow voice.

"Do you need me to do anything?"

He gave her a blank look, as if wondering what she, or anyone, could possibly do at this point.

Franny put an arm around him, steering him over to the sofa.

"This wasn't supposed to happen," he said, shaking his head, his sightless stare directed at the vending machine, where a man in need of a shave stood fumbling for change.

"I know," said Franny, close to the breaking point herself.

"Everything was ready. The nursery, the little outfits. "

Franny nodded in sympathy, her throat tight. "I lay awake at night sometimes, thinking of all the things that can go wrong." She placed a protective hand over the gentle swell of her belly. "Still, you're never prepared for something like this. How can you be? It's beyond comprehension." Even when you know it's coming, like with her mother.

"So what now?" He turned to her, his face painful to look at.

"You pick up the pieces. You move on."

"I'm not sure I can."

"You will. Trust me," she assured him. "You still have Vivienne. And me. I'll be with you every step of the way." He'd been there for her when her mother died. And during the long week of sitting *shiva*, he hadn't left her side.

"Where would I be without you, Franny?" His red-rimmed eyes were no longer vacant but looking straight at her, with such love it was all she could do to keep it together.

"Exactly where I'd be without you—lost," she said, reaching for his hand.

FROM THE INTRODUCTION TO
SOMETHING WARM FROM THE OVEN

My love affair with baking began with a copy of *Betty Crocker's Cookbook for Boys and Girls*, given to me one Christmas by my Aunt Betty (no relation to Ms. Crocker). Inspired, I donned my mother's apron—I had to wrap the ties twice around my middle, I was so small, and went to work mastering such delicacies as pigs in a blanket and three men in a boat. Before long, I was on to blondies and brownies, velvet crumb cake, and molasses crinkles. I learned to make a heart-shaped cake using a square layer and a round one, cut in half. And knew there were so many uses for Bisquick?

Every so often my sisters and I would play what we called "bakery day." We'd each chose a recipe, usually something easy like cookies, and with Mom's blessing (her only rule was that we had to clean up afterward), we'd spend all day making them. By the time the last tray came out of the oven, the kitchen would be a mess and we'd be so sick of it all—literally, given the amount of cookie dough we'd consumed—we wondered what we could have been thinking: This was about as much fun as a trip to the dentist. Amazingly, it did nothing to dampen our enthusiasm the next time one of us piped, "Let's play bakery day!"

Now I think of the days when I'm free to putter around my kitchen as my own private bakery days. No sooner are the breakfast dishes cleared away than I'm measuring flour and sugar, creaming butter I'd taken out earlier to soften. Throughout my roller coaster of a life and career, baking has been the one constant. When I was a young bride, living with my first husband in British Columbia, cut off from family and friends, it was the one thing that connected me to my past. I didn't have an oven and the kitchen was about the size of a smallish walk-in closet; I baked everything in small batches in my toaster oven. Which brought home an important lesson: Where there's a will, there's a way. Baking isn't about loads of equipment and reams of recipe books; it's about the desire to create something from scratch. There's something deeply satisfying to me about kneading dough or frosting a cake, or watching slimy egg whites transform magically into snowy peaks.

Those of you familiar with my novels know that some element of food and baking always seems to figure in. In *Such Devoted Sisters*, Annie becomes a chocolatier. In *One Last Dance*, Kitty Seagrave owns a tearoom called Tea & Sympathy, where her famous cinnamon sticky buns are gobbled up as fast as they come out of the oven. Kitty and her tearoom make an encore appearance in *Taste of Honey*, the second book in my Carson Springs trilogy. The baked goods so lovingly described therein inspired a number of readers to write to me requesting recipes. In response, I posted them on my Web site, *www.eileengoudge.com*. Later, I compiled them in a small book as a promotional giveaway. As a result, I've received mail from all over the country and more than a few from abroad. One woman wrote that my Kahlua brownies were such a hit at her company picnic, several of her co-workers asked for the recipe . . .

KAHLUA BROWNIES

I've gotten more positive feedback on these brownies than for any other recipe on my Web site. They're a cinch to make and they keep well—they're even better a day or two later. If you're feeling adventurous, you can even make your own Kahlua (Recipe below);it requires just a few simple steps and some patience. Around the holidays, when I have the time, I put up a gallon, which I then transfer to inexpensive, decorative bottles from Pier One Imports to give away as gifts. The rest I save for baking.

Makes about 2 dozen brownies
Preheat the oven to 350 F. Grease a 9 x 12-inch rectangular baking pan

3/4 cup (1 1/2 sticks) unsalted butter
4 ounces unsweetened chocolate
4 large eggs
2 cups sugar
1/4 cup Kahlua, or other coffee-flavored liqueur
1 1/4 cups all-purpose flour
1/2 teaspoon baking powder
1/2 teaspoon salt
1 cup chopped walnuts or pecans, optional

Place the butter and chocolate in a medium, microwave-safe bowl; heat in the microwave, covered, for 30 seconds at a time, stirring after each interval (about 1 1/2 minutes total), until melted. Alternate method: Place in a bowl *over* (not in) a pan of boiling water removed from the heat, stirring occasionally until melted. Set aside to cool.

In a separate bowl, beat the eggs and sugar with an electric mixer on low speed until pale and lemon-colored. Mix in the Kahlua and cooled chocolate mixture, until smooth. Add the flour, baking powder, and salt. Beat on low until incorporated, then increase speed to medium and beat *just until blended*. Don't overmix! Stir in the nuts, if using.

Pour into the pan, smoothing even with a spatula. Bake in the oven for 25 to 30 minutes, or until a toothpick inserted into the center comes out with only a few moist crumbs stuck to it. Cool in the pan before cutting into squares.

HOMEMADE 'KAHLUA'

Makes about 1/2 gallon. Allow 4 weeks to cure

4 cups sugar
2-ounce jar instant coffee crystals
Fifth of vodka

In a stockpot or 4-quart saucepan, combine the sugar and 4 cups of water. Bring to a boil. Add coffee crystals a spoonful at a time, stirring until dissolved. Simmer, uncovered, approximately 2 hours, until syrupy. Let the mixture cool several hours or overnight, until room temperature. Pour into a clean, glass gallon jug or two half gallon jugs. Add the vodka and swirl gently to blend. Let stand in a cool, dark place for a minimum of 4 weeks.

Carnival Pride™

April 2–9, 2006
7-Day Exotic Mexican Riviera Itinerary

DAY	PORT	ARRIVE	DEPART
Sun	Los Angeles/Long Beach, CA		4:00 P.M.
Mon	"Book Lover's Day" at Sea		
Tue	"Book Lover's Day" at Sea		
Wed	Puerto Vallarta, Mexico	8:00 A.M.	10:00 P.M.
Thu	Mazatlan, Mexico	9:00 A.M.	6:00 P.M.
Fri	Cabo San Lucas, Mexico	7:00 A.M.	4:00 P.M.
Sat	"Book Lover's Day" at Sea		
Sun	Los Angeles/Long Beach, CA	9:00 A.M.	

Ports of call subject to weather conditions.

TERMS AND CONDITIONS

Payment Schedule:
50% due upon booking
Full and final payment due by February 10, 2006
Acceptable forms of payment are Visa, MasterCard, American Express, Discover, and checks. The cardholder must be one of the passengers traveling. A fee of $25 will apply for all returned checks. Check payments must be made payable to Advantage International, LLC and sent to: Advantage International, LLC, 195 North Harbor Drive, Suite 4206, Chicago, IL 60601

CHANGE/CANCELLATION:
Notice of change/cancellation must be made in writing to Advantage International, LLC.

Change:
Changes in cabin category may be requested and can result in increased rate and penalties. A name change is permitted 60 days or more prior to departure and will incur a penalty of $50 per name change. Deviation from the group schedule and package is a cancellation.

Cancellation:

181 days or more prior to departure	$250 per person
180–121 days or more prior to departure	50% of the package price
120–61 days prior to departure	75% of the package price
60 days or less prior to departure	100% of the package price (nonrefundable)

U.S. and Canadian citizens are required to present a valid passport or original birth certificate and state issued photo ID (driver's license). All other nationalities must contact the consulate of the various ports that are visited for verification of documentation.

We strongly recommend trip cancellation insurance!

ADDITIONAL TERMS
This offer is only good on purchases made from September 27, 2005 through April 1, 2006. This offer cannot be combined with other offers or discounts. The discount can only be used for the Authors at Sea Cruise and is not valid for any other Carnival cruises. You must submit an original purchase receipt as proof of purchase in order to be eligible for the discount. Void outside of the U.S. and where prohibited, taxed, or restricted by law. Coupons may not be reproduced, copied, purchased, or sold. Incomplete submissions or submissions in violation of these terms will not be honored. Not responsible for late, lost, incomplete, illegible, postage due or misdirected mail. Submissions will not be returned. Improper use or redemption constitutes fraud. Any fraudulent submission (including duplicate requests) will be prosecuted to the fullest extent of the law. Theft, diversion, reproduction, transfer, sale, or purchase of this offer form and/or cash register receipts is prohibited and constitutes fraud. Consumer must pay sales taxes on the price of the cruise.

For further details call 1-877-ADV-NTGE or visit www.AuthorsatSea.com.

For booking form and complete information,
go to www.AuthorsatSea.com or call 1-877-ADV-NTGE.

Complete coupon and booking form and mail both to:
**Advantage International, LLC
195 North Harbor Drive, Suite 4206, Chicago, IL 60601**

12936

Not sure what to read next?

Visit Pocket Books online at
www.SimonSays.com

**Reading suggestions for
you and your reading group**
New release news
Author appearances
Online chats with your favorite writers
Special offers
And much, much more!

104